The Intuitives

The Intuitives

Erin Michelle Sky
& Steven Brown

TRASH DOGS MEDIA, LLC

Library of Congress Preassigned Control Number: 2017906039
(hardcover edition)

ISBN: 978-1-946137-01-2

Printed in the United States of America

Cover art by Eugen Zhuravel
Layout & Design by Jordan D. Gum
Edited by Sybil Carey

Trash Dogs Media LLC
1265 Franklin Parkway
Franklin, GA 30217
trashdogs.com

10 9 8 7 6 5 4 3 2

To all the Intuitives out there,
making this world a better place.
You know who you are.

1
ALEXANDRIA, EGYPT
SEVEN YEARS AGO

From the moment the chisel first broke through the stone into the empty air beyond, he knew they had found it. He felt it in his bones—an ache that began in the center of his chest and radiated outward, splintering apart to hurtle around his ribs and pierce his spine, screaming up his neck and along his arms and down his legs, until every last, trembling inch of him was filled with it.

The fools. They had no idea what they'd done.

Amr waited helplessly as Paolo, the foreman, called up to Professor Langston.

"Professor! Come quick! I think we've found it!"

Langston was the lead archaeologist—an American, as luck would have it, still unaccustomed to the heat of the Egyptian sun. Even here in Alexandria, the white jewel of a city that floated impossibly upon the Mediterranean, Langston had been hiding in his tent, mopping his face with his trusty blue bandana four or five times a minute, slowly melting away.

"Yes, yes. I'm coming," he called back, sounding far more weary than hopeful. This was the fifth time today that Paolo had uttered these exact same words, each new "discovery" amounting to nothing more than worthless limestone and bitter disappointment.

But Amr knew. And as Langston approached the end of the long excavation tunnel, he felt it too, finally quickening his pace. The hole in the back wall held a cavernous promise of space behind it, and the old man all but sprinted the last few steps, excitement burning in his wizened blue eyes.

"Dig!" he shouted. "So we can see it, Paolo! Dig!"

Under Paolo's careful direction, the hole began to widen, until they were finally standing on the brink of a man-sized breach in the ancient rock.

"Bring the torches!" Langston ordered, slapping Paolo on the back in his enthusiasm. "Hurry!"

Paolo disappeared down the tunnel and returned in moments, carrying several battery-powered LED lamps designed for precisely this purpose: the distant illumination of large, dark caverns.

"Yes! Yes, good! Here!" The professor beckoned to him, one weather-beaten hand grasping impatiently in the air. Paolo deposited a lamp into his eager palm and took up two more himself, ready to employ them as needed.

Taking a deep breath, Langston turned on the light.

"Paolo! Paolo!" He turned around and grabbed the man's shoulder, tears springing to his eyes.

"Professor! Are you all right?" Paolo looked into the older man's face, clearly worried about his health, but Langston nodded and waved his concerns away, the lamp still in his hand. He was too overcome to speak, but he gestured to the hole, moving aside to make room for the others. Paolo stepped up to it and shined both lamps through as Amr peeked over his shoulder.

"Yes," the professor breathed in his ear. "Look! We are the first! The first in over two thousand years!"

Amr shuddered. He knew far better than they how long it had been.

He watched in anguish as eager hands held up one spotlight after another, a wonderment of statues emerging from the darkness, their shadows slithering over each other only to slip back into the earth below. Imps, gargoyles, minotaurs, gryphons, harpies, unicorns, and even stranger shapes tore at each other's throats—hundreds of creatures locked together in an ancient, raging war, frozen in time.

In the center, two dragons rose above them all, one white and one black, stone wings spread wide, jeweled teeth glistening in the harsh, modern light. But it was what towered between them that made Paolo begin to shout, his yells echoing throughout the underground chamber as the professor pounded him over and over on his back, the promise of untold wealth burning in their eyes. In the midst of the carnage stood an ancient pyramid, its tremendous door emblazoned with a giant image, carved in deep relief: the side view of a life-sized lion, rearing up on its hind legs, its body struck through by a single bolt of lightning.

They stood before the door soon enough, the pyramid looming over their heads. Amr stared at it in wonder—and fear—only half listening to Langston.

"You see, Paolo?" he was saying, his voice trembling with excitement. "It was said in his day that Alexander's mother, Olympias, dreamed on the eve of her marriage that her womb was struck by a lightning bolt, igniting a flame that spread far and wide across the land." As he said this, he pointed toward the door, his hand tracing the line of the lightning bolt in the air. "It was also said that his father, Philip, saw himself in a dream, sealing his wife's womb with the image of a lion."

"But surely that was just a myth, created to support the legend that he became within his own lifetime," Paolo objected, his voice laced with doubt.

"Yes, yes. Don't you see?" the professor replied, shaking his head urgently. "It is what they *said* of him, whether it was true or not. This is the emblem of both dream-myths together, marking Alexander's final resting place, the tomb to which his generals moved him during the civil wars that followed his death."

Paolo nodded along with the explanation. "So what are these markings?" he asked, indicating the carvings that circled the stone frame.

"Ancient Persian. Further proof! The usual warnings—as you would expect to find on the crypt of an emperor in this part of the world."

"You can read them?"

"Yes, of course. It says, 'Here lies the king of two realms, who walked in grace in both this world and the next. With this tomb, the window to the next life is sealed. Disturb it not, lest the great works of his kingdom be destroyed.'"

Close enough, Amr thought. He could read them as easily as he could read modern Arabic, but he kept that knowledge to himself.

Langston stood back and admired the ancient door, his eyes threatening to tear up again, but he wiped them furiously with his bandana and took a deep breath to compose himself.

"We must see it for ourselves."

"But the authorities—" Amr protested.

"No!" the professor almost shouted. "I mean, yes. We will report the find, of course. But not just yet. Please. I am an old man, and I have dreamed of this moment since I was a child. I must see it for myself, while I still 'walk in this world,' as it says."

"OK, Professor," Paolo agreed. "But just the fiber cameras. We must not open it fully without the authorities present. I would lose my license."

"Of course," Langston agreed. "That's all I ask."

They chose a spot deep within the carving, in the ball of the lion's foot, drilling slowly, carefully, until Paolo's patient efforts were finally met by a sudden lack of resistance. For the first time in over two thousand years, the seal on the tomb of Alexander the Great had been broken.

If the very movement of the world seemed to stutter for just an instant, if the tomb itself seemed to take a long, shuddering breath, Amr was the only one who noticed.

This is the beginning of the end. And I am the only one who knows it. They have doomed us all.

He closed his eyes and shook the thought away. He could not afford to lose hope. Not now. There was a plan for this. There had always been a plan for this. And there was still time. They were out there, somewhere—they were out there, and he would find them, wherever they were.

Before it was too late.

2
ROMAN
PRESENT DAY

Roman paused outside the small duplex, his hand resting lightly on the doorknob, refusing to grip it with any real conviction. Refusing to turn it.

The bees might be angry.

Not that standing in the hot Alabama sun was all that appealing. Even in late April, the heat rising off the cigarette-smeared asphalt fell somewhere just shy of egg frying. And the building itself wasn't much to look at either: a narrow, two-story affair with faded green paint that peeled listlessly from the cracked front window. But it wasn't the worst place Roman had ever lived.

It wasn't so dismal as to reach into his soul and tear tiny pieces of him away every time he opened the door.

He had lived in places like that, places that threatened to drown you in your own hopelessness, the constant weight on your chest making it hard to breathe, the constant fear in your belly making it hard to close your eyes at night, listening in the dark to the perpetual scurrying of the wall rats and feeling like maybe they had more of a right to be there than you did yourself.

But this place, with its three tiny upstairs bedrooms and one and a half baths, the extra toilet being a luxury he had once only dreamed of in a family of seven, was no reason in itself not to open the door—no reason not to walk boldly into the small front space that served as a living room and flop down on one of the two squeaky couches, home safe after surviving another day at Grover Cleveland Middle School.

It was just that the house might not be empty.

His mother and Tony wouldn't be home from work yet. His older sister, Kontessa, had gone to a friend's house after school, and the two youngest would be at day care. That left his older brother, Marquon, who was fifteen and went to the high school now, so he got out half an hour earlier than Roman. If Marquon was already home, then Roman would be alone with the bees.

Roman took his hand off the doorknob and moved it gingerly toward the black front door itself, testing its heat after the hours of abuse it had taken in the afternoon sun. He jerked his hand away as soon as his fingertips made contact, nervous about being burned, but the surface was only uncomfortable, not scorching. He reached out again and placed both small, brown hands firmly against the plane this time, palms flat, letting his skin get used to the temperature, and then he leaned in slowly until his left ear was resting against the door itself.

At first, he didn't hear anything at all.

He had just begun to hope that Marquon was out with his friends or maybe had followed some girl home from school, when the TV roared into life, the mad explosion of sound startling him back from the door with a fast shove of his arms. Even several steps away, standing in the small parking space in front of the building, he could still hear the blare of his family's only television, the buzzing notes of its half-busted speakers rattling the window.

Roman's shoulders slumped, but there was nothing for it. He would have to go in. His mother had made it perfectly clear that eleven years old was too young, in her opinion, for a boy to be walking twelve blocks to the corner store or hanging around the park by himself. Especially in that neighborhood. Especially a boy as small for his age as Roman. If he didn't go in, Marquon would tell her that he hadn't come straight home after school, and after everything that had happened three years ago, Roman had to keep his head down.

If his mother thought for even a moment that he might be causing trouble again, well, she would start screaming and crying and carrying on like a banshee, and then Tony would leave (Roman's luck being what it was) and next thing you know they'd be out on the street, this time with baby Xavious in diapers, and with Child Protective Services still sniffing around after the last time...

Roman knew he didn't have a choice. Sighing deeply against the inevitable, he reached out his hand and opened the door.

He tried to do it casually, like he wasn't scared. Acting nervous around Marquon was like squeezing lighter fluid onto a barbecue. So instead of easing the door open like he wanted to and peeking his way around the edge, he just pushed it wide and walked through it, kicking off his shoes and sparing only the briefest of glances in his brother's direction.

Marquon was glued to a video game and acted as though he couldn't care less that his little brother had come home, but Roman knew it was just a ploy. He knew it because the first red bee spiraled slowly up out of his brother's right ear. It angled toward him, flying only an inch or so in his direction until it stopped, hovering in mid-air, staring straight at Roman, a silent vanguard of impending doom.

Roman had started seeing strange things around people when he was only four or five years old. He wasn't clear exactly when it had started because he had had no idea at the time that he was seeing anything unusual. He would tell his mother that a woman in the grocery store had eight arms, or that the preacher on television had a tail like a mermaid, and his mother would either laugh and say, "Boy, you sure do have some imagination!" or would frown and tell him it was about time he started living in the real world, depending on her mood.

In those days, his mother had looked like she lived in the middle of a tornado, just like the one he had seen in *The Wizard of Oz*, that whirled and thrashed around her with a somewhat greater or lesser promise of destruction from one moment to the next. Lately, though, the wind had finally settled down to a gentle breeze that simply twirled her skirts playfully and ruffled her hair from time to time. Tony seemed to have a lot to do with that, and Roman prayed every night that Tony would stay in the picture so the tornado would never come back.

He hadn't realized how dangerous his visions could be, not only to him but to his entire family, until he was eight years old and had just started the third grade. His teacher that year, Mr. Lockhart, had been a particularly disturbed man, despite the outward appearance of propriety that he so diligently cultivated with his pressed businessman's suits and his car salesman's smile.

When Mr. Lockhart had discovered the haunted doodles in Roman's notebook depicting massive, demonic wings growing out of the man's shoulder blades, tearing right through the shadowy material of his favorite charcoal-gray jacket, the walking horror show himself had demanded an explanation on the spot, and a terrified young Roman had insisted that these ominous, though unlikely, protuberances were, in fact, the genuine article, staring at the man in wide-eyed panic and pointing tremblingly into the open air.

Mr. Lockhart, in response, had marched him right down to the principal's office, calling his mother away from the Mexican restaurant where she was waitressing and demanding that she take her schizophrenic son to see a licensed psychiatrist posthaste. Loquisha Smith, however, had never been one to put up with other people's nonsense.

She had issued a scathing rejoinder—with significantly more volume than the situation had probably required—explaining to Mr. Lockhart in no uncertain terms that there was no way she could afford a psychiatrist on a waitress' salary and that in any event there was nothing wrong with her eight-year-old son, and suggesting that the man should spend more time teaching and less time sticking his nose where it didn't belong and taking up good working people's time with such shenanigans, only "shenanigans" was not precisely the word she used.

In tight-lipped fury, Mr. Lockhart had watched her storm away with her son in tow, and as soon as they were out of sight he had called Child Protective Services to report his grave concerns over the child's mental health and his mother's obvious inadequacy as a parent.

That night, her voice quavering with fear, Loquisha had unleashed her frustrations upon Roman's young shoulders, explaining to him that all four of her children (Xavious had not yet been born at the time) could be taken away from her forever if he did not "stop talking all this made-up shit and grow the hell up," and Roman had finally understood in stark and brutal clarity several truths that would stay with him for the rest of his life.

First, his mother had never seen any of the strange and wonderful things that he saw and told her about every day. Second, she had never believed for a moment that he had really seen them either. Third, if she *had* believed him, she would have thought he was as crazy as Mr. Lockhart did. Fourth, terrible things would happen if he didn't start hiding his visions from every other human being on the planet, including his own mother.

Over the next four weeks, Roman had spent several hours of his life convincing a court-ordered psychiatrist that he did not really think there were demonic wings growing out of his third-grade teacher's back. That would be crazy, and Roman was not crazy. He had been drawing scary doodles in his notebook because he had stayed up one night to watch a horror film on TV when he was supposed to be in bed. The movie had scared him. He had had nightmares for a week or two. He had drawn some creepy pictures. Then the nightmares had stopped, and he was fine now. He did not feel like drawing scary pictures anymore. He would gladly draw a picture of his mom and his brother and his two sisters all living together in one big, happy house if the doctor would like to see that. Yes, he would very much like a lollipop, thank you for asking.

But telling people that the visions weren't real did not make them stop. He still saw the winds blowing around his mother. He still saw a gray fog of fear and insecurity wrapping Kontessa so tightly within its grasp that he had trouble seeing her real body through it at all. He still saw young Shaquiya standing in a perpetual ring of sunshine as she pranced about the house, the light soft and ethereal, filtered through a canopy of summer leaves and glimmering off her giant, iridescent fairy wings. And he still saw the swarm of angry, red bees that lived inside his brother, Marquon.

He stared at Marquon now, just for a moment, while his brother pretended not to see him, hogging the television so he could play his video games, the solitary bee of glowing red light standing vigil over his head.

"What are you playing?" Roman asked.

Sometimes, talking about Marquon's games would soothe the hive, and they could sit for a while and have a pleasant conversation about quick scoping and weapon choices and how good Marquon was at blowing his opponents away. Anything to keep the bees from getting angry. Not that the bees themselves could sting him, but when the bees got mad enough to attack, Marquon did, too. With four years and at least fifty pounds between them, Roman never came out well when his big brother lost his temper.

Roman waited a few moments, but Marquon didn't answer.

"Marquon?"

Still nothing. Roman finally decided to head toward the kitchen and dig up something to snack on, but he hadn't taken three steps before he heard his brother's voice calling him back.

"Yo, Romario."

"Yeah?" Roman asked, sighing a little. Marquon always used his full name, mostly because he knew Roman hated it.

Roman had spent almost as many hours of his young life reading as he had drawing, and he had developed a strong suspicion that the name his mother claimed she had 'just made up' for him was, in fact, a moniker mash-up of Romeo, from *Romeo and Juliet*, and Lothario, from *Don Quixote*, as though she expected him to grow up to be as much of a ladies' man as she asserted his father to be.

Roman, however, regarded his father as little more than a drunk and a petty criminal who seemed destined to spend his entire life oscillating in and out of jail on a pathetically regular schedule, and he had no interest in being compared to the man on any basis whatsoever, whether real or imagined. He was also only eleven, so the idea of becoming a great romancer of women was mortifying in and of itself, and he had taken great pains to make sure that everyone referred to him as 'Roman' instead of 'Romario,' thereby guaranteeing that Marquon would do no such thing.

"You hear about that test?" Marquon asked.

"Yeah."

"You think you gonna do better'n me?"

"Naw. No way, man. You know you gonna blow me away."

"Damn straight," Marquon snapped back. "You know why?"

"'Cause you're smarter than me."

"Hell yeah, I am."

"Yeah, I know. You want a soda?"

Marquon's eyes left the television just long enough to size up his brother's attitude, but he must have decided Roman was being genuine because the little bee of red light turned and flew toward Marquon, landing on his forehead and crawling back into him through his left eyeball.

Roman tried not to react to his visions so people wouldn't realize he was still having them, but he hated it when the bees crawled into his brother's eyes or up his nose or into his ears. It was unsettling, and he winced a little as he watched it disappear.

"What?" Marquon demanded, and the bee flew back out of his left eye, accompanied by two more from his right.

"Nothing," Roman said quickly. "I was just thinking about school. I tanked my science quiz. Mama's gonna be pissed."

"Ha! Yeah, she is, dumb-face. Freak-face Romario. Fail-face Romario." He said his name like a taunt each time, and the three bees danced a happy little jig in the air over Marquon's head before disappearing into his right ear.

Roman just shrugged. It didn't matter what his brother thought of him. All that mattered was that Marquon didn't lose his temper and beat the heck out of him before their mother or Tony got home.

"Well?" Marquon asked, when Roman didn't say anything else.

"Huh?"

"Are you gonna go get the sodas or what?"

"Oh. Yeah."

"'Bout freakin' time."

Roman was smart enough not to point out that Marquon had never answered his question and had not asked for a soda. Keeping his mouth shut, he made his way down the short hallway into the kitchen, grabbed two cans out of the fridge, and walked back into the living room.

"Here."

Roman eased a can onto the coffee table, and Marquon grunted in Roman's general direction, never taking his eyes off the television. It wasn't exactly gratitude, but it served as a kind of acknowledg-ment—a subtle cue that they were on truce for the day, at least in Marquon's opinion, which was the only one that mattered.

Roman knew he shouldn't press his luck. He knew he should head upstairs to the tiny room he shared with Xavious, where his private sketchbook was stashed beneath the crib. He kept two sketchbooks now, a 'light' one and a 'dark' one. The light one he carried around, drawing beautiful images of Shaquiya's fairy wings or his mother's smile, but the dark one he kept hidden away.

Most eleven-year-old boys would have hated sharing a room with an infant, but Roman didn't mind it so much. At least he never saw anything strange around his baby brother. He figured he would eventually—he saw things around everyone else. But for now, Xavious just ate and cried and burped and slept, and in between he practiced walking without falling down and saying "NO" and "MINE" and "BOBO," which is what he called Roman, accompanied by Marquon's endless snickering. Roman hated changing diapers as much as anyone else, but it was nice to feel normal once in a while.

And when he wasn't feeling normal at all, when all the evil he had seen during the day decided to get up and start lurching around inside his head, screeching and clawing its way through his brain with no way out, he could grab his sketchbook and spill all that darkness onto its pristine white pages. And Xavious would never tell a soul. The kid would just hobble over to where Roman lay on the floor, sketching furiously, and he would gurgle and laugh as the images flowed into life before his eyes, as though there wasn't anything the least bit disturbing about any of it.

That was what Roman should do now, while he could—while Marquon was busy with his video games and nobody else was home—but he kept thinking about the stupid test. They had just announced it that afternoon. Morning classes would be canceled for every grade from the third through the twelfth for some new test. It made him nervous. Before the whole Lockhart nightmare, he wouldn't have cared. He would have just aced it, whatever it was. But now he lived by certain rules. No good grades. Don't stand out. Keep your head down. See trouble coming.

So even though Marquon was ignoring him and Roman could

have escaped into his bedroom in peace for a couple of hours, he just couldn't stop himself from trying to find out more about it.

"So... did they say what it's for?"

"OMG, you still here, man?"

Roman waited to see if his brother would say anything else, but the silence dragged on between them while the TV blasted screaming guitars and staccato gunfire.

"I thought maybe they told you guys something at the high school," Roman tried again. "About the test? They wouldn't tell us anything."

"Yeah, well, they didn't tell us either. Just sit your asses down tomorrow and take the stupid Is-A-Bitch."

Roman perked up. "Is-A-Bitch?"

"Man, you're stupid." Marquon rolled his eyes. "Intuition Assessment Battery. IAB. Is-A-Bitch. I can't believe I literally have to spell that shit out for you." Just then, Marquon got shot and the game ended, his death playing over and over on the final kill-cam. Cursing, he threw the controller to the ground and stood up, his head whipping around to stare at Roman.

Roman backed away as the entire beehive streamed in vicious red streaks out of his brother's eyes and ears and nose.

"Sorry," Roman said, in a voice that sounded pathetically small and frightened, even to him. "Marquon, I'm sorry."

"Gonna *make* you sorry, Mister Is-A-Bitch!"

He was so close to the front door. Roman wanted to yank at the doorknob and run into the street, but he knew he couldn't. Marquon was already too far gone to stop himself. If Roman ran outside, Marquon would just chase after him, and if the neighbors saw his fifteen-year-old brother beating him half to death, someone would call the cops, and that would be that.

So Roman did what he always did—what he did for his mother and for Shaquiya and for innocent little Xavious so the cops wouldn't come and take them away or run Tony off and ruin everything they finally had. He curled up in a ball and took the beating without making a sound. Marquon kicked him a few times and then fell on top of him, pummeling him without mercy, while a thousand bees of blood-red light swarmed around them.

3
SAM

Had anyone bothered to ask Samantha Prescott what she was doing with her sixteen-year-old life, she would have replied, matter-of-factly and with more than just a touch of bitterness, "Waiting."

But waiting for what, she had no idea.

Ever since she was a child, she had understood—with a conviction that had sailed far beyond the realm of mere belief and landed finally upon the unassailable shores of hard, scientific fact—that every last scrap of popularity and power her classmates squabbled over, when measured on any meaningful scale whatsoever, added up to a sum total value of diddly-squat.

Every day she watched in both fascination and horror as the other sophomores scrabbled and spat their way through the merciless arena of high school drama, acting as though it were a matter of life and death which members of the slave-like masses came out on top for the day, as though the entire spectacle weren't just going to repeat itself again tomorrow.

Really, why did they care? The boys were too childish to fight over. What dared to call itself fashion was hopelessly generic—no one had the guts to wear anything original in this boring, suburban quagmire. And what passed for 'intelligent debate' was just the parroted drivel of the previous generation, passed down from father to son and mother to daughter without any genuine reflection or even a token attempt at independent thought.

How had Sam arrived at this rather pessimistic view of the world? It had all started when she was only five years old. Her father had taken her to a ballet class, not because he had any desire to see his daughter grow into a debutante, but because she had very few friends her own age, and in the absurdly wealthy neighborhood they called home, a ballet class seemed the most logical place to find five-year-old girls.

Sam, however, had taken one look at the room full of leotard-and-tutu-clad miniature divas, twirling their pink-ribboned wands through the air in clumsy, frenetic swirls, turned to her father with her hands on her hips and announced, "Oh, hell no."

Michael Prescott had swept the girl up in his arms immediately, making a beeline for the door and spluttering apologies to the town's most prominent mothers as they stared in open disdain—any furtive, wistful hints of complicit defiance that might have stirred in one ladylike heart or another, yearning toward the sun with grasping tendrils of insurrection, all forlornly renounced under each other's silent, disapproving gazes.

Then again, it might be traced back even farther still.

When Sam was only two, she had asked her mother to teach her how to read. Armed with safety scissors, construction paper, childproof paste, a bouquet of markers, and more women's magazines than any modern woman could reasonably be expected to consult in a lifetime, Sam's mother had crafted stacks upon stacks of homemade flashcards under the child's precise direction, every chosen phrase reflecting her daughter's already eclectic interests, ranging from the somewhat predictable 'good dog' to the far more improbable 'periwinkle raincoat.'

If Jennifer Prescott had expected her two-year-old daughter to ignore the mystical pull of the written alphabet and merely pore over the colorful illustrations for half of an afternoon before losing interest in the entire enterprise, she turned out to be sorely mistaken.

By the time young Samantha encountered the infamous troupe of kindergarten ballerinas, she was already reading *The Wall Street Journal* aloud every morning, perched on her father's adoring (if all-too-transitory) knee. What she took from this exercise, among other things, was that the world seemed to be in serious danger a depressingly large part of the time and that she clearly had better things to do than learn to spin a pink-ribboned baton in ever more elegant circles.

As one might imagine, any hope she might have had of finding even an inkling of common ground with her own kind was doomed from the get-go.

And so it came to pass that although she was now sixteen years old, her general opinion of her peers had changed very little. It bothered her, feeling so alone within the swell of humanity that ebbed and flowed around her, but she tried not to dwell on it. She knew something important was coming down the road eventually—that her life was destined to be of greater significance than even she herself could possibly imagine—and she felt that somehow, deep in her gut, she would recognize this pivotal turn of events when it finally began to unfold.

She just didn't know whether she would be eighteen or twenty-eight or eighty by the time it happened, and in the meantime, nothing she did felt as though it *mattered.*

She didn't care about school. She certainly didn't care about fitting in with the popular crowd. She didn't even care much about other people's feelings if she was being honest. But she did well in school anyway, because it was easy, and she tried not to provoke her classmates too badly—not because it seemed important in the grand scheme of things, but because it made her life that much less difficult at home.

Although both her parents had paid considerable attention to her pre-school education, everything changed once they shipped her off to the first grade, where they were not the least bit worried about her academic success. Ever since that fateful day, Sam's parents had been unlikely to summon the time and energy to 'deal with her' unless they were upset about something.

Her father was a high-priced lawyer, commuting every day from their ocean-view mansion in New Jersey into 'the city,' by which Michael Prescott meant New York City, and more particularly Manhattan. He converted time into money for a living, and his daughter was not immune to these financial calculations. Her requests for his time were invariably weighed against the loss of potential income they represented, leading sadly to the conclusion that the family simply could not afford for him to pay her any significant attention.

This was why Sam tried to make do with what she had, rather than asking for anything special. She wore inexpensive jeans and even cheaper T-shirts to school. She had one pair of black motorcycle boots that she wore every single day. She did the two blue streaks near the front of her otherwise jet black hair herself, which she had learned to do from an online video—the Internet being, in her opinion, mankind's greatest invention.

She certainly didn't ask for a membership to the country club, or the yacht club, or the tennis club, or the beach club, or any other exclusive institution that the girls in her school district expected to attend as a matter of course.

She didn't ask for these things because she didn't want to wonder whether her father's unwillingness to spend weekends at home might have anything to do with the added expense of raising a child. The only exceptions she made to this personal rule were a high-end laptop, a tablet, and a cell phone with a good data plan. If her father wasn't going to spend time with her, he could at least provide her with something to do in all the spare hours he refused to fill with his company.

Not that her mother was any better.

Thanks to Michael Prescott's significant income, Jennifer Prescott had no responsibilities in life beyond raising their only child, who at the age of sixteen was no longer, in Jennifer's opinion, in need of her maternal services. Instead of asking Sam about her friends—of which she had none—or about her classes or her interests or her hopes and dreams and views of the world, Jennifer Prescott spent her time helping the 'less fortunate,' leaving Sam to her own devices as long as her grades were good and she stayed out of trouble.

In fact, it seemed to Sam as though she only ran into her mother by chance these days, as she had just now, both of them standing in their impossibly clean, uber-modern kitchen, which was, as usual, utterly devoid of any sign that anyone had ever cooked in it.

"I have an emergency meeting tonight at the women's shelter." Jennifer spoke these words to her daughter without looking up from the black calfskin handbag she was digging through with her perfectly manicured hands. "Where are my keys?"

This last bit she said to herself, which Sam couldn't help but feel was more typical of their interactions than the alternative.

"You're not seriously taking that bag to the homeless shelter, are you?" Sam settled onto one of the designer-selected bar stools at the high counter, staring at her mother across its glistening, Italian-marble surface.

Jennifer stopped short and looked up at Sam in confusion. "Why on Earth not?"

Sam raised one eyebrow and tilted her head as she made a show of looking her mother over from head to toe. Jennifer Prescott was, at all times, the very picture of elegance. All four of Sam's great-grandparents on her mother's side had been immigrants from

China, and although Jennifer herself had been born in San Francisco and didn't speak a word of Chinese, her lineage showed in the milky-smooth complexion that belied her age. Her thick, black hair was expertly coiffed, her make-up was artfully applied, and her long, gym-toned legs were shown off to maximum advantage by an Akris Punto leather and jersey miniskirt that would have been perfectly at home on a fashion model.

"Because it's Chanel, Mom. You paid more for that bag than most of the women in that place have ever spent on a car."

"I don't appreciate your attitude, young lady." She pronounced every syllable with irritated precision, but both her voice and her manner remained otherwise subdued. Even angry, Jennifer Prescott maintained an air of quiet sophistication. "We've donated a lot of money to that organization. Just because someone else is poor doesn't mean we can't have nice things."

"I'm not saying you can't have nice things. I'm saying you're going to get yourself mugged." Sam grabbed a handful of cherries out of a decorative bowl in the center of the counter and popped one into her mouth.

"Really, Sam. I put those out for guests. If you're hungry, there are leftovers in the fridge from last night. Some brie, I think. And, of course, the duck."

"Of course, the duck," Sam said, rolling her eyes and getting up to spit the cherry pit directly into the trash. "Charity dinner last night, board meeting tonight... what's tomorrow? Book club meeting on *How to Live with a Wealthy Woman's Guilt*? If that isn't a real book, you should write it, by the way."

"Honestly, Sam, what would I possibly have to feel guilty about? Your father works hard for a living."

Dad might, but you don't, Sam thought to herself, but that was a line even Sam wasn't willing to cross.

"I don't know," she said instead, "maybe the baby cow that died for your outfit?"

Jennifer's eyes narrowed dangerously, but she replied without raising her voice in the slightest.

"I really don't have time for this, Samantha." She ended the conversation as abruptly as she had started it, dismissing her daughter by shutting the bag she had been digging through and sliding it brusquely over her shoulder as she turned toward the door.

"Of course, you don't," Sam muttered, but even if she had said it loudly enough to be heard over the sharp click of her mother's heels, Jennifer Prescott was already out the door.

Ugh, what time is it?

5:17 a.m. The answer came to her mind unbidden, as it always did. Sam had an innate sense of time that defied all logic. Her alarm wasn't set to go off for another hour and thirteen minutes, but she knew her father would be up by now, getting ready to leave for 'the city.' At least she could sit with him while he drank his coffee.

Stretching sleepily, she half-crawled and half-fell out of bed, grabbing one of the pairs of jeans that hung haphazardly about the room, yanking a sports bra on over her head, and choosing a T-shirt from the clean laundry she had 'put away' for her mother by dropping the entire pile in the middle of the floor. It was a fitted black tee with an adorable white kitten on the front—with miniature daggers lashed to its tiny claws and big white letters that said, "Don't Even Try It."

Sam grinned as she pulled it on. It was one of her favorites.

She padded downstairs in her bare feet to find her father in the kitchen, just as she had predicted. He was sitting at the black marble counter, already showered and shaved, reading the morning paper, his fresh cup of coffee resting in front of him, with a handful of cherries in his right hand. Sam grinned as he spit a cherry pit directly into the trash.

"Mom said those are for guests," Sam warned him.

Her father rolled his eyes and slid the bowl toward his daughter, who grinned even wider and popped one into her own mouth.

"So what's up, Buttercup? How goes the life of the twenty-first-century teenager?"

Sam shrugged. "Same old, same old."

But Michael Prescott was not about to give up that easily.

"I'm sure you can think of one measly thing you can share with your father. It can be entirely insignificant. I'm not picky."

It's all insignificant, she thought, but she loved her moments with her father too much to ruin them.

"We're taking some new test today," she said instead, between cherry pits.

"Oh? On what?"

"It's not on anything. Well, I mean, obviously it's on *something.* But it's not for a class. It's some new standardized battery they're trying out."

"Really? What kind of battery?"

"No idea," she replied, shrugging. "They're just using us to test it. It won't count this year."

"So let me get this straight. You're going to school to take a test to test a test that isn't testing you on anything?"

"Pretty much. Welcome to my world."

Her father chuckled. "You want out of it? Sounds like a ditch day, to me."

Sam grinned. Michael Prescott looked at education the same way he viewed everything else: as a means to an end. As long as Sam was keeping her grades up, he saw no reason to adhere to the school's attendance policy any more strictly than the law required.

She was about to leap at his offer when a sudden feeling in her gut brought her up short—a profound sense of... importance—and she paused, taking it in, her hand halfway to her mouth with another cherry.

"Sam? You OK?"

"Yeah. Yeah, I'm fine." She placed the cherry back in the bowl. "It's just..." She hesitated, hardly believing what she was about to say.

"Thanks, Dad, but I think I have to go to school today!"

By the time Sam reached the school's broad, white-washed sidewalk, she was already regretting her decision. The strange feeling that something momentous was about to happen had vanished as soon as she had arrived, and now the hulking red-brick building loomed over her, promising nothing but heartache and boredom in approximately equal measure.

There were thirty-seven wide, shallow steps in the walkway, and she climbed every one with an increasing sense of disappointment.

One, two, three, four...

Where had that strange sense of urgency gone? It had been such a beautiful feeling, to think that for once in her life, something she was about to do might actually matter.

Nine, ten, eleven, twelve...

Now she would be stuck in school all day, and for what? Why hadn't she taken her father's offer while she had the chance?

Seventeen, eighteen, nineteen, twenty...

How could she have been so stupid? She had been in a good mood for what? Maybe five minutes? So, of course, she just *had* to start believing her life was actually *important*, that anything she did might actually *mean* something. It couldn't *possibly* be that she was just happy to have her father's attention for half a second, or that she was still loopy on sleep deprivation at 5:28 a.m.

Twenty-five, twenty-six, twenty-seven, twenty-eight...

Now, it felt as though nothing mattered again, like today was just another inconsequential day along the road to old age. Where was that sense of impending *change*? Where was that miraculous feeling she had had for just one fleeting moment, that her life was about to be full of adventure—that she was finally about to step into her destiny?

Thirty-three, thirty-four, thirty-five, thirty-six...

Great, and, of course, as if she weren't already miserable enough, Vinnie Esposito just had to be at the front door.

Thirty-seven.

"Mongol," he said as she walked by.

"Peanut," she replied, her foot crossing the threshold exactly as the first bell rang.

"Why the hell you call me 'Peanut?'" Vinnie demanded, following her down the hallway. He hovered just inches behind her, as he always did, the very weight of his presence making her skin crawl.

Not that she was about to show it.

"I told you to Google it," she snapped back.

Vinnie had called her 'Mongol' ever since the second grade, when a young and hopelessly misguided teacher had commented cheerfully—in front of the whole class, no less—that Sam had such an *interesting* look and was she, perhaps, Mongolian?

Sam had explained in tight-lipped embarrassment that her mother was Chinese and her father was, well, not—with Vinnie snickering maniacally in the back row throughout the entire affair. Sam had inherited her mother's lush black hair, her father's green eyes, and an exotic blend of facial features that was hard for the people of her New Jersey suburb to pin down. Vinnie had started calling her 'Mongol' after that, and unfortunately, the name had stuck.

In return, she called Vinnie 'Peanut' after the dog that had won the World's Ugliest Dog Contest in 2014, a fact she had not let on to anyone, least of all Vinnie.

"How about I just beat it out of you?" he suggested.

He grabbed her shoulder, holding her back long enough to get in front of her and planting one heavy arm against the wall, leaning his body in threateningly, trapping her in the hallway just a few feet from their homeroom.

"Just hit me," she said, staring straight into his eyes. "I'll fall down and scream bloody murder, and when Miss Anderson comes out, I'll get you expelled. I'll miss your ugly face, of course, but I'll do my best to get by. Come to think of it, I might report you for bullying anyway, whether you hit me or not."

"You got no proof, Mongol," he sneered back.

"Hall camera behind you says otherwise, Peanut. Are you going to move, or should I go ahead and call Miss Anderson out here?"

Vinnie glanced over his shoulder at the security camera and then glared at her a moment longer anyway, but Sam stared him down without flinching until he grudgingly removed his arm and let her by.

The second bell rang just as she stepped through the homeroom door.

"Now remember, even though this doesn't count toward your grades, you still need to do your best. Your scores will be matched against those of comparable districts. If the scores here are significantly lower, the entire district will have to take the test again."

There were several groans throughout the room as Miss Anderson walked up and down the aisles, placing scratch paper on each student's desk.

"That's right," she said, nodding. "So do your best—unless you want to spend another two hours of your lives on this little exercise next week."

What difference does it make? Sam thought glumly, but she had no intention of tanking it. If she didn't do well on *any* test, even one that didn't count, someone was bound to call her parents for a conference on 'why our perfect Samantha is behaving erratically.' Those conversations never ended well for her.

Miss Anderson finished handing out paper and started around the room again, this time with a box of Number 2 pencils.

"The test has three sections, each thirty-six minutes long. The first two sections have seventy-two multiple-choice questions. The final section has thirty-six short answers."

Seventy-two questions, thirty-six minutes. No problem. No reading comprehension, that's for sure. Not at thirty seconds per question. Probably math or logic or science.

Sam let herself grin just a little. Those were her best subjects.

Miss Anderson gave out the last pencil and started around with test booklets and answer sheets.

"Fill out your name on your answer sheet as soon as you receive it. Do not turn the test over until it is time to begin."

S, oval nineteen. S is for Samantha. S is for student. Sam composed an acronym for 'Samantha' as she filled in each letter: *S-A-M-A-N-T-H-A. Student... aggravated, answering, arbitrary... Student Aces Maniacally Arbitrary Numbskull Test, Having Answers.*

"You will have exactly thirty-six minutes to complete this section." Miss Anderson returned to the front of the classroom, where she waited until the second hand of the clock was on the number twelve.

"You may begin."

Sam turned her test over.

1. Which color is the best color?
   A) red
   B) yellow
   C) blue
   D) purple
   E) orange

Sam glanced around as a low murmur pervaded the classroom. Everyone was either staring at the test in confusion or leaning surreptitiously across the aisle to see if a neighbor knew the answer. As if there *were* an answer. What color is the best color? What kind of question was that?

Miss Anderson ignored them all. She just sat at her desk, reading.

OK, fine. Let's see. Red means danger, so that's out. Yellow is for cowards... don't eat yellow snow... yeah, not yellow. Blue is for sky... water... blue eyes... blue jeans... maybe blue? Purple is for royalty. Nothing wrong with that, but this is America—not exactly popular here. Maybe that's a trick? And orange... sunrises, sunsets... I guess caution signs are kind of orange? Seriously, what a stupid question. Who wrote this test, anyway?

Sam didn't see why blue would be better than orange, but it was probably more popular, so she chose it on the theory that most standardized tests were not especially inventive.

2. Which of the following best describes humanity?
   A) exciting
   B) well-intentioned
   C) innovative
   D) predictable
   E) resourceful

Really? Sam stared at the question until she knew she was taking too long to answer. As ridiculous as it was, she had to pick one.

She couldn't honestly say she found most people to be exciting, innovative, or resourceful. Some, sure, but certainly not most. That left 'well-intentioned' and 'predictable.' Sam figured she was supposed to choose 'well-intentioned,' thereby proving that she was a healthy, well-balanced teenager with a positive outlook on humanity.

But she just couldn't bring herself to ignore 'predictable.'

People got up at the same time every day, went to the same places, had the same arguments over and over... repeated the same opinions on the same topics of conversation. There was an insufferable rhythm buried within the mind of almost every human being Samantha Prescott had ever met—a numbing monotony that had been threatening to drag her into the depths of despair for years— and if someone was actually going to ask her about it, even if it was only on a stupid test, she was damn well going to be honest.

D. Predictable.

She filled in the answer meticulously, definitively, watching her pencil go around and around, blackening the oval with more than just a small sense of satisfaction before finally moving on.

4
DANIEL

A huge grin spread across Daniel Walker's face as he popped his chin to the funk strains of "Too Hot to Stop" by The Bar-Kays, his shaggy blond hair swaying back and forth to the rhythmic beat of his imagination. Although the room's mission-style architecture was about as un-funky as you could get, that wasn't about to stop Daniel from enjoying a musical interlude, especially if the situation demanded it. And to Daniel's mind, it usually did.

148. How hot is too hot?

As if the multiple-choice questions hadn't been weird enough, the short answer section was downright bizarre. Number 148 had started him in on "Too Hot to Stop." Now it was all he could do not to tap his pencil frenetically on the desk: tap tap tap tap BAP-BAP BAP-BAP BAP-BAP POW! His fingers ached to pluck out the bass line—adding a few embellishments of his own, of course.

He considered writing "When it's too hot to stop" as his answer, but thinking about it as prose, without the music, he suddenly felt awkward, and the song faded away. He couldn't write that on a test—not even one that didn't count. He paused only a moment before his head was nodding again, this time with less pop and more groove, weaving to the sultry beat of "Smooth."

Ask Santana, he wrote.

Daniel decided he liked tests that didn't count. He liked them a lot.

Before moving on to the next question, he finished the melody all the way through in his mind, the easy rhythm of the tune perfectly matching both the title of the song and the gorgeous southern California day.

At lunch, the test was all anyone could talk about.

"Which color is the best color? What was *that*?" Daniel's best friend, Jared, was a short, dark-haired teen with pretty-boy features and unnaturally long fingers that could fly over a bass guitar like a hummingbird's wings.

"Please, brah. Blue's the best color, hands down. Don't be stupid." The reply came from Scott, a heavyset teen with nondescript brown hair and a solid if somewhat uninventive gift for drumming.

The three of them had talked about forming a band for years, but Daniel was the only one who could really sing, and he was too shy even to play his guitar in front of most people, despite his obvious talent. Instead, they held occasional jams in Scott's bedroom, but even these were few and far between, depending as they did on the other residents of the house feeling inclined to tolerate an hour or two of inescapable percussion—which they usually were not.

"Jared's not stupid," Daniel said, quick to defend his oldest friend.

"Aw, don't mind him." Jared flourished his hand through the air as though to sweep the comment away. "A grommet swooped his wave off the line-up this morning. He's been in a bad mood ever since."

"Effing kooks oughta stay on the beach where they belong." Scott scowled at his roast beef sandwich, hardly touching it.

Daniel offered Scott a sympathetic smile, trying to snap him out of it, but Scott's theme song for the day—Three Days Grace's "I Hate Everything About You"—was already on a play loop. Its wailing strains threatened to make Daniel laugh as he imagined Scott behind a mic, howling out the melody in his high-pitched, off-key tenor. He dropped his head as fast as he could, hiding his smirk behind his hair.

"Hey, Daniel," Jared said, interrupting his thoughts with a friendly punch to the shoulder. "Don't look now, but I think Alyssa's watching you."

"If she's looking over here, she's not watching me, she's watching you," Daniel replied, and he laughed at his friend's stunned expression. The shy, petite blonde had been staring love songs at Jared for weeks now. "She's cute. You should ask her out. You two would look good together."

Daniel looked to Scott for confirmation, but Scott said nothing. Only the barest hint of rage passed across his round, cherubic face before he could mask it, but Daniel was onto him.

Apparently, Jared wasn't the only one who liked Alyssa Summers.

Daniel had no idea when that had happened, but underneath Scott's neutral exterior the volatile drummer had already traded in the angst-ridden howling of Three Days Grace for the high-intensity pounding of "Platypus," by Green Day, which echoed riotously in Daniel's imagination, its breakneck tempo contrasting starkly against the brutal hostility of the lyrics.

"You think so?" Jared wanted to know.

"Sorry, what?"

"You think I should ask her out?" Jared tried again, sounding hopeful.

Daniel looked back and forth between Jared and Scott, The Beach Boys' "Good Vibrations" now locked in an epic battle of the bands against Scott's Green Day angst. No matter what Daniel did, he was going to hurt one or the other. How had his beautiful Santana morning come to this?

"Um, hey, you know what? I just remembered I have math homework to finish before class. I'm gonna hit the library. I'll see ya, OK?"

"Yeah, OK," they both replied, each of them staring at Alyssa Summers with vastly different expressions.

Daniel hightailed it out of the cafeteria as fast as he could.

Thankfully, Daniel didn't have to see the two boys together again for the rest of the day, but he did have one class with each of them.

He had math with Jared first, and he spent the entire period enjoying a mash-up of his own invention that ranged from Roy Orbison's "Pretty Woman" to "I'm a Believer" by The Monkees, despite the fact that Jared didn't mention even one word about Alyssa Summers, asking instead in mouthed whispers whether Daniel understood any of this quadratic equation nonsense, to which Daniel replied easily that no, he did not.

History, however, was a solemn affair. Scott pointedly ignored him for the entire class, his chipper Green Day anger having devolved into a seething Eminem tirade. Given Scott's mood, Daniel didn't even want to know what had happened between his friends after he had left the lunchroom. Fortunately, Scott didn't seem inclined to tell him either, storming out after class before Daniel could have said a word.

Not that he was trying to.

Daniel took his time packing up, giving Scott plenty of space to get the heck out of Dodge without another awkward encounter. He hated it when his friends were fighting, and this squabble had all the telltale signs of becoming an epic feud—which was stupid, since Alyssa had started liking Jared weeks ago, and Scott had never even mentioned her before. But of course, that didn't matter. If Scott decided Jared had 'stolen' Alyssa from his unrequited affections, there would be no quarter for his imagined crime.

By the time Daniel reached the parking lot, just about everyone had already cleared out. He sauntered over to his truck, his mood already lifting. Daniel drove a teal, mint-condition 1975 F100 pickup. His grandmother had never much liked driving to begin with and had finally given it up altogether, offering the truck to Daniel on his sixteenth birthday the year before. He had loved it from the moment he first laid eyes on it, and even now, more than a year later, he remembered that initial joy of knowing it was his every time he slid behind the wheel.

It didn't have any kind of sound system worth speaking of, but Daniel didn't mind. He had several thousand songs on his phone and far more stored in his head, and he could listen to them in his memory any time he wanted. Daniel only had to hear a song once to repeat any part of it, even changing the arrangement at will to suit his mood. Although he had been known to dabble in any instrument he could get his hands on, his favorites were lead and bass guitar, and he reveled in them both with equal skill and enthusiasm.

Perching happily on the old truck's bench seat, Daniel paused before starting the engine to take a few deep breaths and let go of the afternoon's negativity. He had promised his father, a firefighter who had seen more than his share of horrific accidents, that he would never drive in agitation, and Daniel took his promises seriously. So he sat in the truck, breathing in the salty tang of the ocean-swept air until he felt the good mood of the morning settling back into his bones, while his empty hands played Santana's lead guitar in the warm California sunshine.

"So, how was your day?" Daniel's mother, Sarah, asked him the same exact question every afternoon. She was an artist by profession, and he found her today, as he usually did, in her home studio, in the midst of a new painting. He took a moment to enjoy the familiar scent of paint, paint thinner, and his mother's lavender shampoo. The question began a ritual they had developed when he was small, and he answered her now in the same way he had begun answering her even then.

"Really good, then good and bad, then funny, then really bad, and now good again."

Sarah Walker laughed. "OK, spill," she said. "Tell me everything."

So Daniel sat on the spare stool while she stood at the easel, painting and listening to her son's day. He told her about the strange test in the morning, about the awkwardness at lunch, about seeing how happy Jared was in math class, and about Scott's cold shoulder in history.

"And what was the last bit?" Sarah prompted him. "The bit about it being good again?"

"That," he said, completing the ritual, "was coming back home. Obviously!"

"Obviously!" Sarah repeated, chuckling at their long-standing routine. She couldn't hug him because her smock was full of paint, but she smiled at him for a long moment before turning back to her work. She was not, however, finished with the conversation.

"So, do you think Scott will get over it soon?" she wanted to know.

"I doubt it." Daniel frowned. "Alyssa has liked Jared for months, and Jared seems to like her, too. So I think that's probably going to happen. But you should have seen Scott. I don't think he's going to get over it soon at all if Alyssa ends up Jared's girlfriend. Maybe not even before school's out."

Daniel's mother sighed in sympathy. Outside of the family, Jared and Scott were about the only two people Daniel spent any time with. If those two weren't speaking to each other, things didn't bode well for him.

"What are you going to do if they ignore each other all summer?"

Daniel just shrugged. "Play guitar, go surfing with Marshall, bring you snacks so you don't forget to eat while you're working. You know, the usual."

"Daniel, sweetheart, you can't spend all summer by yourself."

"I said I'd go surfing with Marshall."

"Your twelve-year-old brother does not count as company your own age."

"Jeez, Mom, you'd think hanging out with my kid brother was a bad thing. Most parents I know would be ecstatic if their seventeen-year-old son started driving his little brother around."

His mother lowered her brush, turning back toward him.

"Don't get me wrong," she started, her tone gentle. "I'm glad you like spending time with Marshall. It's good for him. He looks up to you, and you're a wonderful role model. You always have been. I just think it would be nice if you had a few more friends your own age. Maybe even a nice girl to go to the movies with."

"Mom," Daniel groaned, "don't start."

"I'm not starting anything—"

"You *are* starting something. But I'm telling you, I'm not interested in any of the girls at school, OK? I've seen Jared and Scott go through this more than once, and it's not worth it. I don't want to end up in a fight with one of them—or with anyone else for that matter—over liking some girl who wouldn't even be my girlfriend more than a few weeks before she started liking someone else anyway."

"OK, I hear you," she said, relenting. "Really, I hear you. Be a perfect son and drive Marshall around all summer, making him happy. See if I care." She grinned at him, waving her brush in the air as though to shoo him away. "Go on, then. This canvas isn't going to paint itself."

Daniel grinned back, relieved she had decided not to push the topic—for now, anyway. "I'll be in my room if you need me."

Sarah Walker stared at the doorway until the sound of her son's guitar echoed down the hall, a quick, happy tune that she knew he was playing to reassure her. She stood a while without moving, letting it soothe her, as it always did. He was so talented. Why wouldn't he play for anyone else?

I hope it won't be too long before you find a girl you can share your music with, she thought to herself. *Life is too short to spend it alone.* She knew she should get back to work, but instead she set down her brush, sat on the stool, closed her eyes, and listened to her son play—she in her art studio and he in his room just down the hall, as close as any mother and son have ever been, a lifetime of experience standing between them.

5
ASH

Rush! Behind you!"

"Way ahead of you, bro."

Even before Snark had finish yelling, Ashton Hunt, a.k.a. Rush, had already done a leaping one-eighty and put a bullet between the eyes of two enemy players, and he was hardly even trying. Rush sat with his feet up on his desk, casually holding his controller and watching the screen from a jaunty angle, occasionally reaching out with one hand to sneak a sip of his energy drink between kills.

His top-of-the-line headset and his amped-up controller were both connected by cords to the console, so he had to be careful in grabbing the drink to make sure his arm didn't get caught up in either one. It was, to be honest, more attention than he had to pay to the game itself. He and his friends were just warming up with a free-play match, and the random players they had pulled as enemies were pathetically slow by comparison.

"Seriously, man, you really think you have to warn me about

these noobs?" Rush asked. "I'm tellin' you, I'm goin' pro in August. You'll see."

"Hey, I got faith, man. I believe."

"You sure about that? I heard you and Wingman were taking bets against me."

Snark's laughter burst through the headset, briefly overriding the game sound, but it didn't stop Rush from one-shotting another enemy who had been trying to sneak up behind him.

"Not *against* you, man! Who the hell said that? Me and Wing were bettin' on how many people you'd have to beat out for it. He said two million, but I think it won't be more than one."

"Online mags are sayin' four," Rush countered.

"Whoa. Four million betas?"

"Yeah." Rush blew another enemy away and then tried to hit his drink again, frowning at it when the can ran out.

"I'm out of juice," Rush said. "Cover me, Snark."

"Do my best, Chief."

Ashton pulled his headset off and set the controller on the desk, kicking his feet down onto the floor. He was absurdly fit for a guy who did little more than go to school and play video games, but he wasn't one to eat chips or pound sodas, not even while he was gaming. The energy drinks were his biggest vice, but he only drank the sugar-free kind. Staying lean gave him an edge. Ashton Hunt might not have been anyone important, but when 'Rush' talked about gaming, other gamers listened. Now his whole team stayed fit, following his lead.

He stretched his six-foot frame leisurely, then dropped the empty can into the trash and pulled another one out of the mini-fridge. He popped the top open, took a swig, and then sauntered back to his desk, propping his feet back up and sliding the headset down over his short, dark hair. He picked up the controller, and his ice-blue eyes focused back in on the screen like a hawk's.

"Hey, Snark. You suck."

Snark laughed through the headset again. While Rush had been gone from the game, Snark had gotten them both killed.

"Sorry, man. Team of three got me."

"Meh, no worries. It's just a scrub match."

"Yeah," Snark agreed.

Rush didn't care about random matches. They didn't count in the ranking system. In fact, *Hostage Rescue Team Alpha: Year One* was slated for official sale in August, still several months out, and when the title hit the shelves, rankings from the beta version would be wiped clean. They only mattered to Rush because the top-ranked beta players would be invited in August to compete for spots on the five-man pro team that the game developers were sponsoring.

"They're really sayin' four million now?" Wingman wanted to know. His Texan drawl always made Rush grin.

"Yeah. The beta's gone viral, so they're letting more people in."

"Damn," Snark said.

"Yeah. I don't even care though. They can let five million in. I'll still get a spot."

Rush had been carefully maintaining his *HRT Alpha* ranking, refusing to move higher than number twenty. The launch competition would include the top one hundred beta players in the world, and he wanted to guarantee his spot without attracting too much attention. Everyone would be ganging up on the top five during the competition weekend. He had no intention of starting out with a target on his back.

Rush felt confident he could win it either way, but he was willing to take any competitive edge he could get. The sponsorship wasn't just a couple of free controllers and a pat on the back. This was a genuine, pro team, paid to attend gaming conferences all over the world and play matches in front of live audiences of thousands — even tens of thousands — and far more over the televised broadcasts. The online streaming income alone represented a small fortune.

"Don't forget us when you're pro, man," Snark said, his voice betraying a hint of genuine concern. At seventeen years old, Rush had already been playing with the same four guys for three years. Snark was his oldest gaming friend. He was good, but he wasn't as good as Rush, and they both knew it.

"Naw, man," Rush said. "You know I won't. Ima send you guys my swag. You'll see. T-shirts, games, controllers, snacks... Ima hook you guys up." He meant it, too. Nobody had ever had his back like Snark, Wingman, Fuego, and Stryker.

"Damn straight you hookin' us up, Rush. But I ain't takin' no T-shirts. I'm takin' your women, like it or not, bro." This last was Fuego, always the first to lighten up a serious mood.

"Yeah, OK. We'll see about that," Rush said, laughing.

"Yeah, we *will*, bro. You just wait!"

"Fuego, only girl of mine I'm lettin' you have is my sister," Rush shot back.

"Thought you didn't have a sister," Stryker chimed in.

"Exactly."

And with that, they all dissolved into laughter. They won their match easily, and it was time for Rush to queue them up for another.

"Let's play 'Light It Up,'" Rush suggested.

"Seriously?" Snark complained.

"Again?" Fuego added a few curses in Spanish, just for good measure. *HRT Alpha: Year One* offered thirteen different game modes for player-versus-player beta matches. Rush enjoyed most of them, but 'Light It Up' was his favorite.

"Fuego, you just said yesterday you liked it," Rush countered.

"'Like' is Mexican for 'hate,' bro," Fuego quipped, and Rush laughed. That was Fuego's personal code. If he said a word meant something in Spanish, he was telling you the truth. If he said it meant something in Mexican, he was making a joke.

"I'll play whatever," Stryker said, as he always did.

"Wingman?" Rush asked.

"What's my name?"

"Wingman," Rush said, grinning.

"And why am I the Wingman?"

"'Cause you always got my back," Rush answered. "'Light It Up' it is!" He smiled as he put them in queue for another unranked match. The team was quiet for a while, waiting for the system to find them a game, until Stryker finally spoke up, breaking the silence.

"Did you guys all take that test today?"

Stryker was the quietest of them all. He rarely said anything, and when he did, it was because it was gnawing at him. Rush knew one of the main reasons Stryker stuck with them was because they didn't mind him being so quiet—and because they would always talk to him anyway when he needed to get something off his chest. So when a few long moments passed without a response, Rush stepped up to the plate.

"I think we all did, didn't we? I heard it was in every school in the country."

"Not me, bro," Fuego offered up. "I'm home-schooled."

"If by 'home-schooled' you mean 'illegal,'" Snark replied. It was common knowledge among the team that Fuego was, in fact, an illegal immigrant whose family did not send him to school for fear that he might get picked up by Immigration and Customs Enforcement.

"That's what I said," Fuego replied easily. "'Home-schooled' is Mexican for 'illegal.'"

Rush couldn't help but laugh. "Well, everyone else took it. Why, Stryker? What's up, man?"

"It was *weird*, right?" Stryker said.

"Yeah," Snark and Wingman both agreed.

"I wouldn't know," Rush said.

"I thought you just said you took it?" Stryker asked.

"Well, I kinda did, and I kinda didn't."

"What's that supposed to mean?" Snark demanded.

"Means I read the first three questions, decided it was stupid, and just filled in random blanks after that for the first two sections," Rush admitted.

Snark laughed so hard he finally toggled his mic off to keep from splitting their eardrums.

"You didn't," Wingman objected.

"Truth," Rush said.

"Wow," was all Stryker had to say.

"Hey, guys, wait a sec," Rush interjected, hearing his mother calling him down to dinner. "I gotta go eat. Meet back in twenty?"

"Yeah."

"OK."

"Sure."

"Sounds good."

"Awesome. See you then." Dinner shouldn't take long, and then he could get back to practicing for August. Come hell or high water, he would be ready.

6
MACKENZIE

Even now, several months after they had moved in, Mackenzie Gray hated the carpet in the upstairs hallway. This was due largely to its color, which was ironic, she thought, given her name. But she didn't hate all gray things, or even all gray carpets. It was just this particular carpet, this precise shade of gray, that she found so intolerable.

It was just so... undefined.

She might have liked it, had it been a solid, dependable, gunmetal sort of gray, or if it had evoked within her the thrill of angry thunderclouds on the horizon. A hint of blue could have rendered it more hopeful, like the first gleam of sun in the sky after a long, cold night. Or if it had exhibited any variegation whatsoever, she might have found its contrasts intriguing, like water-polished stones at the bottom of a river—a river you could point to on a map and say, "Here. I'm right here."

In the end, it was just a light, industrial gray, designed to hide the telltale signs of use, cheap to replace, and thoroughly inoffensive, which was perhaps the worst thing about it. Of course, that was what passed for interior design in military housing, a fact with which Mackenzie Gray was intimately familiar, having lived on one Army base or another for all seventeen years of her life to date.

But the dark gray carpet in her last home had at least conveyed a certain sense of place. At least she had felt, standing upon it, as though she were... *somewhere.* The light gray carpet in the upstairs hallway here, coupled with the slightly lighter gray of the walls, left Mackenzie feeling as though she were somehow standing nowhere at all, a feeling so unsettling that she tried to avoid it whenever she could.

Not that she would ever complain about it.

Mackenzie's father, Brian Gray, was a bona fide member of the Special Forces of the Armed Forces of the United States of America. He was—as was every other member of his elite unit—the very antithesis of petulance, and he was not about to let any of his four beloved daughters grow up to be a sniveling little whiner. So Mackenzie Gray did not complain when her family moved from base to base. She did not complain about changing schools or leaving her friends. She did not complain about having to find yet another new Muay Thai coach. She certainly was not about to complain about the carpet.

Nonetheless, she was happy to avoid a bad situation if it was within her power to do so. She had just become very good, very early in life, at knowing the difference between those situations that she could affect and those that she could not. So when it came to the carpet, she said absolutely nothing, but she quietly positioned herself as far away from it as possible.

As the oldest of the girls, Mackenzie got first pick of bedrooms in every new home. This was a long-standing rule in the Gray family, and although one or another of her three sisters had occasionally launched a campaign to challenge its fairness, the familial hierarchy had proven itself highly resistant to insurgence. So when the Grays had moved into this most recent home on this most recent base, Mackenzie had selected the only downstairs bedroom for herself—a room that had been converted from a den-slash-office, with windows overlooking the small but immaculate front lawn.

In any other family, this might have been an odd choice. The room opened directly off the living room, with the noise of the television on the other side of the wall. But Mackenzie slept like the dead, and in any event, the family had survived one paternal tour after another by relying on strict discipline and routine. Bedtimes were adhered to religiously, and the television set was turned off every night by 9:00 p.m. on the dot, without exception.

And because the only rooms upstairs were the bedrooms that belonged to Mackenzie's mother and sisters, Mackenzie never had to brave the gray carpet except under two circumstances: when she put away her sisters' laundry every Saturday, and when she waited in line to video chat with her father every Sunday.

It was this latter event that had her sitting now in the hallway next to Megan, who was fifteen; who sat next to Madison, who was twelve; who sat next to Mia, who was nine. This was the only situation in which Mackenzie's age worked against her, as she was the last one to speak to her father and therefore had to sit in the dreaded hallway the longest.

She sat with her back to the wall, playing with her phone, texting her most recent set of new friends, watching Muay Thai videos, generally embracing the suck, and trying not to think about the disturbing gray carpet. In no way was she going to let her sisters—or the carpet itself, for that matter—know that the stupid thing could unsettle her.

After just a few minutes, Stephanie Gray emerged from the master bedroom and signaled to Mia that it was her turn, an event that was repeated a few minutes later from Mia to Madison, and after that from Madison to Megan, and after *that*, finally, from Megan to Mackenzie. Mackenzie leaped to her feet as soon as the doorknob started to turn, brushing past Megan before her sister could finish getting out the door. Megan, however, was also a daughter of Brian Gray, and if she happened to feel that this was in any way rude, she held her peace on the subject, nodding to her older sister and shutting the door behind her as she left.

Mackenzie hurried to the computer at her mother's desk, her nerves soothed by the warm colors of the bedspread and the abundant family photos that covered the walls, lending the room an aura of home that the hallway, with its industrial blankness, sorely lacked. Her father looked more tired and significantly more tanned than the last time he had been stateside, but his smile was comfortingly familiar. She took in his overall appearance of health and allowed her genuine happiness to shine through for his benefit.

"Hey, Dad. So what's the weather going to be like this afternoon?" It was a running joke between them whenever her father was stationed in a timezone significantly ahead of her own, as he was now.

Her father grinned back. "Hot. Wear sunscreen."

"Roger that," she acknowledged. "You managing to stay off K.P.? Or did they send you over there to peel potatoes?"

"Mounds of potatoes," he replied, winking. "Truckloads. How about you? You managing not to get your ass kicked in Muay Thai? Or are they mopping the floor with you?"

"Oh, ha ha. Let me guess. Mom already told you I won?"

"She's proud of you, Mac," her father confirmed. He was the only person who called her Mac. Everyone else, including her mother and sisters, called her by her full name. "But I want to hear about it."

As it happened, Mackenzie had other news for her father, and she had already been sitting in the hallway for almost fifteen minutes waiting for her turn, refusing to let her impatience show. But she regarded it as an exercise in discipline, so she forced herself to tell him about the competition first.

"It wasn't a big meet. Just eight girls. My first match was the toughest, so if we hadn't pulled each other early, that girl might have made it to the final match. But I'm not sure it would have been as hard to fight her farther into it."

"Really? Why?"

Mackenzie loved the fact that her father always asked questions about her matches. He didn't just care who won or lost. He understood that she loved Muay Thai, and he wanted to know as much about it as he could—to share in what mattered to her. He was the only person who showed that much interest in the sport beyond her own coaches.

"Well, partly because she moved so much. She would have been tired after more rounds."

"Five rounds per match?"

"Yeah, standard rules. So, by the fifteenth, she would have been crazy tired if she had made it that far. But the bad thing was *how* she moved. She kept dancing away from me. Stop laughing."

"I'm not laughing. I'm grinning." But just saying it transformed his handsome grin into a chuckle.

"You're laughing *now!*"

"You're right... you're right... I *am* laughing now," he admitted. "I can just imagine you chasing her around the ring. I know how much you hate that."

"Well, I like to think it wasn't quite as undignified as that makes it sound."

At this, her father laughed even harder before finally managing to bring himself back under control. "OK, OK," he said finally. "So what happened?"

But Mackenzie was grinning by this time, too. She could never listen to her father's charismatic laughter without smiling, no matter what mood she had been in even moments before.

"Well, you're kind of right. I wasn't exactly chasing her, but it probably looked that way. Every time I tried a kick she would back away fast. And then I would do it again, and she would back up again. So I couldn't land anything. But then sometimes she would close for a second, throw a kick or a punch, and then dance away so I couldn't return it. A couple of those caught me off-guard because I was still trying to catch up to her. So she was getting ahead on points even though she was fighting dirty."

"How was it dirty? Was it against the rules?"

"No. No, it's legal. It's just, you know, she wouldn't stand and fight me. Who goes to a competition to run away?"

"But she almost won that way, eh?"

"Yeah," Mackenzie replied sheepishly.

"Sometimes, Mac," and his voice was suddenly serious, a tone she recognized as meaning he was about to impart a gentle life lesson, "running away is the best long-term strategy. Sometimes your opponent is stronger than you. When that happens, you can't stand and fight. You have to be smart about it. Toughness isn't always what wins a battle. Understand?"

"Coach says you're gonna get hit no matter what, though," she protested. "If the other girl is stronger, you're just going to have to take some tough hits. The trick is to take each hit on your own terms."

"I don't think I'm saying anything that different, Mac. But sometimes your best terms are not to take the hit at all."

"Well, that was what *she* thought, that's for sure," she admitted, but her disdain for the tactic was still obvious.

"OK," her father said, relenting, "tell me how you beat her."

"Well, the first two rounds were tied, but she took round three by a point because of all the running. In round four I managed to hold my own again. So in round five I was still down by one, and the match was almost over. I knew I had to score big, right? So I started chasing her for real, throwing lots of kicks, not even trying to connect, just making her run, and then I slowed down, pretending I was getting tired, baiting her to turn back toward me. When she did, she threw a kick at my side, but I caught it the second it landed—I mean I knew *exactly* where it was going to hit, you know? From the second she started the kick, I just read it. And I caught her leg and swept her. Bam! Down on the mat."

"You knocked her out?" her father asked, his eyes wide.

"No," she said, laughing, "but it was a solid take-down. It was enough to win."

"Good," he said proudly. "How were the other matches?"

"Easy, compared to her. I dominated the second girl. She was a total pushover. The last one was a little faster, but not as fast as me. Like Coach always says, 'Take the hit where you want it. Understand why you're taking it so you can hit back harder.' She got a few hits in, but I took 'em where I wanted 'em. And I hit back harder."

"That's my girl," her father said, nodding.

"But, Dad, listen, there's something I have to tell you."

"OK, shoot, Mac, but make it quick. The guys in line are starting to grumble." He smiled when he said it, but she knew he was serious. There were other soldiers waiting, and other families. They couldn't selfishly monopolize the video feed.

"OK. So, remember that weird test I told you about a few weeks ago?"

"The standardized thing that didn't count for anything?" he asked. "The one with all the funny questions?"

"That's the one," she confirmed. Mackenzie and her father had spent their entire chat that week laughing as she regaled him with examples of the test questions. "Well, even though it didn't count toward anything in school, it turns out that it did matter for something after all."

"Oh, yeah?" He raised an eyebrow, waiting for her news.

"Yeah. I got a letter in the mail on Thursday. I didn't even tell Mom yet 'cause I wanted to tell you first." She paused to gauge his reaction to that, but he was smiling at her fondly.

"That's OK, Mac. You can keep things to tell me first. What did the letter say?"

"It's an invitation to this special school for the summer. Here, wait—I'll read it.

Dear Miss Gray,

It is our pleasure to inform you that your recent performance on the nationally administered Intuition Assessment Battery places you at the 99.9th percentile of all students tested throughout the country. In recognition of this outstanding achievement, you have been selected to attend the inaugural summer program of the Institute for the Cultivation of Intuitive Cognition, under the supervision of the United States Department of Homeland Security.

"Homeland Security, Dad! Isn't that amazing? I mean, it's just studying education theory or something, but it's still pretty awesome, right? It says I'd be serving my country, and it says it won't cost us anything either. There's a full scholarship, including food and housing and tuition and even travel. It's totally free because I did so well on the test. That's crazy, right? But it's in Wyoming, and it starts in just two weeks. I know it's short notice..." Her voice trailed off as she waited for her father's reaction.

"Mac, that's tremendous! The 99.9th percentile, and out of the whole country! I'm so proud of you!" He took a moment to beam at her from the other side of the world before voicing his concerns. He was proud of her, she could tell. But Mackenzie also knew he had seen more than his share of bad situations, and his first instinct as her father was to keep her safe.

"But, Mac," he finally said, "what do you really know about this program? Are we sure it's legit? I'm not trying to cast doubt on a good thing here, but—"

"It's for real, Dad," she said quickly, interrupting him. They both knew their time would be up soon. "I asked Cappy to run it through channels before I told you. He said it checks out, but I made him promise not to tell Mom until tomorrow. He said if I got this letter, it's a super big deal, and they really need me. So I can go, right?" Cappy was their nickname for Captain Paul Gillespie, their current next door neighbor. He had made a point of checking in with the family while Mackenzie's dad was away on tour.

"Well... listen, I want to check it out here, too, OK? I don't want you heading off to another state until I've seen for myself that it's the real thing, especially with the invitation coming out of the blue, and it being a government program I've never heard of. But if it is what it says it is, of course you have my blessing.

"But I really have to go now, Mac. Be sure to tell your mother about it tonight so she knows, and tell her I'm looking into it. You said we have a couple weeks, right?"

"Yeah. It says they'll make the travel arrangements, but I'm supposed to let them know by a week from tomorrow at the latest."

"OK. Give me until next week then. I'll let you know on Sunday if everything looks good."

"Thanks, Dad."

"I love you, Mac. Tell your mom and your sisters again for me, too. I miss all my girls."

"We miss you too, Dad. Love you. Be smart." She would have felt stupid telling him to be safe when he was downrange. He couldn't always be completely safe. That was the nature of the job. But he could always be smart.

"I promise, Mac. You, too, OK? Always."

"Always," she agreed, and with that, the feed ended. Mackenzie touched her fingers to her lips and then pressed them to the monitor, sending her father the kiss she hadn't had time for before the screen went dark. She continued to sit at the desk, staring at the blank monitor for another prolonged moment before finally getting up and turning toward the door, bracing herself to brave the long gray hallway one more time.

7
RUSH

No! You don't understand! You can't do this to me!" Rush glared at his father, sitting to Rush's right, at the head of the family dinner table.

"Do this to you? What are you talking about? I'm proud of you, Ashton. This is a tremendous opportunity."

"Seriously? Of all the things to be proud of me for, you choose this? *This? Now???* What about the invitational? I can't go to Wyoming!"

"Really, Ashton, I thought you'd be happy. It's a prestigious program. You'll be able to write your own ticket to any college in the country after this summer. And technically it's with the Department of Homeland Security. Isn't that what you like to do on those games of yours? Play the hero? Now you'll get to serve your country in a way that actually matters."

"Dad, it's not just *playing.* I've told you that so many times! I have the chance of a lifetime with *HRT Alpha.* I'm in the top twenty in the world! Out of over four million people! Do you realize what that means?

My seat at the competition is a lock. And a spot on the team is a real job. Making *real money*, like you always say I should! Did you read even *one* of the articles I sent you?"

Rush had emailed his father countless articles on professional gaming: how it was gaining recognition as a sport, how the top players enjoyed not just national but international recognition, how matches were now televised by the likes of ESPN, and how the best of the best could command salaries that ran into the millions.

"Honestly, Ashton, a job playing video games is hardly a solid career path. Look at Ben, here. He's going to be a college senior next year, and he already has a summer internship lined up, with a guaranteed job when he graduates. That's a career path. Not this... this..." James Hunt struggled for the phrase he was looking for, waving his knife around as though he might be able to skewer the word out of mid-air. "This fantasy world you insist on living in."

Ben looked across the table at Rush apologetically, but he didn't say a word.

"Mom?" Rush begged, starting to feel desperate.

"Jim," she tried, "surely it wouldn't hurt to read one of the articles Ashton sent you. He's very proud of his accomplishments on that..." She looked to her son for the name of the game, and Ashton's heart dropped into his stomach.

"*HRT Alpha*," he offered, but he already knew it was hopeless. His mother loved him, but she didn't know enough about his gaming to help—certainly not enough to raise an argument that the great James Hunt might actually listen to.

"I don't have to read an article to know that video games are *games*," his father declared. "They're fine for children, but it's time for you to grow up. *This* is a once in a lifetime chance, Ashton. A summer program like this sets you apart on your college applications."

"But I won't *need* to go to college once I'm on the team, Dad. I'm telling you, guys like that make—"

"I don't care what they make!" his father shouted. "Not going to college is out of the question! Do you hear me? Out of the question! Another comment like that, and I have half a mind to take away everything *my* hard-earned money ever bought you!"

"I'll pay you back every dime of it," Rush shot back. "Add it all up and send me a bill. Make sure to include interest, too. I don't want to owe you anything."

"Enough!" His father slammed the base of his fork against the table, startling Rush's mother enough to make her jump in her chair. "I'm sorry, Laura," he said, apologizing to his wife, "but I won't hear one more word about it. I'm his father. As long as he's living under my roof, he'll live by my rules. He's going to that program this summer, and that, by God, is that!"

"I won't be living under your roof forever!"

"From your mouth to God's ear," his father snapped back.

The two glared at each other for several long moments before Rush finally stood up from the table and threw his napkin into his food.

"Ashton, honey—" his mother tried, but Rush interrupted her.

"Thanks for dinner, Mom, but I'm not hungry."

"Let him go, Laura," his father said calmly, a forkful of mashed potatoes poised halfway to his mouth. "He'll thank me for this one day."

"Like hell I will," Rush muttered, but this time there was no reply, and Rush stormed away, his dreams shattering like glass with every step.

8
KAITLYN

Kaitlyn, do you have a moment?"

Mr. Hallowell flagged Kaitlyn Wright down before she could make it out the door. The lunch bell had already rung, and as usual, her mouth was watering just thinking about it. But she stopped and smiled at him just the same.

Mr. Hallowell was her chemistry teacher, a portly man with an unfortunate bone structure and a constant air of disappointment. Kaitlyn was one of the few students who had discerned the better qualities that lurked beneath his gloomy exterior. She complimented him on his lectures from time to time, as a purposeful kindness, but only when no one else was listening.

"Sure, Mr. Hallowell. What's up?"

"Well, as you might have heard, the Video Club needs a new sound technician, so of course we thought of you. Don't worry, I know summer is upon us, but I was hoping you might take on the position in the fall, for your junior year? After-school activities do look good on college applications."

Kaitlyn hated to say 'no,' and not just because of Mr. Hallowell's puppy-dog expression. With Tommy Evans graduating, all the other members had approached her individually, begging her to step in. She was starting to wish she could join up just long enough to produce a video declining the position, so she could play it for anyone else who asked.

"I'm so sorry," she said, smiling apologetically. "I really am. I know clubs and things look good for college, but I just can't. I work at the G&G after school, and I don't have time for both."

'The G&G' was the Gears and Gadgets Repair Shop, where Kaitlyn had been working for almost two years, since the day she had turned fourteen. She fixed all manner of small appliances, from blenders to television sets, just barely bringing in enough money to make ends meet. She couldn't afford to give up the job, but she didn't want anyone to know how desperately she needed it either.

"Perhaps you could spare us just a day or two after school? And only the occasional weekend?"

"I'm sorry, Mr. Hallowell. Truly. I just can't." She stared up at him a moment longer, her messy brown hair falling across her soulful brown eyes. She brushed it back off her face out of habit, waiting for him to relent.

"OK, then," he said, finally admitting defeat. "But if you change your mind before September, you'll let me know?"

"I promise," she said, her customary grin lighting up her face. "Thanks, Mr. Hallowell. May I be excused, please? Lunch smells delicious!"

"You may," he said, chuckling.

She flashed him a grateful smile and rushed out the door, all but skipping down the hallway, the alluring scent of hot dogs pulling her toward the cafeteria.

"Hey, Zack-Attack."

"Howdy, Kit-Kat."

"What have you got for me today?" Kaitlyn put down her backpack and slid past the counter into the G&G's workshop. She ran one hand over the utilitarian shelving—overflowing with wires and switches, rags and rust remover, motors and metal housings. Just walking in the door was enough to make her sigh in relief. The smell of grease and old electrical parts settled her.

"Couple things came in this morning, actually." Zack frowned. "I don't know if you'll be able to do anything with them though."

"Really? Let me see!"

He laughed at the way her eyes lit up.

"I swear," he said, "you'd think I was handing you a Christmas present."

Kaitlyn giggled and then 'oohed' and 'ahed' as he pulled her new treasures out from under the countertop.

"This—" he said with a flourish, but she yelped and bounced up and down, interrupting him before he could utter more than the first word.

"An RCA color TV!" she exclaimed delightedly.

"Is an RCA color television, yes," he finished, chuckling at her enthusiasm. "I think the vacuum tube is messed up in it."

"Oh, we can find you another CRT, you adorable little thing, don't you worry," she said, crooning at the television and patting it reassuringly.

"Little? Really? This thing weighs a ton."

"It's still small, though," she said, defending her new charge. "It's just heavy because of the technology. They used tubes in computer monitors, too, for a long time. We can find one. *If* that's what's wrong with you." She said this last directly to the television, staring at it in a thoughtful sort of way.

"Yes, well, before you get too caught up with that to notice me, let me show you the other thing, too."

"Hmm?" she mumbled, already sounding distracted. "Oh! Sorry. What's the other thing?" She giggled, knowing full well that Zack was right. Once she got her nose into a project, she tended to stop taking in her surroundings.

"Here," he said, not even trying to introduce the item this time.

"A Model G mixer!" she exclaimed, sucking in a sharp breath. "Zack, you're full of surprises today!"

"I do my best," he replied, winking at her.

"Did you know Kitchen Aid started building this model on the production line as early as 1927? This is genuine vintage, Zack! What's wrong with it?" She took the appliance from him gently and began turning it back and forth.

"I did not know that, and I have no idea what's wrong with it," he admitted. "I haven't even looked at it. I wouldn't dream of depriving you of that much fun."

"Thanks, Zack! You're the best!" She placed the mixer gently on the counter and leaned over to kiss his lightly grizzled cheek before cradling the mixer in her arms again and carting it farther back into her work area.

"Don't mention it," he replied, shaking his head. "That's just how I roll."

Kaitlyn finally climbed the short staircase in front of her home at 8:00 p.m. The modest house squatted shoulder to shoulder with the others in the row, more of them standing empty than anyone wanted to think about. May was rapidly coming to an end, and the sun wouldn't set until 9:00, but she was exhausted, nonetheless. At least school would be out soon. There would be that many more hours in the day to work and still get home to make her grandmother some dinner.

Kaitlyn had lived with Grandma Maggie ever since she was ten years old, when both of her parents had been killed in a car wreck. Her father had fallen asleep at the wheel, they said. Kaitlyn's grandmother, Margaret Wright, had taken the poor child in—the last line of defense between Kaitlyn and foster care.

Over time, Grandma Maggie had needed more and more help just getting by. Kaitlyn had started doing the dishes and the laundry, and cleaning the house, and eventually making their meals. The house, thankfully, was paid for, but there were still groceries and monthly bills, and after Grandma Maggie's medicines, the checks from Social Security just couldn't cover everything.

The job at the G&G had been a lifesaver—just enough to keep food on the table and the power on and the water running so she could keep showing up at school looking as though everything at home were perfectly fine, so nobody would call the Department of Health and Human Services to go check on them and end up taking Grandma Maggie away and putting Kaitlyn in foster care.

It was an exhausting life, but Kaitlyn didn't mind. She liked fixing things, and she liked taking care of Grandma Maggie, who had always done her very best to take care of Kaitlyn. And she definitely liked living at home more than she would have liked living with strangers. Of that, she was completely and utterly certain.

Kaitlyn turned the key in the front lock carefully so as not to make too much noise. Grandma Maggie liked to nap in the evenings, and Kaitlyn didn't want to startle her. She opened the door and tiptoed into the hallway, avoiding the places where the old floorboards creaked, and then popped her head into the sitting room on the left, where her grandmother was fast asleep in her favorite chair.

"Hi, Grandma Maggie," she said softly. "It's me. Kitten." Only her family had ever called her that, a nickname her mother had given her when she was a baby.

Her grandmother slowly opened her eyes. "Oh, hi, Kitten," she said, and her smile brightened the room. "How are you, sweetheart? How was your day?"

"I'm fine, Grandma," she replied. "How about you. Are you doing OK?"

"Oh, you know me, darling. Couldn't be better. Give me a patch of sunlight and a good book, and I'm as happy as a clam. At least the old eyes are still good enough for that!"

Kaitlyn smiled. "That's good, Grandma. Have you had anything for dinner?"

"Oh, let me see now. I'm sure I must have had something... a sandwich maybe?"

"Yeah? Did you make yourself a sandwich? You think you could eat a little something more for me? You know you have to keep your strength up."

"Oh, I'm fine, Kitten. Don't you worry about me."

"Let's go into the kitchen together anyway, OK? Will you keep me company for a while? I could make us some tea?" It was really just an excuse to get her grandmother to walk the short distance down the hall. The doctor had said she needed to get more exercise to keep her limbs strong.

"Well, OK. I wouldn't mind a cup of tea."

Kaitlyn helped her grandmother up out of the chair, grimacing at how easy that task had become. It seemed to her that Grandma Maggie had lost far more weight than she could really afford to, and Kaitlyn was getting worried.

When they reached the kitchen, she eased her grandmother into a chair and rummaged through the fridge. The loaf of bread she had bought the day before was still unopened, but she didn't mention it. Her grandmother had just forgotten to eat again, and embarrassing her over it wouldn't change anything tomorrow. Instead, she set about making homemade macaroni and cheese, a staple Grandma Maggie would always take a few bites of—even when she claimed she wasn't hungry.

While she worked, Kaitlyn mentioned the Model G mixer she had seen at work that afternoon and then listened happily as her grandmother regaled her with memories of her very first apartment with Kaitlyn's grandfather, who had died not long after Kaitlyn was born, and of the Model G mixer he had bought for her way back when.

"He must have fixed that poor mixer I don't know how many times," Grandma Maggie said, laughing. "He had a gift for things like that. For fixing things. Just like you do."

Kaitlyn was grinning and pouring the sauce over the noodles when there was a knock on the front door. Her first instinct was to panic, but she forced herself to take deep breaths and think. There was no reason for DHHS to come to the house this late in the evening, and even if they did, there was nothing wrong. The power was on. The water was running. She and her grandmother were in the kitchen eating a late supper. There was nothing to worry about.

"Grandma," she asked, "are you expecting someone?"

"Now, Kitten, who would I be expecting? Maybe it's a boy from school, come to call on you, hmm?"

Kaitlyn laughed at this. "I doubt it. Stay here, Grandma. Let me get the door."

"Thank you, darling. These old bones are a bit tired this evening."

The front door had a tall, narrow window next to it, through which Kaitlyn could see a dark-skinned woman with a very personable smile. She was dressed in a skirt suit, but it didn't look like anything Kaitlyn had ever seen on a social worker. The soft, yellow cloth had been tailored to her specifically, its feminine cut lending her an air of gentle confidence—a kind of serenity Kaitlyn would not have thought possible in a business suit until she had seen it with her own eyes.

"Hello?" Kaitlyn said, opening the door.

"Good evening! I'm sorry to bother you so late, but are you Miss Kaitlyn Wright?"

"I am," Kaitlyn confirmed.

"Wonderful!" The woman smiled even more broadly, her teeth flashing brightly against her skin. "My name is Christina Williams. I'm here from the Institute for the Cultivation of Intuitive Cognition—the ICIC, if you will—and I am *very* pleased to meet you!"

A few moments later, all three women were seated at the small kitchen table, Miss Williams having politely declined a plate of macaroni and cheese, but having delightedly accepted a cup of Earl Grey tea.

"So, Kaitlyn, I presume you received our invitation in the mail?"

"Yes, Miss Williams, I did—"

"Please," Miss Williams interrupted her. "Call me Christina. There's no need for formality."

"Well, Christina..." It felt strange to call this well-dressed, grown-up woman by her first name, but Kaitlyn took her at her word. "I did get it, but I'm afraid I threw it away."

"Oh?" The woman raised both eyebrows in obvious surprise.

"Kitten?" Grandma Maggie asked. "What invitation? What's this about?"

"Sorry, Grandma. It's from that test. The one from a few weeks ago. They sent me an invitation to go to some kind of school this summer."

"That's wonderful, Kitten! But why would you throw it away?"

"Grandma, you know I have the job with Zack. He's been good to us. And the school's in Wyoming. I'm not about to leave you alone all summer."

Who would feed you? She wanted to ask. *Who would help pay for your medicine?* But even if Miss Williams wasn't from DHHS, she was still from the government, and government professionals tended to report problems at home. Kaitlyn wasn't about to let on that they were struggling.

"If it's the summer job you're concerned about," Miss Williams responded, "you needn't worry. The scholarship comes with a considerable stipend."

"What kind of a stipend?" That had Kaitlyn's attention. "The invitation said there was a scholarship, but it didn't say anything about extra cash."

"Well, let's just say there are additional benefits available for students who might be otherwise reluctant to attend."

"Such as?"

"Such as..." Miss Williams paused as she dug about in her thin, leather briefcase. "Have you ever heard of this place?"

Having found what she was looking for, she pulled out a brochure and pushed it across the table to Kaitlyn. On the cover was a photo of the most expensive Continuing Care Retirement Community in the entire Detroit area.

Have I heard of it? Are you kidding me? she thought, running the brochure's slick, colorful pages beneath her fingertips.

Kaitlyn researched CCRCs on the Internet at least once a month, dreaming that one day she might be able to set her Grandma Maggie up in a community that could give her the best care, all day long, all year round, so she wouldn't forget to eat, or forget to take her medications, or fall while Kaitlyn was at work and lie there helpless until she got home. That hadn't happened yet, but it was a fear Kaitlyn lived with every day.

But they couldn't afford anything like that, not with a part-time job and a Social Security check as their only income. What kind of game was this woman playing? When Kaitlyn didn't answer, Miss Williams reached one hand across the table and touched her arm, as though she understood what Kaitlyn was thinking.

"When we didn't hear back from you, we took the liberty of making some arrangements. There is a spot for your grandmother here, if she wants it, whenever she's ready." Her voice was gentle and kind, a cool breeze brushing Kaitlyn's cheek on a brutally hot day. She seemed sincere, but Kaitlyn could hardly believe what she was hearing.

"Don't play with me about this," Kaitlyn whispered.

"It's not a game, Kaitlyn. You are... exceptional. Your country needs you, and we are prepared to do whatever is necessary to enable you to participate in this program. Other countries are pulling away from us when it comes to intuitional learning. We need to understand how you do what you do."

"Like, you're going to study me?" Kaitlyn asked, but she knew in her heart she would let them torture her on purpose if it meant her grandmother would be safe and well cared for.

"No," Miss Williams said, chuckling lightly. She had a soft, friendly laugh that reminded Kaitlyn of sunshine and wildflowers. "You won't be a Guinea pig, if that's what you mean. You'll learn things, just like in school, and you'll take tests from time to time, but you won't be graded. We want to teach other people to learn the same way you do, to help them become as exceptional as you are. We want you to show us how to do that."

"But we can't afford that place," Kaitlyn protested. "What if I can't do what you want—"

Miss Williams was already waving her concerns away.

"The offer is in exchange for your attendance, no strings attached. You give us this one summer, and your grandmother can live there for the rest of her life. There's an apartment waiting for her, with a room for you, too, of course. We want the two of you to be safe. And we want you to be together."

Kaitlyn clutched the brochure in one hand and reached out to Grandma Maggie with the other, finding and grasping her small, wrinkled palm in her own.

"I'll go," she whispered, still not trusting her voice. "I accept."

Christina Williams smiled, acknowledging her decision, and for the first time since the death of her parents, Kaitlyn Wright burst into tears.

9
LIAISON REPORT

Do you think they can do it?"

"I wouldn't know, sir. I've only met Kaitlyn so far. She certainly takes her responsibilities seriously."

"Well, that's good, of course, but that isn't what I'm asking."

"I know. I've read the profiles. Their scores are all excellent."

"But is the correlation legitimate? Has the test found what we're looking for?"

"Do we even know what we're looking for, exactly?"

"Don't mock me with my own misgivings."

"No, sir. I wasn't trying to. I'm just asking what we're hoping they can do."

"Hell, we're hoping they can show us what we're dealing with. And how it works. And how to counter it. Preferably without figuring anything out for themselves. The last thing we need is a bunch of kids snap-twitting and face-chatting this thing all over the piss-damn Internet."

"I understand that. But the more we keep them in the dark,

the less they can tell us. The less they can participate in solving the problem."

"How about you let me worry about matters of national security, and you worry about holding their sensitive, participation-loving hands. Is that clear enough for you? Or do I have to find someone else for the job?"

"No, sir. You've made your point."

"Glad to hear it."

10
ARRIVAL

Roman Jackson had not expected to fly on an airplane ever in his life, let alone twice in one day. It was only the one trip so far—from Birmingham to Jackson Hole—but changing planes in Denver had technically put the flight count at two. By the standards of anyone Roman had ever met in his life, he was now officially well-traveled. Anything else the summer might bring was already just icing on the cake, and he wasn't even at the school yet.

Miss Williams had sent a limousine to drive him into Birmingham, launching Marquon into a jealous fit, but Roman had been spared another beating because his mother had gotten up early to see him off. She had said it was the least she could do, given what his stipend would mean to the family.

Her proud dotings didn't make Marquon any friendlier, but Roman didn't care. He had finally done something to make his mother happy, and nothing was going to spoil that for him. She had even bought him a new set of colored pencils as a going-away present, a simple gesture that had made him tear up with gratitude. Gifts were not even guaranteed on birthdays in Roman's family.

After she had hugged him good-bye, the limousine driver—a tall, white man who looked to Roman like he was wearing a red-checkered lumberjack shirt over his suit—had picked up Roman's second-hand duffel and threadbare backpack and placed them both gently in the car as though they were a wealthy man's luggage. Roman had enjoyed that immensely.

At the airport in Birmingham, the driver had stayed with him until Miss Williams had appeared to supervise the next leg of the journey, as though Roman were some kind of precious cargo—an attaché case, perhaps, full of diamonds and handcuffed to a government agent, to be escorted across the country by personal courier.

But Roman wasn't embarrassed by the attention. He was relieved not to be flying by himself, and from the moment he met Miss Williams, he saw her wearing tall, golden boots, with a shimmering golden cape draped across her shoulders, as though she were his own personal superhero. He spent a lot of the trip just trying not to giggle.

When they finally arrived in Jackson Hole, it was still only mid-afternoon, and Miss Williams said they had some time to kill before the others would be landing. She led him to a small restaurant—Roman had not known there were restaurants in airports, but it made sense once he thought about it—and she surprised him by telling him to order anything he wanted. He asked whether he might just have a small order of fries and a drink, if that wasn't too much trouble.

Miss Williams explained that the money she was offering to spend on him was not her own money, that it had been given to her by her employer to pay for meals on the trip, and that if she didn't use it, she would have to return it, so Roman's efforts to save it could not benefit her, personally, in any way.

When he suggested she could just keep the money and *pretend* they had spent it, she then explained, in substantial detail, the specific ins and outs of corporate expense accounts and the overarching importance of receipts, at which point he warmed up to the situation considerably. He finally ordered two cheeseburgers, a large fries, a side of biscuits, a side of hash browns, a soda, and a milkshake, ingesting so much of it at once that he ended up feeling as though he might never eat again. (But he squirreled the biscuits away in his backpack anyway, just in case.)

The last bit of the afternoon passed by in a hazy bliss of *fullness*, the likes of which he had never before experienced in all of his eleven years on this Earth, thereby leaving him in a wonderful mood, despite the long day of traveling, and more than ready to greet his fellow students when they finally arrived.

Daniel flew in on a nonstop flight from Los Angeles. He wasn't sure how he felt about being away for the summer, having only agreed to it upon his mother's gentle insistence, but the mountain view was already lifting his spirits, and the Jackson Hole airport made him feel as though the plane had accidentally landed at a five-star ski resort.

The terminal was inspiring "Billionaire" by Travie McCoy on replay, and it was all he could do not to strut to the beat. His favorite six-string and bass guitars were slung across his back in a double bag, and he carried a small, portable amp in his hand. The song in his head only turned up the volume when he was greeted by a woman carrying a pre-printed sign that said "Daniel Walker."

"Daniel!" she exclaimed as soon as she saw him. "You look just like your photograph. I'm Christina Williams, but you may call me Christina, and this here is Romario Jackson—"

"Roman," the boy said quickly.

"Oh, yes. Yes, of course. I'm sorry, Roman. This is *Roman* Jackson, who will be one of your fellow students at the ICIC."

"Hey," Daniel said, feeling a little awkward.

"'Sup," Roman replied.

"I apologize, boys, but we need to hurry. Another student will be arriving soon at the other end of the concourse. If you'll follow me?"

"Sure," Daniel replied. Roman said nothing, just falling into step behind her.

In truth, Roman was trying not to stare at the new kid, who had a rainbow of light cascading over him like some kind of perpetual cosmic waterfall. Roman found himself even more grateful for the new colored pencils, but he wasn't sure he would ever be able to capture on paper what he was seeing around this blond-haired California surfer. He kept his head down, staring at the floor, but flashes of light sparkled in the corner of his eye whenever Daniel's feet came into view.

Daniel, for his part, was equally intrigued by this small boy who refused to look at him. It wasn't just that the kid was so young; it was the subtle way he would dart his eyes in tiny little glances when he thought no one was looking. The lyrics to OneRepublic's "Secrets" played in Daniel's head—a mellow song, its rhythm fitting the late afternoon sunshine—and Daniel let its melody carry his mind away, content to let the evening unfold in its own time.

The airport wasn't especially large, and it wasn't long before they were standing at another gate, a new pre-printed sign having been produced from Miss Williams' briefcase, this one with letters that spelled out "Samantha Prescott." They waited for a few minutes, Daniel nodding his head along with "Secrets" and Roman stealing glances from time to time at Daniel's living, shifting raiment of color, until the door finally opened and people started filing in off the tarmac.

After several business people came and went, along with a mother carrying an infant in a travel seat and then a small group of twenty-somethings who looked to be on vacation together, Miss Williams called out, "Samantha," and waved at a teenage girl who appeared to be about Daniel's age.

She was wearing faded jeans over what looked like a very heavy pair of motorcycle boots, a black T-shirt emblazoned across the chest with a Batman logo, and a silver ear cuff in each ear. Her backpack was slung over one shoulder—a black leather bag with studs that looked like rivets. The girl didn't walk as much as she sauntered, and suddenly the dystopian lyrics of "Radioactive" by Imagine Dragons were blaring in Daniel's head.

Daniel raised one eyebrow and tried not to smile as she approached them, imagining slow motion strides and smoke effects, the blue streaks in her hair being lifted from below by a high-speed fan, as though she were a model in a music video—assuming the model looked like she was ready to beat someone up.

Note to self, he thought, *this is not the girl to cross.*

"Welcome, Samantha," Miss Williams was saying. "I'm Christina Williams. We're so pleased you could come spend the summer with us."

"Thanks," was all the girl said, dropping her bag at her feet and shaking the woman's hand.

Roman eyed her cautiously, but all he saw around her were a scattering of small, white flames, whizzing around her so fast that they left light trails in their wake. In the first instant, he had been reminded of Marquon's bees, and he had taken an involuntary step away from her, but he saw almost immediately that these were not angry, red bees. They were just lights, flying in regular patterns, several of them crossing each other, but never colliding.

"You OK?" Sam asked him, having seen his reaction. "Don't worry. I don't bite." She said this with a hint of a grin, and Roman decided that he liked her.

"I like your hair," Roman said. "The blue, I mean. It's cool."

"Thank you," she replied, smiling even more warmly.

"I'm Roman."

"Roman," she said. "Like the Coliseum. That's easy enough. I'm Sam." She reached out and shook his hand without seeming to think about it, as though she came from a world in which teenagers shook hands on a regular basis.

"And you are...?" she asked, turning to Daniel, who finally allowed himself to smile a little at her "Radioactive" theme song, trusting that the grin would be taken as nothing more than an attempt to be friendly.

"Daniel," he replied.

"OK then," she said, cocking her head a bit to one side and staring at him thoughtfully. "Daniel. Like Daniel in the lion's den. Got it." But she didn't offer to shake hands, both of hers remaining firmly planted on her hips, and Daniel wondered vaguely whether or not he should be insulted.

"Let's hope it doesn't come to that," he quipped, smiling to show he wasn't taking offense.

"Sorry?" she asked.

"The lion's den," he explained. "Let's hope it doesn't come to that."

"Oh, right. Sorry. Nothing personal. I have trouble remembering names sometimes, so I try to think of associations. Like, you're lions, and Roman here is the Coliseum, which is kind of funny when you think about it. You know, lions in the Coliseum."

"Yeah, I get it," Daniel answered. He really wasn't sure what to make of this girl at all. She was definitely different.

"You can make one up about me if you want."

"Pretty sure I can remember 'Sam,'" he replied. He realized suddenly that he might be insulting her, since she had just admitted she couldn't remember 'Daniel' without a catchphrase, but she only shrugged.

"Suit yourself," she said. "How much time do we have before the next arrival?"

This last was addressed to Miss Williams, who smiled again.

"Seventeen minutes, according to the monitor."

"Great," Sam said, snatching up the bag that she had dropped on the floor and hoisting it back over her shoulder. "'Cause I need to use the bathroom."

Fifteen minutes later, the gathering crew had migrated to yet another gate, and now Miss Williams was holding up a sign that said "Mackenzie Gray."

The girl who emerged through the door this time was a bit taller than Sam, her slim but well-muscled torso clearly defined beneath a tight, brown T-shirt. Her blond hair was tied up in a simple ponytail, and her blue eyes narrowed in on their group immediately. She strode toward them with quick, purposeful strides.

"Mackenzie Gray, reporting for duty, ma'am," she said, standing stiffly before Miss Williams.

"Mackenzie," Miss Williams replied. "I'm very pleased to meet you. I'm Christina Williams, as you have obviously deduced. But there's no need for formality here. You may call me Christina, and these are some of your classmates for the summer: Sam, Daniel, and Roman."

Mackenzie nodded briefly at each of them in turn, repeating their names one by one.

"Sam. Daniel. Roman."

"Reporting for duty?" Sam said, raising an eyebrow. "Really? We're not in the military, Private Benjamin."

"My name isn't Benjamin," Mackenzie replied neutrally. She

had met enough new people in her life to recognize a personality test when she saw one, and she saw this one coming from a mile away. "It's Gray. Mackenzie Gray."

"It's from a movie," Sam replied. If she was expecting a comeback, it never arrived.

"Is it a good movie? I love movies." Her voice was all innocence and sunshine, but something in her eyes said *test me all you want, little girl—I eat civilians for breakfast.*

Sam didn't answer her, so Mackenzie held her gaze a moment longer and then moved on to Daniel.

"Hi," Mackenzie tried.

But Daniel was tongue-tied. It wasn't that she was beautiful, although she was. It was that she looked like she knew how to break at least seven different bones in his body before he could move a muscle. The lyrics of "Fighter" by Christina Aguilera came to mind, and he had the distinct feeling that she might head-butt him to the floor at any moment, despite her calm demeanor.

He nodded, acknowledging her greeting, but he didn't say a word.

"OK," she said, drawing the word out so that it sounded more like, "Ohhhhh kaaaaay."

"How about you, Roman?" she asked, moving on down the line. "Looks like I could use a friend around here. You want to be my friend?"

Roman nodded vigorously. From the moment she had walked through the door, Roman had been mesmerized. In his mind's eye, he saw her skeleton, every bone in her body glowing with soft, white light, but that skeleton stood within a giant golden bear with its own golden skeleton, standing on its hind legs to mimic her posture, its head towering above her, every one of its huge golden bones tied to her own, as though she were some kind of cosmic puppeteer.

When she walked, the bear walked. When she spoke, the bear spoke, mirroring her movements. Bears could be protective, or terrifyingly dangerous, depending on whether they considered you a friend or an enemy. Roman absolutely, definitely, no doubt about it, wanted to be her friend.

"Good. We're friends then."

Roman visibly sighed in relief.

So, Mackenzie thought, *the girl's going to be a challenge, but I know how to handle sarcasm. Eventually, if I can't befriend her, I'll shut her out. Her choice. That Daniel guy is shy, but that's good. The shy ones always warm up to kindness. Roman will be a good ally. I'll look out for the kid, and Daniel will end up in my camp. Not bad for the first few minutes.*

Twenty-six minutes later, Kaitlyn Wright flew in from Detroit.

She had hardly been able to contain her enthusiasm throughout the entire journey, having ensured before she left that her grandmother was settled and happy in their new home. She had hesitated at the last moment, hugging Grandma Maggie at least three times while the driver waited politely, but her grandmother had finally held her at arm's length and looked her in the eye, saying, "Go live your life, Kitten. I'll be fine here. You don't need to worry about me anymore. Go enjoy being young for once. It will be a wonderful summer. You'll see."

So Kaitlyn had hugged her one more time for good measure and then slid into the limousine, closed her eyes for half a minute, and ended up sleeping all the way to the airport, the weight of adult responsibility finally lifted from her shoulders.

By the time she had boarded the plane, however, her excitement had once again reached full throttle, and she had chatted all of her airborne neighbors up a storm. When she finally landed in Jackson Hole, she had so many people laughing with her and waving good-bye that the entire ICIC team collectively overlooked her until she bounced right up to their seats, throwing her arms around Miss Williams without any warning whatsoever.

"Well, hello there, Kaitlyn!" Miss Williams said, laughing, and she hugged Kaitlyn back just as warmly until the girl finally let go.

"Hi!" Kaitlyn giggled at Miss Williams and then looked around at the others.

"These are your classmates—"

"Hi!" she said again, waving generally to them all without waiting for names.

Without even realizing what he was doing, Daniel was already rising to his feet.

"I'm Daniel," he said, and then he paused awkwardly. He thought he might have been about to hug her himself, as though he had known her his whole life, which was not like him at all. Confused, he just stood there, but Kaitlyn's smile never wavered.

"Hello, Daniel," she said easily.

"Smooth move, Romeo," Sam muttered. Roman shot a reflexive glare at her but soon realized that the taunt was aimed at Daniel, not at him.

Daniel frowned, realizing he had just done this horribly inept thing in front of everyone and having no idea how to fix it, when Kaitlyn herself came to his rescue.

"Want to carry my bag for me?" she asked. She was wearing jeans and sneakers and a pretty, white blouse, but her backpack practically exploded with color, tie-dyed in broad swirls of yellow and green and blue and purple, although how anyone had tie-dyed a backpack he had no idea.

"Sure," he said, grateful to have something slightly less awkward to do than just standing there helplessly and listening to Joe Cocker's "You Are So Beautiful" playing in the background of his awareness. He took her backpack in one hand, slinging it over his shoulder, and then picked up his guitar bag, slinging it over the other shoulder, making sure he would still be able to carry the portable amp.

Sam rolled her eyes, reaching past him to shake Kaitlyn's hand. "Sam," she said.

"Kaitlyn!" Kaitlyn replied happily.

"I'm Mackenzie." Mackenzie smiled at her, and Kaitlyn smiled back. "And this is Roman." Mackenzie winked at Roman when she said it, making him blush a little.

"Hi," Roman said.

"Hi, Roman!"

Roman couldn't help but stare as tiny champagne bubbles rose gently from the new girl's hair, floating delicately into the concourse. As each new bubble lifted away, another formed in its place, a few more steadily coalescing and then lifting off from her neck and shoulders, and others sliding all the way up her arms from her fingertips, now that he was really watching. In fact, tiny champagne bubbles seemed to appear everywhere, leaving shimmering, gossamer tracks all over her skin. It was all he could do not to reach out and try to catch one in his hands.

Rush's flight was the last to come in. He arrived at 8:16 p.m. and disembarked just a few minutes later, an *HRT Alpha: Year One* T-shirt on his back and a scowl permanently affixed to his face. When Christina Williams introduced herself, he only nodded, refusing to speak.

"These are your classmates, Ashton: Roman, Daniel, Sam, Mackenzie, and Kaitlyn."

"My name is 'Rush,'" was all he said in reply.

"Of course," she agreed easily. If the nickname surprised her, she didn't show it in the slightest. "Rush. My apologies."

He nodded, somewhat appeased, but the frown never left his

face. After an extended silence, it became painfully obvious that he was not going to greet anyone else.

"OK then, it's been a long day," Miss Williams said finally. "Let's get going. We're meeting our driver outside with the rest of your luggage. Follow me."

The group headed out, subdued in the wake of Rush's open hostility—all except Kaitlyn, that is, who was still trying to be friendly.

"Hi!" she said brightly. "I'm Kaitlyn!" But Rush just stared her down until she fell back a few steps, shrugging.

Daniel had never been so relieved in all his life.

He felt like Rush must look like a superhero next to him, standing easily two inches taller and a good number of well-muscled pounds heavier than his lean, musician's frame. He was perfectly happy for Rush to ignore Kaitlyn—and anyone else he wanted to, for that matter.

As they made their way toward the exit, Roman couldn't help but watch the newcomer. He seemed so angry, but all Roman could focus on was his suit of glorious silver armor, etched in delicate blue markings that glowed upon its surface as though lit from within.

He trailed back as far as their sharp-eyed caretaker would allow, watching them all walk together: racing embers of white flame; a swirling, rainbow waterfall; delicate champagne bubbles; a glowing anime hero; and a giant, golden bear, right in the middle of the group, lumbering down the concourse and towering silently above them all.

This, he thought to himself, *is going to be one crazy summer.*

11
ICIC

A small, private bus waited for them outside the terminal. Sam wanted to ask whether anyone else saw the irony in the short bus picking up the kid geniuses, but she decided to keep the thought to herself.

Kaitlyn climbed in first, sitting two rows behind the driver. When Daniel stopped to hand over her backpack, she patted the seat next to her. He didn't have to be asked twice. Roman sat across from them, trying to stay near Miss Williams, and Mackenzie slid in behind him.

"You want something to do?" she asked. "I have a tablet in here if you want to borrow it. I was just gonna mess with my phone."

Roman looked over curiously. "You have any games?"

She turned it on and flipped to a page full of them.

"Knock yourself out." She dangled the tablet over the back of his seat. He looked up at her hopefully but still didn't reach for it.

"Play anything you want," she said. "For real. There's nothing you can mess up on there. I promise."

With a grin, Roman took the tablet and started looking through the games.

Sam wasn't excited about sitting behind the two love birds, but she didn't feel like sitting close to Mackenzie either. In the end, she sat two rows behind Kaitlyn, opening her bag and pulling out a tablet of her own.

Rush boarded last, walking all the way to the back. The row behind Sam was a whole row of five seats at the very rear of the bus, and he slid into the seat farthest from Sam's, farthest from everyone, tossing his backpack on the seat next to him like a barricade, crossing his arms over his chest, leaning into the corner, and closing his eyes.

"That's everyone," Miss Williams said to the driver, and she took the front window seat, directly in front of Kaitlyn, who smiled at her warmly.

The driver closed the door, and they were on their way.

Rush pulled out his phone, tempted to check in with his team, but he didn't have the heart for it. He knew he couldn't bear the long pauses, waiting for them to reach a break between games to answer his messages, knowing they were playing without him.

Just a couple of weeks ago, he was ready to grab his future in both hands, and now here he was, watching it slip through his fingers. He wanted to throw the phone as hard as he could against the wall of the bus, to feel the primal satisfaction of watching it shatter into a thousand pieces, but he fought to control the impulse, crossing his arms back across his chest and waiting for the urge to pass.

He must have let the temptation show because the Sam girl glanced up at him as though he had startled her. Their eyes met for a long moment before she turned away, obviously embarrassed. It was too bad, really. She had a cute, gamer girl kind of look about her, with the blue streaks in her hair and her big, bluish-green anime eyes. It was the kind of look he would have been into if he wasn't dead set against having anything to do with this stupid program.

Besides, if he really let his guard down with anyone they might figure out that he didn't belong here at all—that he had just filled in the blanks randomly on that stupid test—and if he got sent home, his father would sell his whole gaming setup for real. His only hope was that his mother might still try to interfere for him. Uncrossing his arms, he woke his phone up and sent her a text.

Please talk to Dad. I miss you. I want to come home.

It was only a few moments before he received her reply.

Not tonight. He had a terrible day at the office. Give him a few days to cool down. I'll talk to him then. Love you.

It was a long shot, but it was the best he could do.

Thanks, Mom. Love you, too.

He slipped the phone back into his backpack, grabbed a spare sweatshirt, stuffed it behind his head, and closed his eyes again. All he could do now was wait.

When he woke up, the sky outside was dark, and the bus was turning into a long driveway. The building up ahead looked like the five-star resort version of a log cabin, the exterior lights arranged artfully to show off tall windows, timber framing, and a high, steep roofline that soared above them.

"Wow!" Kaitlyn said, stretching and craning her neck around Miss Williams to see it better as they drove up. "Is that for us?"

"It is!" Miss Williams confirmed. "Welcome to the ICIC. Check your seats for your things, but don't worry if you forget something. The bus belongs to the program, so it will be here on site."

The students gathered their belongings, Roman returning the tablet to Mackenzie with a shy look of gratitude and Sam packing hers back in her own bag. One by one they filed off the bus, locating the rest of their luggage by the curb and then grouping up by the entrance.

"OK, everyone," Miss Williams said, "follow me."

They walked through the front doors into a large gathering room, complete with tables and chairs for eating, several couches for lounging, and a huge, round fireplace in the center. An inviting fire leaped cheerfully behind its curved glass.

"I'm sure you're all tired," she continued. "Let's get you up to your rooms, so you can settle in. There will be plenty of time tomorrow to explore."

They followed her up a wide, curving staircase to the left of the front doors. Both the stairs and the upstairs hallway were covered in a plush, burgundy carpet of which Mackenzie Gray wholeheartedly approved. As they walked down the hall, they passed an ornate wooden door on their right.

"I'll be staying in this suite if you need anything," Miss Williams said. "Don't bother knocking on that first door. Just walk right in. My room is the middle one. The other rooms are empty, so you needn't worry about disturbing anyone else. You'll see what I mean in a minute."

They continued down the hall until they reached another door, also on the right. This time Miss Williams opened it, and she ushered everyone into a kind of living room.

It had a flat-screen television on the wall next to the door, with a console table underneath it and a couch and coffee table across from it. To the left was a small kitchen—differentiated from the living room by a countertop and a pricey tile floor. To the right was a laundry area with sheets, towels, and blankets stacked neatly on the shelves. Three bedrooms opened off the common space: one from the kitchen, one from the laundry, and one from the living room.

"This suite is just like mine. Each of you will have his or her own bedroom, and you'll share these common spaces. Each bedroom has its own bath. Meals will be downstairs in the main hall, but there are plenty of drinks and snacks here in the suite kitchens. Help yourselves to anything. It's all free as part of the program. This suite is for the girls. Feel free to settle in while I show the boys to theirs, which is the next one down the hall."

Miss Williams and the boys all filed out, leaving the girls to unpack.

Kaitlyn immediately started rummaging through the suite, opening all the cabinet doors and looking into every nook and cubbyhole she could find.

"Look! Blu-rays!" she said, opening one of the console table doors. "Hey, there are some good ones in here... mostly rom-coms. They must have known this would be the girls' suite, right? Oh! And a Blu-ray player! That's convenient..." She closed the console and headed for the kitchen.

Sam raised an eyebrow and looked at Mackenzie as though to say, "Is this girl for real?" Mackenzie shrugged, holding back an uncharacteristic giggle.

"Oh, sweet! Cereal! Lots of kinds, too. I totally love cereal. Like, you have no idea. I'm a cereal nut. Well, not cereal *with* nuts, though. I'm not a big fan of nuts. Oh! And instant oatmeal! And coffee? Blech, who likes coffee?"

"I like coffee," Sam and Mackenzie both volunteered at the same time, each turning to the other in surprise.

"Ugh! You guys can have it," Kaitlyn said, not breaking stride. "Wait, tell me there's milk for the cereal... yes! Milk. Good." She continued listing the contents of the fridge and the cabinets in an unbroken litany.

"It's like she's a kitchen announcer," Sam said to Mackenzie. "You know, like a sports announcer, but for kitchens."

"Yeah," Mackenzie agreed. "She should sell groceries on one of those shopping channels."

"OMG, totally," Sam replied. "Look at this *beautiful* cereal, people! I wish you could *taste* this at home, and *smell* the cinnamon, and run it through your *fingers*, just to get the *full sensory experience!* You simply *must* have a box for yourself! You haven't *lived* until you've tried this cereal!"

Mackenzie and Sam both broke down laughing.

"I can hear you, you know," Kaitlyn said, but it only made them laugh harder because she didn't otherwise pause at all in her ongoing inventory. After listing all of her food finds, she moved into the bedroom off the kitchen, and they could hear her voice drifting back to them through the open door.

"Hey, there are books in here!" she called out. "Like, some paperbacks. We can trade back and forth, OK? I mean, assuming we have different ones. And notebooks and pens. And a computer desk. No television in the bedroom, but this window is gigantic! Oh, sweet! The bathroom has little soaps and shampoos and stuff! Like a hotel!" Her voice was even more muffled in the bathroom, but suddenly she came running back out into the suite again.

"Hey!" she said, making sure she had the attention of both girls, as if there were any chance she might not. "I call dibs on the bedroom off the kitchen!"

"Why?" Sam wanted to know. "What's so special in there?"

"'Cause it's closest to the kitchen?" she replied, looking confused. "I thought that was obvious."

Sam and Mackenzie burst into another fit of laughter.

"It's yours," Sam assured her.

"Sweet!" Kaitlyn exclaimed, and she went running back into her bedroom again.

"You want center or laundry?" Mackenzie asked, turning toward Sam.

"You don't care?"

"Nah," Mackenzie said, waving the question away. "I sleep like a log. You could blast a movie in here or do laundry in there at 3:00 a.m. It won't wake me up."

"Um, middle, I guess?" Sam said. "If you're sure you don't mind."

"I don't mind," Mackenzie assured her, smiling. *Huh. Maybe we can be friends, after all,* she thought. And she picked up her bags, carrying them through the laundry room and into the bedroom that would be hers for the rest of the summer.

Settling the boys into their suite was a much quieter affair, the two older boys letting Roman have the middle room by unspoken agreement, Rush ferreting himself away into the laundry-side bedroom and Daniel taking the kitchen.

"Be sure to be downstairs in the main hall by 9:00 a.m. for breakfast and orientation," Miss Williams said on her way out. "I'll tell the girls on my way to bed and make sure they've settled in OK."

"Thank you, Miss Williams," Roman said politely. "We'll make sure Rush knows."

"Thank you, Roman," she replied. "You remember where my room is? In case you need anything? Please don't be shy about waking me up. It's my job to make sure you kids are comfortable here."

"Yes, ma'am," he affirmed.

"Well, all right. Good night, then," she said, casting a moment's worried glance toward Rush's bedroom but then smiling warmly at Roman and Daniel, who had reappeared after depositing his guitars and amp safely in his bedroom.

"Good night, ma'am," Roman replied.

"Good night," Daniel echoed.

"Oh," Miss Williams said, obviously just remembering something, "and Roman, the food in the kitchen? That's budgeted, too, like the airport food. OK?"

"OK!" Roman agreed. The door hadn't even closed behind her before Roman was rummaging around in the kitchen, just to see what was there, while Daniel slid past him and disappeared into his bedroom for the night.

Once Miss Williams was gone, Rush reappeared in the living area with a gaming console that he set beneath the television. Roman watched from the kitchen as Rush began to run his hands along the edges of the screen and then placed his face as close to the wall as he could, trying to see what was behind it.

"Miss Williams said we have breakfast and orientation downstairs at 9:00."

"I heard," Rush said.

"What are you doing?"

"This," Rush replied, without further explanation, but he centered himself in front of the television and pulled it gently away from the wall, having discovered that the set was on a swiveling wall-mount, as he had hoped.

Roman just stared at him in amazement.

"How'd you know it would do that?" Roman wanted to know, but Rush just shrugged.

He disappeared into his room again and came back with two controllers and a headset. He hooked the headset and the console up to the television and then pushed the screen gently back against the wall. Next, he pivoted the console table and found an electrical outlet. He plugged in the console and then moved the table back again. He turned everything on and fiddled with the remote until the picture from the console appeared on the screen.

He grunted, satisfied, but when he tried to go into the system's network options, he hit a snag.

"Damn," he said under his breath.

"What's wrong?" Roman wanted to know.

"No Internet. What kind of five-star resort doesn't have Internet?"

Roman just shrugged.

Rush disappeared again and came back this time with a small, flat box. He hit a button on it, and a green light started flashing, but after a few moments Rush frowned and disappeared one more time.

He cursed then, loudly, and he reemerged from the room with a scowl on his face. Roman watched him carefully, but no bees came peeking out of his ears, nor did any of his beautiful silver armor start glowing red, so he decided it was safe enough to try another question.

"What's that?" he asked, pointing to the box.

"Hot spot," Rush said, and then, seeing Roman's hopeful expression and relenting a little, he added, "It takes a cell signal, like for your phone, and turns it into an Internet wi-fi that other things can hook up to."

"Really?" Roman asked, impressed. "Like for your game?"

"Well, it's supposed to, yeah. Only, it's not."

"Why not?" Roman wanted to know.

"No cell service." Rush held up his cell phone. "No signal, no Internet. I swear, we must be in freaking Timbuktu."

"Where's that?"

Rush chuckled a little. "I don't know. Someplace really far away."

"Oh," Roman said.

"Well, a place like this has to have *some* kind of Internet," Rush said, mostly to himself. "I'll ask them about it tomorrow. Meantime, I'll have to play offline, I guess."

Roman just shrugged and kept looking at him, having nothing else to say.

"You want to play?" Rush asked.

"Who, me?"

"Yeah, you. Why not?"

"I don't really know how to play," Roman admitted. He had tried it once or twice when his mother had made Marquon share the system, but the bees had been so angry that Roman had handed the controller back as soon as she had stopped paying attention.

"That's OK. I can teach you."

"OK," Roman agreed. "I won't talk, I promise."

"What?"

"I won't talk to you while you're playing. So I won't make you die."

"Kid, listen, not to brag or anything, cause it's just fact, but there are very few people in the whole world who could kill me just cause you said something during the game."

"My brother gets mad when I talk. He says I get him killed."

"Well, nothing against your brother, but if talking gets your brother killed a lot, then he's not very good."

"He thinks he's good."

"He's not," Rush said.

Roman was quiet for a moment, taking this in.

"OK, so you ready?" But the question was apparently rhetorical because he didn't stop for an answer. "I'll unplug my headset so we can both hear. We'll just have to keep the TV down some."

"Sure," Roman said, happy to follow Rush's lead.

"Sweet. OK, so we're playing *HRT Alpha: Year One*. It's not even out yet. Pretty cool, right?"

Roman nodded. That *did* seem pretty cool.

"The best game mode is called 'Light It Up.' I'll teach you that one."

Roman nodded again. "OK!" And the grin on his face was suddenly so big that Rush couldn't help but smile back at him.

It took Roman several games to get the hang of it, while Rush patiently ran through the weapon choices and helped him learn the maps, showing him some hiding places and helping him understand how players were likely to move on each one. This one had a bottleneck here. That one had a wide-open space with no good cover there. Rush was impressed with how quickly Roman was picking up on things, so he finally suggested that they play one against each other, with some computer-generated bots on each team, just to make it more fun.

"You'll kill me like every two seconds," Roman protested.

"I probably could if I was really trying," Rush admitted, chuckling, "but I'm not going to go all out on you, OK? I just want you to get the feel of playing against someone else, 'cause it's more exciting than only playing against bots."

"OK," Roman agreed.

They started the game, and Roman had to admit that just knowing Rush was out there somewhere, hunting him, was kind of scary, which made the game more exciting already. When Roman found him, Rush let him have a straight-up shoot-out instead of doing anything to protect himself like dropping to the ground or throwing out grenades. Rush still got the kill because Roman's aim wasn't that good yet, but it was close, and Rush encouraged him.

"That was good, man! You see that? You almost got me!"

Roman grinned and ran out from the spawn point again, ready for action. Roman got a few kills on the bots while Rush practiced some of his faster moves against the bots on Roman's team.

"You're doing great," Rush said about halfway through the game. "If you ask me, playing bots can be harder than playing real people. Bots are less predictable, you know? The AI is never as good as a human brain, so they do stupid things you don't expect."

Just then, Rush ran around a corner and slammed into Roman, who had been standing in the middle of an alley looking at his weapon options. Roman panicked so badly that he dropped a sticky grenade on the ground right on Rush's foot, completely by accident, and Rush was laughing so hard that it killed him before he could compose himself enough to react.

Roman looked at Rush in wide-eyed terror.

How could he have been so stupid? How could he have gotten so caught up in the game that he forgot to keep his head down and stay out of trouble? Now Rush was going to be mad and hate him and never be his friend again.

"I'm sorry!" Roman blurted out.

But no angry red bees flew at his head. No punches flew at his ribs. Rush just sat there, staring at him in confusion.

"For what?"

"For killing you," Roman said, his voice small and uncertain.

But Rush only laughed. "Dude, that's the point of the game! You got me! Good job!"

Roman just stared at him, still coming down from the shock of it, and Rush watched him for a few moments in silence.

"OK, I'll tell you what," Rush said gently. "It's getting kind of late. And you're probably just getting tired. Why don't you call it for the night? But now that you've gotten your first official kill, I can't let you crash until we give you a tag."

"A tag?" Roman asked, glad for the distraction, as Rush pulled them out of the game.

"Yeah, a gamer tag. It's like a nickname. It's what other gamers call you."

"Oh," Roman said. "OK. What should mine be?"

"Well, that's what we have to figure out. It should kind of capture you, you know? Like who you are. What's your favorite thing to do? Besides dropping grenades on my foot, I mean."

Roman laughed and felt a little more of his tension drain away.

"I like drawing," Roman admitted shyly. "You wanna see?"

"Sure!" Rush said.

So Roman went and got his light sketchpad. Rush started flipping through the pages, expecting nothing more than a little kid's awkward renditions of houses and cars and trees, but he slowed down almost immediately, amazed at the seamless blending of realism and imagination.

"Who's this?" he asked, pointing at a young girl standing in a ray of mottled sunshine, with translucent fairy wings growing out of her back. Even drawn in black and white, somehow the *feel* of summer—of sunshine and forest and green leaves filtering the light through a vibrant, living canopy—came through perfectly.

"That's my sister, Shaquiya." He pronounced the middle syllable like the word 'why' with a k in front of it: Shuh-KWHY-uh.

"She's beautiful," Rush told him.

"She is," Roman confirmed.

"Yeah, OK, so we definitely have to make it something about drawing. But a gamer tag has to sound cool, too. So we can't just call you 'Draw.' Art... no... pencils... pens... paper..."

As he continued with the word associations, Rush closed the pad in his hands, preparing to hand it back to Roman, and noticed for the first time the lettering on the cover: 'Sketchpad.'

"Sketch!" Rush crowed triumphantly. "That's it. That's *totally* it. You like it?"

Roman loved it. He had never liked his real name very much anyway, and to have this boy, this young man, really, who was everything his older brother wanted to be but wasn't, give him this name as a friend, to make him, essentially, part of his own tribe... well, Roman was speechless with joy. He just nodded his head vigorously, grinning from ear to ear.

"Looks like a 'yes' to me," Rush laughed. "Sketch it is!"

Roman just sat there staring up at him, the young man worshipping the accomplished warrior, until Rush started feeling embarrassed enough to try to send him off to bed.

"OK then, Sketch. You about ready to crash out, man?"

"Yeah," Sketch admitted.

"All right, buddy. I'll see you in the morning, OK?

"'K," Sketch said. He got up off the couch and headed back to his room, but he had only been there a few minutes before he knew for an absolute fact that he was not going to be able to sleep somewhere this silent, this lonely—not after sharing a bedroom with an infant in a thin-walled house with five other people besides.

He got up and padded back out to the living room, dragging the blanket from his bed behind him.

"Something wrong, Sketch?" Rush asked.

"It's too quiet."

"Oh. Yeah, I gotcha. You want to crash out here a while? I'll be up playing a bit longer. Maybe it'll help you sleep."

Without saying a word, Sketch dragged the blanket onto the couch and curled up beneath it, placing the pillow from the end of the couch up against Rush's leg, laying his head on top of it, and then promptly passing out from exhaustion.

Rush leaned back and stared at him in surprise, but eventually he just shrugged, letting the little guy sleep there while he practiced *HRT Alpha: Year One*, keeping his skills sharp and praying that his mother could get him back home before the August invitational.

12
LIAISON REPORT

Any problems at the airport?"

"No, sir. They all arrived without incident. They're settling in now."

"Good. How would you say it's going so far?"

"There hasn't been much time to observe their interactions yet. We'll know a lot more after tomorrow."

"And we'll know a lot more than that by next week. But I'm not asking you next week. I'm asking you now. We hired you for your touchy-feely people skills, and I'm asking you, in your expert opinion, how things are going so far."

"I'd say they're going as well as can be expected of any group of kids who are only just meeting each other. There was some tension between Mackenzie and Samantha, but Mackenzie has proven herself exceedingly resilient in handling new situations. I think they'll be fine. And Daniel and Kaitlyn are already demonstrating a natural fondness for each other—"

"Which I might care about if we had invited them here for a summer of matchmaking."

"I'm just saying there are early signs of compatibility. Established relationships can form the central core of a new social group."

"Or the pair can isolate themselves away from the rest. I read your brief."

"That's true, but I think we should be more worried about Ashton in that regard. He's already chosen to isolate himself from the others. He appears to be here somewhat against his will."

"Against his will? What good are the damn incentives we put together then?"

"They were good enough to get him here, obviously. But that might have been more his parents' doing than his own. Achieving his presence is not the same thing as achieving his active participation."

"Well then, I suggest you find a way to 'achieve his active participation' ASAP."

"I still think the best way to do that would be to let them know what we're up against, sir. What we're trying to achieve here."

"Then you're going to have to come up with a second-best way because that is not an option. You're a professional motivator, for God's sake. Go be motivational."

"Yes, sir."

13
ORIENTATION

When Daniel woke up the next morning in a strange bed, the smell of the sea having been replaced by an unfamiliar mix of pine forest and wood smoke, he felt uneasy at first, not entirely sure where he was or why he was there. But then a single thought floated into his mind, and he was settled again, everything falling into place, the day suddenly full of hope and possibility.

Kaitlyn.

He couldn't explain it, but he felt as though he had seen her face a thousand times before. That thick, dark hair. Those beautiful brown eyes. The light peppering of freckles across her nose. She was not, at least according to popular standards, the most beautiful girl in the world, but he would have argued the point intensely if anyone had tried to say so in his presence. She was happy—genuinely *happy*—in a way that so few people were, and her smile just lit up the room.

He rolled out of bed, grabbed a pair of jeans and a random T-shirt out of his duffel, and headed straight for his guitar.

He sat on the edge of the bed, fine-tuning the strings and then strumming a few chords just to test the sound. Perfect. He didn't turn on the amp because he didn't want to wake anyone; he just started to play. He didn't have any particular tune in mind when he started, but his fingers, as usual, had a mind of their own, and they started playing "Flower," by Cody Simpson. The words flowed through his mind, but he was too embarrassed to sing, knowing that he shared the suite with Rush and Roman, so he just played through the song and hummed a little.

But when he finished, the tune still echoed in his mind. Hesitating for a moment, he finally plugged the guitar into the amp and turned it to the lowest setting, testing the volume in the stillness of the morning. He turned it up just a little bit louder, so he could sing along quietly and the guitar would still drown out his voice on the off chance that anyone heard him. He played the entire song again, and before the last note had entirely dissipated, his fingers started in on "Gone, Gone, Gone" by Phillip Phillips.

He sang through that one also, turning the amp up just a bit more and then launching into Van Morrison's "Brown-Eyed Girl." The grin on his face just kept getting bigger, and after the final notes had echoed away, he was in such a good mood that he turned the amp up again and started singing "(I Can't) Forget About You" by R5, just for fun.

At this point there was a rather insistent pounding on the door, followed immediately by Rush's head poking through it.

"Dude. We get it. You like her. Could you *please*, by all that's holy, play something that is *not* a love song. Seriously. Anything. Sketch and I are dying in here."

Daniel narrowed his eyes at Rush without saying a word, flashed him his most villainous smile, and then turned the amp up even louder and plucked out the opening bars of "Stayin' Alive" by the Bee Gees with unmitigated zeal, popping his chin and rolling his shoulders to the beat with exaggerated flair.

"This better?" he asked innocently.

"It's time for breakfast," Rush growled. He withdrew his head from the room and stalked out of the suite, followed by a chorus of Roman's uncontrolled giggles.

When the boys arrived downstairs, the girls were already seated around one of the small, round tables, eating breakfast. Miss Williams sat at another table next to them, accompanied by a man they had not seen before. He appeared to be in his forties—a handsome man of just less than average height, with short, dark hair, a swarthy complexion, a proud patrician nose, and a close-cropped beard. He smiled at her gently, almost shyly, as they spoke in muted tones.

A buffet had been set up in the back of the room, complete with large silver tureens of eggs, bacon, sausage, biscuits, potatoes, fruit, and pancakes, with butter and several different choices of syrup for toppings. Silver jugs of milk, juice, and water stood next to an array of plates and glasses and silverware—a help-yourself dream that Roman wasn't sure he was ever going to get used to.

Daniel kept sneaking wistful glances toward the one empty seat at the girls' table, but in the end he joined Rush and Roman, pushing his food around with his fork without ever raising the utensil to his mouth. Fortunately, it wasn't long before Miss Williams provided a distraction.

"Good morning, everyone!" she said, placing her elegant, cloth napkin on the table and rising to her feet. "I hope you all slept well. I'd like to welcome you formally to the ICIC. We hope you'll be as happy here as we are to have you with us. If there is anything I can do to make your stay more comfortable—"

"How do we get on the Internet?" Rush asked immediately.

Miss Williams barely hesitated.

"I'm sorry about that," she said. "The lodge is upgrading its service, and the network is not available yet. We had expected the process to be complete before you arrived. The system should be back up in the next day or two."

Mackenzie frowned.

"You OK?" Kaitlyn mouthed the question silently, having noticed her reaction, but Mackenzie only nodded. If she missed one of her father's weekly calls, it wouldn't be the first time. The news had just taken her by surprise. She shook it off and smiled reassuringly at Kaitlyn.

"There isn't any cell service either," Rush added.

"We will make a land line available so you can call home, of course," Miss Williams assured him. "I only became aware of the situation this morning, and we're already working to rectify it. There should be a telephone in each suite by this afternoon. The Internet, I'm afraid, will take longer."

Miss Williams waited a moment, but Rush just scowled grimly and said nothing else, so she continued with her original speech.

"I'd like to introduce Professor Amr Mubarak. He will be in charge of your training here at the ICIC. I believe he has some opening remarks, and then you'll be welcome to ask any questions you might have. Professor?"

Professor Mubarak stood up to address them. There was a certain stillness about him, even when he moved—a sense of silent, thoughtful reflection. And as he began to speak, his soothing voice (infused with a British accent and a hint of something else) seemed to glide through the air, his words perfectly clear despite their quiet tones.

"Good morning, ladies and gentlemen. My name, as Miss Williams has said, is Amr Mubarak. I am from Egypt, but I have had the pleasure of working with many Americans over the years. You may call me Amr, or Professor, or Professor Mubarak, as you see fit. It is my great honor to meet you all." He smiled when he said this, his expression surprisingly humble.

"You have been invited here, as you all know, due to your excellent scores on the Intuition Assessment Battery. The test is new, designed to identify exceptional students, such as yourselves, whose minds operate in a very particular way.

"All human beings process information in both conscious and unconscious ways. When thought is conscious, we are *aware* of it. We know how we traveled from point A to point B in our thinking process. But we are also very strongly influenced, in the thousands of decisions we make every day, by *unconscious* thoughts of which we are *not* aware. And this kind of thinking is highly intelligent and adaptive in its own right.

"For example, if someone needs to cross a river, they might think, 'I can swim across,' or, 'I can walk across in a shallow place.' But then if a bird lands on a vine and makes it sway a little, most people will suddenly think, 'I can use a vine to swing across.' *But they will not know why they thought this.* If we ask what made them think of the idea, believe it or not, most people will say, 'I just came up with it.' They have no idea *how* the unconscious mind solved the problem!

"What we believe to be special about each of you, is that your conscious mind is in contact with *and aware of* your unconscious mind to a much greater degree than usual. You have the ability to use the power of your unconscious mind *on purpose*, thereby blurring the very definitions of conscious and unconscious thought. You might not see the importance of this right now, but rest assured that to me, the prospect is very exciting. *Very* exciting, indeed."

Professor Mubarak looked around hopefully, but the expressions that greeted him ranged from confused to skeptical. He laughed and waved a hand in the air, dismissing their concerns.

"Over the course of the summer, we will investigate this phenomenon together—cooperatively—both what you can do and how you can do it. My expectation is that each of you has a certain prevalent *pathway* by which your unconscious mind sends messages, if you will, to your conscious awareness.

"This pathway will manifest itself in certain talents that you possess, talents which are far more profound than you might realize. We will spend our time exploring these talents together. If we are lucky, by the end of the summer they will be even more pronounced, and more *conscious*, than ever before, and I will have learned something about how to awaken these pathways in other students, even in those who have not previously enjoyed such wondrous abilities."

He finished with an enthusiastic grin, his gentle eyes smiling at each and every one of them in turn, and then nodded at Miss Williams after waiting a few moments to see whether anyone wanted to ask any questions yet, which no one apparently did.

"Thank you, Professor," she said, rising to stand by his side and addressing the students again. "I'll give you some time to finish your breakfast, and then we'll take a brief tour of the lodge, after which I will return you to Professor Mubarak's capable hands for the remainder of the morning.

"In the meantime, there are a few rules I'd like to go over. The six of you are all exceptional young men and women. These rules are not being implemented out of any concern over your behavior, but only for your own safety.

"The lodge is located on several thousand acres, most of which is forested. That's a lot of ground to get lost in, and there are bears and other potentially harmful creatures besides." Roman couldn't help but sneak a glance over at Mackenzie, suppressing a giggle as the big golden bear nodded sagely. "You are more than welcome to visit the landscaped area around the building itself, but please do not enter the woods—not even on marked hiking trails—without a guide.

"We also ask that you be inside the building by 8:00 p.m., but you do not need to be in your individual suites until 10:00 p.m. on 'school' nights, and until midnight on the weekends. I will be doing head counts, again for your safety. Think of yourselves as national resources. If you go missing, no expense will be spared to locate you, and I do mean no expense. So please be kind to the National Guard and respect the nightly curfew."

She smiled when she said this, but Mackenzie had the feeling she wasn't joking.

"There is an exercise space you may use at will. There is also an indoor pool, but this will be off limits except for specific hours on the weekends when a lifeguard will be on duty. The rest of the time, the door to the pool will remain locked. Please respect this precaution."

She seemed to aim this comment particularly at Kaitlyn, who raised her hands slightly as though to say, 'Who, me?' managing to look both smug and casually offended at the same time.

"I think that's about it," she finished. "Enjoy your meal. If there is anything specific that any of you would like for breakfast in the future, please let me know. Anything that is even remotely within reason can be arranged."

As the students finished eating, they did not speak amongst themselves, all of them intrigued by their new teacher but also profoundly aware that Miss Williams and Professor Mubarak were sitting well within hearing range. Privately, of course, they each had their own first impression of the man.

Kaitlyn liked him, but then again, she liked just about everyone. Mackenzie simply accepted him as yet another new teacher in an endless litany of new teachers, without holding any other opinion on the subject, but Sam appreciated his intellectual nature and found herself looking forward to her studies. Rush had no more interest in Professor Amr Mubarak than he did in anything else about the ICIC. Daniel, however, was reminded oddly of his mother—mostly because he heard the gentle reeds and chimes of her favorite yoga music every time he glanced in the man's direction.

As for Roman, he already loved Professor Mubarak's calm

demeanor, and he was intensely relieved not to see anything dark about the man, especially after the demon-winged Mr. Lockhart of his own personal third-grade hell. In fact, Roman saw very little out of the ordinary about Professor Mubarak at all, which was somewhat extraordinary in and of itself, the only exception being a round, golden seal, about the size of a man's fist, emblazoned in light directly over his heart: the side view of a lion, standing on its rear legs, its body struck through by a single bolt of lightning.

14
TALENTS

Which of you is Kaitlyn Wright?"

Professor Mubarak held a manilla folder open on his lap. He was sitting on the floor in the middle of the lodge's exercise facility, a large, open space without any furniture at all. There was another room next door with weight machines and treadmills, but this one was obviously designed for group classes, its floor covered in a blue mat-like material, soft and springy. Daniel would have said it was for yoga. Mackenzie would have said it was for sparring.

"I'm Kaitlyn," she said brightly.

"Excellent!" He sat cross-legged, facing the group, with his students spread out before him in a rough semi-circle. He turned to Kaitlyn, placing the manilla folder aside.

"These sessions will be informal. They will not be classes in the traditional sense. In fact, I hope to learn as much from you as you will from me! So, please, call me Amr."

"I'm sorry, Professor, but I'm not sure I can."

"I understand that it will be strange for many of you, at first, to call a grown man by his first name—"

"No, no, it isn't that," Kaitlyn said quickly. "It's just that, um..." She trailed off and cocked her head at him, pursing her lips, trying to think of how to say what she was thinking in the kindest possible way. "Well, I'm not sure I can pronounce it?"

At this, Amr Mubarak laughed out loud—a rich, deep laugh that made Kaitlyn smile. "Of course! My apologies. Amr is an Arabic name." He pronounced it with the 'm' running directly into the 'r' and then trilling away with a roll of the tongue that did not exist in English. "Americans find it easier to say 'Umar' or 'Amir.'"

"Which do you like?" Kaitlyn asked, but he shrugged her concern away.

"You may pick either one, or something else you think is closer. I will not be offended at the American pronunciation."

"Hmm..." Kaitlyn thought for a moment. "I really don't want to just say it wrong all the time. What about a nickname instead? Like 'Ammu'?" she asked. "'Am' from your first name, and 'Mu' from your last name, kind of squashed together?"

Amr Mubarak looked at her with an odd expression that she couldn't quite read, and then a huge smile lit up his face. He laughed again. "Why, I think that would be quite fitting, yes! That is a wonderful name!"

Kaitlyn looked at him questioningly. There was obviously something more to her suggestion than she realized.

"'Ammu,'" he explained, "means 'uncle' in Arabic, specifically in my own Egyptian dialect. I had never noticed that about my name before. I would be deeply honored if you would call me this. It would please me greatly." He smiled at each of them in turn. They all nodded or smiled back—all except Rush, who stared at him coldly.

"So!" he continued. "Having worked out our introductions, let us begin again! Kaitlyn?"

"Yes, Ammu?" she replied, grinning.

"Are you aware of any special gifts or talents you have already developed? Anything at all for which you might have a particular affinity?"

"I'm good at fixing things."

"Wonderful! What sort of things?"

"Gosh, anything really. I've fixed all kinds of small things at the G&G, but I've fixed bigger things, too, sometimes. Like Grandma Maggie's refrigerator."

"And what is the G&G?"

"Oh, sorry! The Gears and Gadgets Repair Shop. People bring computers and TVs and blenders and microwaves... stuff like that."

"Why, that is a magnificent talent!" Ammu exclaimed, and Kaitlyn beamed with pride. "And when you fix these things, do you find that you have a special talent for reading their manuals as well? Do the diagrams make sense to you?"

"I don't really use manuals," Kaitlyn admitted. "I take things apart, and then I can just kind of see how they're supposed to work. Maybe there's a wire that isn't connected right, or maybe a gear has worn down so it isn't catching anymore, and then I know that's why it isn't working. I fix the wire or put in a new gear or whatever, and then it works again."

"So if I brought you something broken, Kaitlyn," Ammu asked, "could you show me how you would fix it?"

"Sure! But I'd need a workshop. You know, with tools and parts and things. I mean, sometimes I just need the right screwdriver. But other times I might have to scrounge a new part from the stuff I have lying around."

"Hmm, yes. Yes, I see." Ammu pulled a yellow pad of paper from a stack of them that sat beneath his folder, and he withdrew a pen from a small, white carton. He handed these to Kaitlyn, who took them and then watched him expectantly.

"While I speak with the other students this morning," he said, "would you make a list of the things you would expect to find in a well-appointed workshop? Start with the essentials, and then move on to things you might not use as often but would still prefer to have, if you could. OK?"

"OK!" Kaitlyn licked her lips and wrote 'WORKSHOP' in capital letters across the top of the page. Grinning, she began to scribble furiously.

"So then." Ammu looked back and forth between the remaining two girls. "Which of you is Mackenzie Gray?"

"That's me," Mackenzie said. She remembered Sam's comment at the airport and tried to sound more casual this time.

"Excellent! I am very pleased to meet you, Mackenzie."

"Thank you, sir."

"Please, you do not need to call me 'sir.' Ammu is quite fine with me."

"Yes, s— I mean... OK, Ammu."

"And are you aware of any special gifts you might have developed, Mackenzie?"

"Well, I don't know whether this counts, but I'm pretty into Muay Thai."

"Just about anything can be a pathway of communication between the conscious and unconscious minds. But Muay Thai is not something with which I am familiar. Could you tell me about it?"

"Sure!" Mackenzie said, already warming up to the topic. "Muay Thai is a martial art. You know, like Karate or Jujitsu. But it's really fast. You use your hands and feet and knees and elbows as weapons, so there's a lot of striking. I've studied some Taekwondo also, and some Brazilian Jujitsu, but I use Muay Thai more. I like it because most Muay Thai schools focus on actual sparring, and I like to compete."

"That is very impressive!" Ammu said, and Mackenzie smiled. "Do you go to competitions often?"

"Definitely. I try to go to one at least every three to four weeks. Sometimes they're small, you know, but it's still a competition."

"And I take it you win often?"

"I do OK," Mackenzie said, shrugging a little.

Ammu regarded her for a long moment before replying.

"Please, everyone," he finally said, looking around the room. When Kaitlyn kept scribbling on her pad, Sam nudged her a little with an elbow.

"Huh?" she said, looking up in surprise. "Oh, sorry."

"Thank you. Please, everyone, this is very important. It is admirable not to want to appear boastful in front of your peers. I understand that, certainly. But this is not the time for modesty. What each of you can do is already extraordinary, and I expect your abilities only to grow with time. If I ask you whether you have excelled in a given area, please do not minimize your success.

"If you genuinely feel that you are only doing 'OK,' as you say, then it is perfectly acceptable to say so, but if the truth is more impressive, please be honest. We are here to explore your talents, and to make them stronger. Now is not the time to blend in with the crowd. This summer is about standing out. If anything, you are *expected* to stand out, each in his or her own way. Do you understand?"

Everyone nodded, even Rush. His nod was perfunctory, at best, but at least he acknowledged the request.

"Thank you. So, Mackenzie, do you win a lot?"

"Yes," she admitted. "I take first place almost every time. The only times I don't win are when I'm not feeling well, or when I'm upset about something else that disrupts my attention."

"And can you show me something? What this sport looks like?"

"It doesn't really look like much without someone to fight. I mean, anyone can throw a kick in the air. It's landing it on a moving target that matters."

"Yes, I see," Ammu said, nodding thoughtfully. "And I suspect that fighting a beginner would not be much of a showcase for your talent either, correct?"

Mackenzie chuckled a little. "No, it wouldn't," she admitted.

"All right, then. We will see if we can come up with a sparring partner for you. Thank you, Mackenzie."

"You're welcome," Mackenzie replied politely.

Ammu wrote something down on a yellow pad of his own and then glanced into the folder again.

"Daniel Walker?" he asked.

Daniel raised his hand.

"Good morning, Daniel."

"Good morning," Daniel replied.

"And what about you?" Ammu asked. "What particular interests have captured your attention?"

Daniel shrugged. "I like music," he said quietly.

"Go on," Ammu prompted. "In what way do you enjoy music? Do you listen to it? Do you play an instrument? Do you sing?"

"All of those, really," Daniel admitted. "But I don't sing much."

"Ha! Don't listen to him, Ammu. He sings plenty," Rush interjected, grinning wickedly.

"Oh?" Ammu asked. "So, Daniel, you have shared your talent with your new friends already? How wonderful!"

"Oh, he shared it all right," Rush said. "Shared and shared and shared, didn't he, Sketch?" Roman giggled on cue. "Heck, Mister Stayin' Alive over here won't *stop* singing."

"That is quite enough now, Mr...." Ammu held up one hand, but he did not yet know Rush's name.

"Knock it off, Rush," Mackenzie said at the same time, glaring at him over Roman's head.

"He's 'Mr. Hunt' in your file," Sam offered.

"My name is 'Rush,'" Rush snapped at Sam.

"Yeah, yeah," Sam said, rolling her eyes. "I just said 'in the file.' He's trying to figure out which one you are, genius."

"*Please*, children. That is *enough*," Ammu said, interjecting again.

"We're not children," Sam muttered under her breath.

"Listen to me, please," Ammu continued. "I know you have only just met each other, but it is critical that you try to get along. You will be working very closely together this summer. *Very* closely. Although I do not wish our meetings to be formal, I would ask nonetheless that you not interrupt each other, that you respect one another, no matter how you might be feeling in the moment. Daniel, please continue. Tell me about your musical ability."

Daniel didn't say anything, looking first at Rush and then down at his hands in embarrassment. At least Rush hadn't said anything about the love songs, but still, he was mortified. As the pause dragged on, Kaitlyn reached out and placed one hesitant hand on his knee for encouragement. Daniel looked up in surprise and then smiled just a little. She patted his knee and withdrew her hand, but it had been what he needed.

"I have perfect pitch," he said quietly, looking back down at his hands. "If you play me any note, I can tell you what it is, just from hearing it. I like a lot of instruments, but guitars are my favorite. And I do sing a little, but I really don't like singing in front of people." He glanced over at Rush, still embarrassed. "I just get carried away sometimes."

"I'd like to hear you sing," Kaitlyn said quietly, and she smiled at him, which made him blush.

"As would I," Ammu agreed. "But if you are more comfortable, Daniel, we can start, perhaps, with some guitar music? If you brought such an instrument with you?"

Daniel nodded.

"Excellent! Then will you please bring it to our afternoon session? I would love to hear you play and perhaps engage in some simple exercises."

"OK," Daniel agreed, but inside he was horrified. Kaitlyn was smiling at him, and Daniel wasn't sure whether that made him feel better or worse. There was a part of him that wouldn't mind playing for her, at least a little, but not like this, not in front of everyone, especially not with Rush and Sam watching.

"Very well, then. Thank you, Daniel." Ammu turned toward Roman and smiled. "I take it, then, that you are Roman Jackson."

"My name is Sketch," he said immediately, and Rush smirked just a little.

"Oh? I apologize. Roman is the nickname listed in your file."

"It's new," Roman said proudly. "It's my gamer tag. Cause I can draw."

"I see!" Ammu smiled gently. "And what do you like to draw?"

"Just stuff," Roman said cautiously. "People, mostly."

"That is very interesting. Would you consider that to be your special talent, do you think?"

"I don't know," Roman answered, shrugging a little.

"You're good, man. He said don't be modest. Tell him." Rush shoved Roman lightly in the shoulder, and Roman grinned up at him shyly.

"I'm good, I guess," Roman said.

"He's really good," Rush offered, and Roman beamed with pride.

"Well, if that is the case, then I would like very much to see your work. Would you draw something for me?" He picked up another yellow pad and pen and handed them toward Roman, but Roman hesitated, not taking them. He was afraid Ammu would ask him to draw someone here in the room, and he didn't want them to know how he saw them, not even the good stuff.

"Um, I'm really better with pencils," he said quietly.

"You should bring him your pad this afternoon," Rush told him.

"Oh? Do you have a sketching book here with you?" Ammu asked.

"Yeah. It's upstairs," Roman responded, grateful for a way out of Ammu's initial request.

"And would you be willing to bring it to me this afternoon? Along with some pencils, perhaps?"

"Sure," Roman agreed. That last bit didn't sound promising, but at least now he would have until the afternoon to figure out how to handle things.

"Wonderful!" Ammu said, smiling warmly, and then he turned his attention to Sam.

"So, then. You must be Samantha Prescott, yes?"

"That's right," Sam said. She was already dreading this conversation.

"And what would you say is your field of expertise, Samantha?"

What *was* her field of expertise? Everyone else had these amazing talents: music, art, mechanics, martial arts. Sam didn't do anything like that. She did well in school, but that was it. She didn't play sports. She wasn't musical or artistic. She had been wracking her brain this whole time, and she still didn't have an answer, but now she was on the spot. She had to say *something*.

"I honestly don't know. I get good grades, and my teachers say I'm really good in math?"

"Mathematics can certainly be a pathway," Ammu said encouragingly. "When you solve math problems, do you follow the steps as they have been taught? Or do you tend to see the solution as soon as you look at the problem?"

"I follow the steps," she admitted, already disappointed. She saw what he was getting at. She was good at math, but it was something she did consciously, following logical steps that she understood. She didn't leap to unconscious conclusions about math problems. Math might be one of her strengths, but it wasn't her pathway.

"Interesting," he said, watching her thoughtfully. "Do you, perhaps, find that you often know what people are thinking or feeling?"

"No," she admitted, her voice becoming quieter. If anything, human emotion seemed like an unsolvable mystery. She was much more comfortable in the world of math and science and logical rules.

"And yet," he said gently, "you knew why I was asking about following the steps, did you not? You knew it immediately."

"That was just logic," she said, her voice rising a bit. "You said you're looking for the pathways between the conscious and unconscious minds. I knew that's what you were looking for because you told me. It's not like the vine example."

Ammu pondered her silently, while Sam felt more and more embarrassed. Everyone was staring at her. Everyone else knew their talent. Sam was used to being the very best student in class, and now, suddenly, she wasn't just average, she was *worse* than average. She was the *worst* student in the class.

Do not cry in front of everyone. Do NOT cry in front of everyone! She fought to control her feelings, struggling not to get up and storm out of the room.

Ammu seemed to sense her distress, and he spoke to her again, very gently, which only made her feel worse. Now she was the dumb kid. The one the teacher felt sorry for.

"I think, Samantha, that you have more of a gift than you realize. We will discover it together. You will see. Perhaps you can spend some time over lunch thinking about the things you like to do. It might be a hobby or a simple pastime that will lead us to your special pathway, even if it is not something you recognize as a particular skill."

Sam just nodded, not trusting her voice to speak, and she huddled into herself, hugging her knees to her chest as he moved on to Rush.

"And what might your particular talent be, do you think?" he asked, watching Rush with interest.

Rush had his own reason to believe he might not have one of these special pathways the guy kept talking about. After all, he had answered most of the multiple-choice questions on that crazy test by just filling in random blanks! But at least he had a talent to distract everybody with—not like that poor Sam girl—and he wasn't going to be shy about sharing it.

"I'm a gamer," he said. "They call me Rush because I'm so fast."

"So you consider this to be your talent?" Ammu asked. It was an innocent question, but it reminded Rush of his father's taunts, and he felt a flash of anger and resentment surge within his chest.

"When I left home to come to this place, I was number eighteen out of four million beta players in *HRT Alpha*," he said forcefully. "Four *million*! And the only reason I wasn't in the top five was because I didn't *want* to get that high before the invitational. I'm not just good. I'm *pro* good. I'm as good as it gets."

"I apologize," Ammu said, raising one hand in appeasement. "I was not challenging your claim. I was simply confirming my understanding. A talent for video games could certainly be a pathway between the conscious and unconscious minds. I would like very much to see you play."

"Yeah, well you can't," Rush said, his voice full of bitterness. "Like Kung Fu Barbie over there, I need a real opponent to show you what I can do. In fact, I need a whole *team* of opponents. Only we don't have any Internet, so I don't have anybody to play. Get me on the Internet, and I'll show you what I can do."

"I am afraid I do not have any control over that," Ammu said gently, "but it seems to me that you have a whole team of potential opponents sitting right here. Perhaps we could set things up so that you could play against your classmates here at the center."

"You don't get it," Rush shot back. "Unless any of these guys is a top contender, me competing against them is the same as her competing against someone who has no martial arts training. You admitted we aren't good enough for her, so how come they're good enough for me?" He indicated Mackenzie by thrusting his chin in her general direction over Roman's head.

"Call me 'Kung Fu Barbie' one more time, and I'll put you on the floor whether you're good enough to bother with or not," Mackenzie growled.

"Peace," Ammu said, raising his hands again. "I do not want

Mackenzie to fight an untrained opponent in live combat because I do not want the opponent to get hurt," he said, explaining his reasoning. "I would like to see you play against your classmates, even though they are not at your level, because they can not be harmed by a video game, and because the Internet problem is not, as I said, under my control. Until the system is up, I would like to see something of your skill, even if it is not the best showcase for your talent. It is, at least, a place to start."

"Fine. Whatever."

"If you would write down for me—" Ammu began, ignoring Rush's tone and preparing to hand him a pad and a pen, but Rush cut him off before he could finish his sentence.

"I can tell you what we need right now. Six HD monitors. They don't have to be as big as the ones upstairs. I like a twenty-eight inch, but twenty-four is OK. Five more gaming consoles. I'd use mine. Four more controllers. Sketch can use my extra one cause I trust him not to mess it up." Roman beamed at him. "Five more headsets if you want these scrubs to have half a chance of hearing me coming before I kill them anyway, and the *Internet* to download five beta copies of *HRT Alpha: Year One*, cause it's not out on disc yet, and even if it was, you have to get the updates online. But if you get me the *Internet*, then we already have what we need, cause I can play on my own console and destroy some *actual* competition."

Ammu continued to ignore Rush's tone, calmly taking notes throughout his tirade.

"So if we could get you five more consoles with *HRT Alpha: Year One*—I have that title right?"

"Yeah," Rush confirmed.

"OK. Five more consoles with the game, then you could play against the others here at the center?"

"You can't," Rush said. "Like I told you, it's in beta. It's not out yet."

"I understand," Ammu said, smiling graciously and putting the pad of paper away underneath his folder. "I think that is enough for this morning, everyone. You are dismissed. Lunch will be available between noon and 1:00 p.m. in the main hall. Please be back here by 1:30 to continue where we left off. Thank you for your time and attention this morning, and peace be with you."

15
SAM

S am held it together until she got back to the suite, but as soon as she closed the bedroom door behind her, she threw herself onto the bed, buried her face in a pillow, and screamed her frustration into its infuriatingly plush depths.

She was not in the mood for a soft, goose down pillow. She was more in the mood for a prison-issue, burlap-sack, sorry-ass excuse for a pillow that you could sling at someone in a convincingly threatening, non-comedic sort of way, but instead, this elegant thing that her mother simply would have *adored* was going to have to do. She would just have to suck it up and add it to her list of grievances about this day that was already promising to be the absolute worst day of her life, and here it was not even lunch time.

How had everything gotten this bad, this quickly?

She had been so proud when the invitation had arrived in the mail. The moment she had opened the letter, she had felt it again, for the first time since the morning of that crazy test: an overwhelming certainty that the huge, momentous *thing* she had been waiting for all her life was finally starting to unfold.

She had begged her mother to let her go, explaining (with as little eye rolling as she could manage) that attending a Homeland Security summer camp was not the same thing as joining the military and that a five-star resort lodge in Wyoming was not a likely target for acts of terrorism. Fortunately, her father had taken her side, and she had called the ICIC to accept the invitation, practically leaping out of her own skin with excitement.

But within a day or two, that feeling of impending *destiny* had already begun to fizzle out. Once again, her life felt perfectly ordinary, and she expected her stay at the ICIC to be nothing more than a temporary distraction in a long line of days between sixteen and ninety-six, the meaning of it all once again having been lost, if there had ever been any meaning to it in the first place.

She had clung, however, to the hope that once she arrived, things would turn around again—that the overarching purpose of her life would be revealed, some larger way in which her existence on the planet would actually *matter*.

Sadly, this had not been the case.

At no point yesterday had she felt any of that former sense of destiny, and then this morning, on her very first day, things had already devolved from bad to downright nauseating. She was doing nothing meaningful here whatsoever, and apparently she was going to be doing it from the very bottom of the class, her worst fear having been decisively and incontrovertibly confirmed.

There was, in the final analysis, nothing exceptional about her at all.

Sure, Professor Mubarak had said he wouldn't give up on her, but he was a kind man, far too nice to tell a teenager to her face that she just shouldn't be here. He had said to think about the things she enjoyed doing, but she had already gone over everything she could think of. Nothing was going to rescue her from the looming prospect of failure.

She liked jigsaw puzzles, but she did them consciously, looking for shapes and colors. She didn't intuit the position of each piece by glancing at it like some kind of two-bit psychic. She liked crosswords and logic problems, but she solved them by deduction, using established rules and the occasional thesaurus. She even had a system for word searches, which were highly intuitive kinds of puzzles, and which she hated because she sucked at them.

Now, she was going to have to endure a whole afternoon of pitying glances and awkward silence while the other kids explored their grand, unconscious *talents* in the face of her own obvious mediocrity.

Sam heard a tentative knock at the door, but she didn't respond. She was not in the mood for company and certainly not in the mood for *talented* company that was going to rub her nose in her own failures just by their very existence.

The knock repeated itself, however, followed by Kaitlyn's voice.

"Sam? We're going down to lunch, if you want to come?"

Sam ignored it.

"Sam?" Kaitlyn tried again.

"Come on," Sam heard Mackenzie say. "Just leave her alone." But apparently Kaitlyn chose not to take this advice, knocking a third time, just for good measure.

"Samantha?" Kaitlyn called out gently. "Do you want to talk about it?"

"Take a hint, Susie Sunshine!" Sam finally shouted. "I'm not buying your crazy Kool-aid!"

"Hey," Mackenzie fired back, "she's just trying to be nice! Don't be such a—"

Kaitlyn cut Mackenzie off before she could finish voicing precisely what it was she felt Sam was being.

"Don't be mad," Sam heard her say. "She's just upset."

'*About being a total loser and the only kid who shouldn't even be here,*' you mean, Sam thought. *Thanks a lot, Kaitlyn, cause yeah, that's just what I need on top of everything else today, to be the guest of honor at your little pity party. Well, forget you, forget this stupid program, and forget your swimsuit edition bodyguard. I'm still smarter than all of you. I never needed any 'pathway' to be a genius before, and I don't need one now.*

16
INSTRUCTOR REPORT

Have we found ourselves the right students for the job? Can they do it?"

"I believe so, yes. Most of them are already quite aware of their own gifts, which is more than I had hoped for."

"Most of them?"

"Samantha Prescott was not able to offer me any particular direction in which to begin our work together."

"Should I be concerned?"

"Not yet. It is possible, I suppose, that she is not one of the ones we are looking for, but I believe our time together may still prove fruitful."

"Fine. Just keep me posted. We can wash her out if we have to. The fewer the people who know what's going on here, the better. If she can't do it, she doesn't need to know about it."

"I understand. It may be best to isolate them from each other during the first stage of the project anyway. At least for their training sessions. There is some tension between them, and I do not want to build up any resentments. But they must be able to work together eventually if we are to achieve our ultimate goal."

"Let the liaison worry about that. Is the Hunt kid one of the problems?"

"That is not the word I would choose. He was somewhat confrontational toward his peers, yes, but I believe the underlying issue might be relatively simple to address. He would very much like to have access to the Internet."

"I'm sure he would."

"It appears to be a significant source of irritation for him. And in any event, we might need to allow it in order to test his particular abilities."

"See what you can do without it. I'm not giving them Internet access. If it becomes too much of an issue, we can always wash him out, too. Your report says we shouldn't need them all."

"That is true in theory, yes. But the fewer of them there are, the harder things become. Ideally, they will all be able to do what we need them to do."

"In my entire career, never once have I seen a complex mission proceed all the way to completion under ideal conditions. Hell, even the simple ones usually turn into a soup sandwich. We'll keep them all if we can, but if we can't..."

"I understand."

17
DANIEL

"So, Daniel, in order to proceed, I would like first to explain what it is I mean when I speak about a pathway between the conscious and the unconscious mind, OK?"

"OK." Daniel sat on the floor of the exercise room with his guitar bag lying next to him. He had been relieved to learn that Ammu was going to work with them individually—relieved and just a small bit disappointed, because it also meant Kaitlyn wouldn't be there. But even the thought of playing in front of her made his palms sweat a little, and Ammu had mentioned singing...

Yeah, Daniel decided, he was definitely relieved the others wouldn't be there.

"Throughout history," Ammu began, "there have been a few special people in every generation, revered for their abilities—abilities so profound that their work is recognized not just for years but for centuries beyond their death. Rembrandt, Michelangelo, Beethoven, Mozart, Da Vinci, Galileo, Einstein. They are geniuses, not necessarily for their intelligence, per se, but for their *creativity*. They see art before it ever touches the canvas. They hear music even when they have gone deaf. They imagine the possibility that even the most basic and obvious assumptions about the universe may be wrong.

"I myself have been taught that what makes these people special is their ability to tap into the unconscious mind, to see and hear and feel while awake that which most people can only access in their dreams, or in brief glimpses of intuition that," Ammu paused to wave his hand in the air with a flick of his wrist, like a magician, "slip away, almost immediately, so that we never know from whence they came." Ammu smiled at Daniel, his eyes reflecting the passion behind his words.

"The test that you took was designed to identify the young people of your generation who have the strongest ability to do this—to become aware of the thoughts of the unconscious mind. I believe that by studying what you can do, by learning how you do it and by helping you to fulfill your potential, we will eventually be able to teach others to do it as well. The unconscious mind is perhaps the greatest untapped resource of the entire human race, Daniel. To learn to communicate with it is to unlock the genius that exists within us all."

Daniel couldn't help but feel a little overwhelmed. Him? A genius? He was good at music, sure, but he wasn't *Beethoven*, for heaven's sake. He wasn't *Mozart*. But Ammu wasn't done speaking, so Daniel kept his thoughts, and his doubts, to himself. As though sensing Daniel's discomfort, Ammu smiled encouragingly.

"Do not worry," he said. "I am not asking you to write me a symphony!" He laughed out loud as though they had just shared a private joke. "No, no. I understand that you are still in the nascence of your ability. You all are. My task is to help you see what you can do. To help you *understand* what you can do, and to build upon it. OK?"

"Uh... sure," Daniel agreed, shrugging a little.

"Ha! I see your skepticism! But it will not matter. I ask only that you be honest with me, that you answer my questions to the best of your ability, as thoroughly as you know how, and that you attempt any exercises I give you with the intention of accomplishing the task, even if you are not certain that you will be successful. Is that a fair request?"

"Sure," Daniel said again, nodding his head slightly.

"Wonderful!" Ammu beamed at him in obvious delight, which Daniel couldn't help but smile about since they hadn't even done anything yet.

"So, Daniel, there are certain things we already know, from modern science, that the unconscious mind is especially interested in. If you are consciously trying to solve a problem, your unconscious mind will work on it as well. If you are not trying to accomplish anything in particular, then your unconscious mind is still at work, nonetheless, always scanning your surroundings for things it considers important.

"For example, it is always looking for danger. If you walk along a path in the woods, and you see a stick that looks like a snake, you might jump backward a bit before you realize that it is only a stick. Your unconscious mind identified the threat and responded to it before your conscious awareness could react, to tell you that the stick was nothing to worry about. Do you see?"

Daniel nodded.

"The unconscious mind also watches the people around us, for signs of trouble or stress, for example, or for a smile from a pretty girl, hmm?"

At this, Daniel blushed.

"The unconscious mind watches for danger, and it watches for opportunity, and it tries to get our attention if it identifies either one. It is instinctively interested in the facial expressions and body language of the people around us. Do you have any questions so far?"

"I don't think so. Not really," Daniel said.

Ammu nodded enthusiastically. "So, then! Daniel, we are

looking for ways in which the music you connect to may, in turn, be transmitting these signals from your unconscious mind to your conscious awareness. Have you ever, for example, heard frightening music that warned you of a danger you had not yet seen?"

Daniel thought for a while, but he couldn't remember anything like that ever happening to him.

"No," he said, sounding a little disappointed. "No, I don't think so."

"That is fine," Ammu said, his tone reassuring. "We are only just beginning, yes? Perhaps you have not been surrounded by much danger in your life. That is a good thing! Or perhaps your unconscious mind has been more interested in something else. Do you find that music ever tells you things about what people are thinking or feeling?"

"I don't know about telling me things, but I do imagine songs when I look at people a lot. Like if they're mad I might think about a song that sounds angry." He thought about Jared and Alyssa back home and grinned a little. "Or if I know my friend likes a girl, and I see him looking at her, I might imagine him, you know, kind of singing about her in his head."

He thought about Rush and Sketch hearing him singing and winced a little, but no matter how honest Ammu had asked him to be, he wasn't going to talk about *that*.

"Good, good!" Ammu said. "And do specific people tend to inspire the same kind of music every day? Or is it always different?"

"Both, I guess? Like, my mom always sounds kind of like her yoga music. You know, chimes and flutes and stuff. But my friends tend to change more—happy or sad or angry or whatever."

"Excellent, Daniel! This is truly excellent! Can you play for me what your mother sounds like, do you think?" Ammu waved a hand toward the guitar, but Daniel hesitated.

"Not really. It isn't that I don't want to. It's just... the guitar is the wrong instrument for my mom. That's funny, you know, 'cause

I never thought about it before. I really like guitars, but that isn't what I usually hear around her. I can't imitate a flute with a guitar. I mean, I could play the notes, sure, but it wouldn't be the same at all."

"I see," Ammu said, nodding sagely. "So who sounds more like a guitar to you?"

"Oh, it depends on their mood, really, but most of my friends make me think of different songs I could play."

"I would like to hear some examples, if I might?"

"Yeah, OK," Daniel said, and he pulled the guitar bag into his lap so he could unzip it and take out his six-string. He picked up the instrument and walked to the edge of the room, where he had left his amp when he had first come in. He plugged the amp into the wall and then plugged it into his guitar as well, setting it to the lowest volume setting. He plucked each string lightly, in turn.

"You are checking its tuning, yes? With your perfect pitch?"

Daniel blushed and nodded. "Yeah. It's good," he said.

"OK then, imagine someone frowning, and play for me what you hear."

"Uh..." Daniel hesitated for a long time, his hands poised over the strings, ready to play whatever came to his mind, but nothing did. "I'm not sure it works that way," he said finally.

"Oh?"

"Well, there are lots of different kinds of frowns, for lots of different reasons. I'm having trouble picking one, I think. Like, a particular frown."

"Interesting!" Ammu exclaimed. "Good! In a way, this is very good, Daniel. This is a strong indication that your music is more than mere word association, that it is, in fact, showing you something about the feelings of the people around you. Perhaps—"

But before he could continue, Daniel began to play. He wasn't sure where the impulse had come from, but he plucked out a few experimental notes, and Ammu fell silent, waiting. When he settled into a tune, he recognized it as an Eric Clapton song, but he played it much more slowly than the original. He played the chorus and a single verse, and a chorus again, and then, watching Ammu hesitantly, he began to sing very softly, turning the amp up just a bit first.

The song was "Something's Happening," from the *Behind the Sun* album. Daniel had never been certain what the song was supposed to be about, but somehow, in this moment, the lyrics spoke to him, as though the song itself were trying to tell him something, to convey some higher truth that remained just out of reach. He sang the chorus aloud and part of a verse, but then he stopped playing and looked at Ammu hesitantly, the last note of the guitar slowly fading away, hanging in the air between them.

"Something *is* happening, isn't it?" Daniel wanted to know. "Something big."

"Yes," Ammu said quietly, and he nodded once for emphasis. His face was still kind, but he was not smiling now. He was not smiling at all. "Yes, it is."

18
SKETCH

When it was his turn to meet with Ammu, Roman was nervous. He rarely showed his drawings to anyone outside his own family, not even the good things. But he carried his light sketchpad into the exercise room nonetheless.

Roman liked Ammu, whose calm demeanor reminded him of Tony, but where Tony tended to be quiet in a standoffish sort of way, letting Roman's mother do most of the parenting while Tony sipped a beer and watched television, Ammu was quiet in a *thinking* sort of way. This fascinated Roman, and he found himself liking the man despite feeling anxious about having all that intelligence focused in his general direction.

When Roman handed over the pad, Ammu nodded without comment and smiled, a serious sort of smile that conveyed more respect—more *significance*—than Roman, at eleven, saw from most adults. But as soon as Ammu opened the sketchbook, his face registered surprise, his eyes darting back to Roman, as though seeking something he had missed before, something that might explain the wondrous talent that sat before him in the body of an eleven-year-old boy.

He stared into Roman's eyes for only a moment and then returned his full attention to the pages, silently turning them, one after another, slowly, reverently, taking in each new drawing like a true believer who has been allowed, for but a few precious moments, to gaze upon heaven.

Roman had been careful not to draw anyone from the center, not wanting such an image to be discovered accidentally, but the notebook was filled nonetheless with Roman's mystical visions of humanity, including everything from quick, rough studies to detailed renditions that took Ammu's breath away.

"How long?" the man asked finally, setting the book down on his lap without closing it, the current page open to a particularly fine rendering of Shaquiya's fairy wings, poised delicately above her as she sat curled in a patch of sunlight, reading a book. "How long have you been able to see such wondrous things?"

"I don't see that stuff," Roman said, too quickly. "I just draw things I like."

"I see," Ammu said quietly. He took a deep breath and closed the pad, looking directly into Roman's eyes again, and Roman had the impression that he did see, in fact—seeing everything there was to see about Roman, even the darkness that poured onto his secret pages when no one was looking.

The very thought made him want to throw up.

"It is very important," Ammu said, "for us to be honest with each other. Not just you and me. All of us. But such a thing is not possible if that honesty only flows in one direction. I, too, know what it means to bear a secret so great that you feel you must hide it from the world—a secret that must be carefully guarded, to protect the ones you love."

Roman watched as the emblem over Ammu's heart glowed more brightly, pulsing with the rhythm of a heartbeat. Roman had to believe it was the beating of Ammu's own heart—it was the only thing that made sense—but he also had the unshakable feeling that it was somehow the heartbeat of the world itself, emblazoned in light upon this man's chest.

"I can not tell you about my secret yet," Ammu continued gently, "and I will not, therefore, ask you to tell me about yours. But what I *can* tell you is this: our secrets, both yours and mine, are not about *us*. I carry a secret about how the universe *works*, and you carry a secret about how the universe *is*. These are *not* secrets about how *I* work. Or about how *you* are.

"You are special for what you see, this is true, but the things you see are not within *you*. What you see in the people around you, these are things within *them*.

Roman's eyes grew even more guarded. He lowered his shoulders and his head, instinctively making himself even smaller, but Ammu continued as though he had not seen his reaction.

"What you have chosen to show me here today, I thank you for. Truly. To see your gift in such a tangible way... it is a blessing far greater than you can know, especially for me. But I also know, because of the secret *I* carry, that what you have drawn here represents only half of the human condition.

"There are others in the world who will appear to be surrounded by darker things, more sinister things, and I understand why you would not want to share these with me. I hope you will trust me enough to do so one day, but for now, you must know that the frightening things you see are not reflections of your own mind, or of your own soul—they are true reflections of things within *them*, their own very *real* trials and struggles.

"You must not judge such people for the burdens they bear, but you must be aware of this truth, and you *must* have faith in your visions. Always. Do not trust the intentions of the dark ones. Only trust the light. Do you understand?"

Roman nodded, tears springing unbidden to his eyes.

"Good," Ammu said. "Then that is enough for today. You are already much farther along your path than I ever could have hoped. We will speak again when I can share more of my own secret. But you have nothing to fear from me or from the secret I bear. This much I can promise you."

"I know," Roman said, glancing at the emblem that glowed over Ammu's heart.

Ammu smiled warmly. "Then go, for now. And peace be with you."

19
GAME NIGHT

It had been so late when they had flown in the night before that Kaitlyn hadn't even bothered to unpack. Now, after dinner, she took the time to empty her bags, putting her clothes away in drawers, hanging up a sundress and a couple of blouses in her closet, and setting up her laptop—a treasured present from Zack at the G&G—over at the computer desk.

When she was done, she thought about picking up one of the paperbacks, but she wasn't ready to settle in for the night. If she had been at home, she would have spent the evening listening to stories about what her father had been like when he was a child, or about what Detroit had been like in its heyday, or about what life in general had been like, for that matter, before the Internet, and cell phones, and color television.

Kaitlyn definitely didn't feel like sitting around missing Grandma Maggie, so she wandered back out into the suite to see what the other girls might be up to. Unfortunately, Sam was the only one in the living room, and she clearly wasn't in the mood for company.

"Hi," Kaitlyn tried, but Sam never looked away from the television. She was watching some nature show in which zebras were trying desperately to cross a muddy river, struggling to climb over the dead, bloating carcasses of other animals that had been trapped by the steep banks and trampled to death in the process.

"Ugh," Kaitlyn said. "That's awful."

"That's life," Sam said. "Survival of the fittest. Deal with it."

"Yeah, but I mean, look at that little one. It's so sad."

"It's not sad," Sam retorted, her tone entirely unsympathetic. "It's a zebra. If it makes it across, it'll act like nothing happened. All those dead zebras will be right behind it, and it won't care. See that one, there? That one just got out, and it's already forgotten about the whole thing. Zebras are shits."

Kaitlyn looked, and the zebra was, in fact, calmly grazing within sight of the massacre. Somehow, that didn't make her feel any better.

"Where's Mackenzie?" she asked.

"She didn't say where she was going," Sam said, her eyes never leaving the slaughter, "but she was dressed for a workout. She's probably downstairs doing pushups like a good little soldier. Either that or beating the crap out of something. Hard to say."

"Uh, OK. Thanks."

As Kaitlyn opened the door to the hallway, Sam added, "Hey, if she's beating the crap out of Rush, come back and get me. I'd give it even odds they'd knock each other out."

Kaitlyn didn't reply, but as the door was closing behind her, she heard Sam add, talking more to herself than to Kaitlyn, "I'd actually pay to see that."

As Kaitlyn neared the workout room, she began to hear repetitive grunts accompanied by dull, forceful thuds, and soon enough she saw through the long, glass wall of the gym that Sam had been right. Mackenzie was beating up a heavy bag, using as much energy as physically possible.

She alternated among punches, elbows, and knee slams to its midsection, punctuated by the occasional kick for good measure, as she danced around the bag from one side to the other, her body constantly in motion.

When she circled behind it, she saw Kaitlyn standing in the hallway and nodded without pausing her barrage in the slightest. Kaitlyn went in and sat down on a weight bench while Mackenzie finished a lightning-fast combination, ultimately springing away from the bag and leaping into a nasty, spinning kick that connected with a final, resounding thud.

"Hey," Mackenzie said, breathing heavily. She stopped and caught the bag in her hands before letting it go. "What's up? Everything OK?" She picked up the gym towel that was hanging from a nearby handrail, used it to mop the sweat from her face and neck, and then casually flicked it back over the railing. Then she picked up a water bottle, squirting it into her mouth like a boxer.

"Yeah," Kaitlyn said. "Sam's watching zebras die on TV. I thought I'd find something else to do."

"She's watching what?"

"Never mind. How's the workout going?"

"Good. We've got our one-on-ones tomorrow, so I'm going kinda light."

"That's *light*?" Kaitlyn asked, but Mackenzie only laughed.

Miss Williams had told them at dinner that Kaitlyn's session with Ammu would be in the morning. Mackenzie's would be in the afternoon.

"I'm kinda nervous about mine," Kaitlyn admitted. "Are you?"

"Aw, I wouldn't worry," Mackenzie told her. "I mean, obviously I'm thinking about it, but I'd be here doing this either way. I try to get a two-hour workout in every day, minimum."

"Oh," Kaitlyn said, suddenly feeling like she should go practice fixing things. She dropped her head and started swinging her legs in the air.

Mackenzie chuckled. "Ammu just wants to see what we can do," she said, playfully cuffing Kaitlyn in the shoulder. "You said yourself you're a good mechanic. I'm sure he'll be impressed."

"You think?"

"Definitely." Mackenzie nodded reassuringly and smiled at her.

"OK." Kaitlyn smiled back, but she still didn't feel that sure about it.

"Hey," Mackenzie said gently, "you just need to get your mind off it, you know? If you find something else to do, tomorrow will be here before you know it, and then the whole thing will be behind you."

"Maybe," Kaitlyn said, frowning, "but not dead zebras."

Mackenzie laughed. "No," she agreed, "definitely not dead zebras."

Kaitlyn pretended to shudder, and Mackenzie laughed again.

"You're welcome to hang with me if you want," Mackenzie offered, setting down the water bottle and stretching her back, "but I'm just going to be training. I won't be much company. Maybe you should go see what Daniel's up to. I'm sure he'd like to see you." She said this last bit with a teasing grin and raised her eyebrows suggestively.

"Oh, come on. I can't go to the guys' suite," Kaitlyn protested. "That'd be weird."

"Well, suit yourself. But it's either hang out with Daniel or watch some morbid zebra marathon. If I were you, I know which one I'd pick."

With that, Mackenzie winked and started punching the bag again, leaving Kaitlyn to consider her options on her own.

After dinner, Rush hoofed it straight back to the suite (with his self-appointed protégé trailing loyally behind him) and immediately fired up his console to check on the Internet, which was still down, just as Miss Williams had predicted.

"Sh—" Rush stopped himself and looked down at Sketch, who had settled next to him on the couch. "—ugar," he finished. "Another night offline. This downtime is killing me."

"Playing online is really that much better?" Sketch asked.

"Well, yeah, but it's not just that. You know how I said this game isn't even out yet? That it's still in beta?"

Sketch nodded.

"They let people play it before the release to get them all into it," Rush explained. "So everybody's talking about it."

"So they sell more," Sketch said.

"Right. And with *this* game, as part of the hype, they're hosting an invitational in August. The top hundred players in the world get to compete, and the top five get a spot on a pro team."

"And you're number eighteen!" Sketch exclaimed. "You're so in!"

"Yeah," Rush said, nodding, "so I don't want to lose my rank, and without the Internet, I can't check on it."

"Oh man, you're gonna lose your rank if you can't play?" Sketch asked, his eyes wide with horror.

"Naw. I mean, I hope not. If they were just going by total kills, maybe, but that's not how it works. They're tracking ratios, not totals."

Sketch just blinked up at him, saying nothing.

"The point is, the rankings haven't changed much over the last couple weeks. Things have kind of settled out more or less where they're going to be, I think. But I can't afford to lose my edge."

"Well, I know I'm not that good," Sketch said, wanting to help, "but I can practice with you. If you want?"

"Hey, man, don't sell yourself short. You're good for a beginner." Sketch grinned.

"But sure. I'm gonna play either way. You can join in if you want. That way I can practice kicking grenades back in people's faces."

Sketch laughed and picked up the other controller.

They hadn't been playing very long when Daniel walked in, coming back from dinner.

"Hey, Rush, can Daniel play?" Sketch asked.

"Sure, but you guys would have to take turns. I only brought the two controllers."

"I don't mind," Sketch said. "Daniel, you wanna play?"

"Oh, no thanks," Daniel said, his mind obviously elsewhere.

Sketch glanced up at Rush, who caught the look out of the corner of his eye.

"What?" Rush asked him, but Sketch just looked at Daniel and then back at Rush again.

Rush sighed. "Daniel?" he tried. "You sure you don't want to play? We don't mind, do we Sketch?"

"Naw, we don't mind," Sketch said, holding his controller out to Daniel, but Daniel just shook his head.

"No, thanks. Really. I'm OK."

"You can play your guitar out here," Sketch tried again. "We don't mind, right, Rush?"

"Sketch, why you want to hang out with Daniel so bad? Let him do what he wants to do, man."

But Sketch hated it when he felt like he had to go hide from Marquon in his room, and he didn't want Daniel to feel like he had to hide from them either. Sketch didn't say anything else, but Rush saw him droop his shoulders and hunch in on himself. He sighed again.

"Daniel," Rush said. "For real, man, you can sing or play or whatever out here. You know that, right? The living room's for everybody. There, are you happy now?" He said this last to Sketch, who smiled and nodded his head.

"I know. Thanks," Daniel replied, but he headed back toward his room anyway, and Sketch shrugged, satisfied that at least they had tried.

It wasn't much longer, though, before a light knock came at the suite door. Rush glanced at the door in surprise and then looked down at Sketch, who was looking back up at him expectantly.

"Really?" Rush asked him. "How did *I* get to be in charge?"

"You're bigger," Sketch said, and Rush laughed out loud.

"Come in," he called out, still laughing.

The door opened just enough for Kaitlyn to poke her head past it.

"Why, hello," Rush said. "You looking for someone?" He grinned, and Kaitlyn blushed furiously.

"What are you guys doing?" she asked, dodging the question.

"We're playing *HRT Alpha*," Sketch answered her. "You wanna play? We can share." He held the controller out toward her as a bot shot him in the face.

"I don't know how," she admitted. "I don't get to play games much."

"I can teach you," Sketch offered. "I mean, if Rush says it's OK."

"Dude," Rush said, "some helpful advice for a couple years down the road, OK? Never suggest that you have the right to tell a girl what she can or can't do. Trust me. They hate that."

Sketch laughed.

"It's true," Kaitlyn said, grinning. "That's good advice, actually."

"OK," Sketch said. "So, you wanna play?"

"Sure." Kaitlyn came in and sat down next to Sketch, the two boys both scooting over a little to make room for her, and Sketch started explaining the controls.

Once Kaitlyn seemed to have the basic idea, Sketch turned the controller over to her for a game, and then Rush handed his own controller to Sketch.

"Bio break," Rush said. "Play one without me."

"OK," Sketch said, and Rush showed him how to start a new match.

After disappearing into his room for a few minutes, Rush came back out again, but instead of sitting down on the couch, he made sure Kaitlyn and Sketch were involved in their game and then crossed the suite to knock softly on Daniel's door. When Daniel didn't answer, Rush opened it anyway. Daniel was sitting on the edge of his bed playing his guitar, the instrument plugged directly into a headset.

"Well, that explains that," Rush muttered.

When Daniel finally looked up enough to catch Rush out of the corner of his eye, he jumped a mile and yanked the headset off.

"Don't say I never did anything for you," Rush whispered, walking into the room and putting a finger to his lips.

"Huh?"

"Dude, shh. Just come here. I'm telling you, I'm doing you a favor."

Daniel set the guitar down and walked over to the doorway, looking out to see Kaitlyn sitting on the couch with Sketch, playing video games. Daniel looked up at Rush in surprise, and Rush placed a conspiratorial hand on his shoulder.

"Yep," Rush murmured so that only Daniel could hear him. "*There* you go. Now, follow my lead."

Daniel just looked at him.

"Dude, just do it, OK? I got your back," Rush whispered, raising his eyebrows at him, waiting for Daniel to agree to the plan, such as it was.

Daniel finally nodded, and Rush walked out to the couch, sitting down next to Sketch. Daniel frowned in confusion, but Rush immediately turned and looked in his direction, pretending just to notice him.

"Oh, hey, Daniel," Rush said. "You taking a break?"

"Uh... yeah," Daniel said.

"Sweet. You wanna come play *HRT Alpha* with us?"

"Um... sure," Daniel said, smiling at Kaitlyn, who had turned and grinned brightly at him when Rush had announced his presence.

"Cool. Hey, Sketch, come slide over here so there's room on the end for Daniel."

Sketch dutifully slid over, and Kaitlyn followed him to make room for Daniel next to her.

"Kaitlyn," Rush said, "you think you can show Daniel how to play?"

"Oh! Sure!" Kaitlyn said cheerfully.

Rush nudged Sketch, who handed his controller over to Daniel, happy enough just to sit next to Rush and watch while Daniel did his best to follow Kaitlyn's directions.

The four of them played several games in a row, switching the controllers around between matches so everyone could play. It took two more games before Kaitlyn finally got her first kill—on Daniel, as it happened. Sketch crowed in his seat and turned to give her a high five.

"You got a kill! Hey Rush, she got a kill! Give her a gamer tag!"

"Oh, hey—" Rush almost admitted that giving someone a gamer tag on their first kill wasn't really a thing before he looked down and saw Sketch's expression, realizing all at once just how much that rite of passage had meant to him. "You're absolutely right!" he continued smoothly.

"What's her tag, Rush?" Sketch asked, his eyes bright with excitement.

"Well, let's see..." Rush said, making a show of it. "She's good at fixing things..." He rubbed his thumb and forefinger along his chin, looking at her thoughtfully.

"What was the name of that place you said you worked?" he finally asked.

"The G&G?" she asked.

"Yeah, but the whole thing. Gadgets or something?"

"The Gears and Gadgets Repair Shop."

"Gears!" Rush said. "There we go. That's totally it. In honor of your first *HRT Alpha* player kill, I hereby dub thee, 'Gears.'"

"Awesome!" Kaitlyn said, doing a little dance where she sat. Sketch laughed and grinned from ear to ear.

It was three games after that before Daniel finally got a kill of his own, this time on Sketch. Sketch crowed again in delight and looked over at Rush expectantly, who was ready for it this time, having had more than thirty minutes to think of the perfect gamer tag for Daniel.

"Disco," he pronounced immediately.

Sketch laughed while Daniel scrunched up his face and raised a skeptical eyebrow.

"You want me to come up with something else, maybe, Mr. Stayin' Alive?" Rush asked, grinning wickedly. It took Daniel only a moment to consider his options.

"Disco, it is," Daniel agreed.

Rush nodded, smirking, and started up another game.

20
INSTRUCTOR REPORT

How are they doing?"

"The initial indications are even stronger than I could have hoped. Roman Jackson—who calls himself 'Sketch' now, by the way—is incredibly advanced. I believe he can already do what we need him to do, without any further training."

"Well, that's one at least. And the other?"

"Daniel shows definite signs of higher order processing as well. I would like to work with him on accessing his unconscious knowledge more directly, but he clearly has the potential to move in that direction. He will also need to practice singing in front of others. We can not afford for him to suffer from shyness when it comes time to bring the group together."

"Good. You've reviewed the workshop?"

"Yes, it should be more than sufficient for the morning, but I will need the martial arts expert in the afternoon."

"He's already in transit."

"Excellent! Then I believe we are fully prepared for tomorrow.

I have been exceedingly pleased with our initial results. Hopefully, the test has been equally successful in identifying the others."

"If it hasn't, our careers are going straight into the toilet."

"If it has not, Colonel, our careers will be the least of our problems."

21
WORKSHOP

In the morning, after breakfast, Miss Williams escorted Kaitlyn out of the building, explaining that her session with Ammu would be held in the maintenance shop, where Kaitlyn would have access to tools and parts and the like.

"How have you been enjoying your stay so far?" Miss Williams asked as they walked. The weather being clear, she had chosen to take the long way around, leading Kaitlyn out through the front doors of the lodge and following a pathway that ran through a well-manicured garden.

"Oh, it's been great!" Kaitlyn exclaimed. "I called Grandma Maggie yesterday right before dinner. Thank you for the telephone, by the way. She said everyone at the new place has been wonderful."

Miss Williams smiled. "I'm so glad. You were taking very good care of her, you know. You should be proud of the job you were doing, but I understand why you were concerned about her."

"I didn't like that she was forgetting to eat when I wasn't there,"

Kaitlyn admitted. "But she's eating now! When I called, she said she was having pot roast! And garlic mashed potatoes! She loves garlic mashed potatoes."

Miss Williams laughed. "And what about the other students?" she asked. "Nobody's giving you a hard time, I hope?"

"Oh, no! I played *HRT Alpha* with Rush and Sketch and Daniel last night. It was really fun! I killed Sketch a few times, and I killed Daniel a whole bunch! I couldn't kill Rush though. Did you know he had a chance to get on a pro team this summer?"

"Oh, really?" Miss Williams asked, clearly surprised.

"Yeah. He had to give it up to come here. His dad made him, since it'll look good for college."

"I see," Miss Williams said thoughtfully.

"Oh, gosh! Don't tell him I told you, OK? I don't know if I was supposed to. I just don't want anyone to be upset if he seems unhappy. It's not his fault. He's really nice if you get to know him."

"I promise, Kaitlyn, no one is upset with any of you. We're *very* glad you're here, and I'm hoping to get to know you all much better! Remember, I'll be working with everyone else together today while you're working with Ammu, so be sure to come straight back and join us when you're done, all right?"

"OK," Kaitlyn agreed. During breakfast, Miss Williams had shown them a small classroom that had been set up in one section of the big conference room off the main lounge, where she said they would be working on teamwork and leadership skills.

"And we're here!" Miss Williams announced.

The maintenance shop matched the design of the lodge but was just one story. It sat well away from the main building on an extension of the long driveway, with three large, garage-type doors on the front, all painted dark green, and with a normal door on the far end. The middle garage door was wide open, and Miss Williams walked through it, followed closely by Kaitlyn.

"Hello," Miss Williams called out. "Professor?"

"Yes, yes! Over here. Welcome!" Ammu replied, waving to them from the far corner of the garage as their eyes adjusted to the interior lighting.

"Wow! Nice!" Kaitlyn exclaimed.

"Do you approve, then?" Ammu asked. "You will have what you need here?"

"Oh, definitely!"

The inside of the building consisted of a concrete floor and three vehicle bays. The bay on the right held three lawn mowers, with a variety of trimmers and ladders hanging neatly along the right-hand wall. The center bay contained a large, solid table with several industrial-looking stools scattered around it, and the left-hand bay housed a well-stocked work area, designed for woodworking as well as mechanical maintenance.

A long work bench ran the full length of the left-hand wall and then turned the corner to run along the back edge of the left and center bays. The bench housed a high-end table saw, and Kaitlyn recognized a drill press and a lathe as well. Other than a few standing machines, the middle of the left-hand bay had been left open, with four saw horses stacked along the edge, obviously designed to allow the maintenance crew to work on larger projects there.

"May I?" Kaitlyn asked, pointing toward several closed cabinets, hanging both above and below the workbench.

"Please!" Ammu said.

"I'm going to leave you two at it, then," Miss Williams announced, smiling over Kaitlyn's enthusiasm.

"OK. Thanks, Miss Williams!" Kaitlyn called out, her voice muffled by the cabinet that her head was already buried in.

"It's Christina!" she called back. "I told you, call me Christina!"

"Thanks, Christina!" Kaitlyn said, pulling her head out of the cabinet and grinning before turning and plunging back in, opening various drawers and cubbyholes and oohing and aahing over their contents.

As Christina started up the driveway, she heard Ammu begin to speak.

"Throughout human history," he was saying, "there have been a select few among every generation who have been revered for their abilities..."

"OK, guys. This morning we're going to talk about what it means to be a team."

The classroom held six chairs, arranged in a semi-circle, all facing a whiteboard in the back of the room, where Christina stood now. Rush and Sketch sat in the middle, with Mackenzie on Sketch's other side and Daniel next to Rush. Sam slouched in her seat next to Mackenzie and rolled her eyes.

"I myself have always found," Christina continued, looking directly at Sam, "that being able to express one's concerns productively is critical to a team's success. You look skeptical, Samantha. I'd like to hear why."

"Sorry," Sam said, sighing and sitting marginally straighter in her chair.

"No, no. I mean it," Christina assured her. "That's exactly my point, in fact. I would never ask for your viewpoint if I didn't want you to express it. That's not direct communication.

"You rolled your eyes a moment ago, which implies disagreement or skepticism. My primary goal is to make sure we can all share our viewpoints openly and honestly, without reprisals and without ridicule. I realize that will take some time to establish, especially when we're all still getting to know each other, but the only way to get there is to begin.

"So please, Samantha, tell me why you rolled your eyes."

"Teams are stupid," Sam said, shrugging.

At this, Mackenzie rolled *her* eyes.

"Wow, OK," Christina said, grinning wryly. "I see I'm going to have my work cut out for me. Samantha first, and then Mackenzie. Let's *talk* to each other. Samantha, why do you think teams are stupid?"

"Because they *are*," she answered. "One person is always the best at whatever you have to do, so either that person just ends up doing all of it, which makes having a team useless, or they *don't* do all of it, and then the other people bring your grade down."

"I take it that has been your experience of teamwork in school projects?"

"Uh... *yeah*," Sam said, raising her eyebrows for emphasis.

"OK, Sam, I hear you, and I understand why you feel that way. Mackenzie, I take it from your own reaction that you have a different perspective on teamwork. Can you tell us about your own experience?"

"Teammates watch each other's backs," Mackenzie said immediately. "You can't be everywhere at once. Teams let you get things done in different places at the same time. Even if you don't all have the same skill level, everyone can do *something*. The whole point of a team is that you don't have to do everything yourself."

"Sure, if you don't mind it being done *badly*," Sam shot back.

"Mackenzie," Christina said, quickly heading off any reply, "can you give us, perhaps, a specific example of a team that you have found helpful?"

"My family," Mackenzie replied easily. "My dad's always back and forth on deployments, so we have to get things done at home without him. We share chores like cooking and cleaning and stuff, so that it all gets done. My youngest sister is only nine, but she can set the table, wipe down the counters, things like that. Everyone helps according to what they can do, so nobody has to do everything."

"It sounds to me like those are two very different kinds of teams, with two very different experiences," Christina said when Mackenzie had finished. "I think one important take-away here is that even a simple word like 'team' can mean different things to different people."

Christina wrote 'school team projects' and 'family team chores' on the left side of the whiteboard.

"What other examples of teams can you think of?" She asked, addressing the question to everyone.

"Video games!" Sketch exclaimed.

"OK, tell me about video games," Christina said, smiling. "What's a video game team like?"

"Like, if there's two doors in a room, Rush can watch one door, and I can watch the other one. Then nobody can surprise us."

"That's definitely an example of teamwork," Christina agreed, and she added 'video game teams' to the list on the board. "Rush? Do you have anything to add to that, as our resident gaming expert?"

"It's like Sketch said," Rush responded. "You get each other's backs. But I think it's different from the other two things."

"OK, good! How is it different?" Christina asked.

"Well, it's like Mackenzie said, where you need your team because you can't be everywhere at once, but at the same time it's really like Sam said too, because if some people can't pull their weight, the team's gonna lose." He looked over at Sam, leaning forward a bit to catch her eye across Sketch and Mackenzie, acknowledging her contribution.

He's talking about me, Sam thought angrily. *He thinks I'm not good enough to be here.*

"Daniel?" Christina asked. "How about you? Do you have a different team example? It's OK if you don't have anything to add right now. I'm not trying to put you on the spot. I just want to get as many different perspectives as we can."

"A band," Daniel said quietly. "Or a symphony, for that matter. Or a choir."

"A *band*," Christina said, obviously pleased. "Yes! That's an excellent example. Tell me about teamwork in a band."

"Well, like Rush and Sam both said, everyone has to do their part, but every part definitely adds something important. Nobody can play a whole symphony by themselves. You need everyone, playing separately but together, at the same time, and then when you listen to it, even though you can hear all the individual pieces, together it's still so much *bigger* than that, somehow, like a kind of magic..."

Daniel fell silent, a little embarrassed, but Christina smiled at him. On the left side of the board, she wrote 'band/symphony/choir,' and on the empty right side, she wrote, in all capital letters: 'BIGGER - LIKE MAGIC.'

Back in the workshop, Kaitlyn and Ammu sat next to each other at the table in the center bay, a stack of oversized papers sitting off to one side.

Ammu had begun the morning by asking Kaitlyn to fix a simple table fan. In just a few short minutes, she had taken apart the entire mechanism, twisting and turning the pieces this way and that until she had located the problem: a thin wire that had broken away from the motor assembly. She had fixed the connection in no time, reassembling the device and presenting it to Ammu proudly.

Although he had provided her with several technical drawings of the fan's inner workings, Kaitlyn had not consulted any of them. Now, Ammu placed one of those drawings on the table in front of them, where they could look at it together.

"This first illustration is an external multiview of the fan. As you can see, it shows us what the fan looks like, but only from the outside. We can see the front view here, and the side, and the top." He pointed to each view in turn.

"Now," he asked, "how much does this drawing help us to know how the fan works?"

"Hardly at all," Kaitlyn said, frowning. "It only shows what the outside is supposed to look like. It doesn't show us anything about the internal mechanism."

"Good! Now, look at this one."

He set the first drawing aside and pulled out a new one. This one was drawn at an angle showing part of the back of the fan, part of the right side, and part of the top all at once. Unlike the first print, which had been three separate drawings, this one showed a single view. In it, a significant piece of the back appeared to be missing, leaving the motor visible.

"Oh, hey, that's neat!" Kaitlyn exclaimed. "You can see the motor right through the casing!"

"Yes!" Ammu agreed. "Very 'neat' indeed! This is a cut-away view, in which the mechanism is drawn as though some of the outer casing had been literally cut away. Now, how much does this one help us to know how the fan works?"

Kaitlyn frowned again and chewed at the inside of her cheek, thinking it over.

"It's better," she said finally, "but it still tells us more about how the motor sits inside the fan—like, where it goes—than it does about how the motor actually works."

"Very good, Kaitlyn. I agree!" Ammu said, nodding his head, and Kaitlyn smiled at him. "Now, what about *this* one, hmm?"

With a bit of a flourish, Ammu unrolled a third diagram, and this time Kaitlyn caught her breath.

"Oh!" she exclaimed. "That's amazing!"

"This one," Ammu said, smiling at her reaction, "is called an exploded-view drawing. It is called this, as you can see, because it is drawn as though the entire fan had been exploded apart, but with each of its pieces remaining completely intact, of course!"

Kaitlyn pored over the lines of the drawing, which showed every screw and bolt and wire suspended in midair, oriented properly relative to each other, but with a bit of space between each one, so that she could see from the drawing exactly how every single part fit together with every other one.

"It's beautiful!" she exclaimed.

"Again, I agree," Ammu said. "An illustration of this quality is, unfortunately, relatively rare. It takes great skill to represent the inner workings of a mechanical object in such a clear, and at the same time such a detailed, way."

Kaitlyn couldn't take her eyes off the drawing. It seemed as though someone had reached into her mind and drawn the exact way she saw the fan, without her ever having known that this was what she was seeing until it was right here, laid out in front of her.

"*Now*," Ammu said, clearly sensing her excitement, "would you say that this drawing can help us understand how the fan works?"

"Obviously!" Kaitlyn answered immediately.

"Obviously," Ammu agreed. "Good. Now that you have seen and understood this type of drawing for an object with which you are familiar, I would like to show you some more such drawings, to see whether you can identify them, OK?"

"Sure!" Kaitlyn said. She had been nervous at first about her time with Ammu, but now she was tingling with excitement as he unfurled another drawing.

"A car stereo!" she exclaimed without any hesitation.

"Good!" Ammu said. "And this one?"

"A computer printer!"

"Yes! And this one?"

"A cuckoo clock!" Kaitlyn said, laughing.

"Excellent!" Ammu exclaimed. "Yes! A cuckoo clock!"

Kaitlyn looked up at him with bright, shining eyes. She felt as though his drawings were opening up a whole new world. With drawings like these, she could do more than just fix things—she could build anything from scratch, absolutely anything at all.

"OK," Ammu said, his expression growing more serious. "Next, I am going to show you several pictures of things, and I want you to see whether you can, in your mind, create for yourself a drawing like these for each one. Do not worry. There is no need to draw them on paper." He laughed at her horrified expression, and then again at her relief over his reassurance. "I just want you to see them in your mind. Are you ready?"

"But how can I do that if I've never seen what's inside it?" she asked.

"An excellent question! Your engineering skill is a pathway, as I have said. It is *how* your unconscious mind speaks to your conscious awareness. But what your unconscious mind *knows*, this is your special affinity. Clear your mind, and trust the insights that come to you. You know far more than you think."

"OK," Kaitlyn said. "I'll try." She took a deep breath and nodded, indicating that she was ready.

The first pictures were of simple things: a tape dispenser, a hand-held egg beater, a light bulb. With each new photo, Kaitlyn discovered that she could, in fact, see the diagram that corresponded to it. And the more she focused, the more embellished the plans became, adding various twists and swirls of light to indicate the movement of each part within the whole—and its essential purpose.

Ammu moved on to more complex things, and still the images came to her. A blender. A transistor radio. An electric winch. As the machines grew more complex, the very nature of the diagrams transformed, becoming more symbolic than literal, representing connections and interactions, until all at once she began to see the underlying flows of energy and motion that signified each one.

Almost as though she were in a trance, they poured forth to her now, unbidden, forming in her mind without any effort at all. A dishwasher, a car engine, a solar panel, a gryphon.

What???

She blinked and jerked her head, startled, but Ammu was beaming at her, a drawing of a mythological creature lying on the table in front of him: a lion's body with the head and wings of an eagle. For just a split second, she had seen...

"You saw it!" Ammu crowed. "For just a moment! I know it! I could see it in your eyes!"

He was right, she *had* seen something, but she had no idea what to make of it—a circle of complex runes and lines, glowing in the air before her with perfect clarity for just a moment, until the very shock of seeing it had caused it to disappear.

22
RING

"Everything OK?" Mackenzie asked. She and Kaitlyn were sitting together for lunch, Sam having grabbed a sandwich and headed off to a table by herself.

"Huh? Oh, yeah. Fine," Kaitlyn said, offering Mackenzie a quick smile and almost immediately looking lost in thought again.

"How'd it go with Ammu?" Mackenzie tried to keep her voice casual. As her own session loomed closer, she was starting to feel a bit nervous herself, even though she never would have admitted it.

"Good, I think?" Kaitlyn replied, her voice somewhat distant. "Kinda strange. I'm not sure I'm really supposed to talk about it."

Mackenzie frowned, her eyes narrowing dangerously.

"He didn't get handsy with you, did he?"

"What? *No!*" Kaitlyn blurted out. "Oh my gosh, no! Ammu would never!" At the very idea of it, Kaitlyn started laughing.

"OK," Mackenzie said, mollified. "Just checking. You're acting like you saw a ghost or something."

"No. No, I..." Kaitlyn grinned wryly. "I just have an overactive imagination sometimes."

"But nothing bad happened?" Mackenzie almost winced just hearing herself ask. She wanted to believe she was only looking out for Kaitlyn, but she knew there was more to it than that. She liked Ammu, but he seemed mysterious somehow, in a way Mackenzie couldn't quite put her finger on, and as far as she was concerned that made him unpredictable.

"No," Kaitlyn said, smiling now. "Definitely nothing bad. But what happened with you guys while I was gone? Why's Sam so upset?"

"Who knows?" Mackenzie said, shrugging. "Does she even need a reason? I don't think she likes the idea of having to work with anybody else. Like she thinks we're beneath her or something."

Kaitlyn pursed her lips as though she were thinking about it, but in the end she didn't comment either way, taking another bite of her sandwich instead. Continuing to eat in silence, they both watched as Ammu came into the main hall, walked directly up to Sam, spoke with her for a brief moment, and then led her out toward the new classroom, just the two of them. Alone.

"Oh, now this... this will not do at all," Ammu said as they walked into the classroom together. He looked back and forth between the chairs and the whiteboard with obvious disapproval. "Is this how you were sitting all morning?"

"Yeah," Sam acknowledged, shrugging. "So?"

"No, no. This... *this* is how disconnected we have become from the unconscious mind," he said. "Look! The seating has been arranged so the chairs have their backs to the door. If you sit here, you have to turn all the way around to see anyone coming in." He sat in one of the two center chairs and turned his neck and shoulders far enough to face the door, demonstrating.

"You see?" he asked, but Sam just shrugged again.

"The unconscious mind hates this arrangement," Ammu declared. "It allows the unknown to approach from behind."

He got back up and began pulling the chairs over to one side of the room, one by one.

"The unconscious mind, you know, is actually very, very old," he said as he worked. "It is only recently in our evolutionary history that the rational human mind has become so advanced. The unconscious mind has been a part of us for much, *much* longer, protecting us by watching for threats, and helping us by scanning the environment for food and other opportunities to enhance our chance of survival."

Once he had moved all the chairs out of the way, Ammu wheeled the whiteboard over to one side of the space, placing it with its back to the temporary partition that had been drawn across the room to section it off from the rest of the large conference space.

"As modern human beings," he continued, "we train our rational minds from birth to filter out many messages from the unconscious mind. When we are asked as children to enter a dark basement, we become frightened. The unconscious mind is signaling us to be cautious. We must tell ourselves, 'There is nothing to be scared of. It is just a basement.'

"We learn to ignore these signals so completely as adults that we can walk into our basements without any hesitation, but try to walk into someone *else's* dark basement, and hopefully you will find yourself on alert all over again."

"Why 'hopefully'?" Sam asked. "Why would we want to be scared of imaginary monsters in somebody's basement? Nothing personal, but that seems kind of stupid." She continued to watch him as he set about rearranging the chairs to face the whiteboard in its new position. He paused for a moment and looked at her directly.

"Yes! That is the question! Why 'hopefully' indeed! If we spend so much of our lives learning to ignore the impulses of the unconscious mind, why would we want to hear them again? Yes! Good, Samantha!"

Sam knitted her eyebrows together in confusion. She was not used to adults praising her for calling them stupid.

"Because the unconscious mind is *not* stupid," he explained. "In fact, it is highly intelligent in its own right, and in a very different way than the rational mind. When we can merge the two intentionally, learning to hear what our unconscious mind is telling us and filtering out only that which we *decide* to filter out, that is when we begin to reach our full potential."

"There," he proclaimed. "Much better. Now we can sit more comfortably." He sat again in one of the two center chairs, and this time his left side was to the door instead of his back. When Sam sat down, purposefully leaving a chair between them, she realized that the door was now well within her peripheral vision. She didn't like to admit it, not even to herself, but he was right. This position *was* more comfortable.

"So," he said. "Samantha. I believe that the test has done precisely what it was designed to do. Your scores on the IAB indicate that your conscious and unconscious minds are, in fact, communicating to a significant degree, whether you realize it or not. It might take us some time to identify the pathway by which this is occurring most directly, but I do believe that such a pathway exists for you, and I remain dedicated to discovering it."

He paused, as though waiting for some kind of reply.

What am I supposed to say to that? she thought to herself. *Am I supposed to tell you I think you're wasting your time? That I can't have a very good pathway if everyone else instantly knew what theirs was and I have absolutely no idea? That even if you find it, I'm probably going to be so far behind in learning to use it that you're going to send me home eventually anyway?*

"OK," was all she said.

"Good. I'm sure you spent some time last night thinking about hobbies and interests and the like. Did anything in particular occur to you?"

"Not really," she admitted. "I do well in school. That's the only thing I can think of that I'm good at, but that's not unconscious. That's a formula. I read the assignments. I do all the homework. I study before the tests, and I do well on them. That's it. There's nothing unusual about it. I'm just better at it than most people."

"Anything people do that makes them stand out can be an indication of a deeper talent, Samantha. If you don't have a particular subject that fascinates you or a particular hobby you find engaging, then perhaps you have noticed that you respond in certain situations to what people might call a 'gut feeling' rather than relying upon your intellect. Are you aware of making any decisions in your day-to-day life based on such an impulse?"

Sam could only think of two gut feelings she had ever had in her life, and they had both been completely and utterly worthless. *This whole program is so stupid. I can't believe I signed up for this—trapped all summer with this artsy-fartsy mumbo-jumbo about the unconscious mind and nothing to do for like a hundred miles in every direction and no Internet. What kind of a quack is this guy?*

"What are you a professor of?" she asked out loud, ignoring his question.

"Pardon me?"

"Christina called you 'Professor Mubarak.' What are you a professor of?"

"I see," Ammu said. "I hold PhDs in both archaeology and neuroscience."

"That's a strange combination," Sam commented.

"It is," Ammu agreed. He said nothing else, simply watching

her, but he showed no sign of being even the least bit perturbed about either her question or her commentary. There was an aura of patience about him, a sense that he was merely taking in the world as it came, without any judgment whatsoever, that Sam found both disconcerting and compelling at the same time.

"I can only think of two gut feelings I've ever had. I mean ever," she finally said.

"Go on," Ammu said, his demeanor not changing in the slightest.

"My dad was going to let me out of school the day of the test, but I felt like I should take it, so I did. And then when the letter came from the ICIC, I felt like I should come here, so I did that, too. But then the feelings went away. The first one went away before I took the test, and the second one went away before I left to come here. So I've only had two gut feelings in my whole life, and as far as I can tell they were both wrong, so that seems pretty useless."

"On the contrary," Ammu said, his eyes bright with excitement, "I find it fascinating that you have had only two gut feelings and they both involved this program. I do not believe that to be a coincidence."

"Just because your unconscious mind wants something to have meaning doesn't mean it does," Sam replied. "As a neuroscientist, you should know that."

"Samantha—" Ammu started, his voice gentle, but just then Christina and the other students started filing in for their afternoon class.

"Just because your conscious mind believes there is no connection, does not mean that is true either," he finished, smiling kindly. "To be continued, hmm?"

But Sam said nothing, staring at him coldly as he got up to leave, and when the other students sat down, eying her warily, they left the seat next to her empty.

When Mackenzie arrived at the exercise room, she was eager to size up the competition. She didn't know what she had been expecting, but it certainly wasn't the young black man with the handsome smile, mischievous eyes, and well-muscled body who stood in the center of a Muay Thai ring that had not been there before. He stared back at her with an expression that suggested he was equally surprised to find himself facing a leggy, blond teenage girl.

"Ah, good! I see you have already met," Ammu said, walking in behind Mackenzie.

"Not exactly," Mackenzie replied.

"Staff Sergeant Kyle Miller, at your service," the young man said smoothly, looking back and forth between Mackenzie and Ammu as though he were not yet sure which of them he was supposed to be addressing.

"I am Professor Amr Mubarak," Ammu said, smiling warmly, "but you may call me 'Ammu.' And this is our young protégée, Miss Mackenzie Gray."

"Sir," he said, nodding at Ammu, and then, "Miss Gray," nodding at Mackenzie in turn.

"It's OK," Mackenzie said. "I'm a military brat. You can call me 'Gray' if you want. I'm used to it."

"All right, Gray," he replied easily. "And you can call me 'Staff Sergeant.'" He said it with a hint of a smirk, and Mackenzie grinned at him wryly, rolling her eyes.

"As I am sure you have surmised, Mackenzie, Staff Sergeant Miller is to be your sparring partner this afternoon. Remember, the point of the exercise is not to assess your skill in martial arts, but rather to identify the way in which you may be using your unconscious mind to your advantage in the ring. So do not try to showcase your talent by doing anything unusual on my account. Simply do what you would normally do."

"Got it," Mackenzie said.

"Staff Sergeant Miller," Ammu continued, turning his attention to the young man, "while you are engaged in sparring this afternoon, I would like you to watch for anything that might seem unusual about Mackenzie's fighting style. I am not a martial arts expert, so I am counting on you to notice and draw my attention to her particular nuances."

"Roger that," he said, nodding once for emphasis.

Mackenzie unzipped her sweatshirt, revealing a sleeveless black sports top underneath. She wore no jewelry, but she had a colorful, woven armband tied around each of her upper arms. She donned the sparring mask and gloves that had been provided, while her opponent did the same, and then she climbed over the top of the ropes and into the ring.

"When you are ready," Ammu said.

"Do you mind?" Mackenzie asked the staff sergeant.

"By all means." He gestured to her broadly with one hand, granting her the permission she sought.

Mackenzie placed her right hand on the top rope and began to walk around the perimeter of the ring, keeping her hand on the rope at all times and bowing silently for a few moments in each corner. When she had completed the circle, she started into a series of ritual, dancelike movements. Miller did not join her, and Ammu looked to him for an explanation.

"It's an ancient practice," he explained. "All traditional Muay Thai fights begin with a blessing of the ring, followed by the *wai kru ram muay*. That's what she's doing now. It honors the fighter's school and teacher, and it centers the fighter and bring blessings to her, as well as protecting her against negative energies. Or so they say. The armbands you see her wearing—her *prajioud*—those honor her connection to her family."

"Fascinating!" Ammu exclaimed. "And why do you not do the same?"

"To be perfectly honest, Doc, I'm used to a more western approach," Miller answered, looking a bit embarrassed. "I don't have a *wai kru ram muay* of my own. Each one is specific to its school, its teacher, and to the fighter himself or herself. To perform it badly is a great dishonor. Since I didn't come up in the tradition, I don't do it. Most western fighters don't, at least the ones I know."

"I see," Ammu said, watching Mackenzie with a renewed intensity, clearly intrigued by what she was doing.

The dance continued for several minutes before finally coming to an end. Mackenzie walked calmly up to Miller, bowed—an acknowledgment which he returned in kind—and touched her gloved fists to his.

"Elbows to body only, OK?" he asked.

"Sure," she agreed. "Wouldn't want to mess up that pretty-boy face of yours."

"Nice of you to notice!" he quipped back.

They took a step away from each other and raised their gloves, beginning to circle. Mackenzie had been nervous about the idea of Ammu watching her, but the ritual of the *wai kru ram muay* helped her focus. She forgot about Ammu entirely as she watched her opponent, learning who he was and how he moved. Nothing existed outside the ring, and here, within it, she was in her element.

She waited for him to take an experimental jab, and she blocked it easily. He jabbed at her again, faster this time, and she took the blow to her midsection on purpose. She tightened her stomach muscles and turned slightly to the side so it would be no more than a glancing blow, using the force of her own twist to slam her knee into his gut. He spun away at the last second, sparing himself the full brunt of its force, and he danced backward a few steps, raising an appraising eyebrow at the move.

He closed again, this time aiming two quick blows at her center mass. But Mackenzie could tell he was pulling his punches, not wanting to hurt her, and she used it to her advantage. Instead of dodging or blocking the hits, she took them straight on and surprised him by throwing a right jab as fast and hard as she could at his jaw. He took the blow and danced back again, shaking it off, but it would have been a solid point in her favor if there had been a referee watching.

"Enjoy it, Gray. I won't underestimate you again," he said, his eyes locking onto hers with a new intensity. *Closer*, she thought, grinning at him slyly. *Closer... there!* She winked at him and simultaneously slammed her right knee into his left side. She would have scored on that one too, but he outweighed her by too many pounds—the blow didn't throw his balance despite landing squarely where she had intended it.

Miller laughed, but he was watching her like a hawk now.

"I bet that one usually works," he acknowledged.

"Wouldn't know," she answered. "You're the first guy I've ever used it on."

"Sure, I am." He laughed again, and she took advantage of the moment to fly at him with a flurry of knees, fists, and elbows, grinning wickedly all the while. He continued to dance away, letting her spend her energy on the attack while dodging the worst of it.

"Oh, you don't like that, do you?" he said, taunting her now. "You want me to just stand there and let you hit me. Well, I'm smarter than that, Gray. If you want to hit me, I'm going to make you work for it."

Her blows moved even faster in reply, and she could feel the energy between them changing now. He stopped trying to speak, focusing more intensely on the fight, and he dodged several blows before countering with a fast knee to her left side. She took it on purpose and threw another punch at his face. She was rewarded with another grunt from her opponent, but the knee had taken its toll, making her grimace in pain before she could mask it.

Miller didn't say a word. She knew she had hurt him, too; the only question was how much. They continued to trade blows, Mackenzie only taking his hits when she knew she could connect her own, but as the seconds ticked by, he was slowly gaining the advantage. With his extra height and reach and weight, his blows were hurting her more than hers were hurting him. She couldn't win this way, but she could make sure he didn't walk away from it easily, and she flew at him with a renewed vigor that had him dancing away again.

"Time!" he called. "Hey, easy. Time out!"

Mackenzie came to a halt and flashed him a mischievous grin.

"What's the matter?" she asked, her tone all innocence and sunshine. "Had enough already? We were just getting started."

"Doc," he said, ignoring her jibe, "I think I have something for you."

"Yes? Yes! Good!" Ammu said. "What did you see?" It was the first time Mackenzie had heard him sound even remotely troubled. He had obviously not expected their sparring to be so violent.

"Well, first of all, this wouldn't be considered a fair fight. She's very skilled—that much is clear—but I outweigh her by a good bit."

"Yeah, about that," Mackenzie interjected, trying not to grimace at the bruising she had taken to her left side. "Maybe cut back on the protein bars, huh?"

"I'll take that as a compliment."

They climbed out of the ring as he continued.

"Look, the point is she'd be winning if she were up against someone her own size. She hasn't taken a single blow she didn't want to, OK? Every time I connect, it's because she knows she can hit me back harder. The only problem she's facing is that harder is proportional here. The fraction of the punch she takes is still harder than what she can throw back."

Ammu looked to Mackenzie, but she only shrugged. It was certainly no fault of hers that a grown man in top physical condition outmatched her in strength and body mass, but that didn't mean she wanted to say it out loud.

"I fought her on my own terms, matching my upper body strength against hers, where I knew I could win eventually. I had to. *Because she knew everything I was going to do even as I did it.*"

He paused, giving Ammu a moment to let his words sink in while he locked eyes with Mackenzie again, this time with a level of respect he had not shown her before.

"If she were my size, or if I were her size for that matter, she would have beaten me soundly. She just... she just *knew* everything I was going to do."

"Fascinating!" Ammu exclaimed, his worry forgotten in his excitement. "Mackenzie, when you are fighting, are you aware of what Sergeant Miller is saying?"

"Staff Sergeant," she corrected him automatically, making Miller crack a grin. "And yes, sorry. I always know. I mean, not ahead of time. Like, I don't have any idea how the whole fight is going to play out. But in the moment, sure. I know where each punch or knee or elbow or kick is going to land."

"Doc, if I might suggest an experiment?" Miller offered.

"Yes? What sort of experiment?"

"I'd like to get back in the ring and see how things go if Mackenzie stops trying to hit me back and just tries to avoid getting hit."

"No!" Mackenzie said, more loudly than she had intended. "Look, no, OK? I don't get in the ring to dance. I get in the ring to fight. I'm not going to run away like a damn rabbit."

Ammu considered her quietly for a moment, while Miller just shrugged.

"Hey, it's your party. I'm not trying to crash it. I just wanted to see. I'm not sure I could hit you at all if you were only trying to dodge me, and I've never run into anyone I could say that about before. I just wanted to know if it was true."

He said this last bit sounding a little embarrassed, and Mackenzie found herself relenting. He didn't think she was scared to get hit. He just wanted to see if she was as good as he thought she was. Maybe she should give him the chance to find out...

"OK," she said, changing her mind. "Sure. Let's try it."

"Yeah?" Miller said, his face lighting up.

"Yeah," she repeated, climbing back into the ring. "I didn't knock out your hearing, did I? I know you took a couple solid blows to the head there."

Miller gave her a withering look and followed her. They came together in the center of the ring, bowed, tapped gloves, backed away a step, and entered a fighting stance.

This time, Mackenzie forced herself to adopt a defensive state of mind, anticipating his blows and dodging them without returning the hits. Miller started with two quick jabs that she avoided easily, blocking the first and sidestepping the second. His next blow was a knee to her ribs. She had to step away to avoid it, but she blocked the next punch while spinning back into his personal space, seeing easily where she could have elbowed him in the face if she had wanted to.

She grinned at him and backed up a step, allowing him to disengage and start again.

This time he came at her faster, in a flurry of fists and knees and elbows, but now it felt as though everything were happening in slow motion. She was already moving away from each blow in the very moment he began to throw it. Effortlessly. Mackenzie saw them all, each in turn, the inertia of one flowing smoothly into another, always limited by the ways in which the human body can move.

She stopped taking any steps away from him at all, blocking each new blow as it came until finally, unable to help herself, she caught a punch neatly under her arm, locked his elbow into a submission hold, and forced him down to the mat where she lay on top of him for a moment, her right shoulder driving into his chest, her face mere inches from his own, before she finally moved to let him up, both of them breathing heavily from the speed of their exertions.

As Miller stood up, he stared at her in awe.

"How did you learn to do that?" he asked, his chest rising and falling dramatically with each breath. "I've never seen anything like it! Can you teach me?"

"That," Ammu interjected quietly, "is our ultimate goal, Staff Sergeant Miller."

Mackenzie only smiled.

"So, this morning we were talking about teamwork."

Christina was standing near the blackboard in its new orientation, with her side to the door, the students of the ICIC arrayed in the chairs in front of her. She turned toward the board and underlined the last thing she had written down: 'BIGGER - LIKE MAGIC.'

"We said that sometimes, given the right circumstances, a team can become greater than the mere sum of its parts, able to accomplish things together that they could never accomplish alone. This afternoon, I'd like to focus on the conditions that can bring this about. What is needed to bring such a team together? Anyone?"

Sam sat closest to the door, frowning, her shoulders slouched low in her chair, her arms crossed defiantly in front of her chest, the seat next to her standing empty. No one said a thing.

"Daniel?" Christina finally asked after several painful moments of silence. "You mentioned this morning that a band can be this kind of team. What makes a band become something bigger than just a handful of musicians?"

Daniel shrugged, embarrassed to be the center of attention, but Christina smiled and waited, not ready to let him off the hook so easily.

"Well, they all have to know the music," Daniel offered.

"Good!" Christina exclaimed, obviously trying to sound encouraging. "What else?" She flipped the whiteboard over and drew a vertical line right down the middle of the new, clean side. On the left, she wrote: 'Know the Music.'

"They have to be decent musicians," Daniel said, warming up to the topic a little. "They can't just know the music, really. They have to be able to play it well."

"Excellent," Christina agreed, nodding, and she wrote 'Good Musicians' underneath 'Know the Music.'

"They have to play in the same key," Daniel said, more hesitantly now, "and with the same timing. But that's kind of obvious, I guess."

"No, no. That's very good," Christina said, writing these below the first two items on her list. "Anything else?"

"I don't know... they have to kind of... synch. You know? It's more than just timing. They have to be in the same groove, vibing the music together. They have to... like... *feel* it. Does that make sense?"

"Perfect sense," Christina confirmed. "People who study teamwork have a name for it. They call it 'synergy.'

"People have observed this phenomenon in many different kinds of teams, working under very different circumstances. A team of soldiers might start moving as a unit without any discernible signals between them, or a corporate team might start building on each other's ideas to come up with a whole new product design, or an advertising team might offer up a suggestion for a new slogan and somehow everyone knows immediately that this is the right slogan for the campaign.

"Although there does not seem to be any specific formula for creating a synergistic team, experts agree that certain factors are necessary for it to exist, and believe it or not, you have hit on several of them already with your band example."

Christina beamed at Daniel and turned back to the whiteboard. Next to 'Know the Music,' she wrote 'Expertise' on the right side of the board. Across from 'Good Musicians,' she wrote 'Proficiency.' For 'Key' and 'Meter,' she wrote 'Place' and 'Time.' Then, on the left side, she wrote 'Vibe/Groove,' and on the right side, she wrote 'Synergy.'

"For a synergistic team to form," she said, "the team must co-exist in space and time. This does not have to be literal. Teams can work together in virtual space, for example, and can contribute to a process at different times, but studies have shown that synergy appears much more consistently when a team is located together in the same physical space, collaborating simultaneously."

As long as they all have their own expertise, Sam thought bitterly. *As long as they're all at least marginally proficient and not pathetic losers who don't know what they're doing on the team in the first place.*

Sketch leaned forward and turned to stare straight at her. Sam had no way of knowing that out of the corner of his eye, Sketch had noticed a sudden change in the flames that zipped around her, or that he had seen them start to slow down, changing gradually from their usual white to a deep, indigo blue. All she knew was that he was staring at her, silently accusing her of not belonging there at all.

"What are you looking at?" she demanded. "You're not really a *team* with Rush, either, you know. There's no magical *synergy* there. He totally carries you on that stupid video game, and he only plays with you because he feels sorry for you."

"Samantha!" Christina exclaimed, even as Rush growled out, "What the hell is *your* problem?"

"Oh, please," Sam snapped back. "What are you going to do? *Ground* me from *summer* school? Are you going to take away my phone, too—the phone that doesn't even *work* here? Wait, I know, you're going to tell me I can't go out, right? In case you hadn't noticed, there's nowhere to go! I'll tell you what, I'm going to go *ground* myself to my room and pack my bags. Let me know when you're ready to do me the favor of kicking me out, OK? Thanks."

With that, Sam got up and stalked out of the room. Just as she had expected, not one person went running after her.

23
PENANCE

Sam hit her room with every intention of snatching up her bags, stuffing every last thing she had brought with her into them haphazardly, and then waiting defiantly for one angry adult or another to come drag her off to the airport. But she hadn't even finished hauling her suitcase out from the back of the closet when an overwhelming sense of *wrongness* threatened to suffocate her where she stood.

OMG, seriously? Now? NOW? Of all the worst possible times to show back up, you pick now???

There was no denying it. Her sense of destiny was back, and it was screaming at her, in no uncertain terms, that this was *not* the time to leave.

Really? she thought. *You couldn't have let me know this five minutes before I shot my mouth off and insulted the kid?*

She wasn't sure who she was talking to, exactly, but as she finally began to cool off, she discovered that she was starting to feel kind of bad about what she had said to Sketch. Sam had never had a brother or sister to fight with, but she imagined it probably felt a lot like this—intense rage, followed some time later by the warring emotions of sullen anger and halfhearted regret.

On the one hand, the little snot kind of deserved it for staring at her. On the other hand, though, she had to admit, now that she was thinking a little more clearly, that the look Sketch had given her might not have meant anything quite so accusing as she had made it out to be at the time.

I hate people, Sam thought to herself. *They're so freaking complicated.*

She retreated from the depths of the closet, leaving her suitcase where it was, and took a flying leap for the bed, twisting in the air to land on her back and folding her hands behind her head so she could think properly.

OK, so I feel like I shouldn't leave, but maybe that's just because I don't really want *to leave. Which is weird, because I do* want *to leave... don't I?*

But did she? Sam turned the idea over in her mind for a while, trying to feel it out, but she couldn't seem to wrap her head around it. She thought she wanted to leave, but then again, she felt somehow like she didn't. Eventually, without really intending to, she just gave up and fell asleep.

When she woke up again, it was dark outside her window, and she felt disoriented for a moment until her mental clock adjusted to the unexpected change. 9:47 p.m. Apparently, no one had come to cart her away, which meant they probably weren't going to. But was she disappointed? Or relieved?

Sam rolled onto her side and started idly running her fingers over the luxurious bed cover. If she was being truthful with herself, maybe she didn't really want to leave, after all. Maybe what she wanted was to be special, like everyone else at the ICIC, and to have a pathway of her own. Any pathway. A talent for gardening even. Or for skiing. Or blacksmithing. Or yodeling.

Well, maybe not yodeling.

Sam chuckled to herself. OK, she had to admit, things could be worse. She cheered herself up for a while by imagining all the strange and wonderful talents she was grateful *not* to have: raising leeches, roasting termites, lancing boils...

Somehow I always know exactly where to lance the boil so all the nasty pus just explodes out of it all at once!

Sam laughed and sat up. Honestly, she had been getting far too upset about not having a talent—

And there it was, the real reason she had snapped at Sketch. She wasn't angry. She was hurt. She wanted to have a talent, but she didn't. She felt left out, and ordinary, and boring, and she was taking it out on the kid.

Not cool, Sam. Not cool at all.

She didn't want to admit it, not even to herself, but she knew immediately that it was true. Even worse, she knew what she had to do about it. Sighing deeply, she swung her legs down to the floor and stood up. She was going to have to find the kid and apologize to him.

I freaking hate dealing with people, she thought to herself grimly. *I mean I really, seriously hate it.*

If Sam wondered where everybody was as she walked through her empty suite toward the hallway, her question was answered when she got to the guys' suite and found the door propped open.

She poked her head in to find Rush, Sketch, Daniel, and Kaitlyn all sitting on the couch, with Mackenzie sitting behind them on a chair she had pulled in from the kitchen, watching Rush and Kaitlyn play. All five pairs of eyes locked onto her immediately, making her wish she were just about anywhere else in the world, but she took a deep breath and stepped into the room anyway, her heart rising into her throat, her hands in her pockets to keep them from trembling noticeably.

"Hi," she said lamely.

"Hi, Sam!" Kaitlyn replied. Her voice was as cheerful as ever, but nobody else said a word. "You want to play?" Kaitlyn held her controller out toward Sam, but Rush was already protesting.

"She isn't invited," Rush growled.

"Come on, guys," Kaitlyn protested. "She was just upset."

"I'm sorry, Sketch," Sam said quietly. "I didn't mean what I said. Kaitlyn's right. I was just upset. But I shouldn't have taken it out on you."

"Her name's 'Gears,'" Sketch replied, his eyes watching her closely. The flames twirling around her were still a little bit blue, a little bit slow, but not like before. "And that's Disco," he continued, pointing to Daniel.

"OK," Sam agreed, not knowing what else to say. "I'm still sorry. Are we good? Or am I gonna have to do some kind of penance first?"

"Penance?" Sketch asked, looking at Rush.

"It's when you have to do something to make up for doing something bad. Like a punishment." Rush pretended to eye Sam suspiciously, but there was a hint of playfulness behind it. He and his gaming team blew up at each other on a fairly regular basis. As long as she was apologizing, everything was good in his book. "I'd make her earn it if I were you." He said this with a wink for Sketch, and Sketch grinned back at him.

"Get me some chips," he said to Sam, who rolled her eyes.

"OK, fine. What kind of chips?" Sam wandered over to the kitchen and opened the pantry door.

"Salt and vinegar."

"Ugh," Sam commented, but she took a bag of salt and vinegar chips out of the pantry and brought it to Sketch. She walked behind the couch to hand it to him so she wouldn't get in the way of the television, leaving her standing next to Mackenzie, who was watching her guardedly, her expression carefully neutral.

"Here," Sam said, handing Sketch the bag of chips. "Are we good now?"

"Yeah, we're good," Sketch said, grinning. As far as he was concerned, anyone who got mad and didn't try to beat him up was worth being friends with.

"Dude!" Rush exclaimed. "You can't let girls off that easy, bro! You're seriously going to let her off the hook for a lousy bag of chips?"

"I like chips," he said. He ripped the bag open and stuffed a handful in his mouth, and then he looked up at Rush, grinning while he chewed.

"Ugh. Fine," Rush said grudgingly. "But we're seriously going to have to work on that. You just blew a huge opportunity there, man."

Sketch just laughed and shrugged, throwing another handful of chips in his mouth while Kaitlyn giggled.

"You sure you don't want to play?" Sketch asked Mackenzie over his shoulder.

"No thanks," she replied. "I just want to watch you guys. I'm learning the maps this way."

"OK," Sketch said easily. "Sam? You want to play?"

"That's OK," Sam said. "I don't want to interrupt you guys."

"It's not like that," Kaitlyn assured her. "We're all taking turns."

"You can have all my turns," Daniel said. "I suck."

"You do not," Kaitlyn protested. "You're still just learning the game."

Sam looked at Sketch.

"He does kinda suck, Gears. Be honest," Sketch said.

"Sketch!" Kaitlyn objected, reaching past Daniel and threatening to swat his head.

"What? He does!" Sketch ducked under her pretend blow and laughed.

Kaitlyn put her controller down on the coffee table, got up, and grabbed another chair from the kitchen, shooing Sam out of the way so she could set it behind Daniel. Kaitlyn sat down on it and started rubbing Daniel's shoulders.

"Poor Disco," she cooed at him. Daniel leaned back and closed his eyes happily.

"Go ahead, Sam," Sketch said, picking up the controller and trying to hand it to her across Daniel's slouching body.

"How come I don't get a nickname?" Sam asked.

"You have to kill someone on the game first," Sketch explained.

"Oh." Sam sat next to Daniel on the couch and took the controller.

They played for another hour before they called it a night, but Sam never did get a kill. She could have killed Sketch a few times, but she always let him kill her instead. It was her silent way of making it up to him. As for Rush, he wasn't going to let her off the hook that easily. Every time he found her, he shot her in the face, just for good measure.

24
INSTRUCTOR REPORT

T ell me."

"Kaitlyn is much farther advanced than I had expected. Almost as advanced as Sketch, in her own way. She is extremely open to her potential."

"Potential isn't what we need. We need results. Can she do what she needs to do?"

"I believe so, yes. Only the attempt will prove the matter, of course, but she appears to be ready."

"Good. What about the other one?"

"I am certain that Mackenzie is able to access her unconscious mind through her martial arts. She is quite accomplished. The trainer you provided was excellent. He was able to show me the true nature of her ability."

"So glad you approve. And what was the nature of her ability, exactly?"

"'Exactly' might be too precise for my current understanding, but her instincts seem to provide her with spatial information. Once she began trying to dodge the instructor's blows, he was unable to hit her. I am convinced that she was able to see them in her mind before they happened."

"Fighting isn't what I need her for."

"I am aware of that. But her intuitive understanding of place will be critical to the process."

"Fine. Any problems I should be aware of?"

"Samantha is still struggling to recognize her pathway. It is taking its toll on her emotionally."

"We're not here to hold her piss-damn hand, Professor. I don't give a crap about her emotional well-being."

"Nonetheless, her emotional well-being is crucial to her ability. The unconscious mind is a powerful force in its own right. If her emotions are in turmoil, she will not be able to access her power. We must care about her feelings, whether or not it is within your usual experience to do so."

"You might have to care about her feelings, but I don't. I'm not the one working with her. Just find her talent or wash her out. We're getting closer. I don't want anyone here if they can't do it. It's just another security risk we don't need."

"I understand."

25
HRT Alpha

The next morning, after breakfast, they were all ushered into the large conference room just off the main lounge. The far right side was still walled off for the classroom, but the remaining area had been converted into a gaming center, apparently overnight. Six gaming systems were set up around the large space, each with an ergonomic leather chair, a console table, a wall-mounted LED monitor, and a top-of-the-line headset.

"We wanted you to be able to leave your own system in your suite," Ammu explained to Rush, "so we ordered six, rather than five. I apologize that we have not yet solved the Internet problem, but these machines have all been pre-loaded, off-site, with *HRT Alpha* and have been linked to each other locally."

"This is amazing! We can all play together!" Sketch exclaimed, and he threw himself into the chair next to the door, claiming that setup as his own. "Take that one, Rush!" he said, pointing to the one on his right.

Rush wandered into the room looking a little dazed. The total value of the equipment that surrounded him must have run into the thousands. If the ICIC was willing to put this much money into an entire gaming center just to test his abilities, it must really mean a lot to them. Well, *HRT Alpha* was his game. If they wanted a show, he'd give them a show.

"Let's do it!" he said to Sketch. He sat in the chair Sketch had saved for him, and they fired up their systems. Daniel and Kaitlyn took the two setups along the left wall, leaving Sam and Mackenzie to claim the two on the right. The back wall didn't have any consoles, just a few comfortable chairs so people could watch the gaming. Sam snickered—heaven forbid anybody's unconscious mind had to face away from the door.

Rush told Sketch how to set up his own account on the new console, and everyone else followed along. Sketch proudly claimed his gamer tag, and even Kaitlyn and Daniel logged in as Gears and Disco for fun. Rush set up a game while Sam went over the basic controls with Mackenzie, who hadn't actually played yet.

"I'm putting everyone else on the other team," Rush said, "since it's designed for teams of five. I'll take four bots with me."

"Excellent," Ammu acknowledged.

"Everybody ready?"

A chorus of agreement echoed back to him from around the room.

"OK. Here we go!"

Rush started the game, and they were transported to two different spawn points on the map, Rush on one side and everyone else on the other. The game began flashing its countdown: 10... 9... 8...

"The point of the game is to restore power to a city block by fixing three generators."

3... 2... 1... The game flashed 'Go!' on the screen, and Rush ran toward the closest building.

"See? This is a generator. Each team usually fixes the one in their own territory first, and then there's another one in the middle. You can't win until you fix all three." Rush stood at the first generator for a moment, and soon it lit up and glowed on the screen.

"When I take one of theirs, it will look on my screen like I fixed it—like I'm the good guy. But on theirs, it will look like I broke it—like I'm the bad guy. That way each team gets to play the good guys, and it makes the enemy team look like terrorists.

Ammu raised his eyebrows at this, but he made no comment.

"I'm not going to talk much since I only have bots on my team. So yell if you have any questions. The others can talk through their headsets, but for me there's no point."

"Of course," Ammu acknowledged.

Rush sprinted down a back alley. He figured the others would all be waiting for him in the center building, so he flanked around it instead, sneaking up on the one that the others had already taken. He found Sketch, Disco, and Gears guarding it, and he grinned. That was better strategy than he had been expecting, which only made for a better demonstration of his skills. Mentally, he reevaluated the team. Sam and Mac would try to take the center building together. As soon as he was done here, he would circle back for them.

He took Sketch out with a leaping headshot; the kid had been playing more than the others, which made him the biggest threat. As soon as the kill registered, Rush flipped around toward Gears and dropped to the ground, letting her bullets fly harmlessly over his head as he took her out with a quick burst to her center mass. He rolled left before Disco could adjust, jumped up and over a pile of sandbags, landed on Disco's back and stabbed him to death.

He ran to the generator and turned it on.

One to go.

"That was horrible," Gears said, laughing.

"Sorry." Disco sighed into his headset.

"No, I mean me!"

"Nah, don't feel bad," Sketch chimed in, "Rush is really good. I doubt any of us can kill him."

"I can kill him," Mac said.

"Good luck," Sketch said. "'Cause he's coming your way."

Their screens flashed a message. *The north generator has been damaged.* Rush had activated the generator in their base. But right afterward, the screen flashed again. *The central generator has been repaired.*

"Nice!" Sketch shouted to Sam and Mac.

"Good job!" Gears added.

"Don't get excited yet. There wasn't anybody here. We just turned it on."

Sam's words were cut off by the sound of gunfire, followed by another screen flash. *Rush has killed Mac,* and then, *Rush has killed Sam.*

"See?" Sketch giggled.

Gears has killed Bot 4. Gears has killed Bot 1.

"It's not over yet," Mac said, her voice tight with concentration.

"Nope!" Gears shouted. *The south generator has been repaired,* flashed just before the words, *The central generator has been damaged.* "I got this one back just in time, but it's not going to last. I need backup."

"I'm comin'!" Sketch shouted.

"On it!" Mac confirmed.

"Wait!" Sam shouted to Mac, who had been about to run around a corner ahead of her.

"I have to get to—" Mac started to reply, but then *Rush killed Mac* popped up on the screen. "Damn, he was waiting for me."

"Thus, my suggestion to wait," Sam replied. "Stay where you spawn. Let's take the north generator back together."

"OK," Mac agreed, somewhat grudgingly. "But hurry. If we don't get something else back soon, he's going to win."

"We have a minute. Trust me," Sam replied. She ran up on Mac's position, and they entered the north building together.

Mac has killed Bot 2. Sam has killed Bot 3.

The north generator has been repaired.

"Yes!" Sketch shouted.

Rush has killed Sketch.

"No!" he shouted, and everyone laughed, even Sketch.

Rush has killed Gears. Rush has killed Disco. The south generator has been damaged.

"He's coming here next," Mac said.

"Yeah," Sam agreed.

"I think we should go back south, but I don't know if we have time."

"Yeah, we do," Sam said. Mac had to admit, she sounded pretty confident about it.

"OK," Mac agreed. "Follow my lead. We're taking the back route."

"Fine, but not yet," Sam said.

"What?"

"Wait for it..."

"Why?" Mac wanted to know.

"Get ready..."

Both girls were stacked together just inside the rear door of the north building.

"Now!" Sam yelled.

They dashed through the doorway and ran straight into Rush. He killed Sam with a headshot, but Mac ducked under it and knifed him instinctively.

Mac killed Rush, flashed onto the screen, and there was a brief moment of silence before the team burst into cheers.

"No way!" Sketch exclaimed.

Gears and Disco both shouted incoherently.

"Told you," Sam said, spawning and running back to the north building.

"Stop!" Ammu shouted, but they couldn't hear him over the sounds of the game and their own celebration.

"Wait! Please!" he tried again, but he still couldn't get their attention. Christina put her right thumb and forefinger into her mouth and whistled explosively, bringing everyone in the room to a standstill.

"Samantha," Ammu exclaimed, grinning from ear to ear, "In exploring Rush's talent, I believe we have discovered your own!"

Ammu was so excited that he didn't bother to get Sam alone, walking over to her chair instead and beginning to speak to her right there in the room. Sketch took off his headset and wandered over toward them, sitting on the floor nearby where he could hear better. Slowly, the others followed.

"Samantha," Ammu asked, "how did you know you had time to meet up with Mackenzie before Rush took the third generator?"

"I don't know," Sam admitted. "I just knew."

"But you were certain of it." It wasn't really a question.

"Yeah," she acknowledged.

"And how did you know when the two of you should run out of the building? You could not see Rush on the map."

"No, I couldn't. I couldn't hear him either. I just... I don't know... I just knew when to go."

"Samantha, I believe that you have a very particular talent for timing."

Sam thought about this and started to get excited.

"You are smiling," Ammu said encouragingly. "Tell me what you are thinking."

"Well, I always know what time it is, even without a clock. And I always know when I have to leave to get somewhere on time, or how long I'll need to study for a test. But that isn't very impressive, is it? I mean, it isn't like being an artist, or a musician, or having a knack for machines, or whatever."

"Oh, no, you do not understand!" Ammu protested. "Samantha, the only reason we try to find such a pathway is to tap into our unconscious awareness. You, my amazing girl, do not seem to need such a pathway at all! Mackenzie uses her Muay Thai, for example, to access her unconscious knowledge of place. She understands positioning on an intuitive level. *That* is her true affinity. Our goal is to help her access that awareness in everything she does, not just in martial arts."

"She learned the maps really fast," Sketch interjected. "Does that mean Mackenzie can do it in the game, too?"

"Yes, Sketch! Good! She is already starting to apply her ability in other areas. And Samantha," he announced, beaming at her proudly, "has a true affinity for timing—an affinity which she is already able to access on many levels, rather than through a single open pathway."

Again, it wasn't a question, and she had to nod her head.

"I believe now," Ammu continued, "that the sense of importance you felt about taking the Intuition Assessment Battery, and about coming here, had to do with timing as well. What do you think?"

Sam mulled it over before answering, despite feeling a little self-conscious about everyone watching her.

"I felt like it was important to take the test that day, but then the feeling went away," she said, still uncertain.

"Because you had already made the decision to go to school," Ammu pointed out. "There was no need for your unconscious mind to prompt you any further."

"Oh! And once I had decided to come here, that decision was already made, too!"

"Indeed!" Ammu agreed. "You do not have what you consider to be a special talent because your unconscious mind is not limited to a single pathway. You are already able to access your intuitive knowledge of timing in every aspect of your life. It helps you to be an excellent student in many subtle ways, I am sure, and it brought you here as well."

Sam was so happy that tears started to well up in her eyes. She belonged at the ICIC after all. She looked around at the others, embarrassed, and Rush came to her rescue by changing the subject.

"Don't think this is going to get you out of a nickname," he said, grinning wryly.

"Gamer tags!" Sketch exclaimed. "But wait, Sam didn't kill you. Mac did."

"They killed me together. Mac knew where to be, and Sam knew when to be there. Honestly, Sketch, as if any of you scrubs could kill me by yourselves."

Sketch giggled. "So what are their tags, then?"

"Grid," he said, raising his chin toward Mackenzie, "and Tick-Tock," nodding at Sam.

"Perfect!" Sketch crowed.

"They are indeed," Ammu agreed. "Absolutely perfect."

26
THE COMING STORM

You wanna go play downstairs?" Sketch found Rush sitting in their suite after dinner, his feet up on the coffee table, watching the news instead of playing *HRT Alpha.*

"I think I'm played out for today," Rush said. "You go ahead if you want."

"Naw." Sketch settled onto the couch next to Rush. "What did Ammu say about your pathway?"

Scientists at NASA report that the upcoming Orion test is expected to proceed on schedule, as America prepares to return to space flight. The television reporter smiled for the camera. She was wearing a perfectly normal suit jacket, but Sketch was having trouble seeing it through the puffy ball gown and high, powdered wig he saw on her instead, making her look like some kind of historical French aristocrat.

Rush shrugged. "He said it's something about predicting behavior patterns. He says that's why I'm good at the game. I still think I'm just fast, though." Rush wasn't about to admit to anyone, not even Sketch, that he had completed the IAB by filling in the blanks randomly.

"You're fast, for sure," Sketch agreed, "but you're not *just* fast. You're super talented. If Ammu says you're good at the behavior thing, then you are."

"Look, Sketch," Rush said, "I appreciate the vote of confidence, but I'm not sure I *want* to be that good at it. The only reason I'm not failing out on purpose is because my dad would sell all my stuff and probably kick me out of the house."

"He's not allowed to kick you out until you're eighteen," Sketch replied, matter-of-factly. "If he does, they have to give you somewhere else to live."

Rush just looked at him.

"It's a Child Protective Services thing," Sketch offered, by way of explanation.

"It concerns me that you know that," Rush said, but Sketch just shrugged. "Look, that's not the point. I just don't want to be here, OK? No offense to you, man. I really mean that. This place is great for you. It's like a free ticket to college. But me, I want to be a pro gamer, and if I have to stay here all summer, I'm going to lose my chance. My mom says she's going to try to talk my dad into letting me come home early. So don't get too attached to me sticking around."

Sketch's face fell, but he didn't say anything.

"It's not that I don't like you, or that I don't want to hang out with you. You're cool, man. You really are. But guys only get a few years to be pro gamers before their careers are over. It's so short. You have no idea. And if you don't have a pro spot by the time you're twenty, the odds start stacking against you. I don't have that much time left to make it, and I have to take the chance while I can. Once my mom gets me out of this, I'm leaving. That's just how it is."

Rush got up and walked into his room, closing the door quietly but firmly behind him. Sketch slumped on the couch, but when the next news segment came on, he sat up straight, his eyes glued to the screen.

The president is resting comfortably after a near miss today, when Marine One was forced into an emergency landing just moments after takeoff. Experts say the incident was caused by a sudden burst of wind, combined with an as-yet-undetermined mechanical failure.

But it wasn't the reporter's words that had Sketch staring at the screen. It was the news footage behind her. Just before the crash she described, a strange creature appeared in the air next to the helicopter, taking the blurred shape of a man-sized tornado, twisting and writhing in the air.

Watching in both fascination and horror, Sketch saw a face coalesce within the gusting vortex, with two black holes for eyes and a grimacing maw for a mouth. It reached out with ephemeral hands, crackling with the suggestion of lightning, and with preternatural speed it grabbed the helicopter's rotor, causing the vehicle to spin out of control and come crashing down onto the tarmac below.

27
INSTRUCTOR REPORT

There's been a development. We need to do this thing now."

"And by 'now' you mean…"

"I mean now, dammit. Tomorrow. Hell, I mean yesterday."

"Sketch is ready, as is Kaitlyn, I believe, but Daniel still needs more time—"

"I don't care who's ready and who's not ready. It doesn't matter anymore. The timetable has moved up. End of discussion."

"Some things, Colonel, can not be rushed, no matter how much we might wish it to be so."

"I've been patient with you so far, Professor, which is a compliment to your particular expertise. But in the end, this is my operation. If you won't work with me, I'll find someone who will."

"I am not unwilling to work with you. I will begin the active experiments, but they might not yet be able to complete the task we are about to set before them. Rush, in particular, is not likely to perform at his full potential without understanding the urgency we face. He has sacrificed what he sees as his highest possible career path to be here. If he does not know the importance of the work, his heart will not be in it, which will be devastating to his abilities."

"Telling him is not an option. Keep him in the dark and use him, or keep him in the dark and send him home. That's the choice."

"If I might be so bold, I believe there exists a third option: a win-win scenario, if you will. He could be motivated, under the right circumstances, without divulging the information you seek to contain, but I would need your permission to proceed."

"Well, whatever it is, you've picked a piss-damn good time to bring it up. I'm feeling uncharacteristically open to suggestions."

28
BARGAIN

Ammu pulled Rush aside at breakfast the next morning.

"Please, make yourself a plate and bring it with you," he said. "I would like to speak with you privately in the classroom, and I do not want you to miss your breakfast."

Oh, great, Rush thought to himself. *He's finally figured out that I didn't do as well as they think on that test.*

Ammu didn't sound angry, but then again, Rush had a hard time imagining the soft-spoken man yelling or carrying on. Even if Ammu were furious, he would probably just scold him in the same even tone with which he always spoke. *I am sorry to say that we will have to let you go,* Rush imagined him saying, his voice as calm as ever. *It is a great sorrow to me, as you can imagine, and it will surely be a great disappointment to your father as well.*

Suddenly, Rush didn't feel very hungry at all. He gulped and followed Ammu into the classroom.

"Sit down. Please," Ammu said graciously. "I have a deal I would like to propose to you."

Rush sat one seat away from Ammu, setting his plate on the chair between them as an excuse for leaving it empty. He eyed Ammu warily, but a deal didn't sound so bad. Teachers didn't usually make deals with students they were about to kick out of school.

"First of all," Ammu began, "let me say that I am extremely glad you are here at the ICIC. I do not want yesterday's revelations about Samantha to undermine the importance of your own unique gift. Your ability to predict behavior is impressive. I believe it has contributed to your success in the video gaming arena, and I believe it will be of even greater aid to you here, whether you realize it or not.

"That said," he continued, "I am aware that your preference, at the moment, is to attend an upcoming gaming event—an event which, as I understand it, could lead to a lucrative career for you in the industry, yes?"

"Chance of a lifetime," Rush admitted, but he couldn't meet Ammu's gaze, pushing the food idly around his plate with his fork instead. "How'd you know?"

"Kaitlyn told Christina, who told me," Ammu replied, "but do not be angry with them. Kaitlyn told Christina in praising your abilities. Christina told me because I might be in a position to help you. Knowing what I know now, I would like to offer you a deal."

Rush looked up, hope daring to blaze in his eyes.

"If you will commit yourself," Ammu said, "I mean truly *commit*, with everything you have, to participating in this program, and in the exercises that I ask of you, without question..." Ammu paused, making sure he had Rush's full attention, "I am now in a position to promise you that when your invitational arrives... a few weeks from now, yes?"

"Yes!" Rush affirmed.

"That the ICIC will ensure your attendance."

Rush jumped out of his chair.

"Yes!" Rush yelled. "Hell yes!"

"So, you would say we have a deal?" Ammu asked, grinning wryly.

"Yes, we have a deal! Ammu, you're the best!"

Rush looked like he wanted to hug the older man, so Ammu stood and opened his arms awkwardly, unsure of what the culture of the American teenager called for in such a jubilant situation. Rush saw his uncertainty and just grinned instead, holding out his hand to Ammu, inviting him to shake it to seal their bargain.

But when Ammu extended his own hand, Rush's excitement got the best of him. He pulled Ammu in for a vigorous bear hug and slapped him on the back several times, leaving the older man laughing.

"Yes, yes. OK then. Very good," Ammu said, clearly pleased but also in doubt over how best to respond to Rush's enthusiasm. "Try to eat something now. We have a long day ahead of us." Ammu indicated Rush's plate with a nod of his head, what little food Rush had bothered to take still lying upon it, uneaten and getting colder by the minute.

"Yes, sir!" Rush said, and he all but sprinted out the door, heading for either the pancakes, because he was starving, or for Sketch, to tell him the good news, whichever he saw first.

29
TRAINING

ood morning, everyone! Today, I have something very special for you to try. The exercise is likely to seem strange, as it is an ancient practice from my own part of the world and therefore quite removed from your own experience."

Ammu stood in the center of a strange room they had not seen before. It was located in a system of narrow tunnels beneath the building, the stairwell to which was hidden behind a gray steel door in the back of the lodge's industrial kitchen.

The room held no furniture at all. A large mirror was set into one wall, but otherwise there was not a single mark in the pristine white paint. The whitewashed floor appeared to be smoothly sealed concrete. Round, bright lights lay perfectly flush with the unblemished ceiling.

The space was too large and empty to be comfortable, especially given the complete lack of color. It reminded Mackenzie of the despised gray carpet, making her want to shudder, but she hid it as best she could. She suspected the mirror to be a one-way window.

Who knew how many unknown observers might be watching from the other side.

"I thought unconscious minds didn't like basements," Sam said.

Ammu turned to meet her eyes for just a moment but did not otherwise acknowledge the comment.

"In service of this experiment," he said instead, "I have brought something that is quite precious to me, and I would ask you all, please, to treat it with respect when handling it."

Slowly, carefully, Ammu produced a huge tome from a satchel he carried over his shoulder. It was bound in dark brown leather, the edges of each page delicately gilded, with hand-tooled lettering across the cover, painted in gold. The language was so foreign to them that they could not even decipher its letters, let alone its meaning, and it appeared to be printed either backwards or upside down, the binding positioned on the right rather than on the left.

When Ammu opened the book and turned it around so they could see it, Sketch gasped and took a step forward, reaching one hand out toward the page—until he remembered what Ammu had just said. He looked up, seeking permission to touch the illustration he saw there, and Ammu granted it silently, nodding once, allowing Sketch to run his fingers reverently across its colorful surface.

The vibrant picture depicted a creature with the brilliant body and tail of a peacock but the head and forelegs of a wolf. Watching Sketch closely, Ammu turned to a new page, this one displaying a classic gryphon. Its body and rear legs were clearly those of a lion, but its head, wings, and forelegs were just as clearly those of an eagle.

"That's the picture you showed me!" Kaitlyn exclaimed.

"Almost," Ammu said. "The picture I showed you in the workshop was very similar. It was created by the same artist, but it is not exactly the same. There are subtle differences, detailed here." He pointed to more of the unusual writing, arrayed alongside the photo in a column down the side of the page, the lettering aligned on the right instead of on the left, just like the book's binding.

"That's Arabic." Mackenzie leaned forward to take a closer look. "I can't read it, but I recognize it."

"Very good," Ammu agreed. "As I said, the exercise we are to attempt today comes originally from my own part of the world, as does this book."

"What do you want us to do, Ammu?" Rush asked, and Ammu smiled.

"The exercise is designed to strengthen the connection between the conscious and the unconscious mind. Since each of you commands a different ability through a unique pathway, you will each be performing a different aspect of the whole. To begin, Kaitlyn will set the pattern—the blueprint, if you will—for the exercise. From this image, Kaitlyn, when you are ready, clear your mind and try to see it, as you did in the workshop."

Kaitlyn nodded uncertainly and stepped forward, lowering her gaze to the book. They all stood in silence for several moments, but Kaitlyn just frowned and eventually shook her head.

"I can't see it like before," she said, looking to Ammu for direction.

"Try again," he said gently. "It will come."

Kaitlyn nodded and stared at the image again, this time waiting several long minutes in silence before finally giving up.

"I'm sorry, Ammu. It just isn't coming to me. I'm not getting anything."

"That's because it's not as big as it looks," Sketch interjected, and Ammu looked at him in surprise.

"How so?" he asked.

"The picture looks like a lion's body, but it isn't that big at all. It's more like a cat. Like this." Sketch held his hands out in front of him, indicating something closer to the size of a dog. He looked up at Kaitlyn to see whether she understood what he was saying, but she was already nodding eagerly.

"Yes!" she exclaimed. "I have it! I can see it, Ammu!" In her mind's eye, as clear as day, she could see a circle of glowing runes that somehow, to her, represented the living energy flow of the miniature gryphon.

"Excellent!" Ammu exclaimed. "Both of you! That is excellent!"

Kaitlyn and Sketch both beamed with pride.

"Here," Ammu said. He pulled a square tin out of his satchel and opened it to reveal several pieces of blue street chalk. Sketch started to reach for it, but Ammu surprised him by handing it to Kaitlyn. "Draw what you see on the floor. About this big, I think." He held his hands apart, almost as far as his arms could stretch.

"Sure!" Kaitlyn agreed. She knelt on the floor and began drawing a large circle.

"Now, Samantha," Ammu continued, "You will sit in the middle of the circle. If and when it occurs to you to do something, then do it. Use your sense of timing. If everything goes well, you will know when. Trust your instincts."

"Yeah," Sam said, shrugging, "'cause that's not vague at all." But she did as she was asked, sitting with her legs crossed in the middle of the chalk circle on the floor as Kaitlyn began to draw strange runes around her.

"Mackenzie," Ammu said, turning to her next, "I would like you to bless the circle and 'center' the ritual through any series of movements that seems fitting. Your unconscious mind can already communicate spatial information to your conscious awareness through your martial arts. Use that ability to perform the movements that come to you."

"OK," Mackenzie agreed. "I can do that."

"Wonderful!" Ammu turned to Daniel, who looked like he wanted to throw up. "Daniel, I would like you to sing any tune that represents the way you feel as you watch what Kaitlyn is doing."

"Dear God, don't ask him to do that," Rush couldn't help but interject, and Sketch laughed out loud while Daniel blushed furiously.

"Hmm? OH! Right. Yes, I see. The feelings that come to you through the runes on the floor, I mean," Ammu corrected himself, looking like he was trying not to chuckle.

"Thanks a lot," Daniel muttered, but Rush just grinned without any sign of remorse.

"Go on, Disco," he joked. "Let's hear it. Give us a Kaitlyn-rune melody."

Daniel glared at him, but Mackenzie looked up from her series of movements long enough to say, "Hey! If I can perform an ancient spiritual cleansing by doing slow Muay Thai moves around a chalk circle, you can hum us a damn tune."

"Fine," Daniel muttered. He grew quiet for a moment and then began humming, very softly, an eerie melody that didn't sound quite like anything any of them had ever heard before.

"What do you want Sketch and me to do?" Rush asked, more than happy to do any crazy thing Ammu asked of him now that they had made their deal.

"You will know when Samantha indicates that the time is right," Ammu replied cryptically.

"Good enough for me," Rush said. He folded his arms across his chest and stood back to watch the fun, Sketch mimicking his pose beside him.

"Wait, wait, wait," Sam said, holding up one hand after Kaitlyn had finished her drawing. "Go back to the beginning."

"Beginning?" Mackenzie asked, she and Daniel both stopping and staring at her.

"Yeah," Sam said. "Mackenzie, wherever you feel like the ritual should start, go back there and wait for a second."

"OK," she agreed, shrugging and walking about halfway around the circle.

"Daniel," Sam continued, "wherever that tune starts, I'm going to count you into it, OK?"

Daniel didn't look happy about having to start over again, but he nodded just the same.

"And Kaitlyn," Sam finished, "Go back to the part of the circle where Mackenzie is standing and trace over the runes again, moving in the same direction she does. I'll point to you when it's time to move to the next rune."

"Okie dokie," Kaitlyn agreed.

Sam took a deep breath and let it out slowly. Rush raised an eyebrow but said nothing. Ammu, however, began to watch her with a new intensity.

"OK, everybody," she said. "Here goes nothing. One... two... one, two, three, four."

Daniel began to hum again, but this time he followed the beat that Sam had introduced, while Mackenzie moved to the same rhythm, punching and kicking at the air in slow motion. Sam pointed occasionally to Kaitlyn, who would trace the next rune while Mackenzie bowed in front of it.

As they came back around toward the beginning of the circle, Rush began to frown. He felt a strange sort of hum in the air, and he found himself wondering whether this was what it felt like right before you were struck by lightning.

It was not a comforting thought.

Suddenly, Sam threw her arms up over her head, and a dark void began to open between her hands. It started as a pinprick, so small that Rush couldn't be sure he was seeing anything at all, but he felt it with absolute certainty. It was as though a hole had opened up between himself and something waiting just on the other side, in the same way that a narrow tunnel might suddenly allow you to hear someone's voice through a wall of solid rock, or allow you to catch the scent of winter lingering on the other side.

As the hole grew, becoming as wide as a marble, and then a golf ball, and then a baseball, and then a softball, Rush could *feel* the thing on the other side struggling to shove its way into the tunnel, which was still too narrow for it. He felt it yearning toward him, and at the same time tugging at him, like two powerful magnets drawn inexorably toward one another.

"What the hell?" Rush exclaimed. He took a huge step backward and stumbled into Ammu, who barely managed to keep them both from falling.

"What?" Sam cried out, seeing Rush's reaction. She yanked her hands back into her lap, her wide eyes meeting Rush's across the span of the room between them, and the void snapped closed without a sound.

30
INSTRUCTOR REPORT

So, what went wrong?"

"I thought it was an excellent first attempt, all things considered. With time—"

"We don't have time, dammit! What... went... wrong?"

"Why, nothing, really. The boy just—"

"Nothing? You're trying to tell me that nothing went wrong? Then where are my results?"

"As I have been saying, it is a bit early, in my opinion, to expect the project to come to its full fruition."

"It's full fruition? Nothing happened!"

"I admit the process did not reach completion, but—"

"Completion? It didn't even start, man!"

"I apologize, Colonel, but why do you keep repeating everything I say as a question? I find it very disconcerting as a method of communication."

"Well, I'm sorry to be disconcerting you with my inconvenient questions about your failure today."

"I would hardly characterize today as a failure."

"Don't play coy with me, dammit! We had instruments set up all around the outside perimeter of that room! Everything from microphones to Geiger counters! So when I say nothing happened, I mean I know for a fact that nothing happened!"

"Interesting..."

"'Interesting' is not the word I would use in this situation if I were you, Professor. Not with me. Not today."

"If you want better results, I believe we need to do a better job of preparing the unconscious mind for success. If they know exactly what they are attempting—"

"For the last damn time, we are not telling them anything! I want results, and I want them now. So you had better figure out how to provide them, or I swear to God I will go down there and motivate those kids myself. And I promise you, you are not going to like the way I choose to do that. You are not going to like it at all."

31
CONFERENCE

"OK, what the hell was *that* this morning?" Sam stopped pacing behind the couch and put her hands on her hips, glaring at everyone else as though daring them not to answer.

Rush and Sketch were playing *HRT Alpha: Year One* with something less than their usual enthusiasm. Daniel and Kaitlyn sat next to them, holding hands in silence, looking as though the world were about to end at any moment, which might be the truth of it, as far as Sam knew.

"We don't know any more than you do," Mackenzie finally answered when no one else did. She was running through a series of stretching exercises, but it wasn't doing much to calm her nerves.

"Oh, I beg to differ," Sam snapped. "We've all had individual sessions with Ammu that nobody else got to see. Maybe if we put it all together, things will make some kind of sense. So, spill. What did he say or do with each of you?"

Mackenzie just shrugged. "Mine wasn't anything weird like this morning," she said. "Really, it was a lot like Rush's—which was yours, too, for that matter—and we were all there for that. I just fought this guy named Miller, and I dodged a lot of punches. That's it. No crazy runes or chanting or holes in space."

"You saw that?" Sketch blurted out, turning to look at Mackenzie over his shoulder.

"We all saw it," Mackenzie said. "We might not all be talking about it, but we all saw it." She glanced meaningfully at the back of Rush's head, but Sketch wasn't worried about who was talking and who wasn't. The fact that he wasn't the only one to see the weird thing between Sam's hands was exciting in and of itself, and he turned back around, chewing the inside of his cheek thoughtfully.

"What about you, Gears?" Sam asked. "What did Ammu do with you?" They had been playing *HRT Alpha* ever since dinner—long enough to start using each other's gamer tags out of habit—but they had chosen not to play downstairs by silent agreement, all of them feeling safer in the suite than they would have in the open space of the conference room.

"I don't know. Mine was kind of weird," Kaitlyn admitted. "Ammu was showing me things like blenders and stuff, and I was starting to see blueprints for them in my head. Then he threw in a picture of the gryphon thing, and I saw these symbols glowing in the air, like the stuff I drew on the floor."

"OK," Sam said. "So maybe the runes are some kind of blueprint for the gryphon."

"You can't *build* a gryphon like a blender," Rush interjected, his voice thick with condescension.

"I'm not saying you can *build* it," Sam snapped back. "I'm saying you can, I don't know, call it or something."

At the words 'call it,' Rush's back stiffened, but he kept his thoughts on the subject to himself.

"Look," Mackenzie said, "let's say, just for a second, that calling gryphons through holes in the air doesn't sound completely and totally crazy. And let's even say, just for the same second, that it's what we're trying to do. That still doesn't tell us *why* we're doing it."

"Yeah, that's true," Kaitlyn agreed. "Why *would* they want us to do that? I mean, assuming we are, like you said."

Everyone was silent for a while, the sounds of the game the only distraction.

"All we can know for sure," Mackenzie finally continued, "is that this program is more directly related to Homeland Security than any of us realized. Which means two things: one, they have a good reason for asking us to do it, and, two, they aren't going to tell us what it is. Period. All we can do is serve our country as best we can by trying to do what they tell us to do."

"Really? Serve our country?" Sam asked, her voice derisive.

"What's wrong with serving our country?" Daniel asked before Mackenzie could answer.

Sam sighed. "Nothing," she allowed. "I'm not saying I don't want to... I don't know... help... or whatever. I just wouldn't mind knowing what we're helping *with*, exactly."

"I wouldn't either," Mac admitted. "But it's not going to happen. Homeland Security works on a strict need-to-know basis. And I promise you, they aren't going to think we need to know."

"We could ask," Sam suggested.

"No." Mac was already shaking her head. "Trust me. That would only make things worse. They'll just get mad—maybe even scrap the program if they think we're figuring things out. Whatever we do, we can't look too curious about any of it, and we can't let them know what little we know. Anything we manage to work out about what we're really up to, we have to keep to ourselves. Agreed?"

"Agreed," Rush growled. "I'm going to that invitational no matter what, and nobody's going to screw it up for me. You guys hear me? Don't ask questions. Don't let on you know anything's up. Don't make them mad. Everybody got it?"

"Yeah," Daniel said.

"Roger that," Mackenzie answered.

"OK," Kaitlyn agreed.

"Sure thing, Rush," Sketch chimed in.

Sam was the only one who didn't reply. When Rush turned to stare at her, she finally nodded her consent, but she still didn't look happy about it.

32
LIES

The next morning, from the moment Daniel walked into the strange, white room, he could tell something was wrong. Ammu had not appeared at breakfast, which was unusual in itself, and now he was waiting for them alone, down in the stark, empty space. Even the runes had been washed away.

He smiled when they arrived, but there was something darker in his eyes that made Daniel shudder. The strains of "The Fear" by Ben Howard started playing in his mind, and an icy chill raced along his spine.

Daniel grabbed Kaitlyn's hand, his eyes locking onto hers in silent warning: *Be careful. I have a bad feeling about this.* But the smile she gave him in return was vague, distant, and not at all reassuring.

"Good morning, children," Ammu began, and Sam looked up sharply. He had not called them 'children' since the day she had taken offense to it, and he caught her gaze now, staring at her intently.

"Given yesterday's complete lack of results," he continued. Sam frowned, about to protest, but Ammu's eyes were still locked onto her own, as though silently willing her to understand some private message, intended just for her.

And then she had it. He knew she would challenge such an openly false statement, and he was begging her not to.

She nodded, just barely moving her head, but it was enough. His eyes softened, and Sam felt an overpowering urge to look over her shoulder at the one-way mirror. She resisted it, however, keeping her eyes steadily on the Egyptian, refusing to give anything away to whoever sat behind the glass, watching them.

"I think it best that we start over from the beginning," he finished. "Kaitlyn? Would you like to see the image again?"

"Yes, please," she replied. Ammu pulled the book out of his satchel, opening it to the gryphon page and handing her the chalk.

"Remember," he said, "the exercise is intended to improve the connection between the conscious and the unconscious mind. Nothing more. Think of it as calisthenics for the intellect—a kind of mental conditioning, if you will—and try to be as open as you can to your own individual pathways throughout the endeavor."

Now Daniel heard the chorus of "You Lie" by The Band Perry, the upbeat rhythm making him want to tap his foot despite the song's implications. If Daniel's time with Ammu had taught him anything, it was to seek any clue he could in the music that came to him. The song implied that Ammu was lying, but its tone was telling him not to be frightened, only cautious.

At least, he hoped that's what it was telling him.

"When you are ready, you may proceed," Ammu said.

Kaitlyn drew a rough circle on the floor, and Sam sat in the center, crossing her legs and resting her arms lightly on her knees. Mackenzie found their starting position, and they looked up for Sam's count.

"One... two... one, two, three, four."

Kaitlyn traced out the first rune, Mackenzie moved into her ritual cleansing, and Daniel started to hum. They did everything the same way they had before, but this morning, nothing happened. The timing wasn't any different, and they all moved in unison—Sam knew that much for certain—but still, something felt... off.

Kaitlyn had understood Daniel's concern from the moment he had touched her hand—even as she drew the blue loops and whorls on the floor, she found herself focusing more on his voice than on her own task. His perfect tenor held the same clarity it always did, lending an ethereal beauty to the strange melody, but today every note left her feeling uneasy. Whatever they were doing in this peculiar, underground room, Kaitlyn hoped it wouldn't work this time.

As for Daniel, he was enduring the greatest musical challenge of his life. Songs about fear and lies chased each other through his head even as he hummed the ancient melody out loud. The symphony that resulted from the blending of real and imagined music at once was so discordant as to make him almost feel ill, but he soldiered on as best he could, hoping the song would sound the same as it did yesterday to everyone else.

If Mackenzie noticed anything odd in her teammates, she didn't show it. Her own movements were smooth and flowing, as graceful as ever. But after they had completed four entire circuits of the circle, Ammu finally sighed and called a halt to the exercise.

"Thank you, everyone. That was excellent," Ammu said, clapping his hands to interrupt them. "You have done exactly as I asked, and I am proud of you all."

Ammu looked directly at Sam when he said this, and she held his gaze for a moment, acknowledging the deeper meaning behind his words.

"Take the remainder of the day to rest," he told them. "You have earned it."

33
CLOAK-AND-DAGGER

By mid-afternoon, they all ended up in the gaming room playing *HRT Alpha: Year One* to keep their minds off the strange events of the morning. Sketch had teamed up with Rush against Daniel, Kaitlyn, Mackenzie, and Sam, filling out both teams with bots to play five on five.

Grid has killed Bot 2. Tick-Tock has killed Bot 1. The south generator has been damaged.

"Why are our bots so stupid?" Sketch pouted.

"'Cause all bots are stupid," Rush said. "If you didn't want to play with bots, you should have played on the other team."

"Yeah, but then I couldn't play with you, though," Sketch pointed out, and Rush laughed.

"Life is full of tough decisions. At least I've got one player I can count on, right?"

"Right!" Sketch agreed. Rush caught the boy's proud grin out of the corner of one eye and smiled.

"Oh, get a room. Damn lovebirds, squawking up the channel."

Sam's voice floated over their headsets, and Sketch giggled. Since they were just playing to hang out, Rush had set up the system to let both teams hear each other.

Rush has killed Tick-Tock.

"Poor Tick-Tock," Rush taunted back. "Killed by a lovebird. How embarrassing for you."

"Mwa-ha-haaaa," Sketch crowed, doing his best impression of a maniacal, evil genius laugh, until he cut it short with a gurgling death gasp, still in character.

Grid killed Sketch, flashed on the screen, and they all laughed—even Daniel, who was so quiet over the air that Rush couldn't help but think of Stryker.

"Rush?"

"Yeah, Sketch, what's up? Want me to pick you up at the spawn?"

Rush killed Disco. Rush killed Gears.

"When do you think we're gonna have to go back downstairs?"

"I dunno, man. Probably tomorrow."

"I don't like it down there." Sketch's voice was quiet now. He hadn't fully understood the tension in the room that morning, but he had certainly felt it. The rune over Ammu's chest had dimmed considerably, Rush's armor had glowed with faint, red lines of agitation, and even Daniel's usual cascade of color had been muted somehow, as though viewed through a hazy, gray fog.

"Me either," Daniel admitted, which were the first actual words he had spoken over the comm link all afternoon.

"Can it, guys," Rush warned them. "Let's just play."

Rush killed Tick-Tock. Rush killed Bot 1. The central generator has been repaired.

Grid killed Sketch. Rush killed Grid.

"I don't think Ammu—" Sam started, but Rush cut her off mid-sentence.

"Everybody offline!" he barked. "Now!"

He ended the game, whipped off his headset, and leaped out of the chair. Sketch stared at Rush in terror, his armor's usual blue markings all replaced by angry red slashes, its usual silver hue transformed into a deep, almost bronze gold.

Rush strode toward Sam in long, quick strides, but Mackenzie intercepted him and stood defiantly in his way, the great, golden bear staring him down.

"Oh, for God's sake, I'm not going to hurt her," Rush said, sounding exasperated rather than furious. "Come here. Everybody, come here. Huddle up."

Sketch watched Rush for any signs of violence, but while his armor still glowed in the same ominous colors, he seemed relatively composed. Sketch moved toward him with the others, but he stayed behind Mackenzie, just to be on the safe side.

"We said we weren't going to talk about that stuff," Rush said in hushed tones once they were all together. "We agreed. And we have no idea what they might have done to these consoles. For all we know, they're listening to everything we say on there."

Sam hung her head, feeling stupid. She should have thought of that.

"Let's just go talk upstairs," Kaitlyn suggested.

"Yeah, cause they couldn't *possibly* have bugged our suites," Sam countered. She might have been caught unaware once, but she wasn't going to make the same mistake again.

"She's right," Rush whispered. "We're probably safe here in the middle of this huge room, but we can't stay here. It would look suspicious if someone came in and we were all just standing around like this."

"What about your workshop?" Daniel asked Kaitlyn, and everyone turned to him in surprise.

"Hey, that'd be good," Kaitlyn agreed. "There's no way they'd bother to bug it. Even *I've* only been out there the one time."

"Like I said," Rush growled, sounding even more frustrated,

"we agreed not to talk about this stuff at all. We don't need a *place* to do it. We need to *stop* doing it. I'm not messing up my invitational."

"And I'm not letting this go," Sam argued, crossing her arms over her chest and cocking her hips defiantly. "Yesterday, Ammu wanted us to open that thing. Today, he didn't. I want to know why."

"I hate to say it," Mackenzie chimed in, "but I agree with Tick-Tock. We said we wouldn't let Ammu or Christina know what we know. We never said we wouldn't even try to figure it out."

"Fine!" Rush relented, worried that either one of them might walk in at any moment. "Tonight. We'll go to the workshop tonight."

"What time?" Sam asked automatically.

"After curfew, *Tick-Tock*," Rush declared. "Christina said she was going to be checking on us every night, but I haven't seen her do it. Have you guys?"

Everyone shook their heads.

"OK. So maybe she's not doing it, but then again, maybe she's been listening in so she knows where we are. We'll play it safe. Stay in the suites until 11:15, then meet up here—right here—and we'll wait for a while. That way, if someone comes after us, we can say we wanted to play. We won't get in a lot of trouble for that.

"If we're in the clear, then we head for the workshop. In the meantime, nobody says another damn word about anything weird today. Everybody got it?"

"Yeah," they all agreed.

"11:15," Rush repeated, just for good measure. "Not before."

By 11:17 p.m. they were all back down in the game center. Rush

convinced them to fire up one quiet round of *HRT Alpha*, just in case anyone came looking for them. But no one came. When the match ended, they all signed off and gathered up in the center of the room.

"We should go out the back way," Kaitlyn whispered. "The main doors all have alarms, but there's an access panel between a janitor's closet and a gardener's shed in the back. The shed door isn't on the main system."

They all just stared at her.

"What?" she asked. "Didn't you guys explore the place when you got here?"

"I *thought* I did," Mackenzie said, grinning wryly. "Please. After you."

Kaitlyn led the way out of the conference room toward a series of narrow hallways at the back of the building. Just as she had promised, a janitor's closet offered up an access panel in the rear wall. They used a wrench from the closet to loosen the bolts and remove the panel. The resulting hole was an easy fit for Sketch and just barely large enough for Rush to squeeze through.

On the other side was a small shed that stood against the outside wall of the lodge. Gardening tools hung from metal pegs, neatly filling the top half of every wall, leaving the bottom half free for stacked bags of peat moss, weed killer, and fertilizer.

Rush went first, shoving a few bags out of the way and then standing up to make room for Kaitlyn. The shed was too small to hold more than two people comfortably, but Kaitlyn slid past him and opened the outside door without any hesitation at all—ignoring Rush, who threw one hand up in surprise and then dropped it lamely when nothing happened.

"I told you," she said. "This door isn't on the alarm system. I'm *Gears*, remember? This is my thing."

"My mistake, your mechanicalness," Rush apologized, throwing her an exaggerated bow. "After you."

They all made their way outside and followed Kaitlyn down the path toward the maintenance garage.

"The garage has its own alarm system," Kaitlyn whispered when they reached the normal-looking door at the far end of the building, "but I watched Ammu reset it when we left after our session, so I know the code. We just have to get in."

She fished around in her pocket and pulled out an odd-looking tool set, chose a couple of small tools from it, pushed them into the lock, and started to fiddle around with them. For the second time that night, everyone just stared at her.

"Where the hell did you learn how to do that?" Sam finally asked.

"It's really not that hard," Gears whispered. "Little springs inside the lock push the pins down to keep it from turning. You just push the pins back up, keeping enough tension on them so they don't fall back down again... and... voilà!"

The door opened and Kaitlyn slipped through it. She entered the security code into a beeping alarm pad, and the beeping stopped.

"Aren't you coming?" she asked, popping her head back out to see why everyone was still outside.

"I think maybe your tag should be CIA," Rush said.

"Nah," Kaitlyn replied, giggling. "I like 'Gears'!"

She disappeared into the garage again, and this time the others followed her.

The shop didn't have any windows to give them away, so Kaitlyn turned on the overhead lights. "I officially call this meeting of the Cloak-and-Dagger Society to order!" she said grandly.

"Sure, okay," Sam said, rolling her eyes.

"First order of business: why was Ammu acting so weird this morning?"

"Right?" Sam pounded both hands against the work table. "Like saying nothing happened yesterday."

"And then acting relieved when it didn't work today," Mackenzie added.

"Maybe it's dangerous?" Kaitlyn suggested.

"Maybe," Mackenzie acknowledged, "but if that's all it was, he would have been acting weird yesterday too."

"So, what then?" Sam demanded.

"I think whoever's watching us doesn't know what's going on," Mackenzie said. "I don't think they could see that thing yesterday."

"How could they not see it?" Daniel muttered.

"I don't know," Mackenzie admitted, "but think about it. Why else would he stand in front of that one-way mirror and say it didn't work?"

"Unless he didn't see it himself," Sam said, thinking out loud. "But then he just would have said it didn't work. He wouldn't have acted all weird about it."

"Agreed," Mackenzie responded. "I think he knows it worked, and obviously *we* know it worked—but whoever's watching us, I think they *don't* know it worked, and Ammu doesn't want them to figure it out."

"But why not?" Kaitlyn asked.

"I have no idea," Mackenzie said, and everyone fell silent, pondering the question.

"Whoever we're doing this for, ultimately," Rush said finally, "wouldn't Ammu *want* them to know it was working? I mean, that's gotta make him look good, right?"

"Yeah," Mackenzie agreed. "Something must have changed. But what?"

"I don't know," Rush said. "But that thing..." He paused, not sure he wanted to admit what he'd felt.

"What thing?" Sketch wanted to know.

"I'm pretty sure that thing yesterday was some kind of portal. I swear I could *feel* something on the other side, trying to come through."

"I knew it!" Sam crowed.

"Keep your voice down," Rush hissed. "But yeah, I think you and Grid were right. I think Ammu has us trying to... I don't know... to call something here... from somewhere else... and I think it has to be that gryphon. But I have no idea why."

"Maybe if we actually do it, we can figure that out," Sam suggested.

"But Ammu doesn't want us to anymore," Kaitlyn protested.

"He doesn't want us to do it in front of that mirror," Sam countered. "But there's no mirror here."

"What? *Now?*" Rush glared at Sam. "You're out of your mind."

"I want to see it," Sketch said quietly. He was tired of being the only one who could see things nobody else could see. If his friends could see the portal and the people behind the mirror couldn't, maybe the gryphon would be like that too.

"Look, Sketch—" Rush began, but Kaitlyn interrupted him.

"I want to see it, too," she said. "I mean, come on! It's a miniature *gryphon*! Don't you guys want to see a gryphon?"

Daniel shrugged. If Kaitlyn wanted to see a gryphon, he didn't want to argue against her, but he wasn't so sure about the idea himself.

"Grid," Rush protested. "For God's sake, help me out here. Please tell them we should not be trying to summon something we don't know anything about—especially not all on our own in the middle of the night without any backup."

"Look, I want to know what's really going on," Mac replied cautiously, "but I'm not the one who freaked out. What do you know that we don't?"

Rush just glared at her, refusing to answer.

"Rush?" Kaitlyn tried. "We'll listen to you, OK? If you tell us we shouldn't do it, we won't do it. But can you tell us why?"

"I don't know," Rush said reluctantly.

"Rush," Mac prompted him again, leaving his name hanging in the air.

"Fine!" he said finally. "I felt it coming through, OK? There was definitely, absolutely, no-doubt-about-it something coming through that portal. Wouldn't that have freaked *you* out?"

"Probably," Mac admitted. "But Ammu keeps telling us to trust our unconscious minds, and the rest of us didn't sense anything wrong. You're the only one who felt it, whatever it was. So did it *feel* like something we wouldn't want to bring here?"

For several long moments, Rush didn't say a word. Nobody spoke. Nobody moved. They all just watched him, waiting for an answer.

"No," he finally admitted, sighing deeply. "If anything, it felt happy, like it really wanted to be here. It just freaked me out because I wasn't expecting it."

Not that I even belong here, he thought. *Since I didn't really take the stupid test, and you're all crazy to listen to me at all, let alone hang on my every word.* But even he had to admit that he had seen the portal—and that he had felt the thing on the other side, wanting to come through. Whatever was happening here, he was a part of it, whether he had expected to be or not.

"Then I say we try it," Mac declared, and this time nobody, not even Rush, tried to say they shouldn't.

34
EXPERIMENT

In one of the cupboards, Kaitlyn found a piece of white chalk she could use to draw on the gray concrete floor of the workshop.

"I hope the color doesn't matter. There isn't any blue in here," she said, but she wasn't talking to anyone in particular.

"We'll just have to use what we have," Mackenzie replied. "Either it will work, or it won't."

Kaitlyn nodded, but then she frowned. "We don't have the book either," she pointed out. "I have to see the picture to get the runes again."

"I can show you," Sketch said. "Were there any pencils with the chalk? And some paper?"

"I don't know about paper," Kaitlyn said, "but there are plenty of pencils. Here." She pulled a handful of assorted pencils out of the cabinet and handed them to Sketch, who started looking through them.

"Check in those drawers for paper," Kaitlyn said to Sam, who was standing closest to the work table. "There isn't any in the cabinets. Or, at least, there wasn't a couple days ago. The table's our best bet."

Sam nodded and started opening the drawers that were set into the edge of the work table. In the third one she opened, she found a yellow pad of lined paper.

"Is this OK?" she asked, holding it up for Sketch to examine.

"Yeah, that's good."

Sketch took the pad from Sam and climbed a half-step up onto one of the industrial, metal stools, using the rung that circled the bottom of the stool to reach the seat, which was just a little bit high for him. Hunching over the table, he started drawing on the pad, and the others crowded around him, watching as the gryphon gradually appeared on the page—only in black and white instead of full color.

He didn't want to take all night at it, so he skipped most of the detail work, outlining the creature instead and only filling in the most important aspects of its features: its curved beak, its front talons, its rear claws, a suggestion of feathers.

"Damn, Sketch," Rush muttered.

"What?" he asked.

"That's just really, really good."

"Yeah," Kaitlyn agreed. "That's amazing."

Sketch looked up at them shyly.

"Thanks," he said. "Here. Is this good enough?"

He handed the page to Kaitlyn, who took it carefully and placed it in front of her on the table.

"I see it," she confirmed. "This works."

"OK," Sketch said, and he put his pencil back down on the table.

"We'll have to wash the chalk off the floor when we're done," Kaitlyn said, looking around at everyone. "But it should come off fine, I think?"

"Maybe test it, just to be sure," Mackenzie suggested.

"Yeah, OK." Kaitlyn drew a tiny line on the floor with the chalk and then walked over to a sink in the rear of the central bay, wetting a rag that hung over the side and bringing it back to the place where she had marked the floor. The chalk came away easily.

"It works," Kaitlyn announced. "And it looks like it's drying pretty quickly. Even if we leave the floor wet, it'll be dry way before morning."

"Good," Mackenzie said. "OK. You ready?"

"I think so."

"Let's go, then."

Kaitlyn drew a circle in the center of the left-hand bay, which was the one with the most room since it didn't have either the table or the lawnmowers in the middle of it. Sam sat down in the circle, Mackenzie walked to the place where it felt like the runes should begin, and Kaitlyn followed her, kneeling down on the floor and raising her chalk, looking to Sam when she was ready.

"OK, Sam," Mackenzie said, nodding at her. "We're good. Count us in."

Sam took a deep breath and then exhaled it slowly, trying to concentrate.

"Here we go," she said. "One... two... one, two, three, four."

They began the process in unison, Daniel humming softly but with more certainty—partly because this was now the third time they had done this together, but also because the workshop felt like a much more inviting and natural space than the strange white room in the basement.

As Kaitlyn moved from one rune to another under Sam's direction, Rush began to feel the same odd sensation he had before, like a buildup of electricity in the air. Prepared for it this time, he didn't back away, taking a moment instead to explore it. He soon realized that he didn't feel it in his skin, as he had first believed, but rather in the pit of his stomach. It was internal, not external, but it spread to his extremities so completely that it was difficult, at first, to tell the difference.

When Kaitlyn completed the final rune, Sam suddenly opened her arms in the air above her head, and again the dark void appeared.

"You see that?" Sketch whispered to Rush.

"Yeah," Rush whispered back. "And I feel it again, too."

He could sense the creature on the other side of the portal just as clearly as he had before. He felt it clawing its way toward him, trying to crawl into the gap between them from the moment it appeared, when the tiny void was still nothing more than a pinprick in the space above Sam's head. But soon enough, the portal began to grow—to the size of a golf ball, and then a baseball, and then a softball.

Rush *felt* it as the thing on the other side managed to thrust its head into the tunnel, even though Rush couldn't see it yet, so he realized that the portal itself must have some depth to it. The creature pushed its shoulders through next, and Rush encountered the strangest sensation he had ever experienced, as he *felt* wings that he didn't have, brushing their downy resilience along the tunnel walls. Finally, the tunnel opened just a little more, and Rush could feel the creature's hopefulness as it forced the rest of its body into the portal, could sense its intense yearning to reach him, even as he himself felt drawn to it, just as before.

But this time, Rush was prepared. He did not make a sound. He did not step back from the portal. And with one final, heroic thrust, the creature surged through the tunnel, as though the resistance that had previously met it now suddenly dropped away, and it exploded out the other side, flying through the air straight at Rush, crashing into his chest, and knocking him to the ground.

35
A NIGHT OUT

Holy shit!" Sam still sat in the middle of the circle, her hands high in the air, framing the portal that shimmered in the space between them.

Sketch had been right. The gryphon was not as big as a full-grown lion, for which Rush was now exceedingly grateful. He lay on the floor, rubbing his chest where the creature had torpedoed into it. Then he sat up slowly, all the while staring at the gryphon, which had rolled playfully off his chest after crashing with him to the ground and now stood staring at him, cocking its eagle-like head this way and that, as though trying to decide exactly what sort of creature Rush was.

"This... is *really* cool," Kaitlyn said.

"Be careful," Mackenzie warned. "We don't know what it might do if it gets scared."

"Oh, come on. Look at it. It's just a baby." Kaitlyn crouched low anyway, trying not to scare it as she made her way toward it cautiously.

It had the body and rear legs of a lion cub, but its front legs ended in thick talons, shaped like a bird's, with feathers running from the shoulder to the knee. Its chest and neck were as broad as a lion cub's would have been, but they were covered in feathers as well: white near the top, transitioning to a tawny golden color before blending almost imperceptibly into its fur. Its head looked vaguely like an eagle's, but it had golden, furred ears, long and tufted, more like a lynx than a lion. Its broad beak was the same tawny gold as its fur.

As Kaitlyn came closer, it stood up on its hind legs and spread its wings wide, screeching at her, making Kaitlyn gasp. The feathers on top of its wings were white, like its head, but the feathers underneath were golden, like its fur.

"It's beautiful," Sketch murmured, and the gryphon turned its head to stare at him, bobbing its head up and down once.

"It's like it understood you," Kaitlyn said. "Can it understand us?" She directed the question to Rush, who looked at her like she was crazy.

"How should I know? Do I look like a mythological zookeeper to you?"

But Kaitlyn just shrugged back at him. "Hey, you called it here."

"No way," Rush protested. "*You* called it here. With that circle thing over there. Remember? Miss I-know-how-to-make-that?"

"I never said I could *make* a gryphon. And anyway, Tick-Tock was the one who opened the portal."

"Yes. Yes, I did. So nice of you to remember me," Sam retorted. "I'm not sure why you guys don't want to take credit for summoning magical creatures here on planet Earth, but I'll be happy to take full responsibility for all amazing feats and wonders if someone could please just come hold this portal open for me. My arms are getting tired."

"How do you know it's magical?" Mackenzie asked. "Just because it got here by magic doesn't mean it *is* magic."

"Here on Earth?" Daniel said, knitting his eyebrows together in puzzlement. "I don't think it came from space..."

"Not really the point," Sam said, rolling her eyes. "A little help, please?"

"I don't think you have to hold your arms up anymore," Sketch interjected, staring at the circle.

"Really?" Sam asked hopefully. "Are you sure?"

"Well, the things on the floor are all glowing, and the ones around the portal are lit up now too, so I think the circle is holding them open," Sketch said.

"The ones around the portal?" Sam asked.

"Yeah," Sketch confirmed. "In the air, around the edge of the portal, just like on the floor. You guys don't see that?"

"Just looks like a hole to me," Sam said, shrugging.

"Oh," Sketch said, taking that in. "But you guys see the lion-bird thing, right?" he asked, turning to Rush. "I mean, that's what you guys are talking about?"

"Yeah," Rush said, grinning. "Definitely see that."

"So, uh, what do I do?" Sam asked Sketch.

Sketch shrugged. "Whatever you want, I think. Just don't mess up the ones on the floor."

Sam moved her arms a little bit farther from the portal, watching the gryphon the whole time. It cocked its head at her inquisitively, watching her as she watched it, but otherwise nothing happened. She dropped her arms to her lap gratefully and started rubbing each shoulder in turn.

"Thank God," she muttered.

Rush reached out a hand toward the gryphon, moving slowly, so as not to frighten it. At first it moved away, but when he stopped moving his hand, the cub moved back toward him, stretching its head out and grazing his fingertips.

"Well, that's weird," Rush said.

"You mean the baby gryphon standing in the garage in Middle-of-Nowhere, Wyoming?" Sam asked, still rubbing her shoulders. "Or something weirder than that? Cause if so, we're really having a banner evening."

Rush flashed her a look that managed to say 'Give me a break, already' without uttering a word, but otherwise he ignored her.

"Its head didn't feel... well, it didn't feel like feathers..."

"Really?" Kaitlyn asked, and she crawled up to it slowly, sitting down next to it when she got close enough to touch it and reaching out a hand of her own. The gryphon reached its head out to brush her hand, and Kaitlyn gasped in surprise, snatching her hand back involuntarily and then reaching out to it again.

"What? What's wrong?" Mackenzie demanded.

"Nothing," Kaitlyn reassured her. "I mean, it didn't hurt or anything. Rush is right, though. It's weird. It's like... it's there, but it's not there."

"What do you mean, 'it's there, but it's not there'?" Sam asked, finally standing up and moving out of the runed circle, stepping over the chalk outline carefully so as not to disturb it.

"I mean, when you touch it, your hand kind of... goes *into* it a little," Kaitlyn replied.

"Huh?" This last was from Daniel, who had moved up next to Kaitlyn, kneeling just behind her and watching the gryphon over her shoulder.

Kaitlyn reached her hand out again, brushing its back slowly with her fingertips, but when Daniel looked closely, he could see that her fingers were, in fact, sinking partly into its back.

"Whoa!" Daniel exclaimed.

"It feels like..." Kaitlyn was clearly having a hard time trying to describe the sensation. "I don't know... Almost like dragging your fingers through clay, kind of, only it's not sticky at all. See?" She pulled her hand back out of the creature's back and rubbed her fingertips against her thumb, showing them that there wasn't any residue on her hand.

"OK, that is *not* normal," Mackenzie declared. "I don't think anybody should be touching it, let alone... *merging* with it..."

But Sketch had already started imitating Kaitlyn, only he let his hand push even farther into its back than she had—and then kept right on going.

"Look!" he exclaimed. "You can pull your hand all the way through it!" Demonstrating, he dragged his entire right hand through the creature from one side to the other. He had to struggle a bit to do it, but the gryphon just stared at him all the while, apparently not at all disturbed by this new turn of events.

As soon as Sketch's hand was clear of its body, however, the gryphon cub shivered all over, its fur bristling and its feathers all puffing up slightly before settling back down. Sketch had pulled his hand away at the first sign of movement, but once the gryphon seemed to have relaxed, he tried to drag his hand through it again, only this time it didn't work.

"Hey," he said, sounding disappointed. "It's normal now."

Rush's eyebrows furrowed as he reached an experimental hand out toward the gryphon cub.

"No way! He's right!" Rush exclaimed, sounding a lot more excited than Sketch had. "It feels like you'd expect it to now. With feathers and fur and everything."

The cub stretched out its neck and rubbed the side of its head against Rush's hand, purring like a cat. Kaitlyn reached out and scratched the feathers on the side of its face, and the cub twisted its neck until her fingers were scratching under its chin. The cub purred even louder and then sighed happily, making Kaitlyn giggle.

"You guys are crazy," Mackenzie muttered.

"Sit, boy," Rush said to it. "Can you sit?" He moved his hand up in the air over the cub's head and then toward its tail, forcing the gryphon to tilt its head up to follow his movement. Rush expected the gryphon to sit down on its rump eventually, but instead, the gryphon just continued to bend its neck backward until its head was completely upside down, resting along its own back, making them all laugh out loud, even Mackenzie.

"Well, it works with dogs," Rush said, still chuckling. "Come on, buddy, sit. Sit." Rush placed one hand against the cub's chest and the other on its rump, gently pressing down until the cub suddenly sat.

"Good boy!" Rush said, scratching its chin and praising it enthusiastically. "That's a *good* boy!"

"It's not a dog," Sam commented, but Rush just grinned at her with a wicked gleam in his eye.

"Hey, Sketch," he said. "Go get me a blank page from that notepad."

"OK." Sketch retrieved the pad from the table and tore a page out of it from behind his drawing, handing the yellow sheet to Rush.

Rush took it and wadded it up into a ball, showing it to the gryphon.

"Look, boy! Look what I've got! You want it?" Rush waved the ball in front of the gryphon, which followed its movements with its head. Sam just rolled her eyes. "I'm gonna throw it, OK? Are you ready? Go get it!"

Rush tossed the paper lightly, not wanting to throw it so far that the cub wouldn't chase it, but the gryphon whipped its neck out to the side quick as lightning and snatched it out of the air as it flew by without moving the rest of its body at all.

"Whoa. That was insane," Mackenzie said, and even Sam managed to look grudgingly impressed.

"Do it again!" Sketch begged him.

"Give it here, buddy," Rush said, grinning from ear to ear. "Drop it... drop it..."

The gryphon eyed him curiously for a moment but then dropped the paper ball into his hand, apparently figuring out what Rush wanted.

"You're a smart one, aren't you," Rush's voice was warm and encouraging, and he scratched the cub's chin again. "OK, boy, I'm going to throw it farther this time. You ready? You wanna get it for me? You wanna get it? Go get it!"

Rush threw the ball well over the gryphon's head, but instead of running after it, the gryphon leaped into the air, executed a twisting, mid-air somersault and extended its wings to dive after the ball, snatching it up in its beak before it hit the floor and then landing on all fours—only to keep right on going, thanks to the floor's smooth surface, its paws and talons skidding wildly on the sealed concrete before it finally slid to a halt, making Sketch laugh out loud.

"That was awesome!" Sketch shouted, forgetting in his excitement that they had snuck out of the lodge in the middle of the night and were supposed to be keeping it down.

"Shh," Rush reminded him, but Rush was chuckling too.

The gryphon cub shook its head for a moment, regaining its composure, and then jumped into the air again, gliding casually back to Rush. It used its wings this time to brake so that it landed gently, if still a bit clumsily, and promptly dropped the wadded up paper back into his hand.

"That," Daniel said quietly, "was *so* cool."

"Hey, guys, I hate to break up the party, but I think we should go," Mackenzie said. "We said we were just going to try this to figure out why they want us to do it. Now we know we can do it, but we still don't know why, and I, for one, really don't want to get caught out here."

Rush looked at Sam. "Tick-Tock?" he asked. Mackenzie flashed him a look of annoyance but said nothing.

"She's right," Sam admitted reluctantly. "We still have time to clean up in here and not get caught, but we need to get going."

"OK," Rush acknowledged. Kaitlyn walked back to the sink to retrieve the damp rag while Rush addressed the gryphon cub.

"Come here, buddy," he said gently. He scratched the cub behind the ears for a moment before finally backing away from it, but the cub only followed him, trying now to climb into his lap.

"No, no," Rush protested, chuckling again, and the cub looked up at him, cocking its head questioningly. "Time to go, buddy. Time to go home, OK? Go home." Rush pointed toward the portal, and the cub looked at it obediently and then looked back at Rush.

"That's right, boy. Go home. Understand? Go home now. We can play again later, OK?" Rush pointed to the portal again, and this time the cub lifted up into the air, surprising him by whistling a quick little tune and then shivering again, its fur and feathers bristling up and settling back down just like before. The shiver had caused it to fall about a foot through the air, but it caught itself easily with a downstroke of its wings and then glided toward the portal, glancing back at Rush over its shoulder to screech a final goodbye, and then thrusting its beak into the darkness, slowly pushing itself back through until it finally disappeared.

"See ya, buddy," Rush said quietly.

With a sigh, Kaitlyn knelt by the edge of the chalk circle and wiped the rag across one of the runes. Immediately, the portal shuddered, shimmering in the air for just a brief moment and then vanishing without a sound.

36
INSTRUCTOR REPORT

So, what went wrong this time? Where are my results? Do you have any idea how much pressure I'm feeling from above?"

"I believe that I do, yes."

"Is that supposed to be funny? Because, trust me, you don't. You have no piss-damn idea how much flak I'm taking. I've been doing my best to keep it off you and your little Pollyanna Island of Neverland, but I don't know how much longer I can hold the shit storm at bay. Hell, I've been your piss-damn flak umbrella. What's coming in from above is a lot worse than what I've been dishing out."

"That is a frightening thought."

"It is, isn't it? So maybe you can understand, then, why it's so important to me that we turn this ship around before it turns into the Titanic! What, exactly, do I have to do to get these kids to perform?"

"You have to tell them the truth. Do you really think I have been making this up? That I have been placing imaginary obstacles in your way? I want this project to be successful at least as badly as you do."

"I doubt that very much."

"Do you? Then you know nothing about me at all. This is a mission for you—just one mission of many over a long career—but for me, it is my life's work. And my mother's before me, and her father's before him, extending back more generations than your own precious nation can count. Far more. So do not doubt my commitment. When I tell you that the unconscious mind is powerful, that it knows when it is being lied to, and that it will not cooperate in this work against its will, I am telling you the truth. We will not get what we want until we tell them what they are doing here."

"And I've told you we can't compromise the security of the project!"

"I am not asking you to tell them the details of what they are up against. We do not need to frighten them. But we must at least tell them what they are trying to accomplish. Otherwise, all our efforts here will be wasted. And you can tell your superiors that the expert they hired had the solution and you chose to ignore him."

"Don't you dare threaten me—"

"I am not threatening you! I am trying to help you! Why can you not see that?"

"Fine! ... Fine. Tell them what they're trying to do. But once they know, the Hunt kid doesn't leave."

"But we told him that if he committed himself to the project—"

"I know what we told him. Things change. If he wants to leave, he leaves now."

37
CHOICES

When Rush woke up for breakfast, he still felt mentally drained, as though the half night's sleep he had managed to get hadn't done him any good at all. He forced himself to get up and go through the motions of his morning routine, but even turning the shower to cold didn't manage to shake the dullness out of his brain. It just made his teeth chatter.

By the time he emerged into the suite's living room, he expected to find Sketch either playing *HRT Alpha* or watching cartoons, as he had every other morning since they had arrived, but instead, he was still face planted on the couch, sound asleep.

"Hey, Sketch. Come on, man, wake up." When he didn't move, Rush finally shook him by the shoulder, only to be rewarded by a series of inarticulate groans.

"Uhhhhh…. gnnnn... lem... sl…"

"Sketch. Sketch, wake up."

"Sud lumme slup."

"Sketch." Rush shook the boy's shoulder again, harder this time.

"Said, 'Lemme sleep!'" Sketch protested, grabbing his blanket, hauling it up over his head, and turning his face into the back of the couch.

"I know we didn't get enough sleep last night, OK? I know you're tired. But we can't act like anything's wrong. You have to get up and look awake, whether you feel like it or not, or else we're all gonna get in trouble."

But this was more than just a simple lack of sleep. Rush stayed up late gaming and then got up the next morning for school on a fairly regular basis. It never left him feeling as wiped out as he felt right now. He assumed it had something to do with the summoning the night before, but whatever the reason, they couldn't afford to let it give them away.

"Good," Sketch mumbled. "Let 'em ground us so we can go back to bed."

"That's not how it works, Sketch," Rush insisted, chuckling a little despite his own exhaustion. "Come on, man. Get up."

Sketch finally sat up, rubbing his eyes and looking sorrier than a stray puppy on the side of the road.

"I know," Rush admitted. "I'm feeling it, too. But we can do it, OK? We just have to get through the morning, and then we can try to grab a nap at lunch."

"OK," Sketch agreed. He stumbled off the couch and headed for the bathroom.

Rush walked toward Daniel's room to make sure he was awake, too, but he was only halfway through the kitchen when he heard Daniel's alarm go off, followed by a defiant grunt. The alarm stopped, and after a few long moments he heard Daniel start moving around. It didn't sound like he was moving very quickly, but at least he was making an effort to get up. Rush left him to it and headed downstairs.

When he reached the main lobby, Ammu walked over to him immediately, striding with purpose. Rush made an effort to stand up straight and look alert, greeting the professor with as much of his usual energy as he could muster.

"Morning, Ammu," Rush said. "Something I can do for you?"

"Walk with me."

"Sure." Rush tried to keep his voice light, but this wasn't good. He really didn't feel up to a special session of Ammu and the Unconscious Mind at the moment, but he was determined not to let on just how tired he felt.

Ammu led him out the lodge doors and around the side of the building. At first, Rush was nervous that maybe they hadn't done as good a job of cleaning up as they had thought, imagining that Ammu was going to walk him back to the workshop and ask him what he knew about the chalk lines on the floor or the stray gryphon feather he had found lying in the middle of the empty bay.

But instead, Ammu stopped in the gardens and led Rush to a simple, stone bench, sitting down amidst the flowers and inviting Rush to sit with him so they could talk. Rush managed to stifle a sigh of relief and sat gratefully next to the older man, doing his best to look alert and interested, rather than exhausted and guilty.

"I am afraid I find myself in an unfortunate position," Ammu began. "I must present you with a choice I did not think you would have to make. Please understand, this is not what I intended. I did not know..." Ammu trailed off and fell silent. Rush had never seen the man at a loss for words, and a spike of fear finally managed to clear a bit of the mental fog away.

"You must choose, unfortunately," Ammu said, apparently deciding not to finish his previous thought, "whether you would prefer to stay here all summer, by which I mean not going to your gaming competition but rather staying here to complete the program, or to leave now, in which case you would have ample time to prepare for your competition, but you would not be allowed to return."

"Wait... what?" Rush said, trying to wrap his tired mind around Ammu's words. "But you said I could go!"

"I know, and for this, I must truly apologize." Ammu's voice was deeply sorrowful, but he continued nonetheless. "It is out of my control. I have some influence over this program and its curriculum, to be sure, but in this case I have no say in the matter."

So Grid was right, Rush thought, silently taking in what Ammu had just admitted. *This really is a Homeland Security thing. Ammu isn't in charge at all.*

"Ammu," Rush begged. "Please don't take this away from me. If they were going to let me go before, there has to be a way they'd agree to it now. Something I can do, or something I can promise? It's not just a game. It's my career, Ammu. It's my future."

"I know," Ammu replied gently. "You can still go. Your future awaits. You simply would not be allowed to return."

"It isn't really a choice then," Rush said, slumping his shoulders forward and hanging his head. "If I go home early, my dad's gonna think they kicked me out. He won't let me go to the invitational anyway."

"Ah. In that regard, at least, I can still be of some assistance," Ammu replied, smiling sadly. "You would be sent home with an explanation that the first stage of the program has been so successful as to be redesigned, that you will be invited to participate in future stages during your bright college career, *et cetera* and so forth. You would not, of course, be under any such obligation, but it would suffice to appease your father, I think."

"Really?"

"Indeed. It is in their best interest for people to believe that the program has been a success. For funding purposes, if nothing else. The ruse would be for the program directors as much as for you."

A success, and completely normal, Rush thought. *I bet there won't be anything about summoning gryphons in that letter, either.* But, of course, that wasn't a thought he was about to share.

"As you can see," Ammu finished, "the choice is genuine. If you go home, there is no reason why you would not be allowed to attend the gaming conference. You simply would not be permitted to return."

"How long do I have to decide?" Rush asked, his head swimming.

Ammu stared at him for a long moment, and Rush knew the answer from his silence even before he heard him say the words aloud.

"You must decide now, before we return to the lodge. Even as we speak, our time is running short. I can not apologize enough for the situation I have put you in," Ammu said, his voice clearly conveying his regret. "This was not my intention."

Rush sat on the bench in silence, wondering how this could be happening. If they had offered him this choice even two days ago, he would have leaped at it. But now... now he wouldn't just be leaving some weird kid named Roman and a five-star resort with no Internet. Now he would be leaving Sketch and Disco and Grid and Tick-Tock and Gears. He would be leaving the baby gryphon he could never see again, and who knew how many other magical creatures from Ammu's book—a whole mystical world he would never be able to explore.

But gaming was all he had ever been good at, at least until now, and the ICIC was hardly a career plan. It was like Grid had said, this was just a government program—Homeland Security would use them for the summer and then send them home. Hell, they might even have to promise never to communicate with each other again. And then where would he be?

The answer came to him in a flash of clarity: he would be exactly where he was now, heading home, only it would be after the invitational, without any other future to look forward to. He would have the same damn hole in his heart he was feeling now, but with nothing else left to fill it.

"How am I going to tell the others?" Rush asked, the depth of his pain showing in his eyes. "How am I going to tell Sketch?"

Ammu smiled sadly, recognizing that Rush had made his choice.

"We will tell them together," he said, his voice somehow still gentle and reassuring even with Rush's whole universe crashing down around him. Together, they stood and began the long, slow walk back to the lodge.

38
CAREERS

No! You can't!" Sketch was the first to react, and Rush was afraid the kid might blurt something out to give away their escapade of the night before. But even shocked and upset, Sketch wasn't stupid. He just stared at Rush with a look that managed to convey pain and anger and betrayal all at once.

"I am afraid he must," Ammu said quietly, "but I need you all to understand that this was not an easy choice for him to make, and that it means nothing about his feelings toward any of you."

"Sure it doesn't," Sam said bitterly.

When Ammu had ushered them all into the classroom, Mackenzie had known something was wrong, but she could not have imagined Rush was leaving. He stood next to Ammu in front of the whiteboard, where Mackenzie just stared at him, her face betraying nothing. She was as hurt as the rest, but she wasn't about to show it. If she could say goodbye to her father on one mission after another, she could say goodbye to Rush.

"It doesn't," Rush said adamantly. "I don't want to leave. But they said I had to pick between this and the invitational. I didn't really have a choice."

"You *had* a choice," Sam spat back. "You just *chose* not to stay here."

"It's not that simple," Mackenzie said quietly.

"No, it is not," Ammu confirmed. "Our friend has a rare chance to pursue his dream of a gaming career, and he might never have such an opportunity again. Our sorrow, of course, is genuine, and it is natural to react to that pain. But what we must try to do—what we must *always* try to do—is to see *his* pain, not just our own. He was faced with a difficult choice—bound to incur sadness, no matter what he decided."

"And he had to do what would make him less sad," Kaitlyn offered.

"Not necessarily," Ammu said, shaking his head. "Rush? Would you say that leaving the program is making you less sad than staying would?"

"No," Rush agreed, seeing where Ammu was leading him. "I'd be much happier to stay." He said this directly to Sketch, begging him to understand.

"Then why not just stay?" Sketch demanded.

Because this might be my only chance to get out from under my father's shadow, Rush thought to himself. *Because when this summer is over, if I don't have my gaming career in place, I'm going to have to go back home and apply to colleges and intern at some huge, boring company and turn into my father, just like my brother did, and I'll do anything I have to do to avoid that, no matter how much it hurts, even leaving the best real life friends I've ever had.* But he didn't know how to say any of that. Instead, he just stared at the floor, silently hoping they wouldn't hate him for leaving.

"It's OK," Mackenzie said finally. "I've always wanted to serve my country. If they told me I had to choose today, now or never, I'd leave, too, even though I wouldn't want to."

"Thanks," Rush said, his voice almost a whisper. He was so grateful for her forgiveness that he was afraid he might break down a little if he looked her in the eye, but he did it anyway because it felt like the right thing to do. The smile he got in return felt like a lifeline in the midst of a raging sea.

"I'm sorry, Rush," Kaitlyn said. "I wasn't thinking about it that way. If I had to choose between fixing things for a living or staying here... well, I'm not sure which one I'd pick, to be honest, but I know it wouldn't be an easy decision."

Rush just nodded, not trusting himself to speak. Tick-Tock and Sketch still looked mad, but at least Grid and Gears seemed to understand.

What if we can't summon anything without you? Sam wanted to ask, but of course she couldn't. This was the most amazing thing she had ever been a part of—the first thing in her life that had ever really *mattered.* For all she knew, he was about to ruin it for all of them, and there wasn't anything she could do about it.

"Fine," she said icily. "Do whatever you want. I'm going back to breakfast. *Some* of us have work to do today."

When Sam stood up, Sketch did, too. "I'd never pick a *job* over *you,*" he said, and his words felt like a knife in Rush's heart as Sketch followed Sam out the door.

"He'll understand when he's older," Mackenzie said, repeating what she had heard her mother say countless times about her youngest sister—every time she started sulking because their father was leaving again. "He's too young to have career goals."

She grinned when she said it, and Rush managed to smile a little too. Then she surprised him by hugging him goodbye.

"Take care of yourself," she said. "Don't worry about us. We'll be OK."

"Thanks, Grid," he said, feeling grateful all over again.

"Knock 'em dead," Kaitlyn said, saying goodbye to him next. She hugged him, too, and when she pulled away, she winked at him cheerfully, her smile as bright as ever. Rush knew in that moment that he would remember her that way forever, smiling like the summer sunshine, and he suddenly understood everything Daniel saw in her.

"Take care of her," Rush said as Daniel got up in turn and hugged him awkwardly, clapping him on the back. "And look out for Sketch, too, OK? Maybe watch some TV with him at night or something? He's not used to being alone."

"I'll look out for him," Daniel promised. "I have a little brother at home. We'll hang out. Trust me. He'll be sick of me before it's over."

Rush laughed a little. But the laugh threatened to stick in his throat, so he stopped before he gave himself away.

"Thanks," was all he managed to say, and Daniel nodded.

"God, I still have to pack my stuff!" he exclaimed suddenly, but Ammu shook his head in reply.

"I signaled Christina when we came in," Ammu explained. "It has been taken care of. Your bags will already be on the bus by now."

"Oh. Wow. I guess this is really it, huh?"

"I did not mean to take you by surprise," Ammu said gently. "We felt that a long goodbye would only distract the group further from the work that lies ahead."

"Yeah, I get it."

Rush looked around at his three friends who were still there. Grid nodded at him, and Kaitlyn smiled warmly, holding Daniel's hand.

"Well, I guess this is goodbye," he said. He hugged them each one more time for good measure and then walked out of the classroom with Ammu trailing behind him. As promised, the bus was waiting in the driveway, and Ammu walked him up to its door.

"It has been an honor to know you, Ashton Hunt," Ammu said. "May peace be with you all your days."

"You too, Ammu," Rush said.

He hesitated on the bus steps, looking back at the lodge, but no small, familiar face appeared at the door. After a long moment, he sighed and stepped up into the aisle, taking a seat by the window as the driver slowly pulled away.

He watched the lodge all the way down the long driveway, ready to stop the bus with a shout, but no one came running out to give him a last-minute hug, or to offer him a final smile of forgiveness. All he saw was Ammu, the lone sentinel, who stood waving a silent goodbye until the bus finally turned the corner, and he passed out of view behind the trees.

39
BRIEFING

Christina and Ammu gathered everyone back into the classroom after breakfast, where there was now a television in front of the whiteboard with a DVD player hooked up to it. Mackenzie was grateful when Christina sat down with them at the far end. Leaving one of the six chairs empty all morning would have been a bit too reminiscent of a missing man formation, and if Mackenzie was feeling Rush's absence, Sketch and Sam were taking it ten times harder.

Mackenzie had expected Sketch's glum demeanor, but Sam's vehement reaction surprised her, making her wonder whether Sam had liked the charismatic gamer more than she had let on. Mackenzie sat in the chair near the door on purpose, so that Sam and Sketch would both have to sit somewhere in the middle. Whether they liked it or not, neither one of them needed to feel any more alone right now than they already did.

In the end, Sketch sat next to Mackenzie, and Kaitlyn sat next to Christina. Daniel hesitated for a moment but ultimately sat next to Sketch, and Mackenzie nodded at him thankfully, leaving Sam to perch sullenly between Daniel and Kaitlyn. Ammu took his place near the television, cleared his throat, and began speaking.

"What I am about to tell you has its roots in ancient history, but I believe the historical facts will be difficult to take in—and even more difficult to believe—without a modern reference point. The video I am about to show you took place in Afghanistan. It is one of the events that prompted the development of the Intuition Assessment Battery."

Ammu turned the television on, and the image that appeared was a still shot of a helicopter, viewed from above.

"This footage is highly classified. I can only show you the very brief segment that applies to our work here at the ICIC. It was captured by a drone, which was filming a certain mission, the details of which are not important. What *is* important is what happens in the next seven seconds of real time, so watch closely. I'll play it at half speed to make it easier to see."

Ammu pressed a button on the remote, and the video started moving. There was no sound, but the blades of the helicopter began to turn, and the camera tilted oddly for a moment before returning to its original angle. A second later, something raced into the picture from offscreen. Even at half speed, it moved incredibly fast. The image was blurred by the movement of the camera, but still, it was clear enough—whatever it was flew right up to the helicopter and caught the main blade in its hands, stopping the rotor and sending the copter into a wild spin.

"What the hell?" Sam blurted out, sitting up straighter and staring at the screen.

The image stopped again as Ammu paused the video.

"That, unfortunately, is all I have been permitted to show you. The helicopter crashed not long afterward, killing the soldiers on board. The military believed this to be some kind of bizarre mechanical failure, as they could not see what you have all just seen for yourselves. But suffice it to say they were soon convinced there was more going on than modern science could account for."

"What *was* that thing?" Kaitlyn asked.

"You saw it?" Sketch asked in surprise, looking across Daniel and Sam to catch her eye.

"Yeah," she confirmed.

"We all did, Sketch," Mackenzie assured him.

"I didn't, actually," Christina said, her soft voice sounding troubled. "But I'd like to know what you all saw."

"Sketch?" Ammu prompted. "Would you be willing to draw what you just saw for Christina?"

Sketch looked around nervously. He had not shown anyone any of his dark drawings since the whole Mr. Lockhart incident—not even Rush—and he didn't want to start now. They all said they saw something, but was it the same thing he had seen? What if they thought it looked different? What if his drawing made them scared of him? Or made them think he was crazy?

"I don't have my drawing stuff with me," Sketch protested. "Maybe everyone else could just describe it?"

"Sure, Sketch," Daniel agreed immediately, and Sketch gave him a small but grateful smile. "It looked like a body made of wind. Like a tornado sort of, only more like the size of a person. And it had a face, with dark holes for eyes and another hole for its mouth."

In truth, Daniel was extremely nervous about describing it for Christina, especially given how strange Ammu had seemed yesterday. But Ammu wasn't behaving oddly now, as though showing people videos of wind monsters taking down helicopters were a perfectly normal thing to do. And, anyway, Daniel had promised Rush he'd look out for Sketch. If it had been his own little brother in the hot seat, Daniel would have jumped in for him, too.

"It had lightning in its hands," Kaitlyn added, not wanting Daniel to have to describe it alone, "but I didn't see any feet. Just a tail that narrowed at the bottom."

Sketch quietly exhaled a long sigh of relief. That was exactly what he had seen.

"That's how Ammu described it," Christina admitted. "I just wanted to know how it looked to you."

Just wanted to check Ammu's story, you mean, Sam thought, but Ammu didn't seem troubled. In fact, he smiled at her comment. *Probably glad he finally has someone to back him up.*

Ammu turned the television off and began speaking again.

"What do you know about Alexander the Great?" he asked, seeming to change the subject entirely.

"He conquered Persia for the Greeks in something like three hundred BC, more or less," Sam offered.

"He was a brilliant strategist," Mackenzie chimed in. "They still teach him in military history, even today."

"Excellent!" Ammu agreed. "History remembers him as a conqueror, but he was much more than that. Persian mythology of Alexander's day describes a vast, spiritual realm made up of both light and dark forces that had claimed our own world as its battle-field. There were good spirits and bad, as well as a whole host of marvelous animals and even plants that could fight for the forces of life or death, depending on which side controlled them."

At these words, Daniel and Kaitlyn shared a surreptitious glance over Sketch's head, remembering the gryphon in the workshop.

"This spiritual world was invisible to most people, but Alexander had been a student of Aristotle, who had taught him to master the pathways of his mind. As a result, he could see that these myths were more than just stories. There was a great war between good and evil taking place all around him, and he vowed, when he succeeded his father to the throne as a young man, that he would fight here in our world with the forces of good, taking back those lands in which evil had been winning the battle, unbeknownst to most of mankind.

"He learned how to summon the forces of good to aid him, and he taught others to do so as well—to see through the eyes of the unconscious mind. These men became his most trusted generals. Together, they held the forces of darkness at bay, not only in Greece and Persia but throughout as much of the ancient world as they could protect. Unfortunately, Alexander died while he was still relatively young. Without his leadership, the forces of darkness pushed back against his army, exploiting the weaknesses within his generals to turn them against each other, creating a rash of civil wars that threatened to tear apart all that he had built.

"But Alexander's true mission had had nothing to do with conquering lands or expanding the Greek empire. He had dedicated himself in every spare moment, in every brief respite during the war he was waging against the forces of darkness, to divining the ultimate weapon he needed to end the war once and for all: the secret to banishing all the invisible spirits, both good and bad, back to their own world. The forces of darkness ended his life, but not before he had completed his work and shared it, cautiously, with only the most trusted of all his generals."

With these words, Ammu reached into his satchel and produced his leather-bound book. He opened it to a spot near the back and pulled out several photographs, which he handed to Mackenzie. Glancing through them, she saw a myriad of statues—some of real animals and others of strange, mythological creatures—engaged in battle throughout a cavernous space, with what looked like an Egyptian pyramid in its center.

Not wanting to miss what he was saying, she handed the photos to Sketch, who pored over each one for a long time. When he came to the photograph of the seal on the tomb itself, his eyes widened in surprise, and he glanced up at Ammu to the symbol that glowed over his heart. It was, indeed, one and the same. He chewed the inside of his cheek thoughtfully, deciding to go through all the photos again before finally handing them on to Daniel.

"These generals took his body from its resting place and secreted it away," Ammu continued, "hiding it from all the world. They buried him in a sacred tomb, concealing it within an ancient Zoroastrian temple that had long been abandoned, and there, they performed the ritual he had taught them just before his death, sealing the rift between the worlds, so that no summoner, no matter how great, could again bridge the gap between this world and the other, for as long as the seal remained unbroken.

"The generals then went their separate ways, swearing each other to secrecy, but each promised to protect the knowledge, should it ever again be needed, by teaching this history—along with the ancient secrets of the true summoners—to a single, trusted member of the next generation. Sometimes this would be a son or daughter, sometimes a niece or nephew, sometimes a promising student of no blood relation at all, but always only one, who would, in turn, promise to do the same.

"Over the centuries, some of these lines of knowledge have been cut short, their keepers having departed unexpectedly from this life before their great secret could be passed on. I do not know of any others besides myself who remain, but there may well be a few, scattered throughout the world. How many, I have no way of knowing. It is not as though we advertise."

He smiled when he said this—his usual, humble smile—and Mackenzie realized with a start how badly he had been wanting to tell them what he was finally telling them now.

"Seven years ago, after more than two millennia, a team of archaeologists discovered the tomb of Alexander the Great, buried deep beneath what is today an Islamic mosque—the mosque, in turn, having been built many centuries ago atop the site of the ancient Zoroastrian temple. Without understanding the implications of their actions, they broke the seal, enabling the ancient rituals of summoning to be completed successfully once again."

Sam looked down at her hands and then shared a brief glance with Kaitlyn before pointedly looking away.

"Unfortunately, as you can see from the video, the rituals can be used for devastating results. Whether the knowledge has been retained by another line of descent from those ancient generals, or whether there exists a Zoroastrian sect which has also managed to protect these secrets across the centuries, or whether the process is simply being rediscovered by those who possess the strongest of pathways between the conscious and the unconscious mind, I do not know.

"What I do know is that the forces of darkness must not be released again upon an unknowing world. Which leads me to the ultimate point of this morning's briefing: the true nature of the ICIC. We have brought you here for the sole purpose of completing a summoning ritual—hopefully, in fact, several such rituals—in a place where the process can be controlled and studied, so that we might learn how to put a stop to attacks of this nature."

Ammu paused and turned the television back on, revealing the final image of the helicopter spinning out of control.

"Before more human lives are lost."

40
SKETCH

"I'm sorry, Ammu, but could we try this somewhere else?" Kaitlyn had been staring at the book for what seemed to her like a very long time, but the runes just weren't coming to her the way they had the night before.

"Is there something we can do to make this space more conducive to the process?" Ammu asked in return.

"No, I guess there isn't really anything wrong with the room," she admitted, but her voice sounded dejected, exhausted.

"If there is anything we can do to help you focus more easily here, we will gladly do it, but I am afraid the experiments can not be moved. There are certain safety precautions in place, as well as equipment meant to capture the process."

Kaitlyn nodded. "I understand. Let me try again."

She looked back at the drawing, and after several long, awkward minutes—during which Sam looked more and more annoyed and Sketch actually sat down on the floor, threatening to lie down on his side until Mackenzie hurried over and propped the boy up with her leg—Kaitlyn finally nodded.

"I have it," she said, but she still sounded tired.

"I know you are all sad to see your friend leave," Ammu said, "but try not to think of the moment in which he left. Try to see him at his gaming convention, with a smile on his face, defeating the competition and earning his position on the professional team. Imagine him happy. It will help your minds to settle and focus."

In the silver lining category, Mackenzie thought, *tired and sad look a lot alike. Rush leaving still sucks, but it's covering our asses right now.*

Kaitlyn nodded at Ammu, trying to look grateful for his help.

"Excellent," Ammu said encouragingly. "Places then, everyone. Let us begin."

Kaitlyn took the blue chalk and began to trace the runes on the floor. She wondered how many times she would have to do this before she finally had the pattern memorized, so she could draw the complex figures without an image to prompt her.

"Hey, Gears?" Sam said, breaking her out of her reverie.

"Huh? Sorry, what?"

"Timing, remember? We all have to work together?" Sam sat cross-legged in the circle, watching Kaitlyn draw the runes while Mackenzie was still extracting herself from Sketch, encouraging him to sit up straight without her.

"Oh, gosh! I'm so sorry!"

"That is all right," Ammu reassured her. "But please, everyone, let us focus as best we can. The summoning will not work if your minds are not attuned to the task. A tremendous amount of knowledge has surely been lost about this process throughout the intervening centuries, but of this much, at least, I am certain."

Kaitlyn nodded, clearly chagrined, and she sat back on her heels, waiting patiently for Mackenzie to make her way over to the circle.

"Actually," Mackenzie said, having finally succeeded in getting Sketch to stand back up, "I think Gears can finish drawing the runes first, and then she can trace them over again from the starting point when I come in." *That's how we did it the first time, remember?* She willed the others to understand what she was really saying. *When we almost opened the portal right here, the time Ammu doesn't want them to know about.*

"Oh, um... OK," Sam said. "I... yeah... sorry, Gears. Go ahead. My bad."

"It is fine," Ammu interjected gently. "We are all still learning how this works. Together, we will experiment until we are successful, yes?" He smiled at them encouragingly, and they all nodded in return, trying not to look guilty.

Kaitlyn finished drawing the runes on the floor. By the time she was done, Sketch was sitting down again. Mackenzie gave Daniel a meaningful glance, but Daniel was already moving toward him, taking her place to prop Sketch up since Daniel could stand still while he sang. He stepped behind Sketch, who leaned back gratefully against Daniel's leg, watching the process with drooping eyelids.

"Here," Mackenzie said, choosing their starting point. "Gears? You ready?"

Kaitlyn took a deep breath and nodded.

"OK, Tick-Tock. Count us in."

"One... two... one, two, three, four."

Mackenzie blessed the circle as Kaitlyn drew each rune, but she was as tired as the rest. Given her background in a military family, she knew how to hide things like pain or sadness or sleep deprivation, but she was still performing the ritual more by rote than through any conscious focus. She only hoped it would still work.

Ammu had come clean with them, and Mackenzie had the feeling it had cost him something to do it—that he was taking a real risk by telling them as much as he had. He deserved to share in their success, to get credit for the progress he had obviously made with them, but she just wasn't sure they could do it in the condition they were in.

Like Mackenzie, Daniel performed his part of the ritual by memory, bouncing his knee once in a while to keep Sketch alert. At the fifth such reminder Sketch glared up at him, but Daniel returned the look with a warning glance of his own, and Sketch grudgingly sat up straighter.

As they neared the end, Sketch finally perked up, the runes on the floor beginning to glow with the same magic he had seen the night before. Sure enough, a pinprick of darkness appeared in the space over Sam's head as she opened her arms in the air. Slowly, just as it had before, the portal began to expand.

"Yes! There it is!" Ammu said, his voice quiet so as not to startle them but intense, nonetheless, in his excitement.

Daniel continued to sing softly as the portal expanded. It was the size of a golf ball, and then a baseball, and then a softball, and Daniel felt himself starting to get excited despite his exhaustion when Sketch suddenly slammed back into his legs, almost making him lose his balance.

Daniel looked down in confusion. Sketch was scrabbling backward on the floor, trying desperately to get away from the portal, but Daniel's legs were in his way. He was panicking too much to realize the problem, continuing to shove himself against Daniel's legs as he started shouting.

"Close it!" he yelled. "CLOSE IT! CLOSE IT! CLOSE IT!"

The creature on the other side was shoving its way into the portal, but even though it hadn't yet breached the final barrier, Sketch could already see it in his mind's eye. Its long, rat-like head was rotting away—what passed for flesh draping in tatters off the muscle and bone underneath. One eye was hanging out of its socket, blackened and dead, while the other glowed red with hatred. It was as large as a full-grown wolf, which was the only thing protecting them for the moment as it clawed and scrabbled at the tight fit, trying to wedge one razor-clawed appendage past its head to help pull itself along.

Sam sat frozen in place, staring at Sketch's sudden panic, her eyes wide with fear, while Kaitlyn just watched in confusion, a puzzled look on her face, glancing back and forth between the empty portal and Sketch's obvious terror.

Mackenzie, however, was already moving. As soon as Sketch screamed, she dropped to the floor at the edge of the circle and tried to smear the chalk away with her hand. When that didn't work, she tore her T-shirt off over her head, wadded it up between her hands, licked the fabric for good measure, and rubbed it viciously across the closest rune. In response, the portal shuddered, shimmered in the air for a moment, and then vanished, just as it had the night before.

Mackenzie stood up, unperturbed by her public disrobing—the sports top she had been wearing under her T-shirt still covered her as much as she was used to anyway while working out in a gym full of soldiers.

"Is everyone OK?" she asked, calmly pulling the chalk-smeared T-shirt back on over her head.

Sketch nodded vigorously, gratefully, his eyes still as large as saucers.

"What was it, Sketch?" Ammu asked, his eyebrows knitted together in obvious concern. "What did you see?"

"I don't know," he said, his voice still shaking, "but *that* was *not* a gryphon."

41
CONSEQUENCES

"What are you drawing?" Mackenzie asked, but Sketch just shrugged.

He sat in the middle of the couch in the boys' suite, where everyone had gathered after dinner by unspoken agreement. Mackenzie sat on his right, looking over his shoulder at the art pad on his lap. His pencil glided idly across the page, the image taking shape only slowly, one line here and then another way over there, so that it was hard to tell how any of it was connected.

Daniel sat at the far end of the couch, sitting crosswise so he could rest his back against the arm of the sofa. He stretched his legs out behind Sketch, who sat forward, close to the edge, hunched over his drawing. Daniel had offered to play *HRT Alpha* with the younger boy, but Sketch hadn't seemed interested, so instead he had retrieved his guitar from his room. He reclined casually, his legs crossed at the ankles, slowly picking out the tune of "Why Worry" by Dire Straits. When he reached the chorus, he began to sing softly, the peaceful quality of his voice matching the soothing words, almost like a lullaby.

Kaitlyn smiled, sitting on the coffee table facing him, having pulled it away from the couch so she and Sam could use it as a bench.

"Are you going to draw us what you saw today?" Mackenzie asked, trying again, but Sketch shook his head adamantly. That thing, whatever it was, belonged in the dark sketchpad for sure, if he ever decided to draw it at all.

"Why do you think that happened, anyway?" Kaitlyn asked.

"Isn't it obvious?" Sam's voice was bitter with resentment. "Rush left. He was the one who could feel it, so he was probably the one calling it. Without him, God only knows what we're going to bring through. Lizard people, maybe, or giant bugs, or brain-sucking slimes—"

"We get it. Thanks," Mackenzie said, raising one hand and begging her to stop. She was worried Sketch might panic again, but he ignored Sam's catalog of disaster, his pencil still floating over the page, pausing occasionally as he tilted his head this way or that and then starting back up again, filling in small portions of the drawing here and there in a way Mackenzie still couldn't comprehend.

"We don't know it was that," Kaitlyn said, her voice thoughtful.

"What *else* would it be?" Sam demanded.

"I'm not saying it wasn't a factor," Kaitlyn said, trying not to disagree with Sam directly, "but I know I was pretty tired. I didn't feel as focused as I did last night. I think that might have had something to do with it."

"I was feeling the same way," Mackenzie added. "I felt the energy flowing into the blessing, but it was like I couldn't hang on to it, or like I couldn't *direct* it, or something. It kept... slipping away from me. I'm the one who's supposed to be keeping up our protections. It was probably my fault."

Sam rolled her eyes. "Oh, sure. Everything revolves around *you*, right? Maybe *I* opened the portal at the wrong time. Did you think of that?"

"Is that what happened?" Mackenzie asked, raising an eyebrow, but Sam just stared back at her, pursing her lips in disgust and refusing to answer the question.

"I wasn't focusing well, either," Daniel chimed in. He didn't stop playing, choosing instead to speak over the soft notes of the guitar. Mackenzie had to admit that the tune was soothing, and she found herself grateful for his efforts.

"Can you always see what's coming through the portal before it gets here?" Mackenzie asked Sketch, but he only shrugged.

"Sketch?" she prompted him again. "I know you don't feel like talking right now, but this is kind of important."

Sketch stopped drawing and glared up at her.

"I don't know," he said. "I guess. I thought everyone could, OK? I don't always know what you guys can see and what you can't. You see more stuff than most people, but I still see more stuff than you, and it's not cool. I don't like being the only one who sees *everything*."

It was the longest speech Mackenzie had ever heard him make, and she raised her eyebrows in surprise, not sure what to do with it.

"I'm sorry, Sketch," Kaitlyn said gently. "I can see how that would be hard."

Sketch had bristled up in frustration, but Kaitlyn's tone seemed to appease him. He dropped his shoulders back down, and after looking at her for a long moment, his expression unreadable, he turned his attention back to his pad and started drawing again.

"I'm sorry, too," Mackenzie added. "I didn't mean to upset you. For what it's worth, you really saved our butts in there today. You might not be glad you can see things we don't, but I'm sure glad *someone* can. Whatever was coming for us, I'm glad you were there to warn us."

"Yeah, she's right," Kaitlyn agreed, and Daniel added his own,

"Me, too." Sam was the only one who didn't comment, but she didn't say anything to deny it, either.

Whatever he was thinking, Sketch didn't reply.

"Maybe we *were* just too tired," Sam finally said, and Mackenzie looked at her in surprise.

"I'm still mad at Rush," Sam clarified. "He shouldn't have left. I'm just saying I was exhausted, too. I think summoning things probably... drains us, somehow. Like when you study really hard for a test, and then after you take it you feel like you're ready to just pass out and sleep all day."

"That makes sense," Kaitlyn agreed. "I don't think we should try to summon things on our own anymore, just in case. I don't want to let Ammu down again."

"I don't think we should be doing it on our own, anyway," Mackenzie added. "Not after today. If Sketch hadn't been paying attention, who knows what might have come through."

"Agreed," Daniel said. Even Sam nodded, and Daniel finally stopped playing and looked pointedly at Sketch. When he didn't look up, Daniel nudged him gently in the back with his foot.

"What? Oh, yeah."

But he was still engrossed in his drawing, which was finally starting to coalesce into a meaningful image. When Mackenzie looked over his shoulder now, she was amazed to see a perfect replica of one of the photographs Ammu had shown them that morning: the door of Alexander's tomb, intricately carved to depict the side view of a life-sized lion, rearing magnificently into the air, with a single, stark lightning bolt running it through.

42
AMMU

I t was two more days before they returned to the summoning room. Ammu explained that extra "security measures" were being added after their close call with the unknown, which was just as well. The students of the ICIC finally had forty-eight hours to enjoy everything the resort had to offer—the pool even being open in the afternoons with Staff Sergeant Miller for a lifeguard—but they were too exhausted to do more than nap in the lounge chairs around the water's edge.

The only one who really took advantage of the time off was Sketch, who pushed the kitchen staff to their limits after testing Christina's offer to accept unusual meal requests and discovering that the dedicated chefs of the ICIC would at least *attempt* to create any dish he asked for, bar none. He immediately sat down and made a list, running through every concoction he could remember from the many books he had read, and then asking the others for more ideas.

As a result, they enjoyed a perpetual buffet, transitioning

seamlessly from breakfast, to brunch, to lunch, to tea, to dinner, to supper, to dessert, to late night snacking, all courtesy of what they laughingly dubbed Sketch's Smorgasbord Spectacular. It didn't make them miss Rush any less, but even Sketch had to admit that eating seemed to be doing as much to restore his energy level as sleeping was. By the time their two days of vacation were up, they were all feeling much more themselves again.

When they arrived in the summoning room the following morning, they were surprised to discover a fully-armed Staff Sergeant Miller waiting for them. He stood in the corner on high alert, wearing a jungle camouflage uniform and a grim expression of determination.

"You realize green camo doesn't work in a white room, right?" Sam challenged him.

"I'm not trying to blend in," he said, nodding at her without smiling. "My job is to draw any potential danger away from the five of you, at any cost. Ma'am."

"Oh," Sam replied lamely.

"Good job, Miller," Mackenzie said, grinning at him wryly. "Way to freak out the assets."

Miller's eyes flicked to the one-way mirror behind her before returning her gaze. "I apologize, ma'am," was all he said, and Mackenzie dropped the grin, automatically matching his professional manner.

"OK, people," she said, looking around at the others to make sure she had their attention. "Everybody ready?"

They all nodded.

"Good. Let's do this thing."

Ammu raised his eyebrows in surprise but said nothing, merely handing the book and the chalk to Kaitlyn.

"Got it," Kaitlyn said immediately, kneeling in the center of the room and beginning to draw out the circle.

"Here," Mackenzie said, just as briskly, pointing to a spot on the floor before Kaitlyn had even finished outlining the circle. "Start here. We're going to do this right the first time, today."

Kaitlyn nodded, moving to Mac's position and allowing her chalk to hover over the floor, ready to start drawing the runes.

"Count us in, Tick-Tock," Mackenzie said, rubbing her hands together with enthusiasm. "Here we go!"

"One... two... one, two, three, four!"

Mackenzie circled her hands through the air with renewed energy. She did not move any faster than before, keeping carefully to the pace Sam set for them, but she focused on every movement, no matter how small—aware in every moment of the energy flowing through her back, her legs, her arms, her hands—intending the blessing and protection of the circle with every nuance of position, every gesture, every fiber of her being.

Kaitlyn drew the runes on the floor, tracing each line meticulously, feeling with confidence the absolute rightness of the pattern that glowed in her mind. And as she drew, Daniel hummed the otherworldly tune of the gryphon, calling to it purposefully across the rift between the two worlds.

Sketch watched as the magic began to build, the runes glowing softly this time even before the circle was complete. On Kaitlyn's last stroke, Sam reached up over her head with just one hand, twisting her wrist gently through the air. Where her hand came to rest, a tiny portal hovered just over her palm. She reached up with the other hand and began to shape it, pausing when it was about the size of a baseball, looking at Sketch for confirmation before she continued.

"It's OK," he said, grinning.

Sam grinned back and opened her hands wider, until finally, in a sudden burst of fur and feathers, the gryphon came flying through the portal, braking hard with its wings to keep it from crashing headlong into the wall.

"You did it!" Ammu exclaimed, switching to his native tongue for several excited moments before returning to English.

"I am sorry," he said finally, trying to compose himself. "I have believed in you all from the very beginning. It is important to me that you know that. I just can not tell you how much it means to me to be witnessing a summoning within my own lifetime—to be the one to see it, after so many generations..."

Ammu wiped a tear roughly from one eye with the heel of his hand.

"It's cool, isn't it?" Sketch said, grinning up at him.

"Yes," Ammu confirmed, laughing now. "It is very 'cool' indeed." Ammu reached out a hand and playfully rubbed Sketch's head, making the boy giggle.

Throughout this interaction, the gryphon cub had flown back toward them and landed on all fours, folding its wings and sitting on the floor, looking back and forth with apparent interest from one human being to another.

"Will it come to us, do you think?" Ammu asked of no one in particular.

Sketch had been about to answer him when Mackenzie interrupted by answering first.

"Let's find out!" she exclaimed cheerfully, looking Sketch directly in the eye for just a moment before meeting Ammu's excited gaze.

Oh, right, Sketch realized. *Ammu thinks we've never seen it before.* He made a mental note to be careful about anything he said for the rest of the morning.

"Come here, buddy," Mackenzie called to the gryphon, mimicking the calm, gentle tone Rush had used in the workshop, but the gryphon just stared at her, cocking its head to one side and chirping at her inquisitively.

He's not here, Mackenzie thought. *Trust me, I'm not happy about it either. But at least we've still got each other, right? So do me a favor and work with me, OK? Make us look good.*

Mackenzie took a cautious step toward it, and the gryphon took a step backward in response, eyeing her warily.

"Come on, little guy. It's OK," Mackenzie said, trying again. "We're not going to hurt you." She took another step toward it, but it only moved backward again, placing itself unintentionally within Kaitlyn's reach.

"I can get it," Kaitlyn said brightly.

"No, Gears, wait—"

But it was too late. Kaitlyn had already grabbed it around its waist, trying to pick it up like a cat. The cub immediately spread its wings and started flapping them in a wild panic, trying desperately to get away, hissing and screeching at the top of its lungs.

"Hey!" Kaitlyn exclaimed, as the gryphon managed to wriggle its way through her grasp—literally. Her hands pulled slowly through its body and then through its legs, at last falling uselessly to her sides.

"Well, *that's* not promising," Sam commented, and Ammu gasped in amazement.

The gryphon was not at all pleased with this new turn of events, flying high up into the air and turning to watch Kaitlyn warily as it hovered near the ceiling, well out of reach.

"Please come down," Ammu tried, his voice warm and inviting. "We will not hurt you. You are such a magnificent creature. Please..."

He reached one hand toward it—not to catch it, given its current height, but only to coax it back down. Apparently the gryphon decided that this was the final straw and that it had had quite enough of humanity for today, thank you very much. Quick as a wink, it dove for the portal, moving so rapidly that its head and shoulders were already through before Sam, still sitting beneath it, could react.

But its own resistance against the substance of the portal slowed it down. Sam watched from below, giggling at first and then laughing out loud as it waved its rear legs in the air over her head, wiggling its butt theatrically from side to side, scrabbling ridiculously with its feet until it finally managed to grab onto the portal's edge with its rear claws, gaining purchase and shoving itself the rest of the way through. Only its tail remained suspended impossibly in midair for one final, dramatic moment before finally disappearing after the rest.

43
INSTRUCTOR REPORT

They did it!"

"So it would seem."

"Is that really all you have to say? They summoned a living creature from another plane of existence! Even if you are not impressed
by the feat itself, I thought you would at least be pleased. You will
finally be able to study the process."

"Study it? We can't even see it!"

"But surely, at least one of the instruments—"

"Nothing. Visible, ultraviolet, infrared, audible, ultrasound,
infrasound—"

"Excuse me, Colonel, but do you mean to say it was inaudible as
well as invisible?"

"Did it make any noise while it was in there?"

"It was quite loud, in fact."

"Then, yes, that's what I mean to say."

"Fascinating."

"That's not the word I would have chosen."

"At least we are finally making progress. Whether or not you were able to record the event, I can assure you—"

"Yes, yes, I believe you. We couldn't record... whatever it was... but we could triangulate your lines of sight as you all watched it. I have been assured that no group of actors in the world could pretend to follow the movements of an invisible creature with that much accuracy."

"I see."

"But that doesn't help me with my bigger problem. I was hoping to find a way to block the whole process, but that doesn't seem to be forthcoming. Unless we know where they're doing the actual..."

"Summoning."

"The actual summoning, I'm not seeing a way to stop it before it happens. Are you?"

"No."

"And once it's here, I can't shoot the thing down if I can't track it. If it eats something, can I at least still see what it ate? Can I spray it with a tracking agent? We need to keep working. Bring it back tomorrow, and I'll set up the experiment."

"They can not do so tomorrow."

"I'm sorry, are they scheduled for a damn massage? Whatever you have planned, it can wait."

"That is not what I mean. They are not busy; they are exhausted. The very process of summoning something from another plane takes a toll on the unconscious mind. The longer it is here, and the more control it requires, the longer the recovery time."

"So you've said. But there has to be something you can do. I don't care if you use sugar or caffeine or raw, unadulterated adrenaline. Just get them back in there."

"It will not be of any use. They will need a week, at least—"

"They have two days. I want them back in that room in two days if you have to prop their eyelids open with piss-damn toothpicks."

"You can not be serious."

"Whatever it takes, Professor. Whatever it takes."

44
CHANGES

Their next two days off were neither fun nor especially relaxing. Now, whenever they visited the buffet, as often as not there was a soldier standing at the tables, poring over their whimsical requests, clearly hoping for something more familiar, like a hot dog, maybe, or a peanut butter sandwich. Kaitlyn soon realized there were only a handful of them. The same faces appeared again and again in different places, at different times, but still, it was odd to see any new people at all. And odder still that they were soldiers.

What was most unsettling, however, was that they never smiled—not like Miller, who would at least sneak her a wink now and then, and who would practice Muay Thai with Mackenzie or play lifeguard if they asked so they could enjoy a couple of hours in the pool. The new soldiers always looked serious, all the time.

They never spoke to the students, and they never seemed to be off duty. They never sat around chatting with each other. They never used the gaming room, which had stood empty ever since Rush had left, too painful a reminder of his absence. They did occasionally use the workout facilities, but even then they were on their guard, alert, never laughing or telling stories. Whenever they happened to run into each other, their greeting was nothing more than a subtle acknowledgment—a brief nod of the head, a quick glance that said, "I know you. You may go about your business. You are not a threat."

Mackenzie, of course, was not fazed in the least. If anything, she seemed even more in her element, returning to her workout routine, practicing Muay Thai with Miller, and adopting the same air of professionalism and dedication as though she had been breathing it all her life—which, Kaitlyn supposed, she had been.

Kaitlyn was happy for her in a way. The soldiers clearly made Mackenzie feel more at home. But she couldn't help feeling that her new friend was pulling away from them all, that the more time she spent in the world she had known before, the less she seemed like Grid, and the more she seemed like Mackenzie Gray: on task, serious, and guarded.

When they finally returned to the summoning room, there was yet another change waiting for them. Now, in addition to Miller, there was also a small table pushed up against the far wall, with metal legs and a durable, white plastic top, upon which sat a spray can, a small plate of food, a clean rag, and a bowl of water.

Looking more closely, Kaitlyn scrunched up her face at the food selection. It was clearly someone's idea of what gryphon cubs might like to eat: some treats for house cats; two small, half-thawed fish; and a dead, skinned mouse, which Kaitlyn grudgingly had to admit was a smart choice, as it would appeal to both an eagle and a lion cub. But that didn't make it any less disgusting.

"Let's do this, people," Mackenzie said, her eyes flashing with intensity. She was just as animated as the last time, but somehow today it came across as commanding, rather than merely enthusiastic.

"Aye aye, Cap'n Bligh," Sam snapped back, offering her a sporty salute.

"This isn't a game, Sam," Mackenzie said, using her given name instead of her gamer tag for the first time since Rush had left.

"I never said it was, *Mac*," Sam retorted.

"Today," Ammu said, glancing from one girl to the other, "the intention is to entice the creature to interact with us. We hope to learn what it eats, and we would like to see whether paint can mark it effectively.

"The paint is only temporary," he continued, holding up a hand to fend off Kaitlyn's horrified expression. "Remember, we must find a way to counter something like the creature we saw in the video. We are here to save lives—not just of soldiers, but potentially of civilians as well. Even the lives of your own families. For some of us, these are one and the same."

He said this last while looking pointedly at Mackenzie, and Kaitlyn realized that the change she had seen in her friend might not have anything to do with the soldiers at the ICIC. Mackenzie's father was serving overseas, maybe even in Afghanistan as far as Kaitlyn knew, and just a few short days ago they had all watched a helicopter full of soldiers get killed by something this very program was designed to stop.

Like it or not, Mackenzie was right; this wasn't a game. What they were doing could have life or death consequences for the people they loved.

"I'm ready," Kaitlyn announced.

Ammu reached for the book, but she shook her head.

"I don't need it," she declared. "I have it." And she tapped a finger lightly against her temple.

Ammu raised an eyebrow in surprise but left the book in his satchel.

"Ready?" Mackenzie asked, looking at Sam, who nodded back, at least somewhat appeased for being asked. Mackenzie then looked at Daniel and Sketch in turn, and they both nodded, too. Kaitlyn drew the circle on the floor, and Mackenzie chose their starting position.

"Count us in, Tick-Tock," she said, meeting Sam's gaze and adding, "when you're ready."

"OK." Sam took a deep breath. "It's go time. One... two... one, two, three, four."

Despite the initial tension, their focus was clear. Kaitlyn's runes glowed softly even as she traced them out, Sketch watching in fascination as the perfectly normal chalk in her hand seemed to be drawing in blue light on the floor. Daniel's voice was even more confident today, and he sang rather than humming, the notes ringing out clearly in the strange, white room. When Sam stopped to look at Sketch, he was already nodding in confirmation.

"Letting it through," Sam announced, and a few moments later, the gryphon exploded through the portal, braking immediately this time and flying straight up in the air, surveying the situation cautiously.

"It's just us," Mackenzie said softly. "Remember us? I know we upset you last time, but we want to make it up to you. Look, we brought you something. See?"

Moving slowly, so as not to startle it, she picked up the plate and placed it on the floor below the hovering gryphon cub.

"Give it some room, everybody."

They all moved back toward the walls, trying not to frighten it. Even Sam stepped carefully out of the circle and backed away, crouching low as she moved.

The gryphon turned this way and that in midair, watching them all. When it was satisfied that no one was trying to grab it, the cub finally descended toward the plate.

It landed neatly, coming down on its hind legs and then using its wings to settle down gently until it was standing on all fours. It folded its wings into its sides and stretched its neck forward to examine their offerings, drawing in a few long breaths as though trying to smell the food through its beak.

"That's unusual," Kaitlyn whispered.

"For a *gryphon*?" Sam whispered back, her glance registering obvious skepticism.

"I mean for a bird," Kaitlyn clarified, shooting Sam a wry scowl. "It has an eagle's head, but eagles don't have a great sense of smell. They hunt with their eyes."

"I don't think they have *ears* either," Sam responded, her voice managing to drip with sarcasm despite being barely audible.

"That's true," Kaitlyn conceded, ignoring Sam's tone.

"We must not make the mistake of seeing it as either an eagle or a lion," Ammu murmured, seeing that the gryphon was not disturbed by their words, "or even as a combination of the two. It has surface similarities to both of those animals, but the gryphon is a creature in its own right, neither eagle nor lion, but only gryphon. We must see it as it is if we are truly to understand it."

The gryphon seemed to agree, whipping its head away from the plate in disgust, not having discovered anything upon it that was worth eating—least of all the dead mouse, one whiff of which had caused the gryphon to shove the plate violently away from itself with one strong, taloned foot.

"Well, *that* didn't go well," Sam muttered.

"We need to try the paint," Ammu directed, nodding at Mackenzie, who stood closest to the table with the spray can. "If you would, please."

"It already didn't like the food," Mackenzie argued softly. "If we start spraying paint at it, it's never going to trust us."

"If this creature becomes too suspicious of us, we will summon something else for further experimentation," Ammu said gently. "Please, Mackenzie. The paint can."

But we know it will work with us. It did before, when we summoned it on our own, she thought, but she couldn't admit that, especially here, where they were surely being filmed. *I'm sorry,* she thought to it helplessly. *I'm so sorry.*

She got up and moved toward the spray can, picking it up in

one hand and pointing it toward the gryphon cub, which cocked its head at her inquisitively. Mackenzie took a deep breath, preparing herself for the task, but just as she was about to hit the trigger, she heard a sudden whistle from the edge of the room.

Startled, Mackenzie and the gryphon both turned toward the sound to see Daniel crouching near the wall, trying to appear smaller, less threatening. He motioned to everyone to do the same, and they all did, kneeling or sitting in place. Then he whistled again, several notes this time, repeating a piece of the tune he had sung during the summoning.

Mackenzie trembled in relief, releasing the breath she hadn't even realized she had been holding. She felt as though she had just received a stay of execution, if only a temporary one.

Daniel clearly had the gryphon's attention, and he whistled at it again—but the cub glanced around behind itself, staring uneasily at Miller, who still stood in the corner, armed and alert, completely unable to see what was happening.

"Get down," Mackenzie whispered to him, pressing one hand down through the air to reinforce her words.

Miller stared at her and then glanced back at the one-way mirror.

"Just do it," she hissed, knitting her eyebrows together and tightening her lips, trying to look more adamant without raising her voice.

Miller watched her uneasily, but when no counter order was forthcoming, he finally crouched down in the corner, maintaining a ready stance while allowing one knee to rest on the floor. He shrugged his shoulders and raised his eyebrows at her questioningly, but the gryphon seemed to be satisfied, turning its head back toward Daniel and whistling the notes back to him.

"Awesome!" Sketch whispered. "Do more!"

Daniel grinned and nodded, humming more of the tune. In response, the gryphon took two steps toward Daniel and whistled at him again, repeating the sequence perfectly. Encouraged, Daniel sang to the gryphon softly, not stopping this time, and after a few moments, the cub moved toward him, cautiously at first but then more boldly, whistling along with him where sections of the eerie melody repeated itself. It sat in front of Daniel, cocking its head, and Daniel signaled to Mackenzie to hand the can to Sketch.

Grateful to be out of the hot seat, Mackenzie made her way toward Sketch, stretching out to hand him the paint can as soon as she was within reach and then backing away from them both. Sketch moved the can into position as though to spray it and looked at Daniel for confirmation, but Daniel shook his head. Instead, Daniel reached his hand out toward Sketch.

Sketch placed the can in Daniel's hand, but Daniel just shook his head and handed it back to Sketch, pushing it toward the other boy until he took it. He placed his hand in front of Sketch one more time, and Sketch finally got it. Grinning, he sprayed a mess of wet, neon orange paint into Daniel's hand.

The gryphon looked up at the sound but soon decided that the spray can had nothing to do with it. Returning its attention to Daniel, it began to experiment with harmonies, creating an impromptu duet between them. Slowly, Daniel moved his hand toward the gryphon and stroked its back. He was careful not to penetrate the surface of the gryphon's strange form, allowing the paint to run over its side, which made Miller gasp a little when the paint seemed to remain suspended in midair.

The gryphon, however, was not disturbed in the slightest. It looked curiously at the orange swath that dripped down its side and then shimmered slightly, causing the paint to disappear as it continued whistling with Daniel.

"Thank you, Daniel," Ammu said quietly, acknowledging that they had what they needed.

Daniel stood up and moved toward the portal. The gryphon cub followed him readily, and when Daniel felt that they were close enough, he stopped singing the gryphon's summoning tune and whistled something else instead—the exact notes the cub had whistled to Rush in the workshop, just before leaving.

The gryphon cocked its head at him, and Daniel repeated the notes carefully. The cub narrowed its eyes a little but then whistled the quick tune back to him, flew up into the air, and dove into the tunnel. Once its tail had completely disappeared, Daniel walked calmly over to the table, picked up the rag, dipped it in the water bowl, and returned to the circle, using the rag to wipe the runes away.

45
CONFESSION

"orkshop," Mackenzie whispered into Sam's ear. "Tell the others."

They were walking through the main lobby, but even in the large, open space, she spoke softly enough that there was no chance of being overheard. Sam looked at her in surprise but wiped the expression from her face immediately, nodding at her once, subtly, to signal that she had understood.

Mackenzie dropped back and fell into step with Ammu, who was grinning from ear to ear.

"Ammu?" Mackenzie asked. "May I speak with you a moment?"

"Of course!" Ammu exclaimed, but then his face fell, sensing that she was not as pleased with their experiment as he was. "Is anything wrong, Mackenzie?"

"No, I just... I'm missing Rush, I guess, and I was hoping to talk with you about it. You have such a way of putting things in perspective." She had no idea whether any other rooms in the ICIC besides the summoning room were being monitored and recorded, but she wasn't taking any chances.

"Oh, yes. Yes, certainly. I am very sorry, Mackenzie. I would be more than happy to speak with you, and, of course, to be of any assistance I can."

"Great," Mackenzie said, coming to a halt so he wouldn't walk beyond the main doors. "Could we sit outside for a bit? Would that be OK?"

"Why, I would enjoy some fresh air myself," he agreed, as she had known he would. He strode to the lodge's grand front entrance and held the door open for her. "Please. After you."

"Thanks," she said, but then she didn't say another word, not even as they reached the garden path and began to walk amongst the flowers.

"There is a nice bench over here where we could sit," Ammu suggested, but Mackenzie just glanced at him and shook her head. Ammu gave her a puzzled look but continued to follow her.

When she reached the workshop, she realized suddenly that someone might be using it in the middle of the day, or that it might be locked. Her brain raced, testing and discarding various plans to make it back to the others and warn them away, but when she tried the door, it was open, and the workshop itself proved to be empty. She ushered Ammu inside and closed the door behind them.

He began to look a bit concerned about her behavior, but he sat on one of the stools at the work table nonetheless, waiting patiently for an explanation.

"I'm sorry, Ammu," Mackenzie said. "The others are coming. They should be here soon."

"And is this meeting, in fact, about our friend, Rush?"

"No," Mackenzie admitted.

"I see," Ammu replied, but he said nothing more, apparently content, at least for the moment, to allow the situation to unfold in its own time.

After several long minutes of silence, the others finally arrived: first Sam and Kaitlyn, followed a short time later by Sketch and Daniel. They all sat around the work table, eyeing Mackenzie and Ammu warily.

"We need to tell him," Mackenzie began.

"What? Are you crazy? That's how you ask us? Right in front of him? Oh my God, Grid." The explosion came from Sam, who could hardly believe what she was hearing.

"I'm not asking," Mackenzie admitted. "Today was *way* too close for comfort. He needs to know."

"You're gonna get us in trouble," Sketch said accusingly.

"Ammu," Mackenzie said, turning to address him directly.

"*Here* we go," Sam muttered.

"If I tell you something I did," Mackenzie continued, ignoring her, "can you promise me that no one else will get in trouble for it? No matter what? Just me?"

"Oh, sure. 'Cause, of course, it was *all* you," Sam said, her voice scathing. "As usual. Like nobody else had anything to do with it."

"Look, I'm trying to take the blame, here!" Mackenzie protested.

"Credit, blame, we all take it together. You got it? Nobody's stealing my thunder."

"I wanted to tell him, too," Kaitlyn admitted. "I don't want them to hurt it."

"Excuse me," Ammu said politely, "but I can assure you I do not always consider it expedient to share everything I might happen to know with everyone who might wish to know it, as I believe you have all seen for yourselves."

"Hey, that's true," Daniel pointed out. "He didn't let them know the first time we almost opened the portal."

Ammu nodded.

"Why didn't you anyway?" Sam demanded.

"Tick-Tock—" Mackenzie started, but Sam interrupted her.

"What? Before he gets to hear what *we* know, I want to know what *he* knows."

"It is a fair request," Ammu said, chiming in for himself, "and one I do not mind in the least. It has been my belief from the beginning that we should tell you all why you were here and what we were hoping to accomplish. I could not do so at first, of course, because who among you would have believed it? But once you had seen the portal begin to open, I knew you would be able to accept it. I allowed them to believe you had failed, seeking permission to tell you the truth."

Ammu looked like he wanted to say more, but he fell silent instead.

"Ammu?" Kaitlyn prompted. "What is it?"

"I am afraid it is I who must seek your forgiveness," he said sadly. "In gaining that permission, my immediate superior mandated that once you were told, you would not be allowed to leave until the project had reached its conclusion."

"Which is why Rush suddenly had to decide," Sam realized.

"Yes," Ammu confirmed. "I am so very sorry. If I had not forced the issue, he would not have had to make that choice. I wished immediately to take it back, but it was too late. I had not foreseen the consequences of my determination."

"But it wasn't you who made him choose, Ammu," Kaitlyn pointed out gently. "You would have trusted him not to tell anyone."

"I would have. Yes," Ammu agreed. "But I should have realized that they would not."

"It still wasn't your fault," Mackenzie interjected. "You just wanted us to know the truth. We don't blame you for Rush leaving. Do we, guys?" She looked around the table, staring at each of them until they had all shaken their heads in agreement—even Sketch, who scowled at Ammu for a long moment before joining in with the others.

"Ammu trusted us enough to be honest with us, and we should

trust him enough to tell him what we know, too. Daniel saved our butts today, figuring out the paint thing, but if we don't tell him, then nobody in charge is going to be on our side. And next time, we won't be so lucky. We're going to scare that gryphon so badly it won't ever come back. They might even order us to hurt it, or worse. Is that what you guys want?"

Sketch shook his head adamantly this time.

"So, we tell him. Agreed?" Mackenzie looked around the table again, and this time everyone nodded, including Sam.

"But we're all in it together," Sam qualified. "If we're telling him, we're telling him everything. We were all in on it. Not just you. I'm not watching another one of my friends leave without me," she finished, taking Mackenzie by surprise.

"Me either," Sketch declared, crossing his arms and jutting his chin forward, defying anyone to say otherwise.

"Together," Daniel agreed, chuckling at Sketch's posture, and he reached instinctively for Kaitlyn's hand, who took it eagerly.

"OK, then," Mackenzie said. "Together." She looked at Sam and smiled.

"Well, for God's sake, don't go mushy on me now," Sam complained. "With Rush gone, who the hell am I going to mouth off to if *you* start acting all sentimental?"

"I would not worry," Ammu replied. "A Samantha without sarcasm would be like the sun without its glorious rays. You will simply have to shine your wit upon us all more evenly from now on."

And with that, they all burst into laughter. Everyone but Sam, that is, who just flashed him a wry grin and rolled her eyes.

46
INSTRUCTOR REPORT

How the hell did it get rid of the paint?"

"I could not even begin to guess. We know so little about its—"

"I don't want you to guess. I want you to make an educated *surmise*. That's why I pay for your expertise: so we won't all be standing around like piss-damn ASVAB waivers just making shit up by pulling it out of our asses and calling it an idea."

"Well, if I had to... surmise... I would say it has to do with its composition. Its most basic physiology is very different from our own. It can literally slip through our grasp. I suspect it absorbed the paint into itself, assimilating it into its own form."

"You're telling me you can't even touch it?"

"We can touch it. We simply can not hold onto it."

"So shooting it might not have any effect."

"That is a distinct possibility."

"Well, there's only one way to find out. Let's try it on the next one."

"What? No! They are already emotionally attached to this creature. They have touched it in awe and wonder. Daniel *sang* with it. If we injure it, they will never summon anything for us again. You must understand, it is not a matter of conscious will. They would be so traumatized as to literally lose the ability to do it, at least here, for us. Possibly anywhere. The results would be devastating."

"Well, hells bells, Professor, I don't care what we shoot. Summon something they *won't* be attached to, then. We're the good guys here, remember? Bring me something bad, and then let's kill it. That's our job."

"Yes. Yes, of course. I will ask them to summon something that is moderately aligned with the forces of darkness. But I must warn you—"

"See? That's what I'm talking about. Kill the piss-damn forces of darkness and go home happy. Tuck the kids in, knowing they're a little bit safer, crawl into bed with the wife. That's a good day."

"As I was saying, I do not believe we will be able to control such a thing without Mr. Hunt's presence. If he were permitted to return—"

"You're not listening, Professor. I'm not trying to *control* the forces of darkness. I'm trying to *kill* them. Booyah. Good guys win. Promotions all around. Home to the wife. You follow? Just bring me something to shoot, and let's put this puppy to bed."

47
TROUBLE

After another two days of rest, Ammu led them back into the basement tunnels, but this time, instead of turning into the white room, he led them past it, turning into a side tunnel and opening a new door they had never seen before. Walking into the small, dim space, they realized they were now behind the observation mirror, looking out upon the summoning room.

Whoever might have been watching them before, there was no sign of them today. They were alone with Ammu, and Miller was alone in the summoning room, standing armed and alert in the back corner. The table was still there as well, but now it held a paintball gun.

"Today, I am going to ask you to summon something different," Ammu said. "You would know it as an imp, more or less: a small creature, technically aligned with the forces of darkness, but not as vicious or cruel as... well, as other things that exist—things that you must never, ever try to summon, for any reason. Is that clear?"

"Like what?" Sketch asked.

"Do not try to summon anything unless I ask you to," Ammu repeated, eyeing Sketch meaningfully, and they all looked down at the floor, feeling a little guilty despite having received his forgiveness for their midnight escapade in the workshop.

"Yes, Ammu," Kaitlyn said, speaking for all of them.

"As I was saying, you will be summoning something that is inherently somewhat dangerous, due to its nature, so as a safety precaution, you are not going to be in the same room with it."

"How is that possible?" Mackenzie asked.

"You will perform the summoning here," Ammu explained, "but you will open the portal in there."

"Oh, sure," Sam commented. "Send the Asian kid in alone to die. I see how it is."

"As I am quite sure you have already deduced," Ammu said, raising one eyebrow but otherwise ignoring her sarcasm, "no one will be going into the summoning room to die, as you say. You, Samantha, will be standing here in this room, along with everyone else. You and Mackenzie will open the portal together, with your joint intention: yours for the timing, and hers for the place."

"Where do I draw the circle?" Kaitlyn asked.

"Right here," Ammu said. "The room is a bit smaller, but the space should be ample enough."

Eyeing its dimensions, Kaitlyn decided he was right; she could fit a full-sized summoning circle here. The observation room was just as wide as the summoning room, with the same whitewashed floor and a small table to the right of the long window for the usual rag and bowl of water. The only limitation was the space between the window and the door, but still, it would be large enough.

"This is what you will be summoning," Ammu said.

He opened his book to the page of a strange little humanoid creature, standing in front of a man, just barely tall enough to come up to his knee. It had a bat-like face with a squished-in nose, beady eyes, a mouth that protruded a bit, almost like a small beak, and tall ears that stuck out of its head at an odd angle. The picture made Kaitlyn laugh, but Daniel grimaced, peering at it over her shoulder.

"Its appearance *is* a bit laughable," Ammu agreed, "but I assure you, this creature is potentially harmful, so you must remain here with me, in this room, at all times."

"OK," Kaitlyn promised. "I think I have the pattern. Should I draw the circle?"

"You may," Ammu conceded. "But please do not begin drawing the runes themselves until I am certain that everyone understands how we will proceed."

Kaitlyn nodded, taking the blue chalk and tracing the circle on the floor at their feet, the others all moving toward the left side of the window to give her more room.

"You will, of course, draw the runes here," Ammu continued. "And Mackenzie will bless the circle, as she usually does. I apologize that there will be less space in which to move, but I believe it will suffice for our purposes."

Mackenzie nodded. Whatever Ammu needed, she would figure it out.

"Samantha, you will stand in the center of the circle," Ammu continued. "When you sense that the portal is ready, you will open it, just as you have been doing. Because Mackenzie's affinity is for position, she will hold in her mind, all the while, the intention of placing the portal in *there*. Together, your combined intention should place and open the gateway properly."

"What if it doesn't work, and it ends up in the wrong place?" Kaitlyn asked.

"Samantha will start the portal very small, as she has been, only opening it further once we see that it is in the correct position," Ammu explained.

"Oh, right," Kaitlyn said, clearly relieved. "OK."

"She will also check with Sketch, again as she has been, to make sure that what we are summoning is, in fact, an imp, rather than something else."

"Yep," Sam agreed.

"Now, Sketch," Ammu said, "your job is very important. If the thing that wants to come through the portal does not look like this, you *must* warn us. I am painfully aware that art in 335 BC was not what it is today, but the drawings reproduced in this book were designed, nonetheless, to depict for the summoner the true nature of the thing being summoned. Dark creatures like to play tricks on the mind, so no matter what *we* see, *you* must see *this* creature, or we will not bring it through. Do you understand?"

"Yeah," Sketch said.

Ammu continued to look at him pointedly, as though Sketch's reply might not have fully reassured him.

"I got it," Sketch said. "What I see, goes. This thing here, or shut it."

Ammu chuckled. "Concisely put," he agreed. "Finally, Daniel, the song for the imp will be different than the gryphon's. It might, at times, be a little unsettling, but trust your intuition."

"OK," Daniel agreed.

"The same is true for you, Mackenzie. The movements you will feel called to perform will be different than the movements that protected the gryphon circle. Focus on the imp, intend to repel anything but the imp, and trust your instincts."

"Roger that," Mackenzie confirmed.

"Well then," Ammu announced, "when you are ready."

"Here," Mackenzie said, choosing their starting position. "Count us in."

"It's go time," Sam said somberly. "One... two... one, two, three, four."

Sketch watched as the runes began to glow with power. The blue light did not seem any different, but everything else did. The shapes of the runes were strange, almost twisted. Mackenzie's gyrations were no longer fluid, containing writhing, jerking movements that seemed unnatural. And Daniel's song was now in a distinctly minor key, its notes discordant, leaping dramatically away from the rest of the music before returning to the larger theme.

The overall effect set his teeth on edge, and he watched even more intently when Sam, standing in the center of the circle, began to raise both hands toward the summoning room. She counted backward so Mackenzie would know the exact moment in which she intended to open the portal.

"Five... four... three... two... one... now!"

Sam splayed the fingers of both hands out wide and flung her arms forward as though she were trying to shove the air itself through the observation window. In that same moment, a portal opened in the center of the summoning room. It was small, just as she had promised—no larger than Sketch's own thumbnail. She looked over her shoulder and nodded at him, making him breathe a little easier. She would hold the portal at that size for as long as he needed.

Rolling his shoulders and stretching his neck to each side, he took a deep breath, exhaled it, and then reached out with his mind toward the *thing* he could feel sniffing around the portal entrance. He was nervous, remembering the rotting face he had seen before, but where *that* thing had felt like disease, like decay, like the cold hand of death grasping at your heart, this thing felt more like... trouble.

Sketch relaxed a little. He didn't like trouble, but he was used to it. He could survive trouble.

He saw the thing clearly in his mind's eye, just like the photograph. Its tiny hands reached into the portal, alternating between one and the other, feeling around inside the tunnel up to its shoulders, exploring it. Its pug-nosed, bat-like face was too big to fit into the circle, but Sketch imagined it pushing one beady jet-black eye into the darkness, trying to see through the hole, and he giggled a little.

He pulled his mind back to the here and now enough to give Sam a thumbs-up, and she gradually moved her hands apart, widening the circle until the imp burst through the hole and fell immediately to the ground, the portal having opened waist high in the air.

"Oops," Sam said. The imp tumbled end over end across the floor before coming to rest against the far wall, its head and torso lying supine on the concrete, its legs extending vertically above it. "Note to self: not everything has wings."

Ammu flipped a switch on the wall next to the window. "I have set the intercom system to work in both directions so we can hear Staff Sergeant Miller, and he can hear us as well."

Miller nodded toward the window in reply.

"You have company, as they say," Ammu announced, "on the floor to your right, roughly center of the wall."

"Roger that."

Miller snatched a spray can from one of the many pockets on his camo pants and deployed it in the general direction Ammu had indicated. The imp screeched in annoyance, turning orange for just a moment over about half its body before shimmering in place, absorbing the paint and returning to its original dark gray hue. To Miller, it seemed as though half of a neon orange imp had appeared on the floor next to him for just a moment and then disappeared again.

"I am so not going to get used to that," Miller muttered, his words coming through clearly over the intercom.

"It's moving," Mackenzie called out.

"Where?" Miller looked around the room helplessly.

"Straight at you!"

Miller sprayed the can again toward the floor at his feet, catching the imp in a new coat of orange just as it lunged for his pants leg.

"What the..." he exclaimed. "Hey!"

The imp was already halfway up his body before the orange coating disappeared, but this time Miller was ready for it.

"That was a mistake, little bugger," Miller said cheerfully. "I might not be able to *see* you, but I can *feel* you all right. Ha! Gotcha!"

Grabbing at his own chest, Miller managed to grasp the imp around its waist, but it was moving quickly, already starting to pull itself through his hand.

"Whatever you're going to do, do it fast," Mackenzie warned him over the intercom. "You won't be able to hold onto it."

"Yeah, they briefed me," Miller acknowledged. He reached into another pocket, trading the paint can for a tracking dart, managing to shove it into the imp's back just before it broke free from his grasp.

"Nice!" Kaitlyn cheered.

"OK, per protocol," Miller announced, obviously for a microphone that was recording the session somewhere, "ICIC Experiment 6A, trying paintballs first."

He picked up the paintball gun from the table and shot it in the direction of the dart, which appeared to Miller to be floating in mid-air. Unfortunately, it was no longer in the imp's back. The creature had reached behind itself and tugged the thing out, and it was now holding the tracker in front of it, staring at it curiously. The first two paintballs sailed between the imp's face and the tracking device, causing the creature to screech and drop it to the ground.

Assuming the imp had fallen, Miller aimed the next two paintballs at the tracker on the floor, the first round hitting just in front of it, and the second landing just to its right, both of them exploding to shower the floor with neon paint—first yellow and then pink, as it happened.

Glancing back and forth between Miller and the tracker, the imp picked up the device and held it out in front of itself at about chest height, watching as Miller fired another two rounds at the tracker and then dancing about gleefully. It launched into an impressive series of acrobatics, holding the dart away from itself all the while, letting Miller try to hit the device as it bobbed and weaved through the air, the staff sergeant obviously getting more frustrated by the moment.

"It's just holding the tracker in its hand, Miller," Mackenzie called out—giggling, to be sure, but trying nonetheless to be helpful.

"I figured," he growled back.

"It's to the left... no, right... no, left..."

But the imp was too quick for her directions, and the observation room finally dissolved into laughter as it started tossing the tracker into the air, throwing and catching it twice until Miller finally shot it away, failing to hit the imp entirely but at least ruining its game by sending the tracker spinning into the window, where it hit and fell to the ground.

"ICIC Experiment 6B, attempting rubber rounds," Miller growled, returning the paintball gun to the table and pulling a pistol out of a holster he wore on his right leg. "Tell me when it's going for the tracker."

"Now!" Mackenzie shouted.

Miller took aim in the general direction of the dart and sprayed a barrage of rubber bullets from left to right at about calf level. The imp let out an enraged scream that dissolved into an angry sort of chattering, waving a fist in Miller's direction and then running away into the far corner below the window.

"What's it doing?" Sketch wanted to know, the imp having moved out of view by ducking against the wall of the observation room.

"How the hell should I know?" Miller answered testily. "I hit it, though. I can see one in... damn."

"What?" Mackenzie asked.

"The round disappeared."

"It must have absorbed it, like the paint," Kaitlyn suggested.

"So the bad things eat bullets for breakfast," Sam commented. "Outstanding."

"That wasn't a bullet," Miller interjected. "ICIC Experiment 6C, live ammo exercise. Repeat, this is a live ammo exercise."

"Tell me this is bullet-proof glass," Mackenzie said to Ammu.

"Affirmative," Miller replied, not realizing she wasn't talking to him.

"It is," Ammu confirmed. "And the walls and ceiling have been constructed to firing range backstop specifications, designed to trap bullets without ricochet, for Staff Sergeant Miller's safety as well as our own."

Miller walked over to the abandoned tracking device, picking it up in his hand and turning his back to the observation window, tossing the device across the room so that it slid into the far wall.

"Tell me when it goes for it," Miller said, removing the clip from his gun, making sure the chamber was empty, and then replacing the clip with a fresh one from a different pocket.

"Roger that," Mackenzie acknowledged.

Miller took aim at the tracking device and waited. The imp, seeing that Miller wasn't paying it any direct attention, started sneaking toward him along the observation room wall, but Sketch caught the movement out of the corner of his eye, having pressed his face right up to the glass, trying to see what it was up to.

"It's under the window! Coming toward your right leg!" he shouted.

Miller whipped to his right and fired rapidly along the floor, starting near his own leg and swinging his arms up, sending a steady stream of bullets in a tight, controlled pattern along the floor and then up the wall, again stopping at about calf level, but as soon as Miller had begin to fire, the imp had scampered away across the room, moving back toward the far wall.

"Where is it?" Miller asked, his words clipped and urgent.

"Across from the window," Sam said. "You missed, by the way."

"Where, exactly, across from the window?" Miller wanted to

know, switching out the clip on his pistol and then pulling something large and tubular out of the calf pocket on his left leg.

"All the way back at the wall," Mackenzie answered him. "At your one o'clock."

"Roger that." Miller tossed whatever it was in that direction, aiming it to hit the floor in front of the position Mackenzie had indicated. On impact, a wave of green paint exploded toward the imp, hitting it full on.

"Paint grenade!" Sketch shouted happily, but before the words were even out of his mouth, Miller unleashed another barrage of bullets toward the small creature.

"No!" Sketch yelled, but the imp had already dropped to the floor, squishing itself impossibly thin, absorbing the paint, and slithering away beneath Miller's gunfire.

Apparently deciding that things were getting a bit too serious, the imp chattered at Miller angrily again—this time waving both fists in the air and puffing its little chest out belligerently—and then ran across the floor to leap gracefully back into the portal, looking none the worse for wear over their encounter.

48
BAD, BAD THINGS

he news is boring," Sketch complained. He was sitting on the couch between Mackenzie and Sam, with Daniel and Kaitlyn on the floor in front of them, the coffee table having been moved behind the couch entirely.

"Just for a while, OK?" Mackenzie answered him. "I want to see... just for a while, I promise."

Mackenzie hadn't been able to talk to her father since she had arrived at the lodge. She had spoken with her mother after his weekly Skype call home, so at least she had gotten an update, but it wasn't the same. She wished she could hear his voice, telling her some crazy story about how many potatoes he had peeled that day or about going on rat patrol, as if his job were really that mundane. Her time at the ICIC was bringing home to her just how *not* true that was.

So far, the news segments had been relatively low key—a minor flood in Louisiana and some bill proposal in the Senate—and Mackenzie was relieved not to find what she was looking for. It didn't mean her father was safe, but knowing there wasn't any news out of Afghanistan made her feel better all the same.

"I don't like summoning bad things," Sketch said, looking down at his art pad. He knew the imp was technically bad, but it had made him laugh, and everyone else had seen it too—so he had decided to put it in the light book instead of the dark one. In his drawing, the imp was tossing the tracking device high into the air, and Staff Sergeant Miller was shooting at the tracker, well over the imp's head, while it danced with glee.

"I didn't think it was so bad," Kaitlyn said.

"I know," Sketch answered her, "but he tried to shoot it."

"Hey, Sketch," Mackenzie said gently. "Listen, they're probably going to need us to bring more things like that, maybe even worse things. They have to try to shoot them so they can learn how to protect people."

Sketch didn't say anything, continuing to add details to his drawing.

"Remember the thing on the helicopter?" Daniel added. "You wouldn't want something like that to just run around loose, would you?"

Sketch shrugged, his expression noncommittal. It wasn't that he thought bad things running around would be a good idea, but he saw bad things around people all the time—not usually as bad as Mr. Lockhart had been, but still. He wasn't sure people who looked good on the outside but did really bad things were necessarily better than things that looked bad on the outside but just played tricks on people and made him laugh. It certainly didn't seem right to shoot them for it.

In breaking news, a plane that took off from Atlanta's Hartsfield International Airport this morning, bound for London, has disappeared somewhere over the Atlantic. Airline officials have not yet released a statement regarding the missing aircraft, but our sources tell us that it is no longer appearing on radar and that attempts to radio the crew have, so far, been unsuccessful.

"That's weird," Kaitlyn commented, but she and Daniel were both watching a game she was playing on her phone, so they didn't see the video that flashed on the screen next.

The plane reportedly took off from Hartsfield International on time, under clear skies and good visibility, with no indication of bad weather to be expected along its route.

"Not as weird as that!" Sam said, staring at the television. "Um, guys?"

"What?" Mackenzie asked, looking up from Sketch's drawing.

Suddenly, all eyes were glued to the screen. The news crew was showing airport footage of the plane taking off. It raced steadily down the runway and then lifted off cleanly, with no indication at all that anything was about to go horribly wrong—nothing, that is, except for the gargoyle perched serenely on its tail.

49
NEWS FLASH

You've got two bogies on your six."

"On it."

Rush performed a leaping spin and took both enemy players out neatly with back-to-back head shots.

"Oh, yeah. Who's your Wingman?"

"*You're* my Wingman," Rush said, laughing.

"Damn straight," Wingman agreed.

"Get a room," Snark commented.

"You know, Snark, I met the girl version of you at the ICIC," Rush told him. *Oh, get a room. Damn lovebirds, squawking up the channel.* Sam's voice echoed in his mind, a bittersweet memory of the team he had left behind. He knew he had made the right decision in the long run, but that didn't make it any easier.

"Oh, yeah? What's her name? Better yet, what's her number?"

"Her name's Snark, cause she's even more snarky than you," Rush teased him.

"Impossible. Besides, the name's taken, bro."

"Nope, hers now. We're gonna have to call you something else."

"You heard him," Wingman said, picking up the joke and running with it. "Snark needs a new name, guys. The floor is open for nominations."

"Snark II," Stryker suggested. "The sequel."

"No, no, no," Fuego said, laughing. "Wait, I got it. You ready? Snarknado."

"Seconded!" Rush shouted.

"I have a second on the floor, gentlemen," Wingman announced. "All those in favor of Snarknado?"

"Aye!" Rush, Stryker, and Fuego all said together.

"Hey, that's not bad, actually," Snark said.

"Really?" Fuego asked. "Then I want to change my vote."

"Hey, guys," Stryker said, interrupting their banter. "Check out this plane."

"What plane?" Snark asked.

"News is saying a whole plane disappeared," Stryker announced.

"Ooooh... Bermuda Triangle... spooky..." Fuego commented, laughing.

"No, man, like a real plane. From here. A big one. Flying from Atlanta to London. Says it just vanished. Poof. Gone."

"What? No way. That's impossible," Snark declared.

"Cover me," Rush said. "I want to see this."

"On it," Wingman promised.

Rush turned on his secondary monitor, switching it to live television and scrolling to the news channels. He pulled his headset down and let it hang around his neck so he could hear the report.

Officials say there is still no sign of an aircraft that took off this morning from Hartsfield International Airport. It was bound for London, carrying over two hundred passengers on board for a routine trans-Atlantic flight... that never arrived.

"What the hell?"

Rush watched, stunned, as the missing plane taxied down the

runway and took off with an unmistakable gargoyle, roughly twice the size of a grown man, planted firmly on its tail.

No explanation has been offered by airline officials, who have said only that the disappearance is still under investigation...

"Oh my God. That's what they were doing. That's what *we* were doing." He said it out loud without even thinking about it. *Sketch and Tick-Tock and Grid and Gears and Disco... They're up against freaking real life gargoyles, and I'm not even there...*

"You say something, Rush?" He heard Wingman's question distantly, through the headphones that still hung around his neck, but he ignored it, his mind racing through the implications of what he had just seen.

"Guys!" he said, whipping the headset off and holding the mic so they could hear him. "Guys, sorry, but I gotta go!"

"Go? Go where?" he heard Snark asking. "Is that like a 'guys, I'll be right back' kind of I gotta go? Or is it more like a 'guys, I'm about to abandon your asses again' kind of thing?"

Rush turned off the television with a grimace and ran out of the room.

"Mom! Mom! Where are you?"

"I'm downstairs, Ashton. Is everything OK?"

Her voice floated up to him from her home office, and he flew down the stairs, taking them two at a time. He raced down the hallway, turning the corner into her workspace so fast that he had to hold on to the door frame with one hand.

"Mom, tell me you still have that ICIC invitation," he said breathlessly.

"Of course, honey. It's in your school file. Over there." His mother stared at him in confusion as he pulled open the drawer and started rifling through it.

"No... no... yes!" He snatched the paper out of the file and grabbed his phone out of his pocket, starting to dial the number before he had even left the room.

"Is everything OK?" she asked again.

"What? Oh, um, yeah... I mean, I hope so. Uh... one of the other kids... called me... about another phase... this summer... that they might need me for... I'll tell you about it in a bit, OK? I'm trying to find out... right now..." He stopped dialing and looked at her, bouncing up and down on the balls of his feet.

"OK," she said, smiling. "I have to say, Ashton, it's nice to see you taking something college-related so seriously."

Sure, he thought to himself. *College-related. Let's go with that.*

"Um... yeah... thanks... do you mind, though? Sorry, I kind of have to..."

"Go ahead," she said, laughing now. "Make your call. Love you, honey."

"Love you too," he said, and with that, he was out the door.

50
INSTRUCTOR REPORT

I presume you have seen this evening's news story of the plane that disappeared over the Atlantic?"

"Don't tell me."

"Yes. I am sorry to report that a summoned creature was involved in some way. I do not know the exact details, but it seems clear enough that the creature was the cause. It had already attached itself to the aircraft before it took off from Atlanta."

"Same thing as before?"

"No, actually. This one was larger than the other, and of a different nature. But in the end, I am not certain what difference it makes. It was equally effective in its purpose."

"It's not about the thing itself. It's about whoever's behind it. If it was the same, I might have believed that they had reached their limits, at least for now. If it's different—bigger—then they're still escalating."

"It would appear so. Yes."

"Which means it's even more important that we learn how to

fight these things, and so far we haven't even been able to see one long enough to shoot it at a distance we can measure in paces, for God's sake."

"But if we could control it, then your soldiers could shoot it, yes? If you had a target that would stand still for you?"

"And how the hell are you going to get the piss-damn forces of darkness to stand still and let us shoot them? There's only so far I'm willing to follow you down this rabbit hole, Professor. If it involves garlic, silver chains, or holy water, I don't even want to hear it."

"Quite the contrary, Colonel. I believe we have, as you say, already found the man for the job."

51
MARSHMALLOWS AND A T-SHIRT

Sketch was asleep on the couch when the sound of the suite door opening caught his attention, at least for a moment. He opened his eyes groggily, but it was only Rush coming back from wherever he'd been. He rolled over, turning his face away from the light of the hallway, ready to doze off again, before his sleep-addled brain finally managed to process what he had just seen.

Rush!

Sketch flipped back over and opened his eyes wide. It wasn't a dream. Rush was back, standing right there next to the couch, grinning down at him like he had never left.

"Rush!" Sketch exclaimed, throwing his blanket on the floor and scrambling off the couch to hug his friend.

"Shh," Rush said, chuckling and hugging him back. "Don't wake Daniel up. I'll see him in the morning."

"So you're staying?"

"Yep," Rush confirmed.

"For good?" Sketch asked, eyeing him suspiciously.

"For good."

"What about your competition? You leaving for that?"

"I don't think so, buddy. I don't think they'll let me, but it doesn't matter now."

"Why not?"

"Let's just say you were right. Some things are more important."

"Like *friends*," Sketch said, sounding more than a little accusatory.

"Like friends," Rush agreed, chuckling quietly. "But listen, it's late. You should get some sleep. We're both going to need our rest for tomorrow."

"Yeah," Sketch agreed, frowning. "We're gonna have to summon something bad tomorrow."

"Something bad?"

"Yeah, like the imp, only worse. Maybe like the thing from the plane."

"You saw that?" Rush asked.

"Grid made us all watch the news," Sketch said. "You saw it, too?"

"Yeah. Sketch, I'm so sorry, man. I didn't know what was on the line, you know? I never would have left if they had told me. I swear."

"I know," Sketch said.

"But what's this about tomorrow? What imp? What do you mean they want us to summon something bad?"

"So they can shoot it," Sketch said.

Rush paused for a long moment, letting that sink in.

"You know what?" he said finally. "Maybe we should wake Daniel up after all. It sounds like I have a lot to catch up on."

"Rush! Wait, are you back? Like, *back* back? What's going on? What time is it anyway?"

Rush and Sketch stood in the doorway of Daniel's bedroom, watching him stretch in bed and rub the sleep out of his eyes. They had decided to wake him up by liberating a bag of marshmallows from the pantry and taking turns tossing them at his sleeping body, which seemed like the perfect way to celebrate the occasion.

"He's back," Sketch confirmed, popping a marshmallow happily into his mouth now that they didn't need it for ammunition.

"It's 2:15 in the morning," Rush added, answering his last question.

"Well, that explains a lot," Daniel admitted. "Oh, hey! Do the girls know?"

"Nope," Rush said. "I just got in, but it sounds like a lot's been going on around here."

"Oh, man, you have no idea," Daniel said, rolling out of bed and throwing a pair of jeans on over his boxers. "We better get them."

"Suit yourself," Rush said, tossing another marshmallow at him just for fun. "I slept on the plane. And again on the bus. If you guys want to be zombies tomorrow, that's your problem."

"Are you kidding?" Daniel said. "Gears would kill me if I didn't get her. I'll be right back."

"OK," Rush said, holding the marshmallow bag in front of Sketch so he could grab another one and toss it at Daniel's back as he left.

While Daniel was gone, Rush started to unpack his gaming console, only to discover a new one sitting in the spot where his had been set up before.

"What's this?" he asked Sketch.

"It's from downstairs. It's the one you played on," Sketch explained. "Daniel got it and hooked it up for me after you left, but I never used it. I didn't really want to."

There was an echo in Sketch's eyes of the pain he had gone through when Rush left, and Rush felt fresh pangs of guilt all over again. He was glad to know, at least, that Daniel really had been looking out for the kid, like he had promised.

"Well, that's gonna be one of the first things we fix," Rush declared. "That one's going back downstairs, and mine's going right there. OK?"

"OK," Sketch agreed happily.

Just then, the girls walked through the suite door, and Kaitlyn screamed. It was a subdued, middle of the night sort of scream, to be sure, but a scream nonetheless. She ran right up to Rush and hugged him, grinning from ear to ear.

"Are you back?" she asked excitedly. "Like, *back* back?"

"Yup," Rush declared. "And apparently, I got here just in time. You and Daniel have been spending *way* too much time together."

Daniel blushed, but Kaitlyn only laughed.

"Good to have you back," Mackenzie said. She didn't hug him, but she did look genuinely glad to see him, and that was enough.

Sam was the one he had been the most worried about, given how they had left things. He had known Sketch would forgive him, but he wasn't so sure about the sarcastic Jersey girl with the blue-streaked hair and the anime eyes. He turned to her now, and his worst fears seemed to be playing out. She stood in the doorway with her hands planted firmly on her hips and a scowl on her face.

"Where's my T-shirt?" she demanded.

"I... what?" he stammered.

"When you leave on vacation, you're supposed to bring back a T-shirt for everyone who didn't get to go. It's like a consolation prize. You know, 'Sorry you guys had to stay here and summon nasty little imps to try to save the world while I was home sitting on my ass and eating tacos for a week and a half, but here's a T-shirt to make it up to you.'"

"Oh," Rush said, trying not to smile. "*That* T-shirt."

"Yeah, *that* T-shirt," Sam repeated. "If these scrubs don't want to demand their T-shirt, that's on them. Me? I want my T-shirt."

"Um..." Rush said, stalling, but Sam just held out her hand, one eyebrow raised, both eyes twinkling, clearly waiting for him to do something about it.

"Right!" Rush declared. "I almost forgot. Your T-shirt. Of course. I packed it in this bag here. Hang on."

Sam continued to stand with her arm outstretched, her hand grasping at the empty air, until he selected a T-shirt from his duffel bag and handed it over.

"Thank you," she said, slinging it jauntily over one shoulder and closing the gap between them. She stood on her tiptoes and kissed him on the cheek. "I forgive you for leaving." She sat down on one end of the couch, holding out her prize to examine it.

"Well?" she prompted, looking around at everyone's grinning faces. "Are we going to bring this guy up to speed, or what? We have a world to save, people."

"I want a T-shirt," Sketch said hopefully, looking up at Rush.

"Oh you do, do you?" Rush replied, and without any warning he flopped down on the other end of the couch, dragging Sketch with him into the middle seat and rubbing his knuckles quickly but gently back and forth across the boy's head.

Laughing, Mackenzie, Daniel, and Kaitlyn dragged the coffee table back where they could sit on it, and Mackenzie launched into the story, starting with everything Ammu had told them the morning Rush had left.

52
A Very Bad Idea

L adies and gentlemen," Ammu began, "our job today is to summon something much more closely aligned with evil—not in the interest of taming it, this much needs to be very clear from the beginning, but of destroying it."

He stood in the observation room, surrounded once again by all six students of the ICIC. Rush's return had infused the group with a new sense of energy and purpose, but seeing a living gargoyle on the tail of a civilian airplane had also impressed upon them just how serious their mission was. They watched Ammu attentively, understanding, as they had suspected, that they were about to proceed into much more dangerous territory.

"We will, of course, perform the summoning here, in the observation room, opening the portal on the other side of the glass. As an additional precaution, the weapon to be employed will be an automated turret. Staff Sergeant Miller will control the turret remotely, from here in this room with us, so that no one need be exposed to the creature."

They could see for themselves that the contents of the white room had changed again. The table was gone, and now a gun stood on a tripod just to the left of the window, aimed at the middle of the room. Staff Sergeant Miller took Ammu's words as a cue to demonstrate, and he used a remote to turn the turret to the left and then back to the right again, showing them how it moved.

"Nice," Rush commented, but Miller only nodded in return.

"We are hoping, Rush," Ammu continued, "that you will be able to control the creature well enough to place it directly in the turret's line of fire."

"I'll sure try," Rush promised. He knew the others had told Ammu about the workshop, and he knew they had had trouble working with the gryphon ever since. He understood their theory that he had been controlling it. He only hoped they were right.

"So then," Ammu said, bending down to retrieve his book from his satchel and paging through it until he found what he was looking for, "this morning, I would like for you to summon *this*."

Kaitlyn looked at the image and then glanced back at Ammu, her eyes wide with disbelief.

"It is not, by far, the most deadly thing in this book," Ammu said, his words offering little reassurance, "but it is more closely aligned with the forces of destruction than anything you have yet summoned, as I suggested it would be."

"It looks like a gargoyle, but it doesn't look like the gargoyle that was on the plane," Sam commented after taking a closer look for herself. "What's up with that?"

The creature in Ammu's image looked like it might be about knee-high on a full-grown man when sitting on its hind legs like a dog, as it did in the picture. If it extended itself to its full height, it might be able to reach a man's chest.

It was dark gray and hairless, its body looking a bit like a pit bull's, but with a face that belonged on a gothic building in a graphic novel. Its eyes were black as coals, it had no ears at all, it had two twisted horns protruding from its forehead, and its snout looked like a demented cross between a dog's and a crocodile's, full of four rows of razor-sharp teeth, two rows on the top and two on the bottom. As if that weren't enough, bat-like wings extended out from its shoulders.

The gargoyle on the plane, on the other hand, had shared little in common with this image beyond its wings. That creature had been much lighter in color and twice as tall as a man, looking far more humanoid in both its posture and the shape of its skull, its vertebrae protruding cruelly from its spine, giving its back a ridged appearance, with a long, spiked tail extending behind it.

Its feet had been preposterously long, so that it stood upright by balancing forward on its toes, its heels sticking high up in the air and acting like a kind of second knee that bent the wrong way, giving its legs a ghastly, almost alien appearance. If Sam had had to place the two creatures on the same family tree, they wouldn't even have been second cousins.

"Ah, yes, it is true," Ammu began, answering her question. "The term 'gargoyle' is highly misleading. The creature in this image and the one from the plane are both aligned with the forces of evil, but their natures are not the same, and therefore their preferred appearance is not the same.

"The beings of the other dimension are not limited, as we are, to a single shape, but can adopt many forms, changing their appearance even to those who can see through the eyes of the unconscious mind. This is why Sketch, here, is so very important. He sees the true nature of things, so that even if something evil were to disguise itself as something beautiful, fooling the rest of us, Sketch would see it as it truly is."

"Way to go, Sketch!" Rush said, grinning at him and thrusting a friendly elbow at his shoulder.

Sketch beamed with pride. Maybe being able to see things that everyone else couldn't, wasn't such a bad thing after all.

"The spirits that battled here on Earth during the days of Alexander the Great were of many, many forms, varying widely in shape, from animals very like those that exist naturally in our world, to fantastical and oftentimes horrific creatures, whose alignment with the forces of good or evil was reflected in their natural appearance.

"What we are summoning today was known as a *zairmyangura* in the ancient Persian tongue. The creature on the airplane would have been called a *spengaghra*. But I suppose that 'gargoyle' is as good a term as any for either one, in this day and age."

"OK," Sam said, dragging both syllables out unnecessarily. "Little sorry I asked, to be honest, but thanks for the history lesson."

"If you want the short version, do not ask a professor," Ammu replied, grinning at her. "Or so my students have told me."

"My bad," she agreed. "So are we doing this thing or what?"

"Indeed," Ammu said. "If everyone is ready?"

"I have the pattern," Kaitlyn announced, and Ammu retrieved the chalk from his bag, opening its protective container and handing it to her.

"Here," Mackenzie said, choosing her spot while Kaitlyn sketched the basic circle on the floor as a reference.

Sam stood in the circle and gave Ammu a silent thumbs-up.

"I can hear it," Daniel said. "I'm not gonna enjoy singing it, I can tell you right now, but I have it."

"Sketch?" Sam said, getting his attention. "Same as before, OK? Only if you say it is what it is."

Sketch nodded.

"OK then," Sam said, taking a deep breath. "Counting us in. One... two... one, two, three, four."

Kaitlyn traced the first rune on the floor as Mackenzie started moving in strange jerks and pops around the circle, with Daniel intoning an ominous chant in a minor key that made Rush's skin crawl.

"OK, this is creepy," Rush whispered to Sketch, who only nodded in return. Today's summoning was making Sketch doubly glad that Rush was back. Even Staff Sergeant Miller, usually the picture of stony impassivity during the summoning sessions, looked a bit unraveled by the scene.

"It is appropriate for it to feel uneasy, even frightening," Ammu murmured. "Fear is one of the most primal ways in which the unconscious mind warns us of danger, and we are dealing now with forces that would harm us at any opportunity, make no mistake."

"Fantastic," Rush said. "No pressure, right?"

As the circle neared completion, Sam began the countdown for Mackenzie. "Five... four... three... two... one... now!" Sam raised her arms, splaying her fingers wide just as before and shoving both hands toward the window, causing a tiny portal to appear in the middle of the room on the other side.

"OK, now *that* was cool," Rush muttered, but Sketch didn't answer him, focusing with his mind's eye on the creature that awaited them on the other side of the portal, and soon enough, Rush felt it for himself.

He almost reeled backward in disgust, but he remembered their earliest attempt at summoning the gryphon, when his fear broke Sam's concentration and closed the portal, so he forced himself to stand firm even though every fiber of his body was telling him to run. The... *thing*... on the other side was already clawing at the tiny hole, sniffing at it eagerly, ready to hunt. Rush felt it as it became bound to his will, writhing and screaming on the other side of the portal, its initial curiosity devolving into rage.

It felt grimy and greasy and dingy and dark, making Rush wish he could shower right where he stood, but Sketch gave Sam the thumbs up, signaling her to let it through. It was vicious and cruel, but it was what it was, and the portal opened wide, vomiting the creature into the stark, white room.

It hovered for a moment, getting its bearings, seeking and finding Rush's essence through the glass that stood between them. It wanted to move toward him, but Rush held it in place—forcing it to land and sit quiescently on the floor—his mind straining against the creature's dark intentions.

"Good?" Rush asked through clenched teeth, one hand raised in a posture of both control and defense, pushing against the creature even as it pushed against him.

"I have no idea," Miller admitted. "One second. Can you keep it from absorbing the paint?"

"I can try," Rush said. The others had told him about the targeting problem, and he held the creature in his mind as best he could, ordering it firmly not to respond to its surroundings. "OK. Ready."

Miller pressed a button, and a fine mist of neon orange paint burst forth from several nozzles mounted along the legs of the turret, coating the creature fully. The creature narrowed its eyes and snarled through the glass, but it did not absorb the paint.

"Brilliant," Miller whispered. "OK, hold it right there. Steady... steady..."

The creature eyed the turret as Miller angled the gun slightly to the right and then down, lining up the shot on a viewfinder mounted in the remote.

With a sudden explosion of sound, two things happened instantaneously. The first was that the gun fired several rounds directly through the creature's chest, the bullets slicing through it viciously and embedding themselves in the far wall.

The second thing, however, was entirely unexpected.

The moment the gun fired, the creature roared in triumph and broke free of Rush's mental grasp. Apparently unharmed, despite having been shot clean through by enough firepower to have severed any normal blood-and-bone creature in half, it thrust itself into the air with a single downstroke of its wings, absorbed the orange paint with an angry shimmer, and then hurled itself directly toward the bullet-proof window, colliding against it with a resounding thunk and starting to push its way in, beating its wings vigorously and thrusting with its hind legs to add to its momentum.

In seconds, the tip of its maw was already through, the vehemence of its struggles making it clear that the *zairmyangura* would not be trapped in the glass for long. Kaitlyn shrieked, and Miller, realizing that something must have gone horribly wrong, yanked the door open and tried to herd them out of the observation room.

"There's nowhere safe to go!" Rush yelled. If bullets couldn't hurt it and bullet-proof glass couldn't hold it, then no amount of running was going to save them. The creature was almost halfway through the window, its progress slowed temporarily while its wings were hampered by the glass. Its maw, already free, snapped at him viciously, it claws scratching at the glass as it worked to pull itself through. In desperation, without even knowing what he was doing, Rush reached out with his whole mind.

"Help!" Rush yelled.

"Tell me what to do!" Miller shouted.

"Not you! Him!" Rush hollered back, as the gryphon cub burst through the portal.

With one powerful stroke of its wings, it braked in midair, locating Rush and surging toward him, but when it identified the threat, it stopped again, hovering for a split second and shimmering angrily as a full set of armor burst forth from its body, settling around it majestically.

It looks just like you, Sketch thought, the gryphon's armor matching not just the shape and design of the armor Sketch saw on Rush but also its color, blazing forth in angry red and a deep, bronze gold—in the exact same hues Rush wore at the moment, whether he realized it or not.

Completing its transformation, the gryphon charged at the *zairmyangura*, grabbing it by its hindquarters before it could finish pulling itself through the glass. The beast screamed in pain as the gryphon reached underneath it and sank its beak into its underbelly, but there was little it could do beyond scrabbling at the gryphon ineffectively with its hind legs since the front half of its body was still on the observation room side of the window.

Although bullets had not harmed it at all, the gryphon's bites opened gaping wounds in the creature's belly that did not close, each new gash pouring angry red light out of its abdomen. In moments, the gryphon had torn gruesomely through its body, ripping through its midsection until the hideous thing had been severed in two.

With a defiant screech and a final flash of light that was almost too painful to look at, the gargoyle fell silent, the back half of its body falling to the floor in the summoning room and the front half going limp, its head slumping against the window in which its chest was still embedded. The humans all stared in silent amazement as what remained of the *zairmyangura* shimmered and vanished, leaving nothing behind—all except for Miller, that is, who was still looking around at everyone else, trying to figure out what their sudden stillness meant and what, if anything, he should do about it.

"It's OK, Miller," Mackenzie said. "You can stand down now. The good guys won."

"We did?" Miller asked.

"*Yeah* we did!" Rush exclaimed, and he and Sketch started whooping and hollering, cheering at the gryphon, which shimmered away its armor, descended casually to the floor, and began preening its feathers as though slaying gargoyles was all in a day's work, which maybe it was for a gryphon, for all Rush knew.

"Well, thank God," Miller said, sounding profoundly relieved.

"Indeed," Ammu agreed.

Without wasting any time, Kaitlyn snatched up the waiting rag.

"If you don't mind?" Kaitlyn said, addressing Rush and indicating the gryphon with a tilt of her chin.

"Already?" Sketch complained. "But it just got here!"

"As much as I love the little guy," Mackenzie said gently, "and I do—I mean, I *really* do—I think we've all had about enough of this particular portal."

Rush looked at Sketch and grinned. "It's OK, man. I'm here now, yeah? We can call him back any time."

"Yeah, OK," Sketch agreed sadly.

Rush closed his eyes for a moment, and the gryphon looked up, bobbed its head at the one-way mirror, and flew back through the portal.

53
INSTRUCTOR REPORT

You're telling me this report is accurate?"

"I am afraid so, yes. The bullets were entirely ineffectual. It would appear the only way to defeat one of these creatures is in partnership with another being from the same realm. This, by the way, is also what the ancient texts claim, but, of course, modern weaponry has changed dramatically over the intervening millennia. As a man of science, as well as faith, I was unwilling to take that claim at face value."

"So was I."

"And yet, here we are, nonetheless."

"But how the hell did we get here? Using kids? To fight the new terrorism? That was never the plan."

"You said yourself that every plan becomes eventually—what was the expression, a soup sandwich?"

"Yeah, but there's soup, Professor, and then there's soup, if you know what I mean."

"I am not at all certain that I do, actually."

"Hell, neither am I. Look, just train them. Work with them. Learn more about what they do and how it all works. It's the best use of the time we have left. Maybe we can come up with another way to destroy those things."

"I pray every day that we will do precisely that."

"So do I, Professor. So do I."

54
CONNECTIONS

ow that you have had a day to rest," Ammu said, "I would like
to speak with you about what we learned yesterday and about
where we will go from here."

"We learned I was right," Sam commented. "They *do* eat bullets
for breakfast. Fun fact."

The students sat around Ammu in the exercise room on the blue
mat-like flooring as they had on the very first day, but that seemed
like a lifetime ago now.

Rush's legs were stretched out in front of him, crossed at the
ankles, his arms extended behind him for support. Sketch sat next
to him, to his left, mimicking the older boy's posture. Mackenzie sat
up straight to Rush's right, her legs crossed neatly in front of her,
as was her habit. Sam, on the other hand, had sprawled out next to
Sketch on the end, lying on her side with her body propped up on
one elbow. Kaitlyn was also lying down, on Mackenzie's other side,
stretched out on her stomach facing Ammu directly, using both

hands to prop up her chin and waving her feet from time to time idly through the air, which Daniel, sitting cross-legged to her right on the other end, found downright adorable.

"Sam's right," Mackenzie said glumly. "Epic fail."

"With every experiment, we learn something new," Ammu pointed out. "It might not be what we had hoped, but still, it is progress."

"Progress toward the end of the world," Sam countered. "Helicopter crashes and disappearing planes and burning buildings and the bad guys win. Terrific."

"We must not make such assumptions," Ammu protested. "In every great undertaking, there are times when the situation appears difficult—even hopeless. But humanity's greatest achievements have come about when those who faced adversity refused to be daunted, rising above such appearances and persevering despite all obstacles."

"Ammu," Mackenzie interjected, "I'm all about pushing forward, but I don't know what we're trying to push forward *to* anymore. Bullets don't hurt it. How is the Army going to fight something it can't hit?"

"Bullets do not seem to have any effect," Ammu agreed, nodding sagely, "but the gryphon cub did."

"We can't use the gryphon to fight something like the thing from the plane," Rush objected. "It'll get killed! I mean, battle armor is cool and everything, but it's just a cub. It can't go up against a... whatever that thing was."

"I agree that we should not use the gryphon for such tasks," Ammu said, holding up a placating hand. "But I must add, while we are on the subject, that the cub, as you call it, might not be as young as it looks. Remember, such beings are not limited in appearance; they prefer the form that represents their true nature. Your gryphon might well be hundreds of years old. I do not know this for certain.

I am saying only that it is possible. The fact that it appears as a cub means that it is playful, like a cub, but it does not necessarily mean that it *is* a cub."

"Weird," Kaitlyn said. "So the battle armor—that's not part of its nature? It's like... fake?"

"It's not fake," Sketch protested, his voice adamant.

"The armor is very real," Ammu agreed. "It is one aspect of the gryphon's true nature, just as being protective of your friends is one aspect of *your* true nature."

"Then why not use the gryphon?" Daniel asked. "If you're saying it can take any form, couldn't it turn into a big gryphon and fight stuff?"

"The farther from its own nature a creature appears to be, the more energy it takes to hold that form," Ammu said, "but that still might be a possibility someday, given enough work and commitment.

"In fact, I believe the gryphon may have formed a very special sort of bond with Rush. Most creatures are tied permanently to one plane of existence and to that plane only. They can visit another plane through the portals, but this takes a great amount of energy. The summoner's mind must constantly resist the pull that seeks to return the creature to its own rightful place. The larger it is, and the longer it stays in our world, the more the summoner's mind is depleted. This is why you all need days of rest, such as today, to recover between summonings.

"But some creatures are able to form connections to people of this world, so that the time they spend here no longer comes with a price. Or so the stories tell me. Such bonds connect them, through the people they love, to this world as much as to the other, so that the creature gains a rightful place in both worlds, becoming free of the pull that I just described."

"Let's try it!" Rush exclaimed, pushing himself up straighter. "Let's bring it back."

"That would not be wise," Ammu said, shaking his head. "We need you all to rest and replenish your energy. If I am wrong, calling the creature through and allowing it to remain would tax you beyond an acceptable limit. There are stories also of men and women who lost their minds, and their lives, by attempting a summoning that required too much of them, or by holding a creature here in this world for too long."

Ammu looked meaningfully at each of them in turn, making sure they had understood the danger he described, but Rush was already remembering the effort it had taken just to hold the gargoyle in place for a few moments against its will. He couldn't even imagine trying to control something forcefully for any real length of time.

"Can I have a pet?" Sketch asked hopefully, and Ammu chuckled.

"Perhaps! It is said that most of the ancient summoners eventually established such a bond with a creature from the spirit world, but these relationships must be chosen freely by both the summoner and the creature to whom he or she feels drawn. It is not the sort of thing that can be forced, or hurried; it must appear in its own time.

"In any event," Ammu concluded, "even if we managed to send the gryphon back before any real danger had accumulated, you would still be too drained to continue your training for quite some time, and what we are doing here is vitally necessary if we are to have any hope of protecting innocent lives. The experiment will have to wait for another time, as much as I do, in all seriousness, regret it."

He said this looking directly at Rush, who nodded reluctantly in agreement.

"So, what *are* we going to do, oh fearless leader?" Sam wanted to know.

"Fearless?" Ammu laughed. "You give me far too much credit, I assure you. But to answer your question, you are all going to regain your strength for two more days, and after that, we are going to work on new levels of control, by summoning this."

With a flourish, he pulled the now-familiar book out of his satchel, opened it to a page he had marked with a gold ribbon, and laid it before him on the mat with a grin. Kaitlyn was the first to lean forward, gasping in delight as she took in the large wolf-like creature with intelligent blue eyes, gleaming silver fur, and the most brilliant white wings she had ever seen.

55
PTEROLYCOS

When they reconvened two days later, Ammu ushered them into the conference room rather than the basement. The accordion-like barrier that had been serving as a wall between the classroom and the gaming room had been folded back away into its storage slot, so that the entire space was now one large, open room again, with an expansive, dark foam cushion laid out over the carpet, extending across the room from one side to the other.

The gaming setups that had nestled against the temporary barrier were now sandwiched between the others instead, and the classroom area had been cleared of everything except for Staff Sergeant Miller. The students sat on the floor in front of Ammu, but Kaitlyn kept craning her neck around, trying to get a better look at the cameras, microphones, and other recording equipment that had been mounted high up along the back wall, near the ceiling.

Ammu retrieved the book from his satchel, laying it carefully on the floor in front of him, open to the page depicting the beautiful flying wolf.

"This creature," Ammu began, "was known as a pterolycos. The word, unfortunately, means 'flying wolf,' which is entirely inaccurate. It is not a wolf that flies—just as the gryphon is neither a bird nor a lion—and I would encourage you to embrace that distinction.

"The pterolycos is aligned with the forces of life, so even if we were entirely unable to control it, it would always protect its summoners. Our greatest security measures, therefore, are Mackenzie's blessing of the circle and Sketch's ability to screen the creature coming through, to make sure that it is, in fact, what we intend it to be."

Sketch nodded happily. It was nice to feel important for the very same thing that used to make him feel crazy.

"Today's exercise will require more space than anything we have attempted before, so this room has been prepared for our purposes. When Alexander the Great fought his most critical battles, he and his generals brought forth creatures into this world that were of tremendous power. The men worked in partnership, both with the spirit beings and with each other, to ensure that the forces of good would be victorious.

"All human beings are unique, and Alexander and his generals were certainly no exception. Each had his own affinity within the realm of the unconscious mind, just as each of you has his or her own special awareness of the world. They learned to work together, bringing their individual talents to any task set before them, so that as a team they were infinitely stronger than any one of them ever could have been alone.

"What I would like for you to do today, in summoning the pterolycos, is to interact with the creature *together*. Just as Rush is able to convey the behavior he desires through thought alone, so I believe the rest of you will be able to communicate your own intuitions as well, enabling the team, as a whole, to take full advantage of all of your unique gifts."

He smiled at each of them, silently acknowledging their abilities.

"So!" he concluded. "I am certain that you would all prefer interacting with a pterolycos over listening to me pontificate any longer, yes? You may draw the summoning circle directly onto the floor covering, anywhere you like, when you are ready."

Kaitlyn took the chalk from him and glanced at the picture one more time for reference. "I have it," she said.

"Mark," Mackenzie said, choosing their starting position.

Sam looked at the boys, who all nodded in reply.

"OK, then," she said. "It's go time! One... two... one, two, three, four!" In what seemed like almost no time at all, Kaitlyn was drawing the last rune, and Sam was counting them back down to the portal.

"Five... four... three... two... one... now!"

Sketch nodded as soon as the portal opened, and moments later the pterolycos sailed into the room. It was the first creature they had seen emerge from the tunnel with any aplomb, so when it leaped gracefully from the portal and unfurled its wings, gliding gently to the floor and turning to look at them all with interest, Kaitlyn gasped in amazement.

"It's even more beautiful than the picture!" she exclaimed.

It was easily twice the size of a normal, flesh-and-blood wolf. Its silver fur rippled with light, as though shining from within, and the white of its wings was just as pristine as Kaitlyn had envisioned. Where the gryphon cub had been nervous at first, the pterolycos allowed them to approach with confidence, nudging them each with its nose in a friendly sort of way and shimmering into its more physical form when it realized they wanted to touch its fur.

"How does it *feel*, Rush?" Ammu asked, beaming with their success.

"It's not fighting me at all, like the bad thing did," Rush said, "but it's not like the gryphon either. The gryphon feels almost like a pet. This feels more like a wild thing, but a wild thing that's willing to work with us, if that makes sense."

"It does. Perfect sense," Ammu said, clearly pleased. "See if it will do something for you."

Rush considered his options. He couldn't ask it to sit, like a dog. It felt too *regal* for that. He understood what Ammu had meant about working in partnership with the higher spirits, rather than commanding them. This creature felt elegant, noble—more like a fairy tale prince than a wolf. It was a citizen of its own world, with a keen intelligence—an intelligence that was not even remotely human, to be sure, but nonetheless equal to his own.

"I don't know what to ask it," Rush said finally.

"Good," Ammu reassured him. "We are in uncharted territory together. Anyone? Suggestions?"

"Can we see its battle armor?" Sketch asked Rush.

"Oh, that's a good one. Do you have armor that you could show us?" Rush tried asking it. "How do you look when you fight?"

The pterolycos looked around itself immediately, but seeing no obvious threat, it did nothing but return to staring at Rush, its thoughts unreadable.

"No, it's OK," Rush told it. "There's nothing to fight right now. I just wanted to see what it would look like. Your armor, I mean. If you have any?"

The pterolycos tilted its head as though trying to understand his words.

"Its armor is tied to its emotions," Daniel suddenly blurted out.

"Excellent, Daniel," Ammu prompted him. "Trust your intuition. What does that mean, that its armor is tied to its emotions?"

"It... when I think of it like this," Daniel said, trying to feel out exactly what it was he was sensing, "I hear the tune I sang when we summoned it. But when I think of it fighting, well, I don't know what that looks like, but it *feels*... not angry, exactly, but more... energized? The tune gets a lot more intense, like a symphony going through a different section of the music."

"Fascinating!" Ammu exclaimed. "Can you sing it, Daniel?"

Daniel imagined the tune again with the intention of humming it, but as soon as he heard the first few notes in his mind, the pterolycos snarled, showing its teeth, and the hackles raised up on its back, the fur bristling all along its body.

Kaitlyn, who had been standing the closest, jumped backward so fast that she fell down on her rump, but Rush helped her up and dragged her out of harm's way. Ignoring them, the creature snapped open its wings and raised itself into the air, shimmering into its less physical form, and before their eyes, its body transformed with a single ripple, looking as though it had been coated with the finest steel plating, every feather of its wings suddenly glittering like diamonds.

"It's even beautiful when it's mad," Kaitlyn breathed.

"It wants to know where the danger is," Mackenzie said suddenly.

"And when it's coming," Sam added.

"You can hear it?" Ammu asked excitedly.

"Not in words," Mackenzie said, clarifying. "It's more like... sensing a request for information."

"Ditto," Sam agreed.

"It's mad?" Miller asked, walking toward Kaitlyn. "Why is it mad?"

Seeing the motion, the pterolycos snapped its head toward Miller, growling deep in its throat.

"No!" Daniel shouted, but his sudden fear seemed to agitate the creature even more, and it furled its wings, preparing to dive toward this new threat.

"Stay!" Rush yelled, throwing both hands into the air instinctively, trying to hold the creature back long enough to keep it from ripping out Miller's throat. The pterolycos snapped its wings back out immediately, braking hard and hovering in place, but it glared at Rush, baring its teeth and snapping its jaws in annoyance.

"It's just trying to protect us," Rush said, the tension in his voice reflecting the mental strain of holding such a powerful and intelligent creature against its will. "I can't hold it for very long. Get Miller out of here. We need to send it back."

"Stop!" Sketch shouted at it, his voice as commanding as Rush had ever heard it. Sketch remembered what Ammu had told them about the dangers of trying to control powerful things, and he was frightened by the toll that Rush's efforts were already taking. "Miller's our friend!"

Sketch usually saw a pod of miniature dolphins swimming around Miller, but he was afraid the pterolycos would not understand the image, so he turned to the man now and imagined instead an aura of golden light shining around his body. He had never before tried to imagine someone in a way he did not actually see them, but he could sense the creature questioning Miller, seeking his nature—and where this creature came from, a being's alignment with the forces of good or evil was usually reflected in its form.

"Look!" Sketch shouted. "See?" But even before he said the words, the creature's armor was already disappearing back into its body.

Rush released it with a groan, falling to his knees and holding one hand to his head, continuing, nonetheless, to watch it warily, but it merely landed back on the floor and nodded regally toward Miller, who was staring helplessly at Sketch, clearly trying to figure out what in the world was going on.

"OK, controlling things directly is so *not* the way to go if you can help it," Rush said, gritting his teeth.

"Are you OK?" Sam asked, looking uncharacteristically worried.

"Yeah, I'll live," Rush promised. "Killer headache though."

"I believe that is quite enough for today," Ammu pronounced.

Sam knelt next to Rush, putting an arm around his waist to steady him and ducking under his shoulder. He accepted her help gratefully, leaning against her body more heavily than she had expected, but still, she didn't seem to mind.

"Time to go," Rush said, addressing the pterolycos. "Sorry about the misunderstanding. No hard feelings?"

This much, at least, the creature seemed to understand. It bowed its head to Rush, just as it had to Miller, and it flew back into the open portal, departing just as gracefully as it had arrived. But Kaitlyn had barely closed the portal behind it before Sam yelled for help, Rush's body having collapsed against hers entirely as he passed out cold.

56
INSTRUCTOR REPORT

"How is he?"

"He is resting comfortably and out of danger. The doctors say he will make a full recovery, God be praised."

"How long?"

"Three or four days, perhaps. A week, at the most, until he is back to his full potential. But we must not push them to such limits. The summonings are too close together. We must give them more time in between. We can not afford for any harm to come to them. The attendant risks are too great."

"For once, we agree. I'm giving them the week. They deserve it."

"They will be pleased to hear it, I am sure. But why, might I ask, do I find myself suspecting an ulterior motive?"

"Maybe you're just a cynical kind of guy. But in this case, you'd be right. There are people who'd like to meet them, and this is as good a time as any. I was thinking of sending them to the Orion launch. Kids love that kind of thing."

"And...?"

"And it keeps the meet-and-greet out of my backyard. Hobnobbing it with top brass is like dinner with the in-laws: it's easier to excuse yourself early than it is to kick everyone else out. Remember, we're still funded under the guise of intuitional learning research. It's true, as far as it goes, but it's not exactly the whole story. We don't need people poking around the lodge, looking at things they don't need to be looking at."

"I understand."

"Speaking of which, I want you to go with them. Babysit. Head off any questions they don't know how to answer. Take Williams with you. She's good at that kind of thing. Get them in and out quickly, and then let them enjoy the launch. I mean it about that. Kids love rockets."

57
CAPE CANAVERAL

Sam watched the back of Rush's head as they climbed off the bus at the Jackson Hole airport, where they would catch a plane for the Orion launch. She couldn't help remembering how he had looked, how he had *felt*—a staggering, dead weight across her shoulder that she could barely support—when he had held that same head in his hands and suddenly collapsed.

He had only been unconscious for a few hours, and that had been almost a week ago, but the entire episode had frightened her so badly that seeing him strong and vital again continued to bring her reassurance. She was careful, though, to look away before he turned around, so he wouldn't catch her at it.

Sam, however, wasn't the only one worried.

Whereas Sam's surreptitious glances were reserved for Rush, Mackenzie couldn't walk three paces without scanning the crowd again, as though she expected a demon to jump out and attack them from behind the ticket counter, or from the back of the gift shop, or from the deli where they picked up a lunch for the plane.

"It will be all right," Ammu told her. "Try to enjoy the trip. The intention is for you all to relax—to enjoy some time away from the Institute. You have been working very hard this summer, and you have had a lot to process. We want you to have the time and space to do that."

Mackenzie nodded politely at his words, acknowledging the sentiment, but it didn't stop her from scrutinizing every plane that came and went while they waited for their turn to board, checking them for any sign of wind elementals, or oversized gargoyles, or any other monster with which their unknown enemy might decide to terrorize them.

Sketch, on the other hand, was ecstatic to be taking yet another flight this summer, the disappearing plane having done nothing whatsoever to curb his enthusiasm for travel. He had not expected to journey outside of his own county ever in his life, let alone across the country. Visiting two different states before he had even entered high school was an impossible dream come true.

Daniel and Kaitlyn were oblivious to all of it, holding hands with a shy, quiet sort of happiness. Rush couldn't help but look on with at least a small pang of jealousy—not so much over their relationship, but over how carefree Daniel seemed to be, taking each new day as it came, not seeming to carry any worry in the world about what might happen to them next, what dangers they might face, or whether he could protect them all when the time came.

"Penny for your thoughts?" Christina asked him.

"I was just thinking about how different everything is now from when I stepped off that plane... what... almost a month ago? It seems like so much longer than that. So much has happened."

I'm not even sure what's strangest, he thought. *That I've seen real-life gryphons and gargoyles and flying wolves, that I gave up the invitational for a few more weeks in a lodge in the middle of nowhere, or that keeping an eye on a weird, eleven-year-old kid from Alabama feels like the most important thing I could be doing right now.*

"Whatcha got there, buddy?" Rush asked. Sketch sat next to him with his art pad in his lap, drawing a picture of a man in a business suit sitting two rows away from them in the waiting area.

"He's OK," Sketch replied. "He just has a big clock on his stomach. See?"

The drawing depicted an old-fashioned clock with a droopy, stylized face, not unlike a Salvador Dalí painting, hovering over the man's midsection.

"Maybe he can do what Tick-Tock can do," Rush suggested.

"Maybe," Sketch said, shrugging.

"Hey, is that what Tick-Tock looks like?" Rush asked.

"No," Sketch said, giggling, but he didn't say anything else, and soon enough it was time for them to board the plane.

The trip was uneventful, the brief layover in Denver allowing Sketch to add yet another flight to his running count, and even Mackenzie finally began to relax a bit as they finally touched down without incident at Orlando International Airport.

"Hey, Rush," Daniel said, suddenly making the mental connection, "didn't you say you lived in Orlando?"

"Yeah," Rush confirmed. "This is the airport I just flew out of."

"Really?" Kaitlyn asked. "Is your family going to be at the launch?"

"I doubt it," Rush said, failing to elaborate. His father and brother were always too busy for things like that. He couldn't even remember the last time they had taken a day to do something together as a family. Even living in Orlando, with readily-available season passes to some of the greatest tourist attractions in the world, they just couldn't be bothered to find the time.

"Too bad," Kaitlyn said, letting it go, but Sam read the terseness of his answer. Apparently they shared more in common than she had realized.

"We'll check into the hotel and then get a late dinner," Christina said, taking charge as she led them toward the exit where the hotel shuttles came and went, spitting out departures and picking up new arrivals like clockwork. "We're staying in Orlando tonight and driving to Cape Canaveral in the morning."

As they exited the building, Sketch couldn't help being reminded of home as well. The warm, humid air was reminiscent of Alabama summers, and he found himself wondering briefly what his mother was doing this evening, whether she was working a dinner shift or had the night off at home with Tony, and whether Shaquiya was hosting one of her tea parties, dressing young Xavious up in funny hats and feeding him cookies to get him to sit still.

He was ashamed to admit, even to himself, that it was the first time he had thought of them since Rush came back, but soon enough the lights and palm trees of Orlando distracted him from his reverie, as he added both to his list of new summer experiences, followed not long afterward by room service, which he scarfed down gratefully before passing out on the couch of the hotel suite.

Ammu was preparing to pick him up and carry him to bed when Rush stopped him. "Let him sleep there," he said. "He likes couches." Ammu shrugged and left Sketch where he was, covering him with a light blanket before retiring to one of the two rooms in the expansive suite, Daniel and Rush crashing in the other one, with a huge double bed for each of them.

In the girls' suite, Kaitlyn took the second bed in Christina's room, letting Mackenzie and Sam have the other room to themselves. But long after they had turned out the lights, Sam still lay awake restlessly, thinking about how close the summer was to being over.

She dreaded going back to school—to rich suburban kids obsessing over clothes and cars and designer handbags—but even more haunting was the thought of returning to a life that felt like it didn't matter at all. How could she even begin to bear that again after everything she had seen and done and *lived* at the ICIC? The faces of all her friends—*friends,* for the first time in her life—kept swimming through her mind, and Mackenzie had been snoring for a solid hour before Sam finally drifted off to sleep.

A limousine picked them up early the next morning. The drive to Cape Canaveral took less than an hour, giving them ample time for Ammu to request a very specific detour, so that by 9:30 a.m. Sketch was standing on the beach of Jetty Park, staring out at the ocean for the first time in his life, watching the morning sun as it played over the gentle waves of the calm, summer day. He looked up with the biggest grin Rush thought he had ever seen, and they all stood together, enjoying the moment, letting the waters of the Atlantic wash in and out over their toes.

Unfortunately, they couldn't stay long, so Ammu gathered them up and handed out their shoes, one pair at a time, ushering them into the limo for the short drive back to Exploration Tower.

The brilliant white building was seven stories tall, with a curved back and graceful, arching latticework that came to a point high above the roof. The glass-fronted edifice was tiered by design, so that every level was slightly smaller than the one below it. The fourth floor had a deck extending outward in the front, facing the launch sites of the Kennedy Space Center, as did the open-air terrace at the top of the building.

"The tower has been rented out for this event," Ammu explained.

"There are exhibits that you may walk through after the launch, but we will spend the time before lift-off on the fourth floor, where various military and Homeland Security personnel will be interested to meet you. Many of them have been influential in acquiring funding for the ICIC, so it is important that we make a good impression.

"Remember, what we have been doing this summer is *not* common knowledge. The true nature of the project is highly classified, and you must act accordingly. You have been studying Persian mythology through intuitive learning techniques. You are excited to be part of the program. If you are asked a question you do not know how to answer, get my attention or Christina's. For our purposes today, she is one of your instructors.

"Just before the launch, we will remove ourselves to the seventh-floor observation deck, which has been reserved for us alone, despite the many illustrious guests who are present today. It will provide a magnificent view of the test launch, which I believe you will all enjoy. Do you have any questions before we go in?"

They did not, so Ammu ushered them into the building and led the way up to the fourth floor, which turned out to be a large meeting hall where several dozen men and women had already congregated. Some were dressed in Army uniforms, but most of them wore expensive business suits, as did Christina and Ammu.

Their arrival did not make any great stir among the crowd, much to their collective relief, so they began to mill about idly, Sketch being the first to notice the buffet table that had been set up toward the back of the room.

"I have a question," Sketch said to Christina.

"Yes, you are welcome to eat at the buffet table," Christina told him. "It's free."

Without another word, Sketch made a beeline for the food.

A kind-faced older woman made her way over to the group and spoke with them for a while. Yes, they all said, the classes had been very interesting. They were very much enjoying their stay at the ICIC. They were excited to be part of the program. Thank you very much for the opportunity.

Smiling, the woman moved on.

This conversation repeated itself with a man in a gray business suit and then again with a man in an Army uniform, whom Mackenzie identified as a "full-bird colonel," which sounded important even though the others didn't know what it meant.

As time wore on and no one else approached them, the students drifted apart, Kaitlyn and Mackenzie joining Sketch at the buffet table, and Daniel wandering toward the punch bowl. Sam walked out to the observation deck to take in the view, but it didn't seem like there was very much to see until she noticed the telescopes along the outer railing. She was heading that way when she saw Rush step outside to join her, so she waited for him to catch up.

"View's nice," Rush commented.

"Of the water, I guess," Sam said. "But the launch pad's so far away you can hardly see it at all."

"Yeah, a pamphlet inside says it's a safety precaution. Even the closest setup at the space center itself is more than two miles away from the pad."

"Oh. I guess I thought we'd be closer."

"I was surprised too," Rush admitted. "It'll still be cool to watch, though."

"Yeah, at least they have the telescopes. You want to check them out?"

"Sure," Rush agreed.

They waited for a rather portly gentleman to finish using the one in front of them. He looked through the eyepiece a few moments longer and then relinquished the device, smiling politely before making his way back toward the meeting room.

"You go ahead," Rush said, waving Sam forward.

"Thanks." Sam smiled back at him, bending down a little to look through the eyepiece and then standing up very slowly, turning toward Rush with a haunted look in her eye.

"Tick-Tock? What is it? What's wrong?"

"Houston," she said, backing away from the device so Rush could look through it for himself, "we have a problem."

Rush took a quick step forward and looked through the telescope.

The magnification was spectacular. The launch pad filled the optics, giving him a perfect view of the rocket that was about to launch Orion into space—and wrapped around its hull, just as clear as day, the sinister form of an enormous, pitch-black dragon.

58
ORION

"Ammu?"

"Yes, Rush? Samantha? Is something wrong?" They found him inside the meeting room, chatting amiably with an attractive middle-aged woman about the military strategies of Alexander the Great.

"No! No, nothing's wrong. We just wanted you to see the launch pad. Through the telescopes. It's very exciting." Rush gave Ammu a meaningful stare.

"*Very* exciting," Sam echoed.

"Of course," Ammu said.

He turned to excuse himself from the conversation, but the woman had already taken advantage of their arrival to disappear into the crowd, apparently preferring less historical chit-chat. Rush ignored Ammu's look of disappointment, grabbing the man by the sleeve and shepherding him out to the observation deck, practically shoving him toward the nearest telescope.

"Rush? What—"

"Look," Rush interrupted him, pointing imperiously to the device while Sam stood by his side, nodding adamantly.

Ammu looked through the viewfinder and then stood up slowly.

"I believe it is time for us to move to the seventh-floor observation deck. Help me gather the others, if you would be so kind." He said it easily, even cheerfully, as though there were nothing whatsoever out of the ordinary about either the request or the reason behind it.

"How much time until the launch?" Rush asked.

"Thirteen minutes," Sam replied, her voice tense, the stress of their predicament welling up within her as she fought to maintain a casual front.

Gathering the others and moving upstairs: three minutes. Performing a summoning: one minute, minimum. That leaves nine minutes to figure out what to summon and use it to get rid of that thing, if we even can.

Sam's mind performed the time calculations as naturally as breathing, whether she wanted to or not. As it happened, she did not, in this particular case, want to know that they had nine minutes to work with before the Orion test flight—the *manned* Orion test flight—exploded on the launch pad, or worse. But she was right, nonetheless.

It took exactly three minutes to gather everyone back together, move up to the seventh floor, explain the situation to the others, and post Christina at the door so they wouldn't be interrupted. The high, white terrace was the perfect size for a summoning, but that was the only thing Sam could think of that they had going in their favor, which didn't seem like much under the circumstances.

"We've never summoned anything even remotely big enough to fight that thing," Rush blurted out as soon as they were alone.

"We have one minute to summon something and another nine minutes to do something with it," Sam said. "That's it. So whatever we're going to do, we have to do it fast."

"How do you know it will wait until the launch?" Daniel demanded, his voice rising in desperation. "How do you know it's not going to just rip the Orion to shreds like three seconds from now?"

"It won't," Sam declared. "Nine minutes. Trust me. We have time to fix it. I *know* we have time to fix it. I just don't know how yet, but we have to figure it out. Now. Planning time counts, by the way."

"It doesn't matter what we decide to bring if we don't have the pattern," Kaitlyn protested. "It's not like Ammu brought his book with him to this thing. The point was *not* to let them know what we can do!"

"I do not have the book," Ammu confirmed.

"It doesn't matter," Sam almost yelled. "You're not hearing me. I'm *telling* you, I *know* we have time to fix it—with what we have, here with us, right now—but we won't for much longer if we don't figure this out. Come on, people. What can we summon that has a chance against that thing?"

"This," Sketch said bluntly, and he held out his art pad, pointing to the page he had been searching for. It was his drawing of Alexander's tomb, but it wasn't the tomb he was pointing at. It was the white dragon, standing on its rear legs next to the pyramid, facing down the black dragon on the other side.

"Yes!" Mackenzie shouted. "Sketch! You're a genius!"

But Rush looked almost panic-stricken. "Guys, there's no way I'd be able to control that thing. The pterolycos was almost enough to kill me."

"You do not have to do this alone," Ammu told him. Despite the urgency of the moment, his voice was serene, unflustered, as it always was, his confidence in them palpable. "I know you do not feel prepared for this, but I have seen the six of you do so much, accomplish so much, in such a short amount of time... you can do it, but you must do it together."

"We'll have to figure it out as we go," Sam said. "We don't have a choice. We have to start the summoning *now*. Gears, do you have it?"

"Yeah," she confirmed, wide-eyed but trying to appear calm.

"Sketch," Sam ordered, "give her something to draw with."

Sketch dug a precious charcoal pencil out of his box and handed it over.

"We start here," Mackenzie said, even as Kaitlyn was tracing out the summoning circle on the white floor with trembling hands. "Disco?"

"Ready," he said.

Sam counted them in with no further discussion. "One... two... one, two, three, four!"

They moved around the circle efficiently, but the summoning had an inner rhythm to it that could not be hurried. The dance Mackenzie performed was the most beautiful yet, and Daniel sang as he had never sung before, his clarion tones ringing out into the morning air. As Kaitlyn approached the last rune, Sam called to Mackenzie.

"Just in front of the terrace, on my mark! Five... four... three... two... one... NOW!"

Sam threw her hands toward the empty air in front of the building, and a portal began to open before their eyes, suspended seven stories up in the sky, just beyond the edge of the terrace.

"Sketch?" she asked.

"Bring it," he acknowledged.

The portal expanded to herculean proportions, and a tremendous white dragon emerged from it, turning to bow in the air before them, bellowing gloriously into the sky and glittering in the sun, its scales catching every ray of light as though they were covered in an impossibly fine mist.

"Oh!" Kaitlyn exclaimed, gasping in delight.

"Eight minutes," Sam called out.

"We need to get it into fighting mode," Mackenzie said, realizing immediately that the dragon had no idea there was an enemy waiting for it several miles away. "Daniel, can you do it?"

"But what about what happened last time?" Daniel protested. "There's like a ton of people on the deck just three floors down."

"It was a mistake last time," Mackenzie reassured him. "We got it all riled up when there wasn't anything for it to fight. This time, I know where to send it, and Sketch knows how to protect the people below us, just like he protected Miller. Right, Sketch?"

"Yeah," Sketch agreed. He was already imagining a golden dome extending over the deck below them, and he *sent* the image from his mind to the dragon, just as he had with the pterolycos. Sketch knew for a fact that some of the people milling about on the fourth-floor observation deck were less than innocent, but he would protect them all, nonetheless.

"We're ready," Mackenzie told Daniel. "Do it."

"OK. Here goes nothing..."

Daniel reached out with his mind for the dragon's summoning song and then imagined what it would *feel* like when it was energized. He heard the change in the melody immediately, heard the faster rhythm, heard the way the notes surged in power. He *thought* the music toward the dragon, and it screamed and rippled in the daylight, every one of its glittering scales igniting before their eyes into a brilliant, fiery gold, blazing like the sun.

Immediately, Mackenzie heard the dragon's request in her mind, coming through almost as clearly as though it had spoken. *Where?* She sent back the image of the launch pad, including both distance and direction, and the dragon turned a graceful somersault in the air, forming a momentary ring of fire as its body circled around on itself and sped away.

They rushed to the telescopes along the deck to see what was happening. Precious moments ticked by as the blazing dragon sped across the miles and finally found its prey, trumpeting its challenge at the black. Moving slowly, almost casually, the black dragon shimmered, covering itself in brutal, black armor with wicked spikes running all along its great length, from its head to its tail.

The snake-like creature unraveled its front quarters from the

Orion craft, leaving its legs and tail wrapped around the larger rocket, unfurling its tremendous, bat-like wings, and screaming at their champion—a sickening screech that trailed out into a hiss. In return, they all *felt* the fiery dragon's intention to slice the dark monster in half right where it sat.

"The astronauts!" Rush gasped. "It's going to rip the Orion apart! I can't stop it! It's too powerful!"

"You do not have to command it," Ammu said, grabbing Rush's shoulders and turning the young man to face him squarely. "The six of you must be in *partnership* with the dragon. Not to control, but to advise. Do you think you just heard that scream with your ears from all those miles away? You heard it *with your unconscious mind.* We can communicate with it instantly, across any distance—we need only connect to it. Reach out to it, Rush. Help it. Give it the guidance it seeks. It *must* be calling out to you."

In fact, Rush had felt it seeking out his will, his knowledge, from the moment it had started coming through the portal. He had been resisting the link, remembering what controlling the pterolycos had cost him, but now, trusting Ammu, he let down his defenses and opened his mind.

There are innocents here, Rush thought to it. *They need your protection. You must be careful, or you will cause the very destruction we are trying to stop.* He felt the dragon trying to understand him, realizing that Rush was requesting caution but not yet comprehending why. Braking hard on fiery wings, it pulled back from its dive, holding its position.

"It knows I'm worried about what it's doing, but it doesn't understand my words," Rush told Ammu.

"But you did it!" Ammu exclaimed. "Your conscious minds do not speak the same language, but the unconscious mind can communicate feelings, intentions, images. Do you see? You have stopped it, without having to control it!"

"Yeah, but that doesn't really help if we can't tell it what it needs to know," Rush protested. "It's just sitting there while the clock ticks down!"

"Six and a half minutes," Sam warned them.

"Wait," Kaitlyn interjected. "You said we can communicate images, right?"

"Yeah," Sketch answered her. "We can. Definitely."

"Then let me try something."

Closing her eyes, Kaitlyn *saw* in her mind an exploded-view drawing of the Orion craft, including the cockpit and its human occupants.

"Make the people gold," Sketch advised her, guessing at her intention.

"Sorry?"

"The people in the rocket, that we're warning it about. Make them gold. So it knows they're on our team."

"Oh!" Kaitlyn exclaimed. "Got it!"

She *sent* the image to the dragon, complete with golden astronauts, and the giant creature responded immediately, moving again, circling the Orion and its launch rocket warily, seeking a way to attack the beast without harming the craft.

"It understands!" Kaitlyn called out.

"Yeah, but it can't find a way in," Mackenzie said.

They watched as the blazing creature flitted in and out of range, swiping with a claw here, snapping at a wing there, slicing away at its enemy's armor bit by bit. Its progress was painfully slow, but as the seconds dragged on, more and more thin lines of angry red light appeared on the black dragon's hide, until it finally uncoiled itself from the Orion, screaming in rage.

Rush and the others cheered, but their celebration was short-lived. Once the black was no longer encumbered by its position, it began striking back, and gashes of brilliant white light began to stream through the golden dragon's burning hide, showing where it, too, had been injured.

It took a nasty swipe to the side, and then another to one of its back legs. The champion fought bravely, its attacks precise, its defense calculated, ensuring that the battle did not surge back toward the Orion, but the fact that it was sacrificing itself to protect the spacecraft was taking its toll, costing it too heavily.

"Four minutes," Sam called out, but they could all see for themselves that the noble creature wasn't going to last that long.

Mackenzie watched as the burning dragon began to falter. She had been studying the black intensely, learning how it moved, how its momentum traveled through its body, and she sent that knowledge to the golden dragon's awareness, showing it where each strike would land. But if dodging a blow would lead them back toward the launch pad, the blazing creature took the hit instead.

Taking the hits it wants to take, Mackenzie realized bitterly. The thought reminded her of the conversation she had had with her father, in what seemed like a lifetime ago, but she heard his words again now, echoing in her mind.

Sometimes, Mac, running away is the best long-term strategy.

"Three minutes to launch," Sam announced.

Suddenly, she knew what they had to do. She tried to convey the plan to the majestic beast that fought so bravely for them, but she was already feeling drained, and the great dragon was fading. For several agonizing moments, she wasn't sure it had understood her, but then she saw a new pattern beginning to emerge. Their champion was choosing its hits differently now, moving the battle back toward the summoners themselves.

And then it happened. The black dragon saw their portal, a swirling black disc against the bright blue sky, suspended seven stories up, above the observation deck of the Exploration Tower. Abandoning the Orion, the black dragon streaked toward the platform where they all stood, intent on destroying the humans who dared to challenge it.

The golden dragon, its scales blazing in the sun, continued to battle against the black, but now it heeded Mackenzie's every warning, dodging every attack, using every opportunity in between to weaken its enemy by striking another angry red gash into its jet-black hide.

Their objectives had shifted. Now it was the black dragon that had an ultimate goal—a purpose that began to take its toll on the malevolent creature as it, in turn, was willing to absorb its opponent's fiery attacks, trying to reach the observation deck that much sooner, while it still knew where its true enemy stood.

Their hero fought valiantly, refusing to succumb to its wounds, while brilliant white light spilled from more gashes than they could count. Its attacks finally began to slow, its energy failing, as the grappling behemoths neared the observation tower—the humans on the seventh-floor deck watching helplessly, knowing there was nowhere to run. When the blazing dragon fell, their lives would be forfeit, one way or another, even if the black had to bring down the entire building to ensure it.

The black dragon was close enough now that they could see every wicked spike along its back, every armor-clad scale along its hide, every onyx tooth in its gaping maw. *So this is what death looks like*, Rush thought, as the black dragon, sensing victory, surged toward the gold, catching the majestic creature in its claws and raking a terrible gouge into its belly, splitting it open right before their eyes, from the middle of its chest to the base of its tail, a torrent of white light bursting forth from its dying body.

"No!" Sketch screamed, his lone voice crying out to it for them all.

But in that moment, the golden dragon, with a last heroic effort, wrenched itself farther *into* the black dragon's death grip and clasped the monster's back, digging its claws into its enemy with all its might. The black, realizing its mistake too late, roared in defiance, struggling to break free, but the portal was already too close.

As a final burst of light exploded from the raging inferno that their shining, white defender had become, it passed into the portal, clutching the black dragon to its heart and dragging the furious beast with it, back into the realm from which it came.

59
INSTRUCTOR REPORT

This is really what happened? Everything in this report is true?"

"I have reviewed the tapes personally to verify my memory of the events. I can assure you that they did, in fact, occur exactly as described. The Intuitives protected the Orion project. They saved the launch, as well as everyone in that observation tower, although their own lives represent the most precious resource that could have been lost."

"Intuitives? That's what we're calling them now?"

"It seems appropriate. We can call them summoners, if you prefer."

"Summoners, gryphons, gargoyles attacking planes, dragons attacking the Orion launch... this was supposed to be a civilian program to develop military intelligence, not a military program masquerading as a high school. This whole thing is spinning way out of control."

"I disagree. 'This whole thing,' as you say, might no longer be what it was originally intended to be, Colonel, but I would argue that the change is for the best. The ICIC belongs to the Intuitives—all of them, not just these six—and the first summoners have come fully into their own. The events documented by this report prove that we are in a far better position today than we were a mere month ago."

"So what the hell are we supposed to do? Leave everything in the hands of a bunch of kids while someone else is out there right now—right now, I promise you—planning their next piss-damn demon attack in this... this hidden war?"

"We trust them. We teach them. We depend on them. At the moment, they are our only hope, and this hidden war, as you say, is only just beginning."

"I refuse to believe that these kids are our only option."

"As you have refused to believe from the start. And yet that appears to be the situation in which we find ourselves. It could be far worse, Colonel. They want to help. They are naturally aligned with the forces of light. They are strong, noble, brave—everything you could ask for in the war that looms ahead."

"Fine. So we'll use them. For now. We'll learn how they do it, and as soon as we can, we'll train real soldiers to do what they do. Who knows where the next attack will be. Or when. We're going to need a hell of a lot more than these six kids."

"It is theoretically possible to teach others to do what they do, of course. We have always known this. In fact, we are counting on it. But you will also remember that we tested military personnel long before we ever tested children. The armed forces, Colonel, simply do not favor intuitive thought. Nor does our modern, rational society, for that matter. We live in a culture of skeptics. Even those who are able to access their unconscious pathways are likely to hide that fact from the world. And those who do not bother to hide it will not be soldiers. They will be artists, musicians, inventors—dreamers of every variety. But I do not have to tell you what you already know, what you have seen for yourself."

"For God's sake, Professor, you can't expect me to sit back and trust the security of this nation to a bunch of kids and dreamers."

"Of course not, Colonel. Not all of it. Just the part that requires them."

60
ATLANTA

I call dibs on the pterolycos," Sam declared. She stood in the living room of the Presidential Suite, looking out over the skyline of downtown Atlanta, the floor-to-ceiling windows affording her a bird's eye view of the city. She imagined flying on the back of the majestic creature, its thick, silver fur clutched in her hands as they leaped off the balcony together into the sky, and the very idea of it made her smile.

"Hey! I want a pterolycos!" Kaitlyn protested.

"Sorry," Sam said, shrugging her shoulders, as though the matter were simply out of her hands. "Too late. I called dibs."

"I don't think that's how it works," Mackenzie said, laughing.

"What would you get, Grid?" Kaitlyn asked her.

"I'm going to wait and see what Tick-Tock ends up with, and then I'm going to get Sketch to find me something in Ammu's book that can beat it up," she declared.

Sam rewarded her with a wry glare, and Mackenzie laughed

again. She sat, at the moment, on the couch next to Sketch, watching as his most recent composition took shape.

"Really?" Mackenzie asked him, pointing at a section he had just filled in, and he nodded silently while his pencil continued to glide across the page.

"Is that another illustration for your book, Ammu?" Daniel asked. He held his guitar idly as he sat on the floor, currently between melodies, his back propped up against the overstuffed chair Kaitlyn was sitting in.

"I do not believe so," the man replied, smiling knowingly. "This particular work is in honor of today's festivities, I think."

The book that served as Ammu's catalog of spirit creatures had been printed almost a century earlier, the most recent edition in a long, unbroken line of copies produced since the original collection. Because summoning had not been possible throughout the intervening millennia, the artwork had never been updated—only duplicated by hand and then eventually photographed for preservation. Ammu had suggested that the book would be vastly improved by modern renderings of the creatures within it, based on actual experience, and Sketch had readily agreed.

Ammu had bought him a new art pad for the purpose, and Sketch had accepted it eagerly, happy to assist with the project but also more than ready to abandon his practice of keeping two separate chronicles of his life, especially now that the ICIC had officially become a year-round program, so that he no longer had to worry about who might run across his darker visions and what they might try to do about them.

"And what sort of creature might you like to be your special companion, Sketch?" Ammu asked.

"I want a dragon," Sketch said, his eyes never leaving his drawing.

"Isn't that a little big for a pet?" Sam asked, but Sketch only shrugged.

Just then, the door of the suite opened, and Rush walked in with Staff Sergeant Miller close on his heels.

"I trust there were no signs of trouble?" Ammu asked.

"Not that I saw," Miller reported. "Although it's a zoo out there. But you'd have to ask Rush about any creepy crawlies. I'm only good at the flesh-and-blood security: muggers, kidnappers, assassins, that sort of thing."

"Rush," Ammu asked, grinning. "Did you witness any 'creepy crawlies' in the course of your perambulation?"

"Nope," Rush replied easily. "All I found was this lousy thing."

He grinned as he reached into a bag and pulled out an olive green T-shirt, tossing it in Sketch's general direction. Seeing that Sketch still had his pad and pencil in his hands, Mackenzie snatched the shirt out of the air and passed it over to him.

"My T-shirt!" Sketch exclaimed happily. He held it up to examine it, turning it over so he could read both sides. On the front was the *HRT Alpha* logo, and on the back were the words *Beta Invitational* in large, stylized letters, with a litany of sponsor logos arrayed in three columns beneath it.

"Sorry about the size," Rush said. "It's a limited edition thing, so a men's small was the best I could do."

"It's perfect!" Sketch declared, pulling it on over the top of the T-shirt he had already been wearing, blissfully ignoring the fact that his new prize hung down almost to his knees.

"Thanks for letting me do this, Ammu," Rush said, turning to the man he had come to think of as his mentor, and his friend. "I promise I'll only take the job as long as it won't interfere with the ICIC. I mean, assuming I win, that is. I just want you to know the program is my number one priority."

"So you have said many times this past week," Ammu noted, smiling gently. "There is no need to thank me, or to reassure me for that matter. I have no doubt that you will be taking your place with everyone else when our classes begin in September—and we will be cheering for you proudly today."

"I know you'll win," Sketch declared. "You're the best. It's your special pathway."

"Yeah, about that..." Rush began, looking at Ammu and hesitating.

"Yes?" Ammu prompted.

"Well, I don't think it probably matters now... at least, I hope it doesn't... but there's something I've been wanting to tell you."

"Oh?" Ammu raised his eyebrows, but there was no shadow of concern or prejudgment in his eyes, just the same intelligence, curiosity, and faith with which he had approached every new challenge they had faced together. It was something Rush and all of the Intuitives had come to count on, and what Rush loved about him most of all.

"Well, when I took the Intuition Assessment Battery, I kind of... didn't really take it, you know, the right way."

"How so?" Ammu asked, clearly puzzled.

"After the first few questions," Rush admitted, "I just sort of filled in all the blanks randomly."

"Oh my God," Sam exclaimed, rolling her eyes in disgust. "All the rest of us get here through our genuine braniac test scores, and of course Rush just waltzes in by sheer, dumb luck. Wouldn't you know it?"

But Ammu was only smiling at him.

"What?" Rush demanded, clearly wishing he had waited to unveil his secret more privately.

"Surely you realize by now that I give very little credence to the idea of coincidence, especially when it comes to an occurrence of 'luck' as statistically unlikely as you are proposing."

"Well, what was it then?" Rush asked.

"My dear Rush," Ammu said, his eyes twinkling, "your unconscious mind understands patterns of thought—it is your most profound affinity, just as Daniel understands emotion, or as Kaitlyn understands the flow of energy."

"So?" he said, still not seeing the connection.

"Ammu," Sam scoffed, "you can't be serious."

"So," Ammu continued, "I would argue that you did not need to take the test 'the right way,' as you say. Thanks to your particular pathway, you predicted the thought pattern of the test makers by recognizing the answers they would select. In its own way, the IAB *did* test your intuitive talent. You just did not know it!"

As Rush listened to Ammu's explanation, a smile gradually dawned across his face. He had known he had a role to play at the ICIC, no matter what he had done on the day of the test, but it was nice to know that his place in the program was just as valid as anyone else's.

"If that's true," he said, his eyes gleaming wickedly as he turned to look at Sam, "then in a way I'm *kind of* the most intuitive one here, wouldn't you say, Ammu?"

"Oh, please," Sam said, rolling her eyes.

"Face it," Rush said, continuing to taunt her. "It does take *two* of you to kill me when we play together. So doesn't that make me *twice* as intuitive as either one of you alone? I mean, just speaking mathematically, of course."

Mackenzie snagged a pillow from the arm of the couch and tossed it at Rush's head, but he caught it deftly while Sketch looked on, laughing.

"OK, man," he said to Sketch. "You about done there? Better get moving if you want to come with me instead of sitting in the audience with everyone else. I have a tournament to win."

"Yeah, just a sec—almost." Sketch looked at the drawing on his lap, gave it a few final touches and then picked up the pad, carrying it with him and handing it to Rush. "I made it for you," he said. "For good luck."

"Oh yeah?" Rush said. "Thanks, buddy, that's—"

As he spoke, he looked down at the page, and suddenly his words fell away. It was a drawing of the Intuitives, all six of them: Rush, in the middle of the page, standing in the back row as though they had been posing for a group photograph, wearing a suit of anime armor worthy of any MMORPG on the market; Grid, on his left, with a huge golden bear towering over her head; Tick-Tock, on his right, a classic smirk on her face, as what looked like a stylized array of electrons whirled around her; Daniel and Kaitlyn, each on one knee in front of the others, he with a rainbow aura of light cascading around him, and she with a spray of tiny bubbles that traced glimmering tracks on her skin before flying up into the air; and Sketch, sitting cross-legged on the floor in front of Rush, looking exactly like himself, smiling broadly.

Ammu was there, too, standing to Grid's left and slightly behind her, with the seal of Alexander the Great glowing bravely over his heart. And Christina stood on the other side, slightly behind Tick-Tock, wearing her signature business suit, paired incongruously with a pair of tall, golden boots and a matching superhero's cape. Finally, rounding out the portrait, Sketch had included the gryphon cub, sitting on the floor to Sketch's left, puffing its chest out proudly and wearing its battle armor, which perfectly matched Rush's own.

Rush's eyes pored over every inch of the image, taking them all in — the best friends he had ever had, captured forever as they were today, right now, in this perfect summer — and he had to clear his throat before he could finish his sentence.

"That's really special, Sketch," he said finally. "Thanks. I mean it. Thank you."

Sketch grinned up at him, clearly pleased that he liked it.

"Take care of this for me, Ammu, OK?" Rush asked. "While we're down on the gaming floor?"

"Always," Ammu replied, his smile conveying a deeper meaning behind his pledge, and he took the pad carefully as Rush handed it to him for safe-keeping.

Turning to go, Rush looked around to make sure he had everything he needed. Sketch was with him, he had his backpack, and Miller looked ready to go...

"Hey!" Rush called out. "Where are you? We're going to be late!"

At the sound of his call, the head of the gryphon cub appeared over the back of the couch, flopping over the edge to stare at him upside-down, the cub having spent the entire morning sleeping on the sofa next to Sketch.

"Let's go, you lazy cat-bird. But you're flying this time. I'm tired of taking the blame when people trip over your invisible butt."

With a mild chirp of protest, the gryphon flew up into the air and hovered obediently above and just behind Rush's head.

"Do you think you could teach me to see him someday?" Miller asked, looking up into the empty air that Rush appeared to be petting affectionately.

"Sure!" Sketch promised, and with that, the three humans and the invisible gryphon headed out of the suite together.

"That is why we are here, Staff Sergeant Miller," Ammu said quietly, after they had shut the door behind them. "That is why we are here."

OUR ACKNOWLEDGMENTS

There are so many people we need to thank that we will most certainly forget someone critically important and end up tearing our hair out over it later. Whoever you are, we beg you in advance: please forgive us.

Taylor and Triston Brown—for inspiring us every day to follow our dreams, just as we hope you will always follow your own.

Ruth and Jack Cook; Cleo Marie and David Brunck; Jonathan Cook; Thomas, Christy, and Christian Brown—for a lifetime of love and support.

Dawn Brown—for everything you do.

Miles Morton II—for your unflagging support and enthusiasm. Every Intuitive in the world should have a friend like you.

The Guardians of Azeroth—for always showing up for us, in every sense of that phrase. (Especially the two grumpy hecklers in the box seats. Christopher Brooks and Charles Henderson, we love you both.)

H1D3—for all the FPS gaming inspiration. When we were

strangers in a strange land, you welcomed us, teaching us your language and your customs.

The tabletop RPG crew: Vaughn Slay, Jamie Strickland, Tommy Brown, Sandy Brown, Robert Harris, Doug Stinnette, Brian Funderburk, Chris Koon, Johnny Smallwood, Timothy Akins—for challenging our story-telling from every perspective. Every... single... day.

Andromeda Spaceways Inflight Magazine—for being the first in the industry to see our potential.

Nathaniel L. Smith—for keeping the doors open, both yours and ours.

Antoinette Carr—for moving us forward into this lifetime.

Valerie Noble—for telling us to keep writing.

Dragon Con—for living the dream.

Jake Jake—for always coming back.

Sybil Carey—for being our angel, even when you still walked this Earth.

And finally: Rush, Grid, Disco, Tick-Tock, Gears, and Sketch—for letting us tell your story.

ABOUT THE AUTHORS

As a child, Erin fell in love with llamas and with the books of Anne McCaffrey, whose *Dragonriders of Pern* series inspired her to become a writer. When she finally met Anne McCaffrey at a fantasy convention some two decades later, she wept uncontrollably throughout the entire affair. She does significantly better with llamas.

Steven spent his childhood reading anything he could get his hands on, sharing his favorite stories with his younger brothers and then acting them out, especially if this required sword fighting on horseback. When they ran out of books, he wrote his own, including his brothers as the main characters by sketching original illustrations on magazine clippings.

Together, they are Dragon Authors, writing science fiction and fantasy novels for teens and adults. You can find them online at DragonAuthors.com.